Angels'
Playground

Angels' Playground

A Novel by

Leigh M. Rose

Bellamy-Fleming Publishing
Berea, Kentucky

Angels' Playground
Copyright © 2020
Leigh M. Rose

Published by
Bellamy-Fleming Publishing
A Division of Parkway Publications, LLC.
Editorial and Sales Offices:
Berea, Kentucky

Cover Design
Wizard Graphics

ISBN: 978-0-9969676-7-9

Printed and manufactured in the United States of America.

Dedicated to:

My mother, Jerlene Bellamy Rose,
and my father,
the late William (Billy) Forest Rose

———

Acknowledgment

*Special thank you to Marty Clamp Broadnax,
a life-long resident of Columbia, South Carolina,
whose help with research, providing contact people,
and constant encouragement, made this book possible.
And thank you to my dear friend, Sherri Taylor Whisman,
for reading through all of my drafts and edits, and
helping catch my typos and misspellings.*

———————

Preface

In the Elmwood neighborhood of Columbia, South Carolina, Wardlaw Junior High School sat vacant for a generation, the last class having passed out its doors in 1984. During the two decades I lived in Columbia, I drove past the school many times. What had been Columbia's first junior high had become just another decaying relic, like the once thriving middle-class neighborhood that surrounded it.

Each time I passed by, my imagination would linger with the old monolith. What would it be like to walk its halls? What items would I find that had been left behind? Perhaps a notebook with a lesson assignment, a lonely coat hanging in a closet, a teacher's desk drawer with valentines from students? These imaginings were the seeds of inspiration for this story. What if a murder had happened here....

It was then that I set about researching and trying to find out as much about the school as I possibly could -- its history, the work by local citizens to save it from demolition, and finally, the plans to salvage the old school.

With much help, I was able to get in touch with people who could grant me access to Wardlaw. This allowed me to explore every inch of the building and take photos that would be helpful in describing the school while writing this book. I interviewed a murder detective with the Columbia Police Department who explained their procedures with murder investigations. I interviewed the forensic anthropologist with the University of South Carolina, who explained their process for finding grave sites, the use of ground penetrating radar, estimating the age of bones, and who is allowed to examine samples. All of this helped with making what I hope is not only an interesting story, but also a story that was as technically accurate as possible.

Angels'
Playground

Angels' Playground

Chapter one

In the blistering heat of the South Carolina summer, renovation on the old Wardlaw Junior High School was proceeding at an accelerated rate. The sub-contracted work crew swarmed over the school like fire ants. The project was two weeks behind schedule due to the severity of the water damage in the old auditorium. But overall, the project was going well, given the environmental problems encountered during the initial cleanup. Jason Shealy, the architect on the project, and the general contractor, were confidant that they could make up the time as the decision had been made by the developers to open Wardlaw to shop renters prior to completing the renovations on the auditorium.

Inside the main hall, as he supervised the installation of the ornamental ceiling tiles, Jason could hear the backhoe digging the trenches for water pipes that would feed the outside fountains. Outside, Pat, one of the few women on the crew, watched as the arm of the backhoe forced its way down into the sandy soil and pulled out another scoop of earth. As the bucket dumped the earth beside the trench, Pat noticed something that looked out of place from the roots and debris they had so far encountered.

Pat waved to Jerry, the backhoe operator, to stop digging. He shut off the motor and climbed down. Pat was lying on the ground reaching into the trench pulling on the object. "What are you lookin' at?"

"I don't know. It looks like some kind of bone."

"Probably just some damn dog bone."

"Dogs don't bury bones two feet deep. Now, get down here and help me pull this out."

Jerry reluctantly climbed down into the trench. "I want to get this section finished before lunch, so I don't have to listen to them bosses bitch." Using his pocket knife, he dug into the cool, sandy soil. As he dug, what was clearly a pair of bones became exposed.

Her curiosity sparked, Pat joined him. Some of the other workers noticed and began to stand along the edge to watch. Jerry plunged his knife deeper into the wall of the shallow trench loosening larger clumps of earth. Then his knife struck something else.

"Wait a minute, I hit something. Somebody hand me a shovel!"

One of the other workmen passed a short-handled shovel to Pat, who maneuvered it in the tight confines of the trench to help with the excavation.

As Pat scooped away a couple shovels of dirt, Jerry, with shock yelled out, "Shit, would you look at that."

The circle of people around the trench moved in tighter. "Hey, move back. You're blockin' our light." Jerry tugged on the object and the sandy soil gave way. Quickly he realized the bones he held in his hand were attached to a small leather shoe. Jerry dropped the bones and jumped back against the opposite wall of the trench.

"Shit! It looks like a kid's shoe."

By now Jason noticed the absence of noise, which should have been coming from the backhoe. He and the foreman on the job walked outside to see why the crew had stopped working.

The foreman, Glenn, with his head tilted slightly down and his eyes peering from under his Gamecocks ball cap, strode across the old playground with Jason tight on his heels. Shouldering his way through the crowd of what was now a dozen workmen, who were lined up giving their comments on the find, Glenn looked down into the trench. "What the hell is going on here?"

"Look what Pat and Jerry dug up," one of the workers exclaimed.

In a matter-of-fact tone, Pat simply said, "It looks like a leg bone and a shoe."

"Damn! Where'd that come from?"

"In here," she said, pointing to the side of the trench. "Jerry was runnin' the backhoe and I was watchin,' then I saw this thing stickin' out that looked kinda funny, so I told him to stop. Then we both got down in here and dug out these bones and an old shoe."

Glenn looked at Jason. "Didn't you say this piece of property used to be an old plantation?"

Jason was staring at the bones. "Yes. It was the old Washington Clark place. At one time it was part of a plantation."

14

"See, it's probably just some ol' slave grave. Throw it back in the hole and keep digging; we got a schedule to keep!"

"If it's a grave, we have to report it," Jason said. "You know as well as I do that it's illegal to disturb a grave site. If we find even just one, it has to be reported."

"Shut up, Jason! You wanna' put us behind schedule any more than we already are!"

"No, it's just that…"

Nudging the shoe with the toe of her boot, Pat interrupted the exchange between the two, "Slaves didn't wear no penny loafers."

Both men were silent as they looked at the shoe and the bones lying in the bottom of the trench. After what seemed like a long silence, Jason spoke. "We'd better call the police. This could be a murder victim. Pat, Jerry, would the two of you stay here and make sure no one touches anything? Don't let anything else get disturbed."

Jason walked to the construction trailer, and Glenn, with a string of profanity, ushered the rest of the crew back to work.

As Jason ended the call, Glenn stomped through the door. "Well! What'd they say?"

"I didn't get to speak with anyone except the dispatch. She said she would send an officer to check it out."

"They better not rope off any of this lot! I've got this job to run and your skinny ass needs to worry more about us getting back on schedule than about some damn bones. Probably just some damn drunk that dropped dead and his buddies pushed him in a hole and took his bottle."

"Those bones and that shoe were pretty small. It might be a child."

"OK, so it's a short drunk!"

"Look, Glenn, you're not the only one who has a lot riding on this project. I want it on schedule as much as you do, but if we don't report this and have it investigated, then the police and the reporters will be on us like flies on shit when it gets out. So just shut up!"

Glenn stared at Jason for a moment, then taking in a deep breath and exhaling it with a snort, Glenn turned toward the door. "I'm going back inside. I'll be in the west wing, up on the third floor. Call me when the cops get here."

Jason sat for a few minutes in the silence of the trailer. The work outside had stopped. The crews were milling about the yard, busying themselves discussing the find. Sitting alone, his mind went back to the eerie silence he had experienced months ago, when first detailing the floor plan of the school. The absence of children's voices and laughter had left him with an empty feeling. If this was a child that was buried in the playground, had its soul watched over his sketches and designs? Had it guided his hand when he determined the positioning of the fountains? Had it somehow willed him to find its discarded and forgotten body? Or perhaps it was just that Wardlaw's silence triggered the memory of the quiet of his parent's house after his little brother died.

Just as Jason's thoughts began to drift deeper into the recesses of his memories, through the window of the trailer he saw the police car and the officer step out. Jason picked up his cell phone and called Glenn, brushed his hair out of his eyes, stood up and walked outside.

"Hey, I'm Officer Tyrone Jackson. Who here called the police?"

"That was me. I'm Jason Shealy, the architect on the project."

"You said your crew was digging and you think you've dug up a body?"

"Yes sir, we think so. It's over here. I had the two people who actually uncovered it stay here to help keep people away so nothing would get disturbed any more than it already has been."

As Jason and Officer Jackson walked to the trench, Glenn joined them. "Officer Jackson, this is Glenn Stone. Glenn is the general foreman on the construction job. He is responsible for coordinating the work, and supervising the crews."

Jackson nodded his head in acknowledgment to Glenn then turned his attention to the trench and the bones and small shoe that lay in the bottom of it. Without touching anything, he examined the site and stood up and looked at both Jason and Glenn.

"I'll need to talk to the people who actually found the remains and anyone who watched them dig it up. Other than that, I want you to keep all of your crew away from here while I radio for an additional car."

Jason began rounding up everyone who had watched Pat and Jerry dig out the leg bones and shoe while Glenn ushered everyone else back to work. Meanwhile, Officer Jackson radioed for not only additional officers to assist him in managing the scene, but also the Richland

County Coroner and a detective.

As Jackson was questioning everyone who had been on the scene at the time of the discovery, a car with signs on its doors identifying it as belonging to the Coroner's office pulled up and parked beside the two squad cars. The Deputy Coroner stepped out and walked straight to Jackson. The two men apparently knew each other.

Together they examined the trench and the two leg bones and shoe. As Jason watched the man from the Coroner's office, it was clear that he was directing the activities at the scene. This surprised Jason; he had thought police detectives would be in charge, asking questions, collecting evidence. The Deputy Coroner gave Jackson some instructions. Jason couldn't hear what was being said, he just saw the officer nod and then walk to his car and start making calls. Then he noticed another car pull up and park near the police cruiser and a man and woman step out. He assumed they were the detectives.

Suddenly, with a train of thought Jason was powerless to stop, the image of his little brother came crashing back into his consciousness. He remembered a similar scene twenty-four years before. The lights, the sirens, the police officers and rescue workers.

Jason was snapped back to the present by Detective Edwards' voice. "Who's in charge of this project?"

"That's me. I'm Glenn Stone, the general foreman on this project." Glenn's sudden presence startled Jason. He had been immersed in his own thoughts and didn't realize the burley foreman had walked up behind him.

"I'm Detective Edwards; my partner over there is Detective Porter." As Detective Edwards turned and looked in his partner's direction, he removed a filterless cigarette from a pack, tapped it on the side of the pack, placed it in his mouth and then lit it in motions so quick and fluid, anyone watching would know that he had most likely been a heavy smoker most of his life.

"Mr. Stone, what the Deputy Coroner has decided to do is call in a forensic anthropologist. Just from what is exposed here we can't tell anything about the body. Age, sex, how long it's been here, nothin'. So, what we're gonna do is rope off this area, get the anthropologist out here with his people and start excavating the site."

17

"How long is all this gonna take? I've got a job to keep on schedule."

"Well, I've worked with these people before and they always take longer than we would like. When you find bones like these there usually ain't much left to work with; at least nothin' obvious, which is why we gotta' call in these people."

"How much are you roping off?"

"When the anthropologist gets here, he and the Coroner will identify a perimeter. You'll have to keep all of your people away from that area. And depending on how big that perimeter is, you should be able to keep working on the inside of the building. This is a pretty good size lot. Hopefully, we won't get in each other's way. And one more thing I'd like to ask - don't call the press. They'll find out about it soon enough on their own and be swarming all over the place gettin' in your way, and mine."

With that statement, Glenn was in complete agreement. The last thing he wanted was his project slowed down, because that meant his bonus and the new truck he was going to buy would be out the window. Both Jason and Glenn agreed to keep the discovery quiet as long as possible.

While Glenn and Edwards talked further about how the area would be secured until the forensic anthropologist arrived, Jason watched as Detective Porter walked around the trench, examining it from every angle. She was much younger than Edwards, early thirties tops, with dark brown hair, and he couldn't help but notice she was attractive, even with the nine-millimeter on her hip.

Detective Porter joined her partner and introduced herself. Hello, I'm Detective Angela Porter." She looked at Edwards, "I think I have the names and phone numbers of everyone who was here at the time the bones were discovered. Also, I've collected statements from several witnesses. I guess all there is to do now is hurry up and wait."

The detectives gave their adieus to the two men, and rejoined the uniformed officers and the Deputy Coroner.

It was now almost three o'clock. Most of the afternoon had been shot and in just those few hours the heat had shifted from blistering to oppressive. Jason was tired and ready to call it a day.

18

Chapter two

The stress of the day, the body, memories of his brother, combined with the sun and heat had physically and emotionally drained Jason. When Jason left Wardlaw, Glenn was cursing and stomping through the ground floor stirring up dust and trying to get everyone hustling again. The detectives and uniformed officers were still on the scene. They left the bones and shoe in the trench, but covered it with a tarp and placed an around-the-clock guard at the site. Jason overheard the Deputy Coroner talking on his cell phone telling someone the forensic anthropologist was at the Medical College of Charleston for the day and wouldn't be able to examine the site until the next morning.

Even with afternoon traffic beginning pick up, Jason was back at his office on Taylor Street in just a few minutes. The Wardlaw renovation was not only his dream job, but it was also convenient. If there were no accidents to snarl traffic on the Broad River Bridge, he could make it from his house in Irmo, a bedroom community for Columbia, to the office then backtrack to Wardlaw, all within thirty to forty minutes. With most of his projects, he was finished when the general contractor took over and he only got involved if modifications to the original drawings were requested. But so much money was tied up in this project and, because new problems continued to arise as it progressed, he had been able to stay more closely involved and work directly with the developers and contractors. It was an opportunity to expand the work of his firm and eventually take on more large-scale projects.

Jason pulled his Subaru into his reserved parking slot at the rear of the building where he rented office space. He turned off the ignition and sat for a moment while he collected his thoughts and an armload of floor plans. As he entered the back door, the cold, air-conditioned air hit him and he experienced a slight chill as the sweat on his exposed skin instantly started to dry. Since moving back to Columbia, he had developed allergy-induced asthma. Most of the time it didn't bother him. He was still able to jog and work out, but the spring and fall pollen seasons usually wreaked havoc with his sinuses and sometimes triggered asthma attacks, so he kept an inhaler with him always - just in case.

Cindy, his secretary slash 'office manager' was in the back filing some drawings from their last office project. "Hey, Jason, how'd it go?" Cindy took some of the rolled floor plans from his arms.

"Not too bad. Glenn and I of course, had some words again today."

"Go figure. Y'all two just don't mix. You know, I think you pissed him off when you said professional wrestling wasn't real."

Jason laughed, "I think you might be right. Today it was because of the little excitement we had on the site."

Cindy's eyes got wider and she turned her body to face Jason. "OK, so what's the scoop? Don't leave out a single detail."

"We started digging the trench today to lay the pipes for the fountains in the parking lot. One of the crew saw something sticking out of the trench about two feet down. It looked odd so they stopped. They dug it out and it turned out to be what looks like leg bones and an old shoe, maybe with part of the foot still in it."

"Oh, my god! What'd you do?"

"We called the police. They sent a couple of cars out, and then the deputy coroner showed up, then a couple detectives. They asked a lot of questions. Tomorrow a forensic anthropologist from USC is going to come out and start excavating the site."

"What for?"

"Anytime bones are found like this and they don't know if it could be an old grave, murder victim or maybe something historical, it has to be investigated. The anthropologist is called in because he's the expert in excavations and preserving evidence and identification of skeletal remains."

"Wow. What'd you think it is?"

"I don't know. I'm just guessing, but it was so small, it had to be either a child or a small adult, a woman maybe."

"I wonder if it could be that college girl that disappeared from here several years ago."

"I don't know. I guess anything is possible."

"You okay? You look like something else is wrong."

"No, everything is fine. Just standing around in the heat got to me today. With the air this still, I always seem to feel a little tired. And I've got a couple of drawings to review before I can call it a day."

"You go ahead and start working on the drawings and I'll get us both a big glass of sweet tea out of the refrigerator."

"Oh no! Don't bring that syrupy stuff near me."

"Honey, you spent too much time with those Yankees. They brain washed you."

Jason gave her a sideways glance and a smile. "You go ahead. I know you need to pick up your daughter. I'll lock everything up."

"I'm not going to argue with you, Boss; she has dance class tonight. I'll just take my sweet tea with me. One for the road."

Jason continued to work two more hours, just late enough for the rush hour traffic to hit its peak. Rather than take his normal route which would take him down Elmwood Avenue past the school, he opted for an alternate route. Turning off the satellite radio in his car he switched to the local stations. There was nothing on any of them about the discovery of the bones, but then, none of the area stations were much for news. Snarky comments about celebrities was about as in-depth as it got.

It was after six when he pulled his car into his garage. He kicked off his hiking shoes at the door and headed straight to the bedroom. Sebastian, his feline roommate, came running down the stairs to greet him.

Jason scooped the cat up in his arms and walked up the stairs. "Hello there, little man. Did you think I was going to be late again?" Sebastian purred and rubbed his head against Jason's hand, indicating he wanted his neck scratched. A girl Jason had dated for a few months thought a cute fuzzy kitten from the shelter would be the perfect gift to help create an atmosphere of nurturing and caring, resulting in thoughts of a family. She was correct about the nurturing and caring. However, within a couple months Jason realized he cared more for the kitten than the girlfriend. The girlfriend left in a huff and Sebastian began sleeping on the spare pillow on Jason's bed.

In his bedroom, Jason stripped out of his sweat-soaked, dusty clothes, then stepped into the shower. Sebastian positioned himself on the bed where he could see into the bathroom and supervise the activities. After drying off, he dressed in a pair of flannel boxers and an old T-shirt from the University of Kentucky, his Alma Mater. Picking up Sebastian, who was by now prancing on the bed eager for attention and a meal, he went back downstairs for a drink and to find something for dinner for himself and his feline roommate.

"OK, big guy, first a snack and some cat food for you." Jason pinched off a small piece of ham that was in the refrigerator and put it on a paper napkin for Sebastian, who was sitting on the counter top waiting for his dinner.

Jason opened a bottle of red wine and poured himself a glass, then fed Sebastian a small can of cat food. Nothing in the refrigerator looked inviting, so he walked into the living room and stretched out on the sofa to watch television before deciding what to eat. As he took another large sip of wine, Sebastian jumped on his stomach and the phone rang in the same instance. "Son-of-a-bitch!" Sitting up and wiping the wine off his chin and neck. "Hello."

"Jason?"

"Hey Mom."

"Are you okay, son?"

"Yeah, I just spilled some wine on myself."

"Vinegar is supposed to get out wine stains, but I've never tried it. We don't usually have wine in the house. Your father won't drink anything but beer and his Jim Beam, and I only like…"

"It's okay Mom, I didn't get any on my clothes, just my face."

"That's good, you won't have to worry about it then. Were you in the living room? I'd hate to see you get something on that new sofa you just bought."

"No. I didn't get anything on it – just me."

"Did you just get home? I tried calling about twenty minutes ago, but no one answered."

"I was in the shower. I haven't been home that long. I had to work a little late."

"Work. That's why I called, I wanted to ask you what was going on out at the old school."

Jason suddenly felt flushed. It was the same feeling he used to get when his mother would catch him in a lie or breaking some household rule. His father had lots of rules. "What'd you mean, what's going on at Wardlaw?"

"On the news, tonight they said that the construction crew had found a body buried on the old playground. They said the police weren't willing to comment on it."

"That didn't take long to get out. When did you see this?"

"It was on at six. But they usually run most of the stories again at seven."

"Hang on; I'll switch stations." With the question from his mother about the discovery of the body, Jason's posture had changed. He was literally sitting on the edge of the sofa as he changed channels. Sure enough, there was one of the local anchors, Dorothy Danze, relaying the news of the discovery. They didn't have film, probably that would be tomorrow night after the anthropologist and his crew arrived.

"So, what's going on with this?" His mother's voice had an accusing tone to it, as if Jason was somehow hiding something from her.

"Nothing much at this point. At least not as far as I know."

"What's a body doing out there where you're working anyway? That whole area is still so dangerous. I worried about you going to work out there. Elmwood hasn't been a good neighborhood to live in since your father and I were children. When they started letting all those blacks go to school at Wardlaw and move into Elmwood the entire neighborhood went down hill."

"Stop, Mom. I really don't want to get into this again."

"We always sheltered you. You don't understand what it was like when those people started marching around and demanding to be treated like they were something special."

"You mean like human beings?"

"Jason, you know I don't have anything against them personally. It's just that they're different from us. They don't see things the same way."

"Yes, you're right, Mom. Three hundred years of slavery and

oppression does tend to distort your view of the world."

"Don't get smart with me. I was just stating a point of view."

"Mom, I'm not even going to continue this conversation. It's ridiculous. I need to go. I'll talk to you later." With that Jason pressed the button on his cell phone and hung up on his mother. He was furious with her and with himself for letting her get to him. She had been a bigot all her life and she wasn't going to change now. But even through his anger, he had to laugh at himself. Somehow hanging up on someone with a push button on the screen of a cell phone doesn't have the same dramatic effect as slamming down a receiver.

"Sebastian, I must have been adopted." Jason knew he was different from most of his family. He could remember his only true ally was his father's sister, Aunt Bess. She was the one who encouraged him to be an architect, to move away from home and not go to college here in Columbia. Tommy was his Dad's favorite; his older sister Carol, was Mom's favorite. Thank god for Aunt Bess.

With no more news on the bones found at Wardlaw, Jason got up from his sofa and turned his attention to the daunting task of dinner. He opened the refrigerator and stared inside. He had lost his appetite so he settled for cold spring rolls from the previous night's carry-out.

Chapter three

Six a.m. came early. Jason hadn't slept well. He couldn't remember his dreams, but then he usually didn't when they were troubling. He would just wake with a feeling of dread. He knew he had tossed and turned during the night. Sebastian must have become irritated at some point and shifted from his usual spot on the spare pillow to the far corner at the foot of the bed.

Jason rolled over on his back and tried to make his eyes adjust to the encroaching morning light. Now that he was awake, Sebastian decided to be affectionate. The big tan and white cat gave a lazy yawn and stretched, then walked across the bed and seated himself on Jason's chest. As he petted and scratched his feline friend, his mind wandered: Strengths of beams. Was his favorite green Under Armour shirt clean? Two more residential plans to review. Whose bones were buried in the playground? Why did he move back to Columbia and subject himself to his parents?

"Come on big fella, let's get up so I can go to work."

Showered and shaved and wearing his favorite green Under Armour shirt (it was clean), he went downstairs. Retrieving a couple of diet snack bars from the pantry and a can of diet soda from the refrigerator, Jason stuffed all of what would be his breakfast, and possibly his lunch, into his backpack. He loaded Sebastian up with enough cat food to last into the evening, just in case he was late; then, picking up his car keys from the counter top, he headed for the garage and his Subaru.

It was now almost eight and already heating up outside. Jason was driving across the Broad River Bridge on I-126, heading into Columbia. The car beside him started to move into his lane. Jason blew his horn a long blast. The car swerved back into its own lane. He gunned the engine and sped up, passing the other driver. "Idiot! Where'd you learn to drive!"

25

Jason initiated the voice command in his car, "Call Office." He knew Cindy wouldn't be there to open the office until a little after eight. She was always running late, but he really didn't mind. He knew she had to drop her daughter off at daycare in the summer.

He heard the beep of her answering machine. "Cindy. This is Jason. I just wanted to let you know that I'm going by Wardlaw before I come in this morning. Don't know if you saw it or not, but there was a story on the news last night about the skeleton we found. I want to stop by and see what's going on and check on a couple of things we left hanging in the auditorium. Text or call if you need anything."

Jason pulled into the lot behind the school. He saw the two detectives from the day before, along with some uniformed officers and the Deputy Coroner's car. In a group, a few feet away from the officers, there were three people. They were young and looked like college students. Then there was an older man, maybe in his sixties.

Jason stepped out of his car and walked toward the group. He could see the older man and the Deputy Coroner talking and pointing to specific points around the trench. They were making square shapes in the air with their hands. As he got closer a uniformed officer stopped him.

"Sorry, sir, this is a restricted area. You can't go any further."

"I'm Jason Shealy. I'm the architect on this project. I need to get over there to talk to our foreman." Glenn, with his ball cap pulled down over his eyes and his arms crossed, was standing beside Detective Edwards and intently watching the activity.

"Sir, I need to see some identification."

As Jason began to fish through his wallet for his drivers' license and a business card, Detective Porter saw him. She remembered him from the previous day and yelled across the lot to the officer, "Thompson. It's OK. He works here. He's clear to come inside the perimeter." With a wave of her arm she motioned for Jason to cross under the crime scene tape.

Jason walked up to her. "Thanks, I appreciate it."

"No problem. I remember you from yesterday. You're the architect? Right?"

"Yes, that's right." Jason paused. He wasn't sure if he should linger or excuse himself and leave. He thought quickly. This was the first time he had spoken to a detective. He decided to stay. "Who are these other people?"

"The older guy there on the right is Professor Russell. He's a forensic anthropologist at the University." Detective Porter then pointed to the two young men and the young woman Jason had observed. "He and his graduate students are going to excavate the site and handle the remains."

"I guess it's a little more complex than just using a shovel and a bucket."

Detective Porter laughed.

Jason smiled. She has a nice laugh he thought to himself. "You aren't what I expected. I mean I just expected old crusty guys as murder detectives." Jason paused. "That didn't sound right, did it?"

Porter cast him a sideways glance. The fact that he was nice looking and fit hadn't been lost on her.

"Detective Porter, what happens now?" Jason changed the subject. He felt he had probably made a major blunder with his comment.

"You can just call me Angela. Don't worry about all the formalities."

Jason breathed a sigh of relief.

"After the soil is removed from around the bones, they'll be wrapped, tagged and transported either to the Coroner's office or to Professor Russell's lab for examination. After he has given us everything he can - approximate age, sex, stature, then the hard part starts."

"And what's that?"

With a slight sigh Detective Porter replied, "Finding a missing person that fits the physical profile he gave us to work within."

"Is that difficult? I mean with computer data bases, can't you just sort files?"

"It isn't that easy. If this is a homeless person, then they may never have been reported as missing. Or for instance, if it turns out that the bones have been here for several years, they may not be in the computer data base. Then we would have to manually sort through archived missing person files. In that case, even if there are records, if they were somehow filed wrong, it could be hit or miss."

"So, you might never know who it is or how they got there."

With a sound of resignation in her voice, "Unfortunately, that's usually how these cases end up."

"How long is it going to take them to finish?"

"I've only worked on one case like this where skeletal remains were found, but the dig on that one took about four days."

"Four days! Wow, I didn't think it would take that long. We're coming down to the wire. Four days can make a big difference at this late stage of the project."

Angela's mood instantly shifted to annoyance. "This isn't television. A case isn't wrapped up in an hour." She paused. "You know, the one thing that I get really tired of with this job, other than just seeing day in and day out how cruel people can be to each other, is how everyone always thinks only of how they will be affected by some inconvenience. Never mind that it could be what's left of somebody's loved one."

"I'm sorry. I didn't mean... I was just commenting. I know finding out who this was is important." Jason was quickly trying to think of a way to make amends with the detective he had just pissed off.

Detective Porter looked Jason in the eye with an expression that said she was through discussing the subject. "Like I said, Mr. Shealy, we'll work something out so you don't have to delay your project any more than necessary.

Detective Angela Porter walked away to rejoin her partner, leaving Jason standing close enough to the work that he could observe some of the activities of the excavation team. He watched as the young woman in the team pulled a sketchpad with grid lines on its pages and began sketching a detailed rendering of the site. He heard the older man, Professor Russell, tell the two young men in his group to begin photographing the scene and then erect a tent above the excavation area as soon as the sketch map was finished.

The excavation team would have to work with the sun beaming down on them, so in a lot where the only shade was a large pecan tree at the back edge of the property, the tent would be a welcome relief. However, as Jason learned by listening to the conversations between the Professor and his students, the side-less tent was to protect the bones from the sun as they were uncovered and removed, not the people doing the digging.

Jason looked up to see Glenn walking with his usual long strides across the lot to the construction trailer. "Glenn, wait up." Glenn either didn't hear him or was ignoring him because he didn't turn around, nor did he slow his stride.

With a hurried step that was almost a jog, Jason walked across the old playground and caught up with Glenn just as he entered the trailer. "Wait up Glenn. I was just talking to Detective Porter. She said it could take as long as three or four days to finish up here."

"Yeah, I heard them. I already had that talk with them before you got here. Pisses me off, too. We could've gotten caught up if it weren't for this."

"We can still make it. It's just going to mean some long hours."

Glenn was angry, which seemed to be his usual state of mind. "Look, Mr. Architect, I'm runnin' this job. They're my crews, and it's me and them that'll be putting in the long hours and pushin' to get this finished."

Jason knew Glenn resented anyone who was better educated than himself. It didn't matter if you had worked your way through school or were up to your ears in debt with student loans. College graduates, in Glenn's eyes, were privileged snobs who didn't know how to work for a living.

"Look Glenn, don't give me that hard working bullshit. I've had enough of it. When you and your precious crews ran into problems on this job, it's been me or one of my people that found a way to fix it and keep you on schedule. So just shut the hell up!"

Glenn was silent. Jason knew he wasn't used to being put in his place.

"Shealy, you know as well as I do what's gonna happen. They're gonna say we got too many people in and out of here and they're gettin' in the way. Then we're gonna have to send everybody home till they finish. It's just gonna turn out to be some old grave that's been there a hundred and fifty years. We shouldn't even have to report it."

"I don't care how old it is. You know as well as I do that, legally, we had to report it. And even if it does turn out to be an old grave site, disturbing it would have been a felony if we hadn't reported it. And you saw how fast it got on the news. Both our asses would have been in a sling."

29

Glenn looked at Jason with surprise; he obviously hadn't watched the evening news the night before. "What do you mean, on the news?"

"It was on the local news last night. I saw it myself."

"Shit! What'd they say about it?"

"Not much really, just that a skeleton had been found on the Wardlaw school grounds while the crews were digging."

Glenn was becoming more subdued at this point and regaining his composure. "Damn, that means we're gonna have people comin' down here to look around and gawk. Shit, I wonder if the developers have heard about this."

"I don't know, but one of us should probably call before the newspaper or TV station does. You want me to?"

Glenn had an exasperated look on his face. "No, I'll call them."

"OK. I've got to check on a couple of things in the auditorium before I head to my office. Let me know if you need anything."

Glenn already had his cell phone to his ear. Without looking up he gave Jason an acknowledging wave with his hand. For Glenn, this was the equivalent of a "thank you."

Jason ended up staying at Wardlaw until almost noon. Periodically, he would look out an upstairs window to see any progress the team from the University was making. With the canopy covering the section of trench, it was difficult to know what had been done. All he could see was that they had used string tied to stakes to make a grid above the area where they were excavating and once or twice it looked as if the young woman in the group was drawing more sketches.

Jason stayed just long enough to see the last of the ornamental tin tiles put in place in the ceiling of the auditorium. This portion of Wardlaw was probably in worse condition than the rest of the school when the renovation had first begun. Portions of the hardwood floor had buckled from rain pouring through a gaping three-foot hole in the ceiling. Plaster had fallen off the walls and the old theater curtains which, surprisingly, were still hanging, had dry rotted. But this was his favorite part of the old school. The one million dollars it had taken to restore just this one section had been worth every penny. Soon, if everything went as planned, a local theater group would share the space with a string quartet, and a ballet troupe had already signed up for a season of performances scheduled to begin in the fall. All this would be such a plus for, not only the Elmwood community, but for Columbia as a whole. Everything was better here now, if only he could just deal with his own ghosts.

Chapter four

Three days passed, Glenn and Jason worked steadily on the school renovation. Work had slowed but not to the snail's pace they had feared. The news crews had shown up only once. They recorded some video footage for the evening news, but with nothing new to report other than triangular trowels of soil being removed, less than a quarter of an inch at a time, they never came back.

It was Sunday; no one was at the school except the officers guarding the site and Professor Russell and his students. The bones had been wrapped in newspaper, labeled, placed in a box and transported to the lab the day before. All that remained to be done was to dig down, and sift through a few more layers of dirt to see if anything was below where the body had laid.

Just as they were ready to pack up for the day, one of the students pushed his trowel into the soil to pick up another scoop when he hit a metal object. "Hey, look over here! I've found something!"

Professor Russell and the other two students hurried to his side. "What've we got there, my boy?"

"I don't know. It looks like some kind of chain."

Professor Russell called to the other young man in his team, "Jack, hand me that brush and let's clean this off."

With a fine bristled brush, Russell carefully brushed the soil away from the links in the chain. Each link had a flattened surface on its outside edges. Without picking up the chain they could see an open clasp at the end of the exposed eight links. Tina, the student responsible for the sketch map, made a revision to the map to include the chain, and then took several photographs to ensure it was fully documented.

"This is good. This is the first thing out of the ordinary we've run across yet. Good find, Kevin. Let's keep working."

After Professor Russell and Kevin had brushed away most of the soil from around the chain it was obvious that it was an I.D. bracelet. Not the medical alert type, but the kind that people usually have their names or initials engraved into with some message on the back stating the occasion for which it was given. Having been sketched and photographed from several angles, only then was it picked up and examined more closely. Tina helped Professor Russell brush off the flat face of the bracelet. "Looks like it has writing on both sides."

Tilting his head up to look through his bifocals, Russell agreed with Tina's observation. "I think you're right. Let's see if we can get some more of this dirt off here and see if we've got a name."

Tina carefully worked the bristles of the brush into the finely cut grooves of each letter until they were clear. Tina exclaimed with excitement in her voice, "It's 'Peggy'! We've got a name to look for!"

Russell looked at the name as she held it up for his inspection. "That's great. Now see if you can clean off the back, looks like something else is there."

With the same care, she cleaned out the grooves of each letter. "Professor Russell, I've got it all. It just says, 'Happy Birthday'."

"Well, it's still more than we had. This ID bracelet could help us identify the person."

Tina held the bracelet in her hands, turning it over, examining it from every angle, and then stopping to stare at the name as if reading it again. She rubbed her thumb across the letters as if to make a promise. "We'll find out what happened to you Peggy." Then she dropped the bracelet into a bag and turned to fill out the evidence list.

Russell was encouraged by the find. "OK team, that was a great find. Now let's keep up the pace, maybe there's something else here." The team moved back to life. The heat index had reached a level that could only be described as oppressive. The air was stagnant and even with the canopy to shield them from the sun there was no relief from the heat. The crew continued to work into the afternoon, removing quarter inch layers of dirt, one trowel at a time, then sifting it through a screen to find any piece of evidence that might remain. The only thing they found were two more buttons which appeared to match the four found the day before and a metal zipper. From where it was positioned in relation to the body, the zipper was most likely under the left thigh of the victim near the pelvic bones. Tina commented that if this were a female that wouldn't be unusual due to some women's pants having zippers in the back or side, rather than the front.

It was now late in the afternoon. Everyone in the group was fatigued from working four days in the heat. Tina removed her ball cap and wiped the sweat from her forehead with the lavender bandanna that always hung from the back pocket of her hiking shorts. "Professor Russell, I'm going to take a break for a few minutes. The heat is making me feel a little light headed."

"Of course, go ahead. I don't want anyone to have a heat stroke."

With that Tina stood up and brushed the sand from her knees, then taking a bottle of water from the cooler, she walked the few yards to the back of the old playground to sit beneath a pecan tree.

Tina watched the slow work of the others as she contemplated the examination that was still to be done in the lab after they completed their work here. The police would need as many clues as possible to identify the body. She knew not to kid herself. Many remains that are discovered like this are never identified. First, the person would have to be listed as missing for there to be a record of the disappearance, then, depending on how long ago it happened, they may or may not be in a computer database which would make it easier to find. The NCIC computer system that tracks missing persons had only been in place since the 1980s. If this person had been reported missing prior to that time, finding the right records would be a hit or miss. Approximate age and race wouldn't be difficult to establish, approximate age could be determined by examining the long bones of the body such as the arms and legs, with the skull providing clues as to race. Depending on the age of the victim, sex would be a guess based solely on the artifacts found with the body since sex can't be accurately determined until about age seventeen or eighteen.

When all there is to work with is a box full of bones, cause of death can even elude the best anthropologists or examiners. Unless there was evidence of trauma, poison, or something else that can be evidenced

35

in bone, no one may ever know how this person died. She had learned much working under Professor Russell. There was so much work still to be done and, for all their work, the riddle may never be solved.

Tina's mind wondered from first one subject to the next. Even without a breeze, sitting in the shade of the pecan tree felt good. The soil was softer here, not hard packed from over fifty years of children playing, like the rest of the old playground. There was also more grass, and it was thicker. When she was in elementary school in Georgia, she had sat in a spot much like this and let Marky Wright give her a first kiss. As she watched a squirrel roll a pecan along the ground across a depression in the earth she wondered what ever happened to Marky.

Tina smiled at the thought of that first little kiss. But the smile slowly began to fade from her lips and her brow furrowed as her eyes followed the outline of the depression. She looked around her to compare the spot to the rest of the ground and noticed other depressions. They appeared to be aligned in two neat rows. She stood up quickly, walking around each depression mentally estimating its dimensions. She began speaking out loud to herself. She had a habit of doing this when she was in the lab or in the field. "The size of the depression looks about right. They are all lined up together." She continued to walk around each depression and talk to herself. "Can't be. But this looks weird. Why over there and then here?" When she was confident in her assumption she waved her lavender bandanna in the air she called to Professor Russell. "Professor Russell, come here. I think I've found something. You need to look at this."

Russell and the others got up from their work. With the site completely excavated and all the soil sifted through, most of it more than once, they had begun collecting their tools. The three men dusted off their knees and shorts and walked in the direction of the pecan tree to join Tina. Looking over the tops of his bifocals and wrinkling his nose, Professor Russell stood by Tina's side. "What did you find?"

"Look at the ground. Do you notice anything odd about it?" She watched Russell's face as he stood for a minute contemplating the question.

"Point it out to me." It was his habit to make his students think by answering a question with a question.

"It's the depressions in the ground. Do you see them? Stand over here and look from this angle."

As the professor moved to stand by Tina's right shoulder, he clearly saw what she had spotted. There were six, maybe seven depressions in the ground, each one approximately the same size and shape and they were in neat rows like in a cemetery. "Hmm. That does look odd." Russell walked around each depression, and then stood back a few feet to look at them again as a group.

"What'd you think?" Tina was anxious for some type of confirmation from her Professor.

"I think we need to examine these a little closer and see what we might have." With his hands on his hips, assuming a posture that looked like a gunfighter from an old western, Russell walked around the depressions again. "Kevin, go back to my truck and get the steel rod out of the back please."

Kevin returned with the six-foot-long steel rod and handed it to Russell. With the pointed end of the rod, Russell struck the ground in several places, staying well away from the depressions. The ground was hard and unyielding. Russell then attempted to push the rod into the soil at the center and the edges of each depression. In each instance the rod penetrated the surface. The ground had, at some point, been disturbed in each of the six depressions. "Let's get the Coroner out here. I think you may have found something. Good observation, Tina."

Chapter five

While they waited for the Coroner to arrive, Professor Russell took the liberty of telling the uniformed officer to rope off the area under the pecan tree and keep people away from it, as well as the excavated area the officer had helped guard the last four days. Russell then sent his students home to relax for what was left of their weekend. After talking with the Coroner, he would decide how to proceed. If they didn't want to excavate this other area he might need to have ground-penetrating radar brought in. But he knew the radar's effectiveness would be limited. It worked great with rocks, stumps and other debris, but not so well with skeletal remains. Even though it appeared crude, the metal probe he used was sometimes his most effective tool. Soil, when it's disturbed like this, can sometimes remain softer than the surrounding soil for as long as a hundred years. He knew Tina's observations were correct. Something had been buried here.

Russell walked back to his truck and made a call to the Coroner.

"Hello."

"How's your weekend?"

"Is that you Russell?"

"Yes, Doug, it is. And I've got something for you down here that you need to see." The two men had worked together on other cases and even though they did not have a social friendship, they had a friendly working relationship."

"What'd you have?"

"When we were wrapping up, one of my students made an interesting find." Russell could hear Doug Brazell let out a heavy sigh into the receiver of the phone.

"Does interesting mean you're about to fuck-up my Sunday afternoon?"

"Probably so, Doug."

"I think we have possibly as many as six additional graves."

"Shit! What makes you think you have more?"

"Well, actually it's pretty standard stuff - depressions in the ground, healthier, more abundant vegetation in the close vicinity of the depressions, which could just be a coincidence in this case, but also the soil in the depressions is softer than the surrounding soil."

"You're sure they're graves?"

"I'm almost certain of it. But there is one difference. These are lined up in two rows of three each. The grave we just excavated was about twenty yards away near the edges of the old basketball court."

"You think this could be some old cemetery and not some more bodies that were dumped there?"

"Since the school was built on what was left of an old plantation it's very possible. But I think we definitely have graves here."

"You said you were packing up. You mind hanging out there for a few more minutes? I want to come down and look at this myself."

"Sure, I can stay. I've already sent my students home for the afternoon. We were actually just starting to pack everything up when one of them found the graves."

"Thanks. I'm at home right now in Shandon. I need to change. Give me about 30 minutes."

"No problem. See you then."

Brazell pulled into the Wardlaw lot and parked beside Professor Russell's truck. When he opened his car door the heat and humidity hit him like a wall. The two men shook hands as they greeted one another. Brazell then pulled a handkerchief from his pocket and wiped sweat from his forehead. "Damn, it's hot out here! I don't think I even remember what rain looks like."

"Yeah, it's been like that out here all week." Russell wasn't sympathetic to Brazell's lack of tolerance for the heat. "Let me show you what we've got."

The two men walked the fifty or so yards to the pecan tree. "Okay, show me what I'm looking at."

Russell, pointing to each of the depressions, explained to Brazell why he agreed with his student's observations. Brazell's experienced eye knew Russell was correct. And Will Russell was seldom wrong. There were six visible graves. He also hoped it was nothing more than an old cemetery long forgotten. Most of what was now Columbia had once been farmland. The Elmwood neighborhood where Wardlaw Junior High sat did not begin establishing itself until somewhere around 1890. But under the current circumstances, the graves had to be excavated. Even if there were no more murder victims, the dead deserved better than to be covered over by a parking lot.

The two men made plans for excavation of the graves. Will Russell would contact his students and begin first thing Monday morning. As for the remainder of his weekend, he would work in the lab examining the remains and preparing the official report for the Coroner's office.

As the two men bid each other good afternoon, on the other side of town, Jason sat on a bar stool at his kitchen counter with his tablet reading the account of the discovery of the skeleton.

Jason had managed to pick up bits and pieces of information from ease-dropping on the students' conversations. He wanted to know more.

Jason looked up from the tablet to be greeted by Sebastian, who proceeded to walk across the screen and with his back arched and then rub his head against Jason's chin. "You don't like anything to get more attention than you, do you little man?" Sebastian purred. "Do you want some lunch?"

Jason was hungry. He had slept late and had only a small bowl of cereal about ten that morning while Sebastian had his normal breakfast of cat food then finished off the milk left in Jason's bowl. Jason got up from the barstool where he was seated, picked up Sebastian and walked to the other side of the kitchen. Setting his feline friend on the countertop, he opened the refrigerator door and stared inside.

"Not much in here. Sebastian, why is it that after I go to the grocery store there's never anything to eat?" His refrigerator was, for the first time in almost two weeks, fully stocked with fruit, vegetables, and baked fish, and seafood from the deli. Jason hated cooking when he had to eat alone.

As he picked up an apple and bit into it, he heard two short horn blasts in his driveway. He knew it had to be Cindy. She always announced her arrival by blowing her horn twice. He thought it was an odd habit and an annoying one for the neighbors, but it was part of her personality. He had never asked why she blew the horn, but he assumed she either enjoyed making a noisy entrance or was giving a warning blast in case he had a date over. A date. He couldn't remember the last time he'd had a date.

Jason walked into the foyer to open the door and greet Cindy. "Hey, Jason. What're ya doin'?" Cindy was in a good mood as usual and she had her daughter with her.

"Hi Jamie." The little girl smiled and moved a little closer to her mother. She was always just a little shy for the first few minutes she was with Jason. Jamie had a little girl's crush on him and once asked if he would marry her mommy. The request made Jason a little uncomfortable. He was afraid that Cindy might have prompted the comment. Cindy was a terrific person but he had never thought of her as more than a friend and co-worker.

"Hey Jason," Jamie said with a smile as she moved a few inches away from her mother. "Is Sebastian awake?"

"Yes, he is. You can go inside and give him some kitty treats." Jason didn't have to say another word. Jamie quickly squeezed between him and the door facing and rushed into the kitchen.

"You busy? We just left Wal-Mart; I had to get her some new shoes. She's already worn out the ones I got her at the start of the summer."

"No, I'm not busy. I was just trying to decide what to eat. Have you had lunch yet?"

"Hey, we'll go. I don't want to interrupt your lunch."

"You're not interrupting. If you stay and eat with me, I'll have something healthy. If you leave, then I'll probably eat another bowl of cereal or have microwave popcorn."

"I don't see how you keep going on what you eat. It's probably why you look like you've lost weight."

"Trust me, I haven't lost weight. Do you want to stay for lunch?"

"We did get a late start today. We're both starting to get hungry. If you twist my arm, we'll stay for lunch."

"Consider it twisted."

Cindy seated herself on the barstool at the counter while Jason began pulling food from the refrigerator. Jamie went into the living room to entertain Sebastian. Cindy looked down at Jason's tablet. "I see you're reading about the bones at the school."

"What? Oh yes. I was just looking to see if there was any more news.

"Jason, you've been thinking about that body a lot, haven't you?"

Jason continued slicing a cucumber into small pieces. "I wouldn't say I've thought about it a lot. It's just hard not to think about it when I see them out there digging every day."

"When you think about it, what do you think?"

Jason furrowed his brow as he contemplated Cindy's question. "I overheard them talking. You know, the people excavating the site."

Cindy's curiosity was now sparked and she leaned forward on the barstool. "What'd they say?"

Jason laid down his paring knife and wiped his hands on a dishtowel. "Please don't repeat this. I wouldn't want anything to get out and me be responsible for damaging their investigation in any way."

"Come on, Jason, you know me better than that. I can keep a secret."

"I really didn't hear that much. Just that the bones probably belonged to a child. Somewhere between eleven and thirteen years old. And it was definitely white."

"Was it a boy or girl?"

"They said they can't tell when they are that young because there are no differences between the skeletons at that age. I also heard them say that if the bones have been there more than about five years, they probably wouldn't be able to tell exactly how long they have been there. He said the only way they would be able to date it would be if they found any artifacts."

"Artifacts?"

"Yes, you know, like things buried with the body that they could identify and date."

"What about cause of death?"

"I did a little research on the web myself. Unless there was damage to the skeleton or something that would remain in the bones, like poisons, they wouldn't be able to tell that either."

"Wow. That's a lot different from what you see on television."

"I know. I was pretty surprised. It's sad to think that out there somewhere there is probably a family that has no idea what happened to their son or daughter and probably never will. There is no way to get any kind of closure. You just keep hoping that someday they'll either come back or you will at least know what happened."

"Jason, don't you think maybe you're taking finding this body too personally? I mean, there's no telling how long it could have been there and you can't solve the case for the police. They're the experts."

"I wonder how hard it would be to get access to missing person records. I think that would be the first place they'd start, don't you?"

Cindy frowned. "What do you want to do, go through their files?"

"No, not at all. I just want to know how the police are going to handle this case. I want to know the procedure."

"There's a guy I went to high school with who's a cop over in Cayce. Why don't I give him a call and ask how they search through records."

Cindy had friends all over Columbia, and could get everything done, from free work on her car to fixing speeding tickets.

"You think he'd help me?"

"No, you're not his type; but he'll help me."

Jason smiled.

Chapter six

As Jason, Cindy and her daughter Jamie sat down to eat lunch, detectives Rob Edwards and Angela Porter were receiving a call from the Richland County Coroner's office.

Edwards sat at his gray metal desk tapping the end of an unlit cigarette against his black appointment book. Angela Porter was seated in a chair opposite him. After twenty-five years as a police officer, and fifteen of that as a detective, Edwards still had an office in the basement of the police station that wasn't much bigger than the janitor's closet. The concrete block walls were covered with faded brown paneling. The lighting was so dim in the small room that, without the desk lamp for reading, anyone who spent much time in there would have found themselves straining to see the words on a page.

Porter's office wasn't any better in terms of size, but since being promoted to detective she had taken time to at least make it a little brighter. Now she sat down the hall in Rob's dim office listening to the grim news from the Coroner's office as it was relayed over the speaker phone.

Angela leaned forward placing her elbows on her knees and cocking her head to better hear the voice on the other end of the line.

The frustration in Edwards' voice was obvious. "So, let me get this right. You're telling me we have six more graves out there?"

The faceless voice repeated the message. "Yes sir. There are possibly six more graves located a few yards from the one that was just excavated. The Coroner has made the decision to excavate those as well."

Angela, still leaning forward, interjected, "When were they found?"

"I believe within the last hour or so Ma'am."

"Who's on the scene now?"

"There are two officers guarding the site. The Coroner extended the

45

perimeter and had an additional officer added to the scene."

Edwards' face was changing from its normal ruddy light tan to flushed red. "Why the hell didn't anyone call me and let me know about all this?"

"I'm sorry sir, but I am calling you."

"Would you call the Coroner and tell him to contact me."

"Yes sir. I'll give him the message."

Edwards' tone was sarcastic. "Thank you." Edwards hung up.

"Edwards, there's no need to shoot the messenger." That guy at the Coroner's office was just following directions."

Ignoring her, Edwards pushed back in his chair. "Son-of-a-bitch! I've had to deal with that prick Brazell more than once. The son-of-a-bitch thinks that he can run an investigation for the police. If that body wasn't a bag of bones the moron wouldn't even be able to tell if it was dead or not."

Angela didn't understand the extreme dislike Edwards had for the corner. "Whether we like it or not, the law in this state says the Coroner has control of the bodies."

Edwards leaned back in his chair still tapping his unlit cigarette on the desk. "You saw those bones, too. You know some sick bastard killed a kid and buried it in that old playground. Now we have maybe six more."

The redness was starting to leave his face but he was still simmering inside. "They should've called us sooner."

"Maybe so, but they called. Now we need to go back and look around again, then wait for the forensic anthropologist's report so we'll know where to start."

Edwards laid down the cigarette and started fumbling with a Matchbox police car his grandson had given him. "Damn, I hate waiting around."

"I know, I hate it, too. But it's not like the murder happened yesterday and there's a fleeing felon and an evidence trail that's getting cold. That body's been there for a while. You and I both know we might not even be able to get I.D.s on the bodies."

Still holding the toy police car, "Yeah, I just hate it when it's kids."

Edwards paused for a moment. "I think I'll swing by there on the way home and just check it out. You want to come?"

"No, I'll see it tomorrow. I need to get home. Hanging out with you wasn't how I planned to spend my Sunday afternoon."

Edwards looked up from the toy police car. "There you go, hurtin' my feelings again."

Angela stood up and took a couple of steps toward the door. "You're the tough guy. You can handle it." Edwards smiled and, without speaking, gave her a wave good-bye then turned his attention to his toy police car. As Angela reached the end of the basement hallway, before ascending the stairs to the ground floor, she turned to look at Rob Edwards. Despite all the things about his personality she disliked, she respected the man. He was completely dedicated to his job and she suspected his family life had probably suffered for it. He was almost the age of her father, but today he appeared older, and tired.

Chapter seven

Across the city of Columbia, Monday morning came too early for almost everyone. It was only seven and already in the low seventies when Jason walked to the end of his driveway to put out his recyclables. He surveyed his lawn. Most of the grass was brittle and it cracked under his step. Every morning, he hosed the flowers and shrubs. Even if he wasn't supposed to water the lawn he could at least salvage the plants.

It had been almost one week since the discovery of the bones at the old school, and it had consumed much of his thoughts. He knew the Professor and his crew of students would be gone. Their work was to be completed Sunday. Unless he caught an update on the news, if the story even made the news again, he would never know what became of the case.

Standing in the driveway looking around at the flowers and shrubs in the yard, Jason decided he wasn't in the mood for watering. They could survive one day without it. He wanted to get to the school and look over the excavation site even though he told himself it was to double check the third-floor wiring to the schematics. Climbing into his Subaru and adjusting the radio to pick up the local public radio station instead of his favorite satellite station, Jason backed out of his driveway onto the street. He then headed for Saint Andrews Road, which would connect him with the interstate, then the I-126 connector across Broad River.

Jason zigzagged in and out of traffic as he crossed the Broad River Bridge. On the radio was another political commentator giving comment on what Congress was or was not doing. The morning rush hour traffic was clipping along at no less than ten miles an hour over the speed limit, with commuters tailgating and cutting one another off. Even though Jason paid attention to the traffic conditions around, him he was absorbed in thought. He felt as if there was something he should remember, something important. He was almost certain it had something to do with the old school.

When Jason arrived at the school he was surprised to see a car from the County Coroner's office, the detective's car and Professor Russell's truck. At the far end of the lot near the pecan tree he saw what looked like Glenn Stone arguing with one of the people in the group.

He walked across the lot to join the group. "Excuse me, but I'm guessing you're from the Coroner's office?"

"I am the Coroner. Who are you?"

Jason extended his hand to Doug Brazell. "I'm Jason Shealy, the architect on the Wardlaw renovation. Is there some problem here?"

"You tell that foreman of yours to shut up and cooperate with us or I'll shut down this whole job site."

Jason turned and looked at Glenn. Glenn had his ball cap off his head and was running his fingers through his short, thinning hair. Jason turned and again faced the Coroner. "Give us a few minutes to talk."

Jason and Glenn walked to the fence-row at the side of the school "So what's wrong, Glenn? What's happened?"

Glenn pulled off his ball cap and hit it against his leg then placed it back on his head with a forceful snap. Glenn took a couple short steps away from Jason then turned and stepped toward him again. "That son-of-a-bitch is going to shut us down!"

"What'd you mean, shut us down? They finished up yesterday afternoon, didn't they?"

"Oh yeah, they finished with that one over there," Glenn pointed to the trench. "But now they want to dig around and play in the sand over there." Glenn pointed in the direction of the pecan tree. "They say they gotta dig up that whole area and they want to inspect the rest of the grounds."

Jason was trying to calm Glenn and make some sense from what he was telling him. "Slow up; you lost me. First, why do they want to dig in another area?"

"They say they think they've found some more graves. There ain't no more graves here!"

Jason knitted his eyebrows and again questioned Glenn. "Wait a minute. They said they found more graves? How could they find more graves when they only dug in that one spot?"

"You tell me, you're the college graduate."

Jason gave a frustrated sigh. "Arguing with them isn't going to get us anywhere. We need to find out why they think they have more graves, and try to cooperate. If we don't cooperate then they will probably restrict our access. At that point we might as well be shut down. Let's just be calm. Let's cooperate with them so we can keep working."

"You go dick around and talk to them. I'm gonna call the developer and get someone out here to take care of this."

"We have to cooperate with the police. The developers can't do anything about that."

In reality, work had slowed very little, with the exception of the parking lot and some exterior finishing work to the back side of the building. "Whatever! You go work with them! I'm getting the developers out here!" With that Glenn stormed off for the construction trailer.

From a distance, Detectives Edwards and Porter watched the angry Glenn walk off. Edwards took one last long draw on his cigarette then tossed it on the ground and mashed it out with the toe of his shoe. He lit another cigarette and squinted as the cigarette ignited into life and smoke circled his head. "I'm goin' to see how our buddies from the University are doin'."

Detective Porter took this as an opportunity to speak to the Coroner. "Excuse me, Mr. Brazell; we've meet before but we have never had an opportunity to talk at any length." She extended her hand.

Brazell shook her hand. "Detective."

"Mr. Brazell, when do you think we can expect to receive a lab report from Professor Russell?"

Brazell turned so that his left shoulder was toward Detective Porter. Porter knew his body language was a brush off but she pretended not to notice.

"Interesting how they can determine so much about a person and how they died just by examining the skeleton," she said.

"Yes, it is. Russell's a smart man."

"I've never worked directly with him, but I know of his reputation. I hope there's enough there for him to give us something to go on. Most of these end up as a John Doe."

Brazell turned his head slightly in Porter's direction. "Well Detective, if there's anything there to give you, he'll find it."

"I hope so. Have you all known each other long?"

"I met him when he first came to the University. We called him in on a case. I was the deputy coroner then, that was maybe nine, ten years ago." Brazell and Porter were now standing shoulder to shoulder about a foot from each other. "Did they put you with old Rob so he could teach you everything he knows?"

"That's very possible, but hopefully he'll learn something from me, too."

Brazell laughed. "You've got your work cut out for you then. You know what they say about teachin' old dogs' new tricks."

"I don't discourage easily."

Brazell turned to Detective Porter and with a smile and lightly touched her upper arm. "It's been nice talkin' to you Detective, but I've got to get back to the office. Looks like Russell has everything under control here."

"Mr. Brazell, when can we expect to see a lab report on the remains?"

"Russell told me he'd have it to me in about two days unless something unusual showed up."

"Thanks, I'll be looking for it."

With that Doug Brazell walked to Russell's side and bid him good day.

Jason was still standing in the same place where he was when Glenn had walked away. There wasn't much he could do to help the situation and he knew it. Glenn was calling the developers. The police and anthropology crew were busy with their work. He knew the renovation work would possibly come to a halt. The uniformed officers were roping off the entire playground and the lawn on either side of the building leaving the front door as the only access in or out of the building. Jason wasn't the project manager and he would be paid regardless of when they finished, but still, this project meant more to him than just the money. He had put a lot of energy into the Wardlaw renovation, now with the discovery of the body he was allowing himself to develop an emotional involvement on a whole new level. Was it just morbid curiosity, or emotional baggage from his little brother's death? He really wasn't sure.

Jason was lost in his thoughts when Detective Edwards walked up behind him. "Looks like you didn't have much luck calming down your foreman."

"Oh, hey. I didn't hear you walk up."

"Yeah, sorry about that. Sand doesn't make too much noise when you walk on it. So like I said, your foreman sure does get upset."

"He's always like that. We've had so many arguments over this project I usually just ignore him."

"Why do you all argue so much?"

"I don't know. He's a good General Foreman, and a pretty smart guy. I guess we just have personalities like oil and water."

Edwards took another long draw on his cigarette. "What'd you think about all this?" He nodded his head in the direction of the students who were busy preparing a sketch map.

Jason began to feel as if he was being questioned and it made him nervous. "What do you mean?"

"Oh, I don't know. It's just kind of spooky findin' a skeleton buried on a playground. Makes ya kinda wonder what stories those walls would tell if they could talk. Old buildings like this have lots of stories." Edwards was reading Jason and playing on it, trying to draw him out and get him to volunteer information about himself. Not that he considered Jason even remotely a suspect. It was just that the probing and subtle inquisition was second nature to him. Drawing someone into conversation; getting them to betray even the smallest pieces of information.

As Edwards talked about the building Jason began to feel more at ease. Buildings, he understood. They had a language all their own, especially the very old ones. It was people whom he didn't always communicate with well. "Yes, this is a pretty neat old building. I've loved working on it; it's been like a dream project for me."

"I bet it's been kind of hard to see the work slow down? You've probably got a lot riding on this."

"I get paid regardless. But having a project this big under my belt could really boost business. I think Glenn's the one that'll probably get hurt if we don't finish on time. He gets a bonus if we finish on schedule."

Edwards squinted as the smoke from his cigarette stung his eyes. "Is that so? How big a bonus? Maybe I should change to a different line of work."

"I'm not sure. But I've heard him talk about buying a new truck so it must be a fairly decent one. Which is probably why he is so bent out of shape."

"Well, you tell your buddy that if we're lucky we won't find anything in these holes and he can go back to work full tilt. Otherwise, we'll all be here for a while longer."

Hearing the word "longer" from Detective Edwards brought back Jason's feelings of anxiety. "How long is longer? Are you talking about days or weeks or what?"

Edwards tossed his cigarette on the ground in front of him. "Don't know. Could be a few days or a few weeks, it just all depends on what they find over there."

"Do you think they'll find anything?"

"Well, let me put it to you this way. If they are going to find anything they'll find it pretty quick because when a murderer's tryin' to get rid of a body, you got one of two situations, sometimes both. He's either lazy and doesn't want to dig down too far, or he's in a hurry because he's afraid he'll get caught so he still doesn't dig down too far." With that the detective walked away from Jason and joined his partner Angela Porter. She was looking over the shoulder of Tina, the student who was busy drawing the sketch map.

Jason looked at his watch. "Damn!" It was almost nine. He had a meeting with a prospective client in fifteen minutes. He had let the time slip away. Jason looked at the construction trailer. He knew Glenn was inside on the phone with the developers. He wanted to give them his opinion, but now he didn't have time.

Chapter eight

It was late Tuesday afternoon. Angela sat at her desk in her tiny office in the basement of the Columbia City Police Department. The paperwork never seemed to stop. Often, she felt she spent more time filing reports then actually doing the investigation. As she picked up another case file from the stack on her desk, the phone rang. "Hello, this is Detective Angela Porter. May I help you?"

It was a woman's voice on the other end of the line. "Hello, Detective Porter. I'm from the Coroner's office. Mr. Brazell asked me to call to see if you have a few minutes to talk about the Wardlaw case."

It had been a week since the skeleton was discovered and Angela was eager for any information. "Of course. When would he like to talk to me?"

"Detective, if you stay on the line I'll put you on hold for just a moment then connect you with Mr. Brazell."

"Okay, sure." There was a short silence then a clicking sound.

"Hello? Detective Porter?"

"This is she."

"Detective. Good to talk to you again. I think I've got something here you've been waiting for." Doug Brazell was friendly, almost jovial as he spoke with Angela.

"And what would that be, Mr. Brazell?" She was hoping it was the lab report on the bones Professor Russell and his students had excavated the week before.

"You don't have to be so formal with me Detective, just call me Doug. I'm sure you've heard your partner call me lots of things." Brazell drew his words out longer and tried to add a touch of Charleston to his speech.

"Actually, Doug, Edwards has rarely mentioned you. But then this is the first homicide I've worked with him."

"Well, we've got a little love-hate relationship," Brazell said, drawing out the syllables of relationship.

"I wouldn't know about that." She paused. "So, is the report ready?"

"Have it right here in front of me." Again, Brazell added the long draw to his words. "Looks like there's not goin' to be much for you to go on, Detective."

"When can we get a copy?"

"Oh, you can get one right now. I can send someone over with a copy, but it might be a while before I can get someone freed up to deliver it. Or you can come over and pick it up yourself."

Angela thought for a moment. She wondered if he thought she was so stupid that she couldn't see through him. Men like him were so transparent, and she had met plenty. "I could probably leave here in a few minutes and pick it up. Probably won't make that much difference. But I would like to have something to get started on."

"It'll be right here waiting for you."

"Thanks. See you then."

Angela looked around the station for Edwards. She wanted to tell him about the call and the report. She tried to call him, but after a few minutes wait there was no call back. "Shit. I'll just leave him a voice mail and pick the thing up myself." She picked up the car keys from her desk and closed the office door behind her as she left.

*****

In his office Jason sat mindlessly drawing circles, squares and triangles, one after another on a note pad. Still he had the same nagging feeling that had troubled him for the last few days. There was something about Wardlaw he should remember. Somehow it was connected with the school itself, not about the renovation project. He knew it was something he must've passed over in the research he did, but what?

As he drew another interlocking row of triangles his cell phone rang. Jason was instantly snapped back to the present. He looked at his phone. It was his mother.

Jason closed his eyes and rubbed the bridge of his nose at the sound of the voice bombarding his ear. "Jason, this is your mother. You do remember me, don't you? I'm the woman who gave birth to you."

Jason replied with a touch of sarcasm in his voice. "Actually, I can't recall much prior to about five years old and the rest I try to block out."

"Very funny. I haven't talked to you in almost a week. I was wondering if you had dropped off the face of the earth."

Still rubbing the bridge of his nose in an attempt to massage away the headache that was quickly developing, Jason let out a sigh. "I've just been busy, Mom."

"Too busy to call your mother?"

"I just have a lot going on right now. I'm trying to be successful and make you proud." Again, Jason had the same hint of sarcasm in his voice.

"Well, we're already proud of you. We just worry. Sometimes we wonder if starting your own business was the right move. You know it can be risky going out on your own like that."

Despite his irritation with his mother, Jason could hear the genuine concern in her voice. "No Mom, you worry too much. As for Dad, he's just afraid that if I go broke, I'll want to move back in with you. We both know how much that would upset his world." All their conversations had a pattern. Jason knew his mother would next try to defend his father and rationalize his actions.

"Honey, I wish you wouldn't be so hard on your father. He loves you. He just doesn't do a good job showing it sometimes. Men from his generation are like that."

Hearing what he knew was genuine pain in her voice, Jason was now more irritated with himself than his mother. Why was it so easy for her to make him feel guilty? "Mom, please don't start about Dad again, I'm just not in the mood to talk about him."

"Okay. I didn't call to talk about your father anyway. I just hadn't heard from you in a few days and wanted to make sure you were all right."

"I'm fine mom, really. I've just been busy."

"Jason, I heard on the news this morning they were digging up more bodies on the old Wardlaw playground. Is that true?"

Now Jason knew the ulterior motive for the phone call. Typically, about seven days had to pass before he would get an I-never-hear-from-you call from his mother. Since it hadn't been exactly seven days something had to be up. "They're doing more digging because they feel they have reason to suspect there could be more bodies. Not that they have actually found more. There's a difference."

"I understand there's a difference, but I didn't hear all the news. I just caught the end of it. That is so terrible! I can't imagine someone killing people and burying them like that. That must be so terrible for the families. Not knowing what happened to them. Just like that girl that disappeared from down in Five Points years ago."

"I know, Mom." Jason's head was now throbbing. It felt as if a rope was slowly being tightened around his skull. He rubbed his forehead to ease the pressure, but he knew it would only get worse. His mother couldn't talk about anything even remotely related to death or dying without bringing up the subject of his brother.

"At least I have a little peace knowing what happened to your brother. My heart still breaks for him, but at least I don't have to live my life not knowing."

Jason had enough. "Mom, could we talk about something else?" Jason closed his eyes. He knew there was no stopping his mother.

"I remember when that girl in your Aunt Bess's class ran away from home. They looked everywhere for her, but never found a trace of her. You and your brother and sister were so young then. And I just remember thinking how her parents must have felt."

Even though at this point Jason had all but stopped listening to his mother and her lamenting, her comment about the run-away triggered a vague and distant memory. "Mom, what was that about the girl running away?"

"I was just saying how her parents…"

Jason interrupted before she could start another round of lamenting for the dead and missing. "No, I mean about her being in Aunt Bess's class and running away. Who was she?"

Delighted that Jason was showing an interest in what she had to say, the tone of her voice changed from despair to almost cheerful. "Oh my gosh, that was so long ago I don't remember her name. I just remember how it troubled your aunt so. It was so sad."

"So Aunt Bess was teaching at Wardlaw when that happened? Seems like I remember something about that."

"You probably do remember a little about it. I think you were probably eight or nine when it happened…or maybe that was your sister. Anyway it was on the news. This girl and one of her friends were going to run away from home, but she was the only one that went through with it. The other one changed her mind."

"And you don't remember what year it was?"

"No. I just remember how awful it was…"

Again, Jason cut his mother off in mid-sentence. "Do you think Aunt Bess would remember?"

"I'm sure she would. You know how she remembers everything."

Jason could hear the resentment in his mother's voice. Bess was his father's sister and had always been considered the shining star of the family. Bess finished college and became a teacher, then went back to school and got a PhD, then eventually landed a professorship at the University of South Carolina. She painted and traveled, and pretty much lived life on her own terms, but her greatest sin in the eyes of his mother was the influence Bess had over him when he was a child. To Jason, Bess was the only person in his family he could count on. To his mother, she was more educated than any woman needed to be, and most likely lived an immoral lifestyle.

Jason knew about the "immoral" lifestyle his mother hinted at in conversations, but would never actually talk about. The summer after Tommy's death, Bess took him to Cape Cod for a trip that was only to last a couple of weeks. Bess eventually talked his parents into letting him stay for the summer. Jason considered those three months, living in the small rented bungalow with Aunt Bess, to be the best summer of his life. Her friends, who were also summer residents of Provincetown, were all so very interesting. They took him out on their rented sailboats where he saw whales for the first time. Often in the evening they would build bonfires on the beach and sing while one of the women played guitar. Sometimes the women would dance together and sometimes he would join them. They were so much fun to be with; especially one or two of the women who dressed a little like men and took him fishing. Bess and her friends doted over him and made him forget the guilt he felt over Tommy's death.

Jason felt more strongly than ever that there was something about Wardlaw he needed to remember. "When's Aunt Bess going to be back in town?" She had flown to upstate New York to visit an old friend from college who had recently been ill. It was one of the women Jason remembered from that summer and who had helped him fish.

The annoyance sounded in his mother's voice. "I thought she would've been back by now. I mean I don't see why she had to go all the way up there anyway. That woman has family that can take care of her."

Rather than argue with his mother and defend his aunt he chose to ignore her remarks. "You don't know what day she's coming back? I would like to ask her about that girl that ran away."

"Why do you want to know about some girl that ran away? That had to have been thirty or forty years ago and it broke her parent's hearts? Things were starting to change back then and it just keeps getting worse every day. I worry about your sister's children, with all the drugs and crime now-a-days."

Jason could feel his headache begin to throb against his forehead. Like a chameleon changing its colors, his mother, in a span of less than five minutes, had shifted her moods from despair, excitement and now to anger and resentment. "Okay Mom, I'll call Aunt Louise and ask her if I can't reach Aunt Bess."

"I didn't realize you were friends with Louise." He could hear the resentment in her voice.

"Of course, I'm friends with Louise. She's lived with Aunt Bess for over thirty years at least. She stops by the house all the time." Jason instantly knew he had made a mistake by mentioning Louise. Usually Jason was better at volleying his mother's remarks, but with the headache and his preoccupation with the discovery of the remains he wasn't as careful.

"She sees you all the time! I'm your mother and I can't even get an invitation for coffee. For the life of me I'll never understand why you want to associate yourself with those people. Your Aunt Bess is one thing. She's family. You have to be civil to her. But that woman and their friends… I just don't understand."

"Well Mom, I'm sorry you don't understand why I like spending time with Aunt Bess and Aunt Louise."

"Don't you get smart with me, I'm still your mother and how dare you call that woman an aunt. She's not welcome in this family."

"The rest of the family welcomes her. It's just you and Dad who don't. She is my family. Why don't you just go ahead and say what an ungrateful son I am. Tell me how Tommy would have never turned out like me."

"Don't you use your dead brother's name like that!"

"By the way Mom, just so you'll know, in the last election, I voted for all Democrats." With that Jason hung up on his mother. Jason stood up and paced back and forth across the floor of his small office while he rubbed his forehead. As he paced off the adrenaline he replayed the conversation in his head and began to smile. Talking to himself he said, "I'll have to tell Aunt Bess and Louise about this one. They'll love the voting Democrat comment."

Jason looked at his watch. It was almost time for everyone in the office to start packing up to go home for the day and he still had more work to finish. Louise wouldn't be home for at least another three or four hours if she had any afternoon appointments. She sold real estate in the Columbia area and made good money doing it. Louise was the one who located the office building for Jason when he was starting up his firm and she often helped out by recommending him to clients who needed remodeling or renovations.

Jason stuck his head out his office door. "Cindy, you got a minute?"

"Sure, I'll be right there."

Cindy walked in to Jason's office to see him frowning with his eyes closed and rubbing his temples with his fingertips. "You okay?"

"I'm fine. I just got off the phone with my mother."

"Oh." Cindy knew about the relationship Jason had with his parents. Her relationship with her own parents was probably just as dysfunctional, but in a different way.

"What was she going off about this time?"

"Have a seat. Oh, she went through the entire range of emotions. She went from why didn't I call her to ranting about Bess and Louise. Finally ended with me telling her I voted for Democrats in the last election."

Cindy laughed. "Boy, that must have been a knock-down, drag-out if you said that."

"We've had worse."

"What got her going this time?"

"I asked when Aunt Bess was going to get back in town."

"She really hates your aunt doesn't she?"

"I think actually she's jealous of my aunt's life."

"You mean your mom secretly wants to date women."

Jason smiled. "No, smart ass. My aunt has had a fun, interesting life and Mom likes to play the role of southern belle and homemaker. She wanted to be a member of a country club and drink ice tea on the veranda, only Dad has never made enough money for her to have that life style."

"Your parent's house doesn't have a veranda."

Jason laughed.

"So how did the subject of Bess come up?"

"I had forgotten about it, but before Bess finished her PhD she taught at Wardlaw. There was a girl in one of her classes that supposedly ran away from home."

"Okay, so what are you saying?"

"I'm just wondering if there is some connection between the runaway and the remains that were found."

"You think it could be the same girl?"

"Who knows. But I'm trying to remember something I saw when I was researching Wardlaw. Something about a couple of missing children, but I didn't really read it because I was looking for information about the building itself. I need to go back to the state paper and see if I can find those articles again. I just wish I knew what I was looking for. The two probably have nothing to do with each other, but I just have a funny feeling about it."

Cindy's curiosity was sparked now, too. She started running various disappearance and murder scenarios through her head. "Have you listened in on any more of their conversations?"

"No, the police have so much of the school grounds roped off I can't get near them."

"You are just going to have to let the police do their work."

"I just don't think they'll look in the right place."

"In the right place for what?"

Jason was frustrated. "I don't know. They'll just miss something. I just feel it. There is something I found. I just need to find it again."

"And you'll find this something?"

Jason was silent for a moment. He knew Cindy was probably right, but he didn't want to listen. "I need to go to *The State* newspaper office before they close and look through their files again."

"Are you going to review those drawings I did of the stair detail for the Masterson house before you leave? I've never done a stair detail before."

Jason was gathering up his papers and stuffing them into his messenger bag. "I know you haven't done one by yourself before. I'll look at it tomorrow. I have to get going before The State closes."

"The library stays open longer. You could review the drawings, then look at microfilm there."

"I have a friend in the circulation department that helps me find information when I need something."

"Jason, you're ignoring work!"

Impatiently, Jason replied, "I'm not ignoring work. I know exactly what we have to do."

"Yeah, but we can't do some things without you. You're the licensed architect in the office, not the rest of us!"

"I know how much time I need. Don't worry about it."

Looking her in the eye, Jason again told Cindy, "Don't worry. I'm not going to let work go and nothing is going to happen to the firm. We're doing great right now. Actually, so great we can barely keep up."

"I know. That's why we need you here and not chasing some ghost story."

"I'm not chasing a ghost story. This was a real child that was murdered; at least, I think it was a child, and now maybe there are others. I just think I can find something that could help."

"Help what, bring Tommy back to life?" As soon as the words were out her mouth Cindy regretted saying them. "I'm sorry. I shouldn't have

63

said that."

Jason looked at her in silence. There was a wounded look in his eyes.

Cindy tried to apologize. "Jason, I'm really sorry I said that. I just don't know when to keep my big mouth shut sometimes. It just starts going in high gear and my brain is still in neutral."

"Cindy, it's okay. Don't worry about it. If I got upset every time someone brought up Tommy, then my parents would have driven me crazy years ago and I would've been locked up in a psychiatric ward by now." Jason threw the strap of his messenger bag over his shoulder and put on his Ray Bans. "Would you lock up for me please?"

"Sure thing," Cindy replied as the door closed.

Chapter nine

Sitting opposite Doug Brazell, Angela looked up from the report. "There's not much to go on here: white, somewhere between the age of eleven and thirteen, sex couldn't be determined, has been interred in excess of five years, possibly sometime around the late sixties to mid-seventies due to the clothing and artifacts found with the remains. That's a pretty wide time frame to look for a missing person. The victim could even have been wearing vintage or second hand clothes."

"Yes, I know, but unfortunately that's about as good as it gets sometimes. At least you have the I.D. bracelet, that could shed some light on who this child was."

"Was there any indication of cause of death, even if it is just speculation at this point?"

"I spoke with Professor Russell myself and he told me that there were no marks on the skeleton which would indicate a cause of death and the toxicology reports were all negative."

"What about strangulation? Was the hyoid bone broken?"

Brazell furrowed his brow. "Most people aren't aware of this Detective Porter, but the hyoid bone isn't always broken during strangulation."

"Oh really, I didn't know that."

"Don't feel bad, crime novels and television make such a big deal about it even professionals like yourself aren't informed. They really don't teach you officers enough about forensics. I see it as an oversight of most police departments."

Angela was getting pissed. She wanted to tell Brazell that Edwards was right when he described him as a self-absorbed pompous ass, but she knew at least one of them needed to be able to get along with the man. "Well, maybe you can propose that we detectives take some classes in forensics."

The corner of Brazell's mouth turned up slightly and his blue eyes had almost a cheerful look in them. "Angela. It is all right if I call you Angela, isn't it? I mean we'll be working together on this case and Detective Porter and Mr. Brazell sounds so formal. I'm that way with all the people here in the office that are under me. I want them to use my first name so that they feel we work together as a team, not just that they work for me."

"That's fine. Whatever you prefer." Angela felt she should stick to calling him Mr. Brazell and she wasn't sure why she agreed so easily to being on a first name basis with him. The way he described his style of management and his interactions with the people who worked for him sounded almost condescending. "Mr. Brazell, I believe Detective Edwards may be at the school right now checking on the excavation work. I need to get back and give him a call and see how it's going."

"Please, its Doug, remember."

"Okay, Doug." The words hung in her throat. "As I was saying, I thank you for calling me so quickly with this report. I need to go now and check on how things are going at the school."

"Of course, Angela. You detectives are always loaded down with cases." Brazell stood up and straightened his tie.

Angela shook his extended hand. "Thank you, Doug. Let me know as soon as you have anything else for us."

"Well Angela, you all over at the police station track down some names for us to start working with and we'll match them up with medical records," he said, holding on to her hand just a little longer than was appropriate.

Angela pulled her hand free. "We'll see what we can come up with."

Angela was caught in traffic on I-26. Another tractor trailer had taken the taken the ramp from I-26 to I-20 too fast and snarled traffic on both sides of the interstate.

She knew her friend Becky Thompson was probably already waiting patiently in the food court and most likely eating either a chocolate chip cookie or a soft pretzel. Becky was one of the few close female friends she had outside the police force. Most people didn't understand the demands of her work. Becky's father had been a state police officer, so at least she could relate. She could tell Becky how sometimes she could feel the badge, the work consuming her from the inside out. It was gradual but it was consuming her all the same. She was young compared to some of the other detectives, but already she had seen the darkest sides of human nature.

Becky was a good friend, patient and understanding. She wasn't part of Angela's work life. She was someone Angela could be herself with, the other self, the small part that wasn't focused on being a detective.

Angela picked up her cell phone and tried again to call Rob Edwards. Finally the cars in front of her were moving. She punched the accelerator and maneuvered in and out between the three lanes of West bound traffic. As she shot up the ramp which would throw her out onto Harbison Boulevard and in the middle of rush hour mall traffic, her cell phone rang.

The phone rang a couple of times before she could take her hands off the steering wheel to answer.

"Hello."

It was Edwards. "Hey, what do you want?"

"What do you mean, what do I want? I've been calling you all afternoon."

"You're startin' to sound like my wife."

"Yeah, and your wife is a saint. I have the lab report on the remains."

Instantly Edwards' voice changed from annoyance to anticipation. "So what does it say?"

Angela was now negotiating the turn from Harbison Boulevard into the Mall parking lot while she held the phone in place with her shoulder and shifted gears. "Not much, partner. Not much other than a starting point."

"So what's our starting point?"

"It's a child somewhere between the ages of eleven and thirteen, white and has been in the ground in excess of five years."

"Shit. This ain't gonna be easy, is it. Anything else?"

"That's about it other than the I.D. bracelet with the name 'Peggy' on it and they did say the shoes, zippers and clothing artifacts could be from the sixties or early seventies."

"So, we got a kid that went missing sometime in the last fifty years. They didn't start that missing persons data base until the eighties so if its earlier than that we ain't gonna have much luck."

"We could always get the face reconstructed and run it on the news. It's worked before."

"I'm gonna go see if I can start runnin' some missing persons reports. You want to join me?"

Angela's phone began to crack and pop. "I think I'm about to lose the connection. I'll see you tomorrow. I'm out at Columbiana Mall right now. I'm meeting a friend of mine."

"Yeah, sure. See ya in the morning."

Angela pulled into an empty parking spot near the main entrance. She let out a sigh as she checked her hair in the mirror on the back of the sun visor. She looked tired and she knew it. She stuffed her phone into her pants pocket. Hopefully, she and Becky would be able to finish shopping and actually have a nice relaxing dinner without being interrupted. Angela needed to purge her mind of police work even if only for a couple of hours.

Chapter ten

Jason arrived at The State newspaper office just as they closed for business to the general public. "Damn it! I should've just gone by the library instead of coming all the way out here." Jason hit his steering wheel with his hand, then sat in his Subaru and tried to decide what he should do next. He knew going by the school would be useless. The excavation crew would still be working, but he wouldn't be able to get close to them.

Jason started the engine and turned the air conditioning on high. The summer heat was oppressive and there was no rain in the forecast. Sometimes he felt he should have stayed in Kentucky. At least there the summers didn't last as long and when it did get hot there was still a breeze in the air. It was difficult to reach his Aunt Bess; her cell service in that part of New York was spotty, so he sent Louise a text message. Hopefully, she wasn't tied up with a client and would call him.

Pulling out of the parking lot, Jason headed down Shop Road toward the I-177 connector so he could get on I-26 and bypass the downtown afternoon traffic. His mind was a jumble of thoughts and emotions. He felt almost desperate to find out something, anything, about Wardlaw, the runaway girl, the remains that were unearthed. Deep inside his body he felt a tension and anxiety that was reminiscent of arguments with his father, but now it came from a new source. Jason knew these feelings weren't emotionally healthy, but he didn't care. He was consumed with the need to know what happened and who put the body in its lonely, secret grave.

The cell phone rang as he approached the Bush River Road exit. "Hello."

"Jason, you sent me a text."

"Yes. Do you have time to talk?"

"I just finished up with a client. I'm on my way to the airport to pick up your Aunt Bess."

"Really! So she's back now?"

"Her plane should land in about twenty minutes."

"That's great. I was going to ask you when she was coming back. I tried to reach her a couple times, but the call and text didn't go through. I need to talk to her about when she was teaching at Wardlaw."

"Where are you now? You could just meet me at the airport. She'd love to see you."

"Well, you two probably want to get home and spend some time alone. And I know she probably needs some time to chill and settle in."

"Yes, but you could still meet me there. It would be a nice surprise."

"Tell you what. I have some things I need to check on tonight. How about I have you all over for dinner tomorrow night?"

"That sounds wonderful. But I need to check with Bess first. But don't go to any trouble cooking, you know Bess doesn't care."

"Don't worry. You're family. I know I don't have to impress you. Oh, tell Aunt Bess to bring her Wardlaw yearbooks if she has any."

"Which one do you want her to bring?"

"Just tell her to bring all of them. Hello, hello, you still there?" The phone was silent, the call had dropped.

As he pulled into the driveway he could see Sebastian on the second floor looking out the bedroom window. No matter the time of day or night Sebastian was always waiting for him to come home and was always glad to see him. Work and Sebastian seemed at times to be the only two constants in his life. His relationships with his parents and sister were strained at best. In the past his sister tried to play the role of mediator. But she gave up long ago. The emotional scars were too deep and their parents were unwilling to compromise. Now that his sister was married, with children of her own, she didn't want to waste the emotional energy and spent more time with her husband's family.

At least he had Aunt Bess. Sometimes he wondered what he would do when she was gone. Perhaps he would be married by then and have children of his own, but that thought frightened him. His parent's example made him reluctant to enter into any type of emotional commitment to another person. Having a cat and good friends was so much safer.

Jason pulled into the garage and turned off the engine before lowering the door. Once securely inside, he stuffed some papers into his messenger bag and threw the strap over his shoulder as he slid out of the car. He put his door key in the knob and as he turned it, the door swung open. Instantly, Jason knew he had forgotten to lock the deadbolt that morning. It was a minor thing, especially with the security system he had installed last year – his Christmas present to himself. Still he didn't feel the house was secured without the deadbolt locked as well.

"Sebastian, I'm home." Before he could call again the fuzzy orange and white cat was arching his back and rubbing against Jason's leg.

"Are you glad to see me little man? Boy, I'm glad to see you." Jason picked up Sebastian and rubbed his face into the soft fur of the cat's neck and head. Sebastian gave loud rhythmic purrs as Jason scratched behind his ears. The sound was soothing and helped calm some of Jason's tension.

After emptying a can of cat food into Sebastian's dish Jason walked to the living room and stretched out on the sofa. A few minutes rest might do some good. He adjusted the pillow beneath his head. His green eyes slowly scanned the room. Cindy was right. He had worked too hard to build up his still fledgling business and buy a home to let his obsession with the remains uncovered at Wardlaw jeopardize it.

He picked up the remote and surfed channels until he stopped on his preferred station for local news. He was tired from lack of sleep and the summer heat had only drained him further. It was almost time for the six o'clock news. Jason struggled to keep his eyes open but sleep was overtaking taking him. As Jason slowly drifted out of consciousness and into sleep, the face of Dorothy Danze flashed on the television screen. "Hello, this is Dorothy Danze. Tonight I'm joining you from what was once the playground of the Wardlaw Junior High School. Now this playground is the scene of what may become a murder investigation as six additional sets of remains were unearthed…" Jason was asleep.

Chapter eleven

It was only eight in the morning, but already the sun had evaporated what little dew had formed on the parched and drought-stricken grass of the Carolina Midlands. With the television broadcasts from the day before and a front page story in *The State* newspaper by mid-morning, most of Columbia would most likely be discussing, analyzing and giving their opinions on the discovery of what had become a total of seven sets of skeletal remains buried beneath the former playground of the old school.

As the sun began to rise higher in the sky and the humidity increased, so did the community's apprehensions. Since no information describing the few artifacts found with the first skeleton had been released, some believed the bones belonged to former slaves who had worked the fields of the old Clark Place. The South Carolina natives, who spoke of the Civil War as if ended only last year, were convinced the bones were most likely those of people killed by some of Sherman's Yankee soldiers.

Most residents of the greater Columbia area who had followed the news reports feared a much more chilling scenario behind the presence of the skeletons. They knew it was much more likely that another serial killer, someone reminiscent of Gaston, was walking among them, stalking one innocent person after another, their only objective the thrill of slaughtering their victim without mercy.

Professor Russell had added two more students to the excavation crew so the work would proceed faster than with the first set of remains. The police now knew they were dealing with the worst type of murder investigation. This was a case that would probably go unsolved. The bodies had been in the ground too long and if they were even able to identify the remains, whatever trail the killer may have left would most likely be gone. Their only chance to find some justice for the young victims and their families would be to identify them and then look for a common thread. A thread that would pull the pieces together and then, like a compass, point them in the proper direction. The direction that would eventually lead to their killer.

Detective Edwards, with the back of his white shirt wet from sweat, stood a few feet away from professor Russell and his students, watching in silence as they carefully wrapped in newspaper one of the six newly discovered skeletons. He and his partner had their work cut out for them. At least there was a starting point – a kid named Peggy missing for at least five-plus years. He had to go back to the station and get started on the missing persons reports. Angela was probably there already, searching the names. She was efficient, and eager like he used to be before the job ate away at him. Edwards pulled out another cigarette and lit it.

Angela walked up and broke his train of thought. "This place is starting to look like a circus."

"Hey, there. I thought you'd be at the station going through missing person files."

Angela moved a couple steps in front of Edwards so his cigarette smoke wouldn't drift into her face. "No, I started going through them, then thought I'd better wait until we had information on all the remains. No use going through the files looking for one person, then going through them all again."

Edwards took a long draw from his cigarette then flicked it on the ground in front of him. "Russell said they didn't find anything with these skeletons like they did the other one."

Angela, puzzled, knitted her eyebrows. "Nothing at all?"

"Not a thing. No buttons, no shoes, no zippers, no nothing. But the funny thing is that, so far, it looks like these six were laid in their graves just like that first one that was dug up."

"What'd you mean?" Angela wasn't following Edward's train of thought.

"That girl over there, Tina, one of Russell's students," Edwards nodded his head in the direction of the excavation crew as he snorted cigarette smoke out his nostrils. "She pointed out when they got that first skeleton uncovered…" He put his hands together. "It's hands were like this, like it was praying. Like in the pictures you see of sleeping children looking like angels."

"Yes, I know the kind you're talking about. So all of these are posed the same way?"

"That's right."

"That's interesting. I wonder if they'll turn up anything when they start sifting the dirt. They didn't find the I.D. bracelet until after the entire skeleton had been removed."

Angela slowly turned her head, surveying the activity. "Is he going to be able to get us a report on these skeletons in a reasonable amount of time? That first one took too long."

Shifting his stare from the excavation work to the sand that had left a dusty residue on the toes of his brown wingtips, Edwards breathed in deeply then let out a raspy cough. "Yeah, I talked to him earlier. He said he would give us approximate age, race, and sex if he can. He said he would have the x-rays done while we're lookin' for a match on the physical description."

Angela looked at Edwards. He was still staring at his shoes. "Are you going back to the station?" she asked.

"Right behind you. Hey, this is going to be a tough one. Don't let it get to you."

"I'll be okay. See you there. And you need to get that cough checked. It sounds terrible."

"I'll get my cough checked as soon as you get your headaches checked."

"I hear you." As Angela walked back to her car she saw Jason standing just beyond the crime scene tape watching her. When he realized she had seen him, he waved and began walking along the parameter of the tape so he could intersect her path to her car.

As she approached him she began to take notice of his appearance for the first time. Not bad, she thought. Nice build. He must exercise. Kind of boyishly cute. Other than the hair that's a little long, pretty clean cut looking. Seems a little tense though. Probably just worried about his renovation project. A little too interested in this case. Must be a crime buff. Angela thought all people who were into reading crime novels, and

75

obsessing over police work, were a little odd. He doesn't look like a nut; too bad he probably is one.

It had been a long time since Angela had been involved with anyone. Her last boyfriend couldn't handle the demands of her job and most of the men she met through work were either cops or on the wrong side of the bars. Her friend Becky had fixed her up with a guy six months earlier, but on their first date he wanted to try out her handcuffs. There wasn't a second date. It wasn't that she didn't think the handcuffs weren't an interesting idea with the right person, but this guy was too forward for a first date, or the fifth date for that matter.

"Hi, Detective Porter, remember me? I'm Jason Shealy, the architect on this project."

"I remember you." Angela noticed for the first time that Jason's eyes were a deep green and had small lines at their corners when he smiled. He was nice to look at.

"Detective, I was just wondering if you had managed to identify the remains." Jason was apprehensive about talking with Detective Porter. He felt almost desperate for any information he could get his hands on. He thought about mentioning the missing girl his mother spoke of but he doubted she would think it significant.

"We haven't identified the remains yet."

"Do you have a physical description of the person?"

Angela was slightly annoyed with Jason's questions. He sounded like a reporter. "That information, Mr. Shealy, has not been released to the public."

"Is it going to be released?"

"After reviewing all the missing persons reports, if we don't have a match, then we might have to release that information and ask the general public for help." Angela was short and concise with her answers.

Jason could now detect the irritation in Angela's voice. "I'm sorry, I don't want to be a pest, but I do have a legitimate interest in how the case is progressing."

As Angela looked at Jason there was a moment of silence between them. Maybe she was wrong and he wasn't a nut. How could someone with green eyes like that be a nut? If he wasn't a nut, then he was probably only interested in how the investigation affected him and this job, not the victims or their families, which meant he was shallow and self-centered. Which was he?

"I'm sorry, I'd like to tell you more but I'm not at liberty to discuss it." Angela watched as a look of disappointment, and what seemed almost like sadness, come over Jason's face. "Maybe I can tell you more after all the remains have been recovered."

"That's quite alright, I understand. You have regulations to follow and an investigation to protect." Jason reached into his back pants pocket and pulled out a brown leather business card holder that had his initials "JMS" embossed on the cover. "Here, let me give you one of my business cards and I'll write my personal cell number on it too, just in case there's anything I can do to help."

"Mr. Shealy…"

"Please, just call me Jason. Mr. Shealy makes me feel too old."

"Okay, Jason. I have to be honest with you. If there is any information released, you'll probably hear about it on the local news first."

"So, you're saying you won't call."

"I'm just telling you now that I can't give out information. And I don't make it a habit to call people to chat just because they're curious about how a case is progressing. And I don't involve civilians."

Jason looked at Angela. There was an invisible wall around her not unlike his own. "Just keep the card in case you need it."

Angela slid the business card into the front pocket of her slacks. "If you'll excuse me. I've got to get back to the station. Missing person files to sort, remember."

"Yes, I have to go myself. Work at the office has been getting a little behind the last few days. Nice talking to you again."

Angela felt an awkwardness between them almost as if there was something more he wanted to tell her but wouldn't. Probably just uncomfortable talking to a cop – a lot of people are. Angela began second guessing her impressions of Jason. Since their initial encounter the day the first remains were discovered, Jason seemed to seek her out at the crime scene. Because of his interest in the details of the investigation, she had been certain his only concern was the impact of the investigation on the Wardlaw renovation. Today when she spoke to him she seemed to sense a sincerity about him. Perhaps there was some other reason he was interested in the case. Professor Russell's report stated only that the body had been interred in excess of five years, and the artifacts were from clothing from the late sixties. Could have been used clothing. Maybe it would be worth her time to find out where Mr. Jason Shealy was five years ago.

Jason sat in his Subaru with the air conditioning running full blast. He had known he wouldn't get any information from the detective, but he felt desperate at this point. He had to try.

Jason looked down at his watch. "Damn, it's after ten. Cindy is going to be on my ass about those drawings." Since Jason had been so preoccupied with the discovery of the skeletons Cindy had taken upon herself the responsibility of reminding him of impending deadlines and work he still needed to complete. Sometimes he wondered who was really working for whom.

Jason left Wardlaw and headed for his office on Taylor Street. As he drove past the Township Auditorium, which was only a block from his office, he read the marquee to see who was in concert. It was a group he remembered from his high school days. He knew he probably had some of their CDs tucked away in a box in the closet in his spare bedroom.

It had probably been two years since Jason had seen a good concert. As with most things he just didn't take the time. Business was good. They almost had more than they could handle right now, but he had to keep new jobs coming in to keep bills paid, and hopefully, expand.

Jason pulled into his parking spot and began to gather up his things. "Shit!" Jason held up his hand. His palm and fingers were covered with chocolate goo. While he was watching the activities at Wardlaw and waiting for an opportunity to speak with Detective Porter, his partially eaten breakfast bar had melted. Jason looked around the car for a discarded paper napkin or piece of paper to wipe his hand. Seeing nothing, he used only his left hand to throw the straps of his messenger over his shoulder, then slid out of the driver's seat.

As Jason entered his office building he was greeted with smiles from Cindy.

"Boy, you are sure in a good mood this morning. Did you win the lottery?"

"I wish. If I had you wouldn't be seein' my smilin' face right now."

"So what's up?"

"I have good news and I have bad news. Which do you want first?" Cindy added.

"I always like to hear the bad first, because then I can listen to the good news and cushion my fall."

"Do you want it now?"

"Go for it."

"Okay. We are so behind schedule and so backed up you are probably going to have to add some temporary help to get us through this. And it's only going to get worse."

Jason took a deep breath and let it out. He knew they were behind because he had spent so much time at Wardlaw chasing ghosts.

"Is that it?"

"No. Our friend Mr. Grover, the guy that probably has a sheet with eye holes hangin' in his closet, called."

Jason was afraid this was more of the bad news. "What did he say?"

"Nothing much. He just wanted to tell me that he liked your designs. He thought they gave his storefronts kind of that old south, plantation kind of feel to them."

Jason's eyes widened. "Really? I mean he liked them okay?"

"Yes. He sounded excited about them."

"That's awesome." Jason raised his chocolate covered right hand to give Cindy a fist bump.

"Ew, what is that crap on your hand?"

"Sorry. I forgot. I left my breakfast bar in the car this morning and it melted. I didn't notice it until after I picked it up and it squeezed out on my hand."

"Out watchin' them dig again?"

"You don't have to say anything else. You're right. I've spent too much time out there doing nothing but watching them dig up skeletons. I haven't been focused on our clients at a time when everyone has needed me here. So you're right and I don't want to talk about it." Jason excused himself to wash his hands.

Standing in the doorway to the bathroom, Cindy continued. "There's a second part to my good news."

Jason turned off the water and stood waiting. "What is it?"

"My friend with the Cayce police department said he would try to get a copy of the lab report, but didn't think he would have any luck."

"How is that good news?"

"He said he would make a couple calls and find out as much as he could about what is in the report. He will let us know what's in it."

"You're kidding."

"No, seriously."

"That's great. When does he think he will have the information?"

"He said probably today. He said to meet him at Breaker's Bar and Grill in Five Points tonight. He is going to be out there."

"What time?"

"He said around eight-thirty."

"Okay. Sounds like a plan." Jason was excited about the prospect of getting more information from Cindy's friend. "You know. I'm not sure why this is so important to me. It may have something to do with Tommy drowning and Dad saying it was my fault. Or maybe I'm just crazy, but it really matters to me that I know who these people were and what happened to them."

"Your dad really blamed you for your brother drowning? Wow. So how did you handle all that?"

"I didn't at first. Fortunately, my Aunt Bess could see what was going on with me. She knows my parents are loons so she sort of emotionally adopted me. By the time I was out of high school I was spending so much time with her I might as well have moved in. So she probably saved my sanity."

"You talked about them before, but I didn't realize they blamed you. I'm sorry."

"It's okay. That was a long time ago. I'm okay, but they are still loony."

Cindy laughed.

"Now, if you will clear out, I will get busy and get caught back up. I'm behind and I promise to do better so we can keep the bills paid around here."

"I was just fixin' to leave." Cindy replied.

Jason laughed. Lately, Cindy had been more dedicated and focused than he. He knew he needed to regain his focus on work, but he didn't want to turn loose of the idea that he could somehow help with the police investigation. If he only had access to the police information.

Jason closed his eyes and rubbed his temples then spoke out loud to himself. "Come on, focus. I've got to stop thinking about this and concentrate on work."

Staring at the blueprints in front of him, Jason picked up his red pencil and began to check calculations to confirm the correct size and spacing of support beams. For several hours he worked, stopping only long enough to give Cindy some money so she could bring back lunch. Jason ate while he worked and wiped up the occasional drop of mustard before it could soak into his note pad of calculations. When he finally looked at his watch, he realized it was after six. He would have just enough time to get home, feed Sebastian, change clothes, then get to the Breakers Bar and Grill to meet Cindy and her friend.

Cindy had already left for the day. As Jason was checking the computers and printers to make certain everything was shut down, the phone rang. Looking again at his watch, he wondered who would call his office that late. Probably Cindy calling to remind him of something. Jason picked up the phone on the fourth ring. "Hello, Shealy and Associates. Jason speaking."

"Jason. I was going to hang up. I thought you had probably already left."

"Aunt Bess?"

"Yes. It's me. How've you been? Louise said you called her yesterday. Why didn't you come out to the airport and meet us?"

"I thought the two of you would probably want the evening alone since you'd been gone for almost a month. And anyway, I needed to feed Sebastian."

"I was pretty tired. Had a zillion flight delays, but I'm always glad to see you. How is the little eating machine you call a cat?"

"Oh, he's fine. Just as spoiled as ever. How was your trip?"

"The trip was great. Getting a break from the heat was wonderful. But poor Sharon. You remember her don't you? She was the woman

81

who taught you how to fish that summer you stayed with me in Provincetown."

"Of course I remember her. How's she doing?"

"Physically she's doing okay. The doctors think they got everything, but mentally it's really shaken her. She was always the heartiest of all of us. Now she has suddenly been hit with the realization that she isn't invincible. Plus, having a breast removed can be very traumatic for a woman. Imagine having part of your penis cut off."

Jason winced. He should have been ready for that comment, but he wasn't. Aunt Bess was always blunt. "I'd like to get her address and send her a card if you think it would be okay."

"Oh, she'd love it. She asked about you while I was there. She wanted to know if you had gotten any better at baiting a hook or did it still make you gag."

Jason laughed. The thought of baiting a hook brought back pleasant memories. He had almost forgotten that the first time Sharon made him put a piece of squid on a hook he almost threw up. "I'll have to tell her I only use plastic worms now."

"Oh, before I forget. Change of plans. You are coming to our house for dinner instead of us coming there."

"No. You just got back. I know you are probably tired."

"We insist. We have a new dish to try on you."

"Okay, if you put it that way. Can I bring anything?"

"No. Just yourself. Now, Louise said that you had some questions about a little girl that went to Wardlaw when I was teaching there. And you wanted to see my year books."

"Actually, yes, I did."

"What's up?"

"I was talking to Mom yesterday…"

"My lovely sister in-law. I'm sorry. She's your mother and I shouldn't make remarks."

Jason let out a sigh. "I know. Anyway, Mom said that while you were teaching there, a girl ran away from home. They never found a trace of her. These days it doesn't seem that unusual for a child that age to run away. But back then it was kind of odd. I was just wondering if you remember anything about it."

"I remember it happening. I don't remember many details."

"Do you remember what year it was or her name?"

There was a silence on the other end of the phone for a moment. Then Bess spoke. "I can see her face, but I don't remember her name. I'd have to go through my yearbooks to get her name for you. Why are you asking?"

"Well, I really don't want to get into it over the phone. It's kind of a long story."

"Does it have anything to do with those remains they dug up at the Wardlaw school grounds?"

His aunt's question surprised him. Back in town only one day and she was already up on all the news. But that was typical of Aunt Bess. If she wasn't in the middle of something she at least had the details on it. "Honestly, I don't know if it does or not. I'm kind of going off a gut feeling."

"So you think one of sets of remains could belong to the runaway?"

"Maybe."

"You know, I didn't teach there that long. Just four years. But this runaway you're asking about wasn't the only girl that went missing."

Jason's heart rate increased. "She wasn't? There were others?"

"Only one that was in one of my classes. But in the time that I was teaching, there was another girl. But then, I think there may have been another before I started working there. Maybe it was after I left. I don't really remember."

"I was out there this morning and was able to talk to one of the detectives for just a few minutes. Of course she wouldn't tell me anything that I couldn't get off the news. I at least know for sure there are seven skeletons. Six were under a tree at the back of the playground. The seventh was buried at the edge of where the basketball court was."

"Is there any chance they are from an old cemetery? Most of downtown Columbia was farmland at one time."

"I don't know anything about the six. But I was there when the first one was found, the one by the ball court. It was wearing penny loafers."

"Oh. I bet that was an eerie sight."

"You're not kidding. It was like something out of a movie. It really creeped out a couple of the guys working on the job that are your big, tough, redneck types."

"They're usually the biggest wimps."

Jason looked down at his watch. "Aunt Bess, I'd love to talk longer, but I have to meet a couple people tonight for pool. One of them may have some inside information for me on this."

"In that case you'd better get going. Don't want to be late for that game.

"Thanks for not telling me I'm crazy."

"Who am I to judge crazy? If half our relatives had their way they would've had me locked up years ago. You go play pool and I'll look through year books."

"Thanks again. Love you."

"Love you too, Jason."

Jason laid down the phone and paused for a moment to think about his conversation with his aunt. "I don't know what I would've done all these years without you, Aunt Bess." Jason picked up his messenger bag, and tossed in a small note pad. Standing up and scanning the office one last time to make sure he hadn't forgotten anything, Jason flipped off the lights and exited the building, making sure the door was securely locked.

Chapter twelve

The evening was hot and still. There was no breeze to evaporate the sweat from a person's skin. No stars could be seen; they were obliterated by the lights from the city sprawl. Angela Porter stood in the lab watching Professor Russell examine each skeleton and make notes on a legal pad. Occasionally, he pointed out interesting details about the human skeleton. He explained how to determine approximate age by examining the long bones of the arms and legs. In most people, up into early adulthood, the ends of these bones are actually a combination of bones that have yet to fuse together. The degree of fusion is an indication of age. Sex however, isn't easily determined until the person is in their late teens or sometimes early twenties. Now, with the use of birth control pills by increasingly younger girls, identifying the correct gender was becoming more difficult in some victims.

Detective Rob Edwards sat in the back of the lab reading Russell's notes on the first two skeletons which had been examined. Russell was still working on the third. Four more had yet to be completely exhumed.

Angela was eager to start searching through missing person files. "Professor. Do you see any similarities between the three skeletons? Is there anything significant for us to go on?"

Russell looked up, peering over the top of his glasses. He looked first at Angela then at Edwards. "Sorry. Other than telling you they are Caucasian, between the ages of eleven and thirteen, and have been interred for at least five years or longer…there's nothing I can say until my official report is complete."

Without looking up from the legal pad, Edwards interjected. "You're wastin' your time, Porter. The Doc here plays by all the rules. Isn't that right, Russell?"

"That's right, Rob."

"I've been working with Russell since he came to Columbia. Where was it you were at before USC?"

"Florida."

"That's right. I remember. Anyway, he ain't goin' to tell you nothin' until the official lab report is finished. That's why, when he's not looking, I just read his notes."

Russell again looked over the top of his glasses at Edwards. "And that's why you aren't going to find anything in my notes that you don't already know. So far we haven't found any artifacts with these two. They were possibly buried nude or in some type of cotton cloth that has decayed."

"You haven't found any buttons or zippers like with the first one." Angela asked.

"Nothing so far, but we haven't finished sifting the ground under these two bodies." Russell pointed to the skeleton he was examining and the one on the table nearest him. "Which is why I don't make statements outside the official report, Edwards."

"Okay Doc, I got you. We'll head outta here and let you get your work done. We at least have a starting point to start looking for missing kids. Thanks. See you later." Edwards stood up and as he walked passed Professor Russell toward the door he patted the professor on the back.

Outside the lab in the hallway their footsteps echoed. "Looks like there's not going to be much to go on." Angela said. Her voice drifted down the long hallway then vibrated in her own ears.

"No. Probably not. At least we have that I.D. bracelet for one of the kids."

"Do you think the same person is responsible for all seven?"

"I have no idea. I would guess it was the same guy, but they were in two different locations. The first one was buried in its clothes. The others probably weren't."

"Maybe the guy perfected his ritual." Angela added, "From some of the things I've read about serial killers, their M.O. and ritual can change over time as they evolve, become more confident, more comfortable with killing."

Edwards was quiet for a moment as they walked down the stairs to the first floor. Angela recognized the silence. She had seen it before.

Edwards was analyzing the details in his mind. Developing a hypothesis based on the facts, as he knew them to be, trying to determine a course of action.

As they exited the pale green building that housed the anthropology department, they paused to stand on its steps in the warm stagnant night air. Angela asked Edwards, "You think we'll actually find anything?"

Edwards reflected for a moment. "We have to."

"I didn't mean not try. I was just trying to look at this realistically. I mean, there have been a couple cases in the last few years where no trace of the victims was ever found.

"I know what you meant. We'll just have to start hitting the missing person files tomorrow morning. We'll start with 2010 and work our way back. Can't solve a case until we know who the victims are."

Angela stood with her hands in her pockets watching the cars drive by on Pickins Street. "I've never had a case like this one," she said. "The other murders I worked, there was a body with a face and a name. It was just a matter of collecting evidence and figuring out who did it."

"I've worked on missing person cases where all we had was a skeleton or part of one. But I've never had one that could be a serial killer."

Angela looked at Edwards. "With as many years as you've been a detective I thought you would've seen it all by now."

"Not everything – but pretty close to it. Don't get too many serial killers in Columbia, South Carolina. At least not that we know of anyway."

"You want to go down to Five Points and have a beer?"

"Nah. That crowd's too young for me. Besides, the wife is waitin' on me. Said she'd like to have dinner with me one night this week, even if it's a late one."

"I don't want to be responsible for getting you in trouble with your wife. Tell Mary I said hello."

"Will do. See you in the morning."

"I'll bring the Danish."

Edwards nodded and winked. Then waved good-bye over his shoulder as he walked away.

Angela stood in the dark. Except for an occasional passing car or pedestrian she was alone with the hissing sounds of palmetto bugs and distant car horns. Edwards had been acting strangely the last few days. He was quieter, almost melancholy. Twice he had disappeared for hours at a time and she wasn't able to reach him on his cell phone. Perhaps this case was getting to him in a way he hadn't expected. He always seemed more personally involved in cases where children were the victims. Now, what might be his last big case before retirement, could end up a fruitless search for the identities of dead children, and a killer who would possibly never be caught.

Angela looked at her watch and pressed the button on its side to illuminate the face. It was almost nine. "Shit, I didn't realize it was this late." Angela walked quickly down the steps and to the street corner. She checked for on-coming cars then crossed to her car.

While Angela was driving home and planning a nice soak in her tub before turning in, Jason was buying Cindy's friend his third beer.

"Hey man, thanks for the beer. You don't have to keep buying us rounds. Let me get one."

Jason put his hand up. "No. Don't worry about it. I'll just write it down as a business expense. Gotta entertain clients, right?"

"Thanks. I appreciate it. So, your business doing okay?"

"It's not bad," Jason said. "The first couple of years when I was just getting started things were pretty tight. Columbia has been rebounding the last few years. Things have been pretty good for me."

"Hey, that's great man."

"How long have you been on the force?"

"About ten years."

"Are you going to stay where you are?"

"No. It's about time to move on. I'm thinking about applying to larger departments. I may move to Charlotte or Atlanta." There was a pause. "Okay, so let's cut the small talk. You want to know what they found. Honestly, not much at this point. But it's early."

Jason was suddenly discouraged. "What exactly do they know?"

"They found an I.D. bracelet with the name Peggy on it. It was with the first set of remains. They found some clothing artifacts. A zipper and some buttons. They couldn't tell much from the zipper and buttons. The shoes are from the sixties. The bracelet, now that was the big find."

The name on the bracelet gave him encouragement. "Did they find anything with the others?"

"No, not yet."

"When do you think all the skeletons will be examined?"

"It shouldn't take too much longer. Maybe a few days. The forensic anthropologist is still working on the lab report. According to my source they haven't finished sifting through the dirt."

"I wonder why they found buttons and zippers and shoes and nothing else."

"If they're wearing cotton clothes when they're buried about the only thing that holds up over time are the zipper's and buttons. Now, if they're in polyester or synthetics, those hold up pretty well. Leather shoes will last a long time, too."

It was after ten by the time Jason left the bar. As he drove home he mentally analyzed the information he had received from Cindy's friend. He had a gut feeling the remains belonged to the runaway girl. She probably hadn't run away at all, but even if she did, she didn't get far. Someone murdered her, then the sick bastard buried her body on the same playground where she played.

"How could they bury a child on a playground and not get caught," Jason asked himself aloud. "Someone had to have seen what was going on." Jason exited I-26 at the Harbison exit. To his right the Columbiana Mall was nearly dark. He could see a mall security officer's car driving slowly through the parking lot. "Maybe whoever buried her there worked at the school. I'm jumping to conclusions. What I need now is to get with Aunt Bess. Then somehow get my hands on the police department's missing person files."

Jason pulled into his driveway and waited while the garage door slowly opened. I'm starting to talk to myself way too much. Maybe I am nuts. At least when I walk around the house talking to Sebastian I don't feel crazy." Jason paused then threw his hands in the air. "There I go again – talking to myself." Jason pulled into the garage, turned off the engine, and lowered the garage door.

As he stepped into the kitchen he was greeted by Sebastian, who, seated on the counter top, began to meow his disapproval of Jason's late return.

"I know I'm late. I'm sorry. How about I give you some tuna to make it up to you? Does that sound good?" Retrieving a small can of tuna from the pantry closet, Jason opened it and placed half its contents in Sebastian's dish. Sebastian jumped off the counter and immediately began devouring the tuna.

Exhausted, Jason climbed the steps to the second floor and once inside his bedroom changed into a T-shirt and boxers, then laid down across his unmade bed. By the time Sebastian jumped onto the bed to take his place on the spare pillow, Jason was asleep.

Chapter thirteen

Jason awoke to the sound of his cell phone ringing. As he rolled over and stretched his arm out to pick up the phone, his hand brushed Sebastian's tail. The sleeping cat jumped up with a start and, with claws extended scampered across Jason's back to the other side of the bed. Jason winced as two of the claws pricked his skin.

"Hello."

"Jason. Is that you?"

"Yes. Who is this? Cindy?"

"Yes, we were a little worried about you since you usually call when you aren't going to be here first thing. Just wondering if you made it home okay last night."

"Yes, I'm fine. I only had three beers all night. What time is it anyway?"

"It's almost ten."

"Ten! Shit. I must have forgotten to set my alarm."

"You're getting old. Can't run with the big dogs anymore."

"What? Oh, yeah." Jason was having trouble waking up. He had to concentrate on every word before he could respond. "What time is it again?"

"Almost ten."

"Okay, right. I'll get up. I think I can be there by eleven if I get up now. I need to call my aunt."

"We have it under control right now so take your time. But we're going to need you to look at some drawings this afternoon. Have to have that LPA stamp."

"Okay, I'm moving. I'll be there."

Jason sat up in bed and rubbed his eyes, blinked and looked around the room. Sunlight was pouring in through the open blinds. Usually this much light in a room would have awakened him but the tension and anxiety from the last few days had drained his energy. "Sebastian. Why didn't you wake me up, little man? You're usually my back-up alarm." Sebastian closed his eyes and purred as Jason scratched his ears and chin.

"Are you ready for breakfast? I am." Jason was hungry and wanted more than his usual breakfast bar. Picking up Sebastian, he slid his feet into his slippers and walked down stairs to feed them both.

Entering the kitchen, Jason noticed he had left Sebastian's dry food bowl down. "Looks like you were snacking all night. Is that why you didn't wake me up? You weren't hungry?" Sebastian purred and pushed his head against Jason's chin. Jason retrieved a can of cat food from the pantry shelf, then, setting Sebastian in front of his dish, emptied the contents.

Jason poured himself a glass of iced tea from the pitcher he kept in the refrigerator as he dialed his Aunt Bess. He knew she would probably still be at home. USC, where she was a professor was still out for the summer and she usually managed to not teach summer school.

"Hello."

"Aunt Bess?"

"How are you Jason? This is Louise."

"Oh, I'm fine. I can't tell you two apart on the phone sometimes."

"Please don't tell me that. That would mean after all these years I've finally picked up a Southern accent."

"I hate to break the news to you – but you have one."

"Oh no," Louise faked a moan of anguish. "Well, after all these years I guess it was to be expected."

Jason, playing along added. "Well, you don't sound like a native. You just sound like you've been here a long time, and a native had a corrupting influence on you. Linguistically speaking, that is."

"Thank you. Now I guess you want to talk to your aunt."

"Yes please." Jason could hear Louise call for Bess. There were a few moments of silence.

"Jason. What can I do you for?"

"Hey, Aunt Bess. I need that favor now."

"You were able to get some more information?"

"Sure was. I have a basic physical description, approximate age, time period that artifacts were from that were found with the remains, and a possible name."

"Oh," Bess squealed. "Good job. I'll go dig my yearbooks out of the attic right now. When you come over tonight, we'll do dinner and start going through them."

"What time?"

"How about seven?"

"Works for me. You have a date." Jason had a broad smile on his face as he hung up the phone.

"We might be on to something, Sebastian." Sebastian looked up from his dish, and with an unconcerned expression on his face, returned to nibbling on his food.

"Now what was I doing?" Jason asked himself as he turned and looked around the kitchen. "Oh yeah. Breakfast." Jason knew he needed to go into the office and get some work done, but he still hadn't taken time to find the Wardlaw news article that he only half remembered. He thought he had read something that referenced a missing student, but he wasn't sure. When he first began his research on the old junior high ,he was more concerned about the history of the building itself, not the lives of the people who had once walked its halls.

As Jason leaned against the kitchen cabinet sipping iced tea and debating with himself whether he should go into the office or skip out to *The State* newspaper office, hunger pains returned. He thought for another moment, then pulled a slice of turkey from a lunch-meat package and a slice of cheese from another package. Rolling the two together, he picked up his glass of tea and ate as he ascended the stairs to the second floor. He would shower then go to work. *The State's* archives would have to wait a few more hours.

*****

Detectives Porter and Edwards sat buried in computer print-outs and hard copies of unsolved missing person reports. The computer records went back only until the early eighties. After that it was a manual search through every file.

"I'm not having much luck finding a match," Angela said in disgust.

"What were you expecting, kid? For a name and a face to jump out at you after an hour of looking?"

"No. But I did expect to find at least a few possible matches. We have several possibilities from the regional computerized records, but nothing from the hard copies."

"Don't get too discouraged. We might not be back far enough." Edwards' tone offered little encouragement.

"If there is a missing person report from the hard copies, and it wasn't filed correctly, then we might never find the person. And, we might never find them if they're from out of state."

"Then just hope that 'interred more than five years' also means less than fifty and they were from South Carolina." Edwards changed the subject. "I'm getting hungry. How about a break for lunch?"

"Good idea. My stomach feels like it is going to wrap itself around my ribs. You want to go get something?"

"Actually, I have a couple errands to run during lunch. I just wondered if you were ready to take a break."

Angela knew she wasn't invited along to run the errands or do lunch. "Sure, okay. A break is good with me. All the words on the pages were starting to run together anyway. I have a couple errands, too."

"See you in about an hour or so." Edwards stood up from the table and, collecting his note pad and pin, walked down the hallway and up the stairs to the first floor.

Again, Angela noticed the difference in her partner's mood. Maybe he and his wife were having some problems, or perhaps he was worried about money since he was so close to retirement.

Angela sat alone staring at the stack of missing person reports. Finding a match seemed daunting. Even though she knew they needed to search all the most recent records first, Angela felt with what was more instinct than anything else, that this first child's remains had been hidden in the ground a very long time ago. She wanted to skip over all of the more recent records and dig through the records from fifteen, or twenty, or even thirty years ago. But what was the cutoff point? A wrong guess could cause her to overlook the one piece of paper she needed to give this child a name.

No. She would continue to work her way backwards, one year at a time. Pull out every file that was even remotely a possible match. Then, with Professor Russell's help, try to find the correct puzzle piece. Angela placed her elbows on the table then leaned over and placed her face in her hands and rubbed her eyes. She was tired and hungry and could feel herself developing the beginnings of a migraine. She knew she needed to eat before the pain in her head worsened. If she did get a migraine she would be of no use to anyone until she had time to go home and sleep it off.

She looked down at her watch – only half past eleven. If she hurried she could make it to Motor Supply Company, a little restaurant located in an alley off Gervais Street, and be enjoying an appetizer by the time the lunch crowd began pouring in.

Angela hated eating alone. There was something about sitting in a restaurant by one's self that seemed so sad. She thought of herself as a pathetic looking creature, sitting alone at one of the small tables tucked away in a corner of the restaurant, hidden from the sight of people who actually had someone to dine with.

She could call Becky and ask her to meet her at Motor Supply. Becky would understand and would be satisfied with quiet conversation and not expect her to be entertaining.

Angela stood up from the table and, exiting the room, closed and locked the door behind her. As she reached the top of the stairs and rounded the corner to exit through the always locked, glass security doors, Grace, one of the desk officers stopped her. "Detective Porter, I've got a call for you that just came in."

"Who is it Grace?"

"It's the Coroner, Mr. Brazell."

Angela rolled her eyes. "There goes lunch."

Grace handed her the phone. The black cord stretched taunt across the counter top knocking over a pencil holder. Angela reached for the falling pencils and pens with her one free hand, but only succeeded in propelling them further across the counter top and Grace's desk. "Shit. Sorry."

"That's okay. Don't worry about it. I got it, honey." Grace replied as she bent down to pick up two stray pens that had rolled under her desk.

"Hello, Mr. Brazell. This is Angela Porter."

"Angela. Good to talk to you again." Brazell had an almost cheerful tone to his voice. "Remember our deal. It's Doug."

"Okay Doug. What can I do for you?"

"Do you have a few minutes to talk?"

"Well, actually I'm standing in the hall on someone else's phone. I was just on my way out."

"Did I catch you at a bad time?"

"Not really. I was just on my way to lunch. I wanted to try to beat the noon rush so I could eat and get back here."

"Well, if you don't already have a lunch date would you like to join me? Or I could join you if you've already decided on a place to eat."

Angela wasn't sure what she should do. She hadn't called Becky yet and knowing her luck Becky wouldn't be able to get away. Brazell may be full of shit, but at least she wouldn't feel pathetic eating by herself. Angela decided Brazell was the lesser of the two evils.

"No definite plans, I was just thinking about going to Motor Supply Company. They're close and the food is good."

"Good choice. The food is always good. Do you mind if I invite myself along and we can talk shop."

"No. I don't mind at all," Angela lied. "But I have to warn you. I've been staring at reports all morning and I'm working on a headache, so I may not be the best company in the world."

"Not a problem. I'll see you there in a few minutes."

Angela knew Grace had listened to the conversation. "The Coroner. He wants to talk shop. Oh well, I guess talking shop with a coroner over lunch might be good way to lose weight."

Grace laughed. "I think I'd rather take a diet pill."

Angela smiled then left the building and walked to her car. Angela was wearing navy colored slacks, and even though the fabric was light-weight and supposedly designed for summer, she was certain the designer had never spent an August in South Carolina. In just the few minutes it took to walk the length of the parking lot, she could feel sweat running down her back and her legs. Even with reflective shades in the front and rear windows, her car was an oven. She hoped the air conditioning was working well at Motor Supply.

Angela parked her car on the street. Doug's Mercedes with the license plate spelling out "BONES" was parked at the meter in front of her. She rolled her eyes. "Oh my god." She felt her headache suddenly worsen. She wasn't sure why she had agreed to lunch, since he couldn't tell her anything about the lab reports she couldn't read for herself, but she didn't want hostility to exist between the two offices while working on something as important as this investigation.

As she entered the building, she saw Doug sitting in a dimly lit corner of the restaurant. He had a broad smile and straightened the bottom of his tie as he stood up to greet her.

"Hope this table is okay with you. It's out of the line of traffic. This place gets pretty cramped during lunch."

"It's fine. As long as I'm not sitting next to the kitchen door, I'm good-to-go." She paused. "So what's up, Doug?"

"Good, you remembered to use my first name. Mr. Brazell just seems too stuffy for me." Another broad smile.

Angela unrolled the linen napkin and arranged her flatware, out of habit and training – dinner fork and salad fork on the left, with knife (blade facing inward) and spoon on the right. Then she moved her stemmed water glass so that it was positioned just above the point of the knife blade. These habits were a carryover from her childhood. Angela had been raised in an upper-middle class family. Her mother was a homemaker who regularly entertained business associates and their wives for Angela's father. Good table manners and knowing which utensil to use was a requirement in their household. From an early age she realized her mother cared about appearances and making a good impression. Angela tilted her head slightly and rubbed her forehead.

"How's your headache?" The expression on Doug's face looked as though he had some genuine concern.

"I've been working on one for the last hour, but it's not bad. It'll probably go away once I get something to eat. A lot of my migraines I can head off if I just eat something."

"I'll see if I can get the kitchen to put a rush on an appetizer. Don't want you not enjoying your lunch with me because of a headache."

Again another big smile and the drawl in some of his syllables was just a hint longer. Angela knew he was trying to add a touch of Charleston to his accent.

Doug waved for a waitress, a young girl, probably in her early twenties. She was wearing a white long-sleeved blouse which was tied at the ends and exposed her midsection. Her black mini skirt and platform boots accented her long legs, and with the burgundy streaks in her hair and the nose ring through her left nostril she would have looked strangely out of place working in some of the less "trendy" restaurants around Columbia. "Hi. My name is Sharon. I'll be your waitress. Can I take your drink order?"

"Sure honey. And we'd like to get an appetizer out here pretty quickly. My friend here has a little headache and would like to get something in her system." Another broad smile from Doug. This one was more condescending.

The young waitress turned to Angela. "We have several items on the menu and a couple that are specials today. Would you like to hear those? Then I'll get you a menu."

As the waitress spoke Angela noticed Doug's eyes drift down the length of the girl's torso and then follow the curves of her long legs. Angela was convinced more than ever that Doug had ulterior motives for the lunch meeting. Not that she was trying to flatter herself, but she knew she was, in her own opinion, reasonably nice looking; others might say attractive. She knew his type and he was working up to asking her out.

"Actually, I think I already know what I want. Do you still have the spinach and artichoke dip?"

"Yes, we do. Would you like that?"

"Yes. And a glass of unsweetened iced tea."

"Yes ma'am. And for you, sir?"

"Just sweet tea. And if you could get a basket of that bread of yours out here that would be great."

"Of course. It'll be right out."

Doug leaned back in his chair and, stretching his shoulders backward, threw his left arm over the back of the chair. Again he straightened his tie while glancing for a moment at the young waitress's behind as she walked away from the table toward the kitchen.

"Doug," Angela looked at Doug who quickly turned his eyes from the waitresses' behind to give his attention to Angela. "Any word on how the excavation is going today?"

"As a matter-of-fact I spoke with Professor Russell just before I called you. He should have all six sets completely out of the ground by tomorrow morning and then he'll be able to provide you with a preliminary report on all six at one time."

"That's great. While we're looking through missing person files I'd rather look for all of them at once. Instead of going through the files seven times."

The waitress returned with the glasses of tea. "Your dip will be out in just a few minutes. Can I get you anything else while you wait?"

"No, I'm fine thank you." Angela smiled at the girl.

"Honey," Doug lifted his right hand pointing his index finger into the air. "Basket of bread."

"Yes sir, it's coming."

What a jerk, Angela thought to herself. Many times Angela felt that the only men she had attracted in the last few years were one of two extremes. Either they were like Doug, married and chasing any half-way decent looking female that crossed their path, or they eventually became intimidated by her being a cop. This was one of the job hazards they failed to mention at the academy.

The waitress returned and set the basket of bread on the table, bringing Angela's thoughts back to the present. "Are you ready to order now or would you like a few more minutes?"

"I think I know what I want. How about you, Doug?"

"Sure, go ahead."

Angela gave her order. "I'll have the blackened mahi-mahi." She usually didn't eat such a large lunch, but with the pain in her head continuing to pound, she thought it would be better to eat a little more then just cut back on dinner or skip it completely. She would probably just go home after work and go to bed anyway.

"Would you like a salad with that?"

"No, thank you."

"And for you, sir?"

"I'll have the grilled chicken with honey – Honey." Doug laughed and gave another big smile to the waitress and then to Angela. Doug was clearly pleased with himself for being, what he considered, clever.

The waitress gave an annoyed smile, took the menus then exited for the kitchen.

"Nice looking girl isn't she," Doug commented to Angela. "If she didn't have her nose pierced and I was twenty years younger I'd ask her out."

"Somehow Doug, I can't picture you letting a nose piercing stop you." This time Angela gave a broad smile to Doug.

Doug laughed in response, but Angela could tell he wasn't sure of the intent of her remark.

Angela quickly changed the subject back to the Wardlaw case. "So you say Professor Russell will have a report to us by maybe late tomorrow afternoon?"

Doug applied a generous amount of butter to a dark grain roll. "He'll give you a basic body type and profile to look for. Then by the time you come up with some possible matches, he'll have a more extensive report finished, complete with x-rays."

"Will he be able to narrow down the amount of time they've been buried?"

Doug leaned back in his chair while he swallowed his bite of roll and butter. Straightening his tie, he seized the opportunity to share information with Angela that made him feel he had a superior knowledge of forensics.

"Unfortunately," he said, "when these poor children were buried in the ground may continue to be a mystery unless we can put a name and a face with them. But if there was a large enough span of time between each murder or burial, then he may at least be able to give you the sequence that they were buried." Doug changed his facial expression to add a degree of drama to his statement.

Angela added her thoughts to the conversation. "So for example, if we can find a match for number three, and we know that one and two disappeared a few years before and four, five, six, and seven were later, we narrow it down that way."

"Exactly. Hit or miss."

Angela had almost finished her spinach and artichoke dip, with a little help from Doug, when the waitress arrived with their main course.

"Is there anything else I can get you?" The young waitress asked as she placed their plates in front of first Angela, then Doug.

"We'll both be needing some more iced tea." Doug drew 'iced tea' into a long drawl. Doug and Angela continued to discuss the points of the Wardlaw case through lunch. Occasionally, Doug would throw in pieces of information about himself. Star athlete in college, self-made man, neglected by the wife. Angela ignored most of it and always brought the conversation back to work related topics.

When they were finished, Doug, of course, insisted on paying and Angela obliged with little more than an obligatory offer to pay for her own lunch. She felt that, even though her headache had somewhat subsided, a free lunch was compensation for spending the hour with Doug.

With another "thank you" and a firm hand shake, Angela bid Doug good afternoon and returned to the police station to resume her search through missing person files.

Chapter fourteen

Arriving late, Jason closed the door to his office to minimize his interruptions. He had several drawings to review and phone calls to clients to return. He wanted to leave early but knew he shouldn't without first making sure he was caught up enough with his share of the work so that everyone else would be able to stay busy the remainder of the day and into Friday morning. Jason knew himself well enough to know that if his aunt had any information that could help identify the child, then he wouldn't want to spend the day in his office. He would want to track down every possible lead.

By three o'clock he was far enough ahead that he felt he could safely leave and begin his search for information at *The State's* archives. "Cindy. I'm out of here for the rest of the day. If there's an emergency or you need to reach me just text me."

"I thought you were going to be here all day."

"No. I've reviewed all the drawings that are complete and, at this point, I'm far enough ahead of everyone that you won't have to wait around for something to do tomorrow if I come in late."

"You're coming in late?"

"Maybe. Depends on if I get lucky tonight."

"You've got a date?"

"Yes. With my aunt."

Cindy knitted her eyebrows and formed a puzzled look on her face.

"I'm having dinner with my Aunt Bess tonight."

"Oh."

"Aunt Bess used to teach at Wardlaw and she remembers a little girl that went to school there disappearing. As far as she knows they never found her."

"But, there are seven skeletons."

"I know. But if we can figure out who one of them is, then maybe that will help with identifying the others, or point to a possible killer. I mean, think about it. Who would kill seven children and bury them on a playground. That's beyond sick."

As Jason spoke about the possible murders and helping find the killer, his demeanor changed. He went from moody and almost sullen to what bordered on cheerful. It was as if he was becoming obsessed.

"Is there anything I can do to help?"

"No. Just handle the office." Jason picked up his messenger bag and threw the strap over his left shoulder.

"What if someone calls in the morning and needs to talk to you?"

"Just do what you always do. Take a message and text or call me if it's an emergency. Well, I'm out of here. See you sometime tomorrow." Jason leaned around the corner and waved to the others. "See you tomorrow. Text me if you run into any problems."

With that, Jason was out the back door and climbing into the seat of his Subaru. If he hit the lights just right he could be out Shop Road and in the parking lot of *The State* newspaper in ten minutes. He was excited. He knew there would be a story about the missing child or children. Columbia was still too small, especially back then, for a missing child to not be front-page news.

Wesley, his friend at *The State*, was expecting him. Knowing how efficient Wesley was, the guy had probably already found the articles and copied them for him. Actually, Jason was counting on that.

Jason parked his car in *The State's* visitor parking and placed a sun shield in his front window to help block the sun's rays.

As Jason opened the front door to the newspaper's office he felt a momentary chill as a blast of air-conditioned air hit him. Jason approached the receptionist desk where a woman who looked to be in her mid-twenties was talking on the phone. Jason stood in front of the desk waiting for her to set the phone down and ask what he needed. From her body language and the tone of her voice Jason knew she was involved in a personal conversation.

The woman glanced at Jason then returned her eyes to her note pad and with a slight laugh began drawing geometric shapes as she continued her conversation. Jason was angry with her lack of attentiveness. He would never let people in his office treat customers with so little regard. "Excuse me. Excuse me."

The young woman covered the mouth-piece of the phone and with a sarcastic tone replied to Jason. "Is there something I can help you with?"

"Yes. As a matter of fact there is. I'm here to see Wesley Martin. He's the Circulation Manager."

The young woman removed her hand from the receiver and in a low tone of voice told the person on the other end of the line she needed to hang up but she would call back later. She looked up at Jason. "Who shall I say is here?"

"Jason Shealy."

"Mr. Martin. A Jason Shealy is here to see you."

"He said to come on up."

"Thank you." Jason was pissed by the woman's rudeness. "Miss, I have just one quick question."

"What's that?" the young woman asked as she smiled at Jason.

"Does your boss know you spend so much time on the phone making personal calls?"

The woman's smile quickly changed to a disgusted frown. She had no reply as Jason walked past the desk toward the elevator.

"Jason, how're doing buddy?"

"Pretty good. Better if you were able to find any information for me."

"I found some things. I don't know if it's what you're looking for or not, but I have a hunch it is."

"What'd you find?"

"Well, you told me anything having to do with Wardlaw and anything associated with Wardlaw students that were kidnapped or went missing, or anything about murder suspects."

"Right." Jason confirmed the instructions he had given his friend Wesley.

"That was a pretty wide field. I did the search all the way back to the start of the sixties, but I concentrated on the mid-sixties to mid-seventies. That was the time period you wanted to focus on. Well, I did come across several articles on Wardlaw, most of which dealt with it closing, busing students, and so forth."

"Anything about missing students or deaths?"

"That's where this got interesting."

"What do you mean?"

"I found this one article written by one of our reporters and it talked about more than one missing child. But the children went missing over a period of years." Wesley handed the copy of the article to Jason to read. "Basically, what the guy is saying is that there were, I think he said, three girls that disappeared. And he is implying that there is a connection between the three. Then he goes on to talk about the irony in all three being Wardlaw students."

"Wow. This is great. This may be what I need," Jason was excited.

"There's more."

Jason looked up from the article. "More?"

"Yes. Get this. In what looks like a sequel to his article he writes about three more girls that disappear. The sequel was written a couple of years before Wardlaw closed for good. But the second article was several years after the first one."

"No shit. So this guy is implying there is a connection between six girls and the connection is that they all went to Wardlaw."

"Actually, if you look at the second story, it says three of the girls weren't students there."

"So why is he making a connection?" Jason asked as he began to quickly skim the articles for himself.

"I read them both pretty closely, but I'm not sure. It's just the way it's written and one brief reference to his previous article. I think he wanted the reader to connect the two."

"Do you think he could be doing that just to sensationalize the story and sell more papers."

"Could be. If he did, he sure wouldn't be the first journalist to do it."

"Or the last," Jason added. "Does this guy still work here?"

"Way ahead of you. I knew you would ask that, so I've already checked. Human resources told me that his employment ended in 1982. They had records for him up until November of that year."

"Did he quit or transfer or retire?"

"They couldn't tell me. They said some of their records are incomplete."

"They had no idea?"

"No. Sorry."

Wesley handed Jason a folder with additional news clippings. "I don't think I need to ask what you're doing. Especially since I know you're the architect on the Wardlaw renovation. Everyone in the state knows about the remains they found out there."

"I don't want you to say anything about this yet, Wesley. I just have this feeling those remains out there have something to do with someone who may have worked at the school. I don't think the police will look in the right direction, at least not soon."

"So you think these missing girls in the articles are the skeletons they just dug up?"

"I don't know," Jason continued to skim the two articles. "They have a total of seven skeletons and he only talks about six."

"Could be another kid was killed after he wrote the last article."

Jason looked up at Wesley. "My Aunt Bess was a teacher out there when one or two of them disappeared. One supposedly was a run-away. That doesn't sound right for back then. I mean I know there have always been kids who ran away..." Jason paused. "I think I can help figure this out. I don't think the police will look for this kind of information."

"Apparently this reporter here thought there was something funny about all those girls going missing. Maybe you're onto something. I'll wish you good luck, buddy. Keep me in the loop. If you find out anything and give me the scoop, it won't hurt my raise any this year, that's for sure."

"Don't worry. If I get anything I'll let you know."

"Thanks, man."

"Wesley, is there any way I could find out where this reporter..." Jason looked down at the article, "Mark Harris, where he lives now?"

"Human resources isn't going to be any help. They couldn't even tell me why he stopped working here. Best I could do was his last known address."

"An address that is what, thirty years old?" Replied Jason.

"Exactly."

"What about a social security number?"

"Good idea. Why didn't I think of that?"

"Because you're not as sneaky as I am."

"You always were the sneaky one in school. Maybe that's why you never got detention."

The left corner of Jason's mouth turned up in a smile. "I never got detention because the teachers thought I looked too innocent to be guilty."

"Innocent, my ass! You were the damn mastermind." Wesley laughed. "Hang on a minute and I'll call down there and see if they will give me his social."

While Wesley dialed human resources, Jason again read the two articles written by Mark Harris. Just as Wesley described, the first article had been written shortly after the third Wardlaw girl disappeared. In the article Harris made many references to the first two disappearances. The intent of the story wasn't clear. Jason still wasn't sure if Harris was trying to sell more papers by inventing connections between the three disappearances where none existed; or was he truly just pointing out the obvious parallels and reporting the facts as he saw them.

Then there was the second article written a few years later. This time the missing girls were not Wardlaw students, but he drew the same parallels. The tie to Wardlaw School was tenuous at best. Harris talked about girls who had disappeared at least ten years prior to the article. Mark Harris went out on a limb with this one. Jason wasn't certain he was on the right track. None of the missing girls were named "Peggy." Perhaps Cindy was right.

Whether Mark Harris really did see something there and only alluded to it in the stories, or was just another journalist fighting for space on the page, Jason realized that if he couldn't track him down he might never know.

Jason heard Wesley express his thanks to the person on the other end of the phone line.

"Well? Did you get anything?"

"Sorry buddy. They said his file is incomplete."

"What do they mean incomplete? They don't have a social security number for him? What about for their tax records?"

"Apparently a lot of the old files are in bad shape or worse – lost. Seems with some of the turnover we had in HR a few years ago and with purging files and going to off-site records storage, a lot of archive information was lost. Sorry I can't help you there."

"Just these articles are a big help – hopefully. I'll just have to try this old address. After this long the guy has probably moved."

"He might be in the phone book. Just google him."

Jason looked up at Wesley in amazement. Google him. It was too simple. Why didn't he think of that? "That's too easy."

Wesley just shrugged. "You never know. Anyway, I don't want to be rude and run you off, but my little boy has a soccer game this evening. I want to be able to get there on time for once. And I got a shit load of work to do to before I can get out of here today."

"You and your ex-wife getting along any better?"

"About like when we were married."

"Sorry to hear that."

"Oh well, life's a bitch, then you divorce her." Wesley laughed.

Jason joined him because he felt he should, but he had known Wesley a long time and he knew the circumstances behind the divorce. If Wesley said his ex-wife was being a bitch then he was probably giving her good reason to be.

"I've got to get going myself. I'm meeting my Aunt Louise for dinner tonight."

"Tell them I said hello."

"Sure thing. Maybe we could all meet out one afternoon after work and have a couple of beers, and play pool. I know they would love to see you."

"You just tell Louise I've been practicing. She isn't going to run the table on me like she used to do when you and I were in high school."

"I'll tell her. But she'll probably take that as a challenge and hunt you down."

"Tell her I'm waiting."

Jason smiled. "I'll see you Wesley. And thanks again. Seriously, let's get together before the next Super Bowl party."

Wesley waved as Jason exited the office and walked down the hall.

Chapter fifteen

Jason parked his Subaru in the driveway of his Aunt and Louise's house. From the front it appeared to be a modest brick home with a curved drive and large azaleas and dogwoods partially obscuring it from the view of anyone passing by. Once inside, the true size of the house became apparent. With over two thousand square feet of living space, which Jason liked to describe as looking like it came from the pages of Architectural Digest, there was plenty of room for its occupants' hobbies, only one of which was collecting art from their vacation travels.

Jason rang the doorbell, then waited as he heard Louise's beagle, Bella, bark the announcement that company had arrived.

"Jason, come in." Jason was greeted with a hug from Louise, and a sniff around the ankles by Bella. "You look good. Have you lost a little more weight?"

Jason looked down at his clothes. "I don't think so."

"Well you look good. Just don't lose too much."

Aunt Bess walked out of the kitchen wiping her hands on a dishtowel. "There's my favorite relative." Bess gave Jason a tight hug and a kiss on the cheek. "I haven't seen you in almost a month but it seems like longer. Have you put on a little weight? Your face looks fuller."

Jason laughed. "Louise just said I look like I've lost weight."

"Oh what does she know? Her mother is Jewish and her father was Italian. They always think people need to eat more."

Louise gave Bess a gentle slap on the shoulder. "Oh you. We don't want him to waste away. He works all the time and doesn't eat."

"I eat. I eat if I'm hungry." Jason said in defense of himself.

"Well, I hope you're hungry tonight because we cooked – a lot."

"Aunt Bess," Jason frowned. "I told you not to do that. We could have just ordered pizza."

"Are you kidding? We haven't seen our favorite nephew in a month and I'm just going to order pizza? I don't think so."

"Besides, I haven't had a decent meal since she left town," Louise added.

"Well, it smells great. I've been so busy lately I haven't really taken time to cook for myself."

Louise arched her back and straightened her posture until she looked to be almost standing on her toes. "See, I knew it. He's lost weight."

"Come on in the kitchen. You can sit at the bar and talk to us while we finish cooking."

"Is there anything I can do to help?" Jason asked as he followed his Aunt and Louise into the kitchen.

"Yes." Bess replied. "You can go to the wine cooler and pick out a wine to go with dinner. Something red and foreign."

"You know I can cook. And I'm pretty good at it, too."

"I know you can, honey. Louise and I taught you, remember? We wanted to make sure you made some woman a good husband one-day. Speaking of which. Are you and Cindy seeing each other yet?"

"Aunt Bess. She works for me. I can't date her. Besides, she's not my type."

"What is your type?"

"I don't know. I haven't met her yet."

"Cindy is a really sweet girl. And that daughter of hers is priceless. So smart and well mannered."

"She's quiet, too." Louise added. "Most children these days can't sit still and have the attention span of a gnat."

Bess had a reflective look on her face as if recalling a memory from long ago. "She reminds me of you when you were little, Jason. Children today don't use their imagination. Everything is blasted at them in sound bites while they stare at a TV screen and eat food that's loaded with sugar. But she's very creative, like you were at that age."

Jason's Aunt Bess, having worked as a junior high teacher and then later a professor, had very strong opinions about the problems of children. She felt that our society was failing them and, in-turn, as adults they would fail society.

Jason opened the wine and poured them each a glass. He positioned himself at the bar while his aunt finished the entrée and Louise sliced fresh tomatoes she had picked from her small vegetable garden in their back yard.

"What nationality are we eating tonight?"

"Spanish. Louise and I fell in love with Spain and its food when we were there last year."

"It smells fantastic."

When the three sat down to eat, with the cats and dog receiving hand-outs under the table, the conversations were not of bodies and missing children. Instead, they talked about Bess's recent trip and the piece of sculpture she found in a little gallery. It was tucked away in a turn-of-the-century building down a little cobblestone street that tourists rarely found. Jason talked of work and how his business was expanding, almost faster than he could keep up. As always, his time spent with Bess and Louise was his most relaxing and happiest.

*****

Across town, Angela was cooling off from her evening run. She had cut her run short. The heat and humidity were unbearable. Normally, it didn't bother her this much but, half way through her run, she began to feel over-heated and fatigued and opted to walk back home rather than try to get in her usual three miles.

She stood in her small kitchen holding the refrigerator door open staring at its contents. She was too overheated to eat. She closed the refrigerator door and opened the freezer. Angela weighed her options and decided on a strawberry frozen fruit bar. At least it was cold. Angela picked up the remote and turned on the TV. She still had time to catch the seven o'clock edition. Sitting in the floor in front of the television so she wouldn't get sweat on her sofa, Angela finished off her fruit bar while she watched the introduction of the news anchors.

The male anchor, whose name she could never remember, began the headlines of the evening's stories. "In our top story tonight, Dorothy Danze is on the scene at the old Wardlaw Junior High as the last body is removed. And in other stories tonight…"

Angela hit the mute button and picked up her cell phone. She called Rob Edwards.

"Hello," a woman's voice answered.

"Hello. This is Angela Porter. Is this Mary?"

"Yes. How are you, Angela?"

"I'm fine. I was wondering if Rob was there. There's something coming on the news I thought he might want to watch."

"He's here, but he's resting right now. But I'll tell him you called."

Angela could hear a waver in Mary's voice that sounded as if she had been crying. Angela hesitated for a second. She didn't know if she should ask if something was wrong. She didn't know Mary that well. She and Angela and only met briefly a few times. Angela decided she should ask. If she didn't, then she would worry all night. "Mary. Is everything okay? You sound like something's wrong."

There was a moment's hesitation. "No. Everything is fine." Mary's voice faltered slightly. "It's been a long day and everyone's just a little tired. Rob's lying down right now. I'll give him the message."

"Okay. You sure everything is okay?"

"Yes. Thank you for asking. Good-bye now."

Before Angela could say goodnight, Mary hung up. Angela, still sitting in her living room floor, stared at the TV screen. She ran her fingers through the sweat-dampened hair at the base of her neck and pulled it loose from her skin. Something was wrong. She had felt it all week.

Realizing the news cast about Wardlaw had begun, she picked up the remote to take it off mute and focused her attention on the news anchor.

"This is the scene where just barely over a week ago, a single skeleton of what is reported to be a child, was removed from what was once the playground of Wardlaw Junior High. Now a forensics team prepares to remove the seventh and hopefully, last remains of this now vacant lot. A week ago construction crews who were working on the renovation of Wardlaw found the first remains while they were laying pipe. Then during the recovery work, the six additional sets of remains were found."

Angela closed her eyes and shook her head. Dorothy Danze was trying to sensationalize the story.

"We have not been able to obtain a statement from authorities, but inside sources close to the investigation tell us that items have been found with the bodies that may shed light on who these victims are and how long they have been buried here. Hopefully, police will be able to identify them and provide some solace to the families."

The camera switched to the television news studio.

"Dorothy, the first body was recovered several days ago. Has there been any word on how close the police are to identifying it?"

"No, John, there hasn't. Our sources tell us that these children have probably been here a long time – several years at least, which would make tracking down the right missing person records, and finding a match that much more difficult."

"Dorothy, I know down in Charleston on the campus of the Citadel, old Confederate graves were discovered several years ago. Is there any chance that this could be an old burial site?"

"Actually John, initially there was some speculation that this was the case here. At one time the Wardlaw school grounds were part of a plantation and then later, a farm. But that was ruled out early on due to the degree of deterioration of the bones and also, the types of items that were found with the children's bodies."

"What are the items you mentioned?"

"That information hasn't been made available yet. We just know that items were found with the bodies."

"Thank you, Dorothy. Keep us posted."

"Thank you, John."

"Shit!" Angela bent over and hit her fist against the floor. "Damn!" Angela closed her eyes and rubbed her forehead with her fingertips. Even though the account wasn't totally accurate, the first skeleton was the only one where artifacts were found. Someone had obviously leaked information.

Angela reached for the phone. Her first reflex was to call Rob Edwards, but she had stopped herself. Angela sat with her hand suspended in mid-air, hovering above the phone. She was pissed and she wanted to talk to someone. None of her friends could be told anything about the case. Venting to any one of them was an exercise in futility. For a split second she thought of Doug Brazell. "No, don't even go there," she told herself. If she called him now, it would be telling him it was opening day of deer season and she was Bambi.

Angela thought about calling the TV station to complain, but that would only fuel the rumors and speculation.

"Damn!" Angela stood up and paced across her living room floor, taking short, contemplative strides. Who could be the leak? Or was there one? Angela mentally questioned herself. Most of what Dorothy Danze reported could have been picked up around the excavation site. All she really needed to do was listen in on a few conversations and ask a question or two to a couple of key people. Then she would have her story. The only thing that concerned Angela was the mention of items found with the bodies. Still, that was probably a guess, or misinformation someone had given her, since she had alluded to items being found with all seven children.

Angela knew, other than the aggravation she and Rob would have to endure, in the long run it probably wouldn't matter. They would most likely have to go to the press and appeal to the public for help in identifying the children.

Public appeals had worked in the past. In Professor Russell's lab, he kept on display the clay likeness of a woman's face. A badly decomposed body had been brought to him for identification. After boiling off what little tissue remained on the skull, clay was used to construct a likeness of the woman. Fortunately, the nameless woman had unique bone structure. After running a picture of the likeness in *The State* newspaper and broadcasting it on the evening news, a family member came forward and identified the woman. Unless the missing person reports yielded more than she expected, this procedure would be used to, hopefully, identify the seven children.

As quickly as Angela had shifted her attention from her partner Rob Edwards, to the news broadcast, she shifted again. Her train of thought skipped from one unrelated topic to the next, like a flat stone skipping across a pond. This time her mind jumped to her personal life. For a moment she began to feel sorry for herself. She wanted so badly to talk to someone. Because Becky's father had been a cop, she had a second -hand way of understanding what Angela was going through when the stress of a case was getting to her. But even so, there was only so much you could tell a friend. She hadn't had a serious boyfriend in two years.

The last one, Mike, was just like the others. As soon as things started getting more serious, he suddenly was no longer fascinated by her job. He began asking when she was going to change careers. A wife and mother couldn't be a cop – the hours, the atmosphere. What if something happened?

To Angela, there was no difference. A man would leave behind a wife and child. Why is that different for a woman? Eventually, both she and Mike could see that they were at an impasse. Neither of them could or would change. Angela's career meant too much to her to give it up, and Mike didn't want a wife with a career. Let alone one who wore a badge and carried a gun.

Angels' Playground

Chapter sixteen

Dinner was relaxing for Jason. Since the time of his brother's death his Aunt Bess had provided an emotional haven. She had given structure and security to his life at a time when he needed it most.

"Jason, would you like another glass of wine?" Louise asked as she held up the nearly empty bottle of Malbec.

"No thanks, Louise. I've had my limit. If I have any more I'll need to spend the night."

"That's no problem. We have clean sheets on the bed in the guest room."

"Sebastian wouldn't like it if I spent the night. I've been keeping some pretty odd hours lately and he's spending too much time by himself."

"What about you?" Bess asked as she joined Louise and Jason in the living room.

"What'd you mean, what about me?"

"Don't you spend too much time alone?"

"Not really. I'm interacting with people all day long at work. I have the two of you and at home, I have Sebastian."

"Sebastian is a cat."

"He doesn't know that. He thinks he owns the house. I just go to work and abandon him for the day so I can pay the bills."

Jason could see the look of concern on his aunt's face. "Okay, Aunt Bess. I would like to have a girlfriend. I admit that. But I haven't found one yet and I love Cindy to death, but there's just not anything there." Jason changed the subject. "Now, let's get down to business. Where are those yearbooks?"

"I have them right here." Bess patted the small stack of dusty yearbooks resting on the corner of the coffee table."

"Have you already looked through them?"

"Not yet. But it shouldn't take us that long to figure out if these little girls are in the yearbooks or not. Actually, I think I may have even saved the news clipping. But it's probably stuffed away somewhere."

With Louise sitting to Bess's left and Jason to the right, Bess slowly scanned the pages of the yearbooks. Jason and his aunt decided it would be best if she didn't look at the names from the news clippings beforehand. Nor did Jason give her the name that was engraved on the I.D. bracelet that had been unearthed with the first body. None of the names in the article matched the bracelet and Jason didn't want to influence Bess's recollection of the missing girl.

After about thirty minutes of carefully looking at each of the school photos of the sixth, seventh, and eighth graders, Bess was satisfied the missing girl she remembered was not in the 1966 yearbook.

"You sure she's not in there?" Jason asked with an anxious voice.

"Positive. I remember some of the faces and the names, but she's not in this group. Ready to try 1967?"

"Sure."

Louise handed Bess the second yearbook from the stack and laid it in her partner's lap. Again Bess slowly turned each page, taking time to scan each snapshot. She wanted to closely scrutinize the group photos as well as the individual photos. There was a chance the missing girl had missed picture day, but had been present the day group and club photos were taken. "Nothing in the sixth grade."

Jason gave a sigh that was barely audible. He had what he knew to be an unrealistic hope, that his Aunt would open the first yearbook and the names and faces would spring from the pages.

After turning the first three pages Bess paused. She tapped her finger below a photograph of a girl that stared out from the page with a solemn expression on her young face. "This is her. This is the girl that everyone said ran away from home."

"Are you sure, Aunt Bess?"

"I'm positive. I remember her so well now. She always seemed like such a sad little girl. Very smart, and talented, too. She gave me a drawing she had done. I kept it and put it up somewhere. Probably with the news clipping."

"She gave you a drawing?" Jason had an excited tone in his voice. His aunt had a tangible connection to the girl.

"Yes. She wasn't in one of my classes. But I used to see her sitting in the courtyard by herself. She would always eat out of a brown paper bag and draw in her note book. Wardlaw had a courtyard at its center that was enclosed by classrooms on one side and the gymnasium and stairwells on the other three sides."

"Yes, I know. It's going to be an open-air seating area for a café that's going in on the ground floor." Jason stopped himself. He had interrupted his aunt's train of thought. "I'm sorry. Go ahead with what were you saying?"

"That's quite alright." Bess patted Jason's knee. "Anyway, she would eat out there on pretty days rather than sit with the other children. Sometimes I would go talk to her and give her a mini art lesson. I think she developed a crush on me. Young girls do that a lot."

"Do what?" Jason inquired.

"Get crushes on female teachers that are nice to them or that they look up to. It's harmless and goes away the first time the cute boy sitting next to them smiles at them."

Bess paused for a moment then turned to Jason. "So is Annie our girl?"

Jason looked at the copy of the news clipping he held in his hand. "Annie is the missing girl, but that isn't the name on the bracelet."

"You said there were others."

"Yes. But Peggy doesn't match any of the names in the articles I have. I was hoping you would point out a Peggy in the photographs. The articles only talk about six girls. There were seven skeletons found. Peggy could be the seventh."

"Peggy? Now that name rings a bell, too."

Both Louise and Jason looked at Bess.

"Let me see something." Bess quickly flipped back through the pages of school pictures she had already scanned. "Here. This is Peggy. She was Annie's best friend."

"I thought you said she didn't have any friends." Louise reminded her.

"She didn't, not really. None, except for Peggy Anderson."

"You think she would have had Peggy's bracelet?" Jason asked, the excitement returning to his voice.

"Actually, I wouldn't be surprised. Peggy was pretty and popular. Annie was pretty, too, but she was shy and quiet. Some of the other children would tease her because she wore old clothes and brought her lunch in a used, wrinkled paper bag."

"That's sad. Children are so cruel to each other sometimes." Louise commented as she reached over and turned the pages back to look again at the picture of the sad young face staring out at them.

"I know. But children learn those things at home. Anyway, Peggy befriended her and I used to see the two of them together a lot. They would play together on the playground. Most of the time, they would just sit under the magnolias on the front lawn and talk."

"What would they talk about?" Jason asked.

"I don't know. Secrets young girls tell each other, I guess. Actually I think they had crushes on each other."

"Really? At that age?" Jason was surprised.

"Like I said, sometimes girls that age do that. Children then weren't as clued in on sex and everything, like they are now. A crush then was usually pretty innocent."

"So it was a deep friendship kind of crush?"

"Probably. If the remains they found were Annie's, that could explain why it had an I.D. bracelet with Peggy on it."

Louise was still staring at the pictures. "What happened to Peggy?"

"I don't know. I remember she was there through eighth grade. I used to see her in the library reading. I tried to talk with her a few times after Annie disappeared. She was pretty withdrawn after that. Her whole personality changed."

The excitement Jason had felt at finding a connection between one of the names in the article and the bracelet was gone. He understood loss. As a child he had learned how emotionally devastating it could be. His excitement was replaced with empathy.

"That poor little girl. That had to have been so terrible – for both of them."

Jason's Aunt looked at him. He was staring at the page, but his eyes were looking through it. Jason was inside himself. His eyes saw another place, another time.

"Honey, are you okay?"

"Yes. I'm fine. Let's see if there are any more names in the yearbooks that match the names in the articles."

"I have two more year books. We'll finish up the seventh and eighth grades in this one and then look at the others."

"Sounds like a plan."

Louise stood up. "I'm going to get some coffee. Would anyone else like something?"

"No thanks, Aunt Louise. The caffeine would keep me up. But I'll take a bottle of water."

"It's decaf."

Jason paused for a moment as if contemplating his options. "No thanks. I'm not much for coffee. I'll stick with the bottled water."

The aroma of fresh brewed coffee filled the lower floor of the house as Jason and Bess meticulously scanned the first of the two remaining yearbooks. They were careful to not miss a single photograph or name. The girl they were looking for could be hidden away in a group shot or a club photo.

"You know honey, just because she wasn't in this yearbook doesn't mean she wasn't a student. Let me see that article again." Bess read the names of the missing girls. "When was the article written?"

"I don't have the exact date. Looks like it was cut off when Wesley copied it. But he did say that this article was written after the three girls disappeared."

"All of the girls were twelve?"

"The three in this article were, but in the later article I don't think it listed any ages." Jason held the copy of the second article in front of him so both he and Bess could read it. "No. I wonder why he didn't give names and ages in this one, but did in the other."

"Who knows. Anyway let's look at our last yearbook."

Jason handed his aunt the 1969 yearbook. Bess quickly flipped to the individual photos of the children. The photos were arranged alphabetically by class. Their search of the first half of the sixth grade yielded nothing.

"We probably won't find anything else."

"Don't give up yet, Jason. Does the article say exactly when they disappeared?"

Jason quickly reread the first article. "It just says she was twelve and gives a time of year, not an exact day." Bess flipped past the pages with sixth grade photographs, then went to the seventh graders.

"S, T. Here, I bet this is her." The face smiling out at them, with braces on her teeth, belonged to Susan Thompson. She was a small girl with blond hair and eyes that sparkled and gave just a hint of what must have been a playful and mischievous personality.

Jason looked at the photograph. "That's the right name. You think that's her?"

"Perhaps. You know I don't remember anything about this happening. I just vaguely recall something about a missing girl. I don't remember anything going around the school about it."

"Could it have happened during summer vacation?"

"Possibly. If it happened early in the summer, then the excitement would have died down by the time school started again. Or it could have been after I left." Bess paused. "I'm trying to remember exactly when I went back to school to work on my doctorate. Let me tell you, when you are working on a dissertation full time, you aren't always tuned in to the rest of the world."

"How could we find out if this is the right one? You don't have any more yearbooks do you?"

"No. That was my last one. And all the yearbooks would tell us, anyway, is if she was there for the next school year – maybe. My suggestion is to go to the police with what you suspect."

"I really don't want to do that yet."

"Why not?"

"I want to do it when I have more information. I want to be able to tie all of these together correctly."

"Then my suggestion is to find the reporter who wrote the articles. He obviously thought something odd was going on here."

"Wesley checked with human resources for me. The last record they have on him is 1982. Apparently, their records from back then are in a mess. They couldn't even give Wesley a social security number or tell him why he left *The State*."

Bess arched her left eyebrow. "Couldn't, or wouldn't." She replied with a tone of suspicion in her voice.

"I think they couldn't," Jason said. "Wesley said they were pretty screwed up down there. And, technically, they can't give out the social security number, but Wesley has a friend."

"Still, it's odd that nothing more was said about the disappearances, than these two articles. You would think that the public would have been pretty keyed up over this."

"I wasn't even born when these girls were in junior high," Jason pointed to the yearbooks whose pages were still open to the faces of Annie and Susan. "I wasn't even in elementary school when this second article was written."

"Louise," Bess yelled into the kitchen to get her partner's attention. "Do you remember anything back in the early- or mid-eighties about children disappearing in Columbia?"

Louise walked into the living room with her coffee in one hand and a bottle of spring water for Jason in the other. She handed the water to Jason then sat down in the large, slightly overstuffed chair opposite the couch and propped her bare feet up on the ottoman. "Not really, dear. Seems like every few months some child is either missing or found dead, but nothing really stands out. Why do you ask?"

"Well, we were just talking about this. For the reporter to have two articles about missing children and allude to connections between them, it just seems odd to me."

"In what way?"

"It's just that I can't remember a community reaction to it. Not intending to use a cliché, but I don't recall any out-cries of public concern over a rash of children disappearing."

Jason interrupted, "It doesn't give exact dates in the article, but it sounds like this happened over several years. Look at Annie and Susan. They were probably at least two or three years apart. Maybe they were just spread out so far that no one noticed except this guy."

"That is always possible," Louise agreed. Then holding the mug with both hands, took another sip of coffee.

"I still think you should go to the police with this."

"I will. I promise. But I want to get some more information first. I want to find this reporter – Mark Harris, and talk to him."

"Jason, you could have information the police need."

"Aunt Bess, these children have been dead all these years; another two or three days isn't going to make any difference. I'll tell them what I've found. I just want to try to find a little more first."

"If whoever killed these little girls is still out there walking around on the street, then they probably know the remains have been found. If you go poking around in this, you could put yourself in danger."

"Aunt Bess," Jason replied with exasperation.

"Don't roll your eyes at me young man. This is work for the detectives. You're the most important part of my family. Don't go playing Barnaby Jones or Joe Mannix on me."

"What? Who are they?"

"They were television private investigators. Sometimes I forget just how young you are."

"Now if we are talking investigators, then I could be Charlie and the two of you could be my angels."

Louise laughed. "I want to be Kate Jackson. Back in the day I had such a crush on her."

"Okay, but I was thinking more along the lines of Cameron Diaz."

Louise shook her head. "You really are such a youngster."

"I've seen the new ones. Lucy Liu is rather hot," Bess added.

"I'll say!" Jason added. "She could investigate me any day of the week."

"Anyway," Bess changed the subject. "Promise me you'll go to the police."

"I will. I just want to talk to Wesley. I want to ask him if anyone still works there who knew Mark Harris."

"Is there anything else I can help with?"

"If there is, I'm not sure what it would be right now. I just need to figure out where to go from here."

"Okay." Bess patted Jason's knee. "Do you want to take these yearbooks with you?"

"Yes, please. If you don't mind."

It was after ten when Jason finally pulled out of their driveway and headed home. He was tired and felt mentally and physically drained from the combination of work, recent family stress, and now preoccupation with the "Wardlaw murders," as the press was calling it. With the store spaces in Wardlaw only two-thirds filled, Jason was concerned that some merchants would begin to pull out because of the negative publicity.

The economy in Columbia was better. After the long recession, new businesses were moving into the metropolitan area. Realistically, for every one business that pulled out of Wardlaw, there would probably be another to take its place. People wanted places to spend their money. Some businesses might even feel that the murders would be a draw for business.

As Jason pulled into his driveway and waited for the garage door to open, he looked up at his bedroom window. His ever-faithful best friend was at the window awaiting his return. Jason smiled when he saw Sebastian's head disappear from view. He knew his little friend was, at this very moment, running down the stairs to greet him when he entered the house.

Chapter seventeen

Angela awoke to the blaring sound of a disc jockey pitching cars for an area dealership. She rolled over and hit the snooze on her alarm. There had to be a better way to wake up in the morning. Some days she didn't feel like getting out of bed. This was one of them.

She tried to drift off to sleep again. Just a few more minutes of sleep she told herself. If she only had another half-hour that would make all the difference and she would feel great. But Angela knew a half-hour or even an hour wouldn't really matter. She had always loved her work, but lately she had begun to feel dissatisfied and sometimes even resentful. These feelings weren't healthy and she knew it. This past week had been the worst. Looking at the skeletons of seven murdered children had only intensified the feelings that had been slowly building within her. "I'm not going to get burned out, not this early," she kept telling herself.

Now something was wrong with Edwards, her partner. Even with his sometimes brooding disposition he was still too distant, even for him. Angela had worked with Rob Edwards long enough to know that lately, even when he was concentrating on the work, a part of him was somewhere else. Somewhere that was dark and troubled.

The radio sounded again, signaling another reminder that it was time to get up. Angela turned it off and rolled closer to the edge of the bed and slowly pushed herself upright. As she sat on the edge of the bed allowing her eyes to slowly adjust to the light that filtered in through the closed blinds, she thought about an earlier conversation with her friend Becky. Becky had commented that she thought Angela sometimes seemed depressed. That she didn't have the same spark in her eyes that she used to. At first Angela disregarded the comments. However, as she thought more about Becky's observations, she began to agree with her.

Angela knew she loved her job but her lack of a personal life, other than occasional drinks or dinner with Becky and the running to keep herself fit, was not enough to ward off the stresses inherent to being a police detective.

"I'll go see a movie this weekend or go to that concert in Finley Park," she said out loud to herself as she stood up and walked into the bathroom. "I just need to start making time to have fun."

As Angela showered and dressed for work, Jason was already at his office making electronic images of the photographs from the yearbooks. He printed them out on heavyweight paper that was coated on each side, perfect for photo images. He held the 8x10-inch sheet up in front of him and admired his work.

"Perfect!" He said out loud. "Anyone should be able to recognize you from this."

Jason printed pictures of all the girls, Annie Walker, Susan Thompson, and Peggy Anderson, the little girl who had befriended Annie. Jason stared for a long moment at the photograph of Peggy.

"If I could find her and this reporter, I bet I could find the connection between all the girls. Then I'd know who did this."

Jason looked at his watch. It was still too early to call Wesley. Wesley probably wouldn't show up for another half hour. He also planned to call a friend who worked at the Department of Motor Vehicles. If Mark Harris was still in the system, then his friend could find him. His own Google searches had resulted in nothing. There was no digital footprint of the Mark Harris who wrote the articles.

Jason stood over the printer watching the last image of Peggy come out of the machine. It was a group shot of her in the science club. Most of the other members of the club were boys. Peggy must have been an exceptional little girl. It wasn't until well into the seventies and early eighties that attention was drawn to the fact that little girls were being discouraged from pursing interests in the sciences. Jason wondered if she still lived here. She would be almost sixty. Googling her might not work if she had married and changed her name. Without a social security number, even his friend at the Department of Motor Vehicles might not be able to find her, especially if had she moved out of state.

Jason brushed his sandy brown hair back from his eyes. Pulling his hair back made him remember the last time he had spoken with his father. All he had said to Jason was to ask when was he going to get a hair cut and start looking respectable. Jason's only reply was, "After I get my nose pierced."

As Jason drifted deeper into his thoughts, he heard a sudden hard pounding on the front door of the office. The pounding was so loud and sudden that it startled him. Stepping from behind the cubical wall where the printer was located, Jason looked down the short hallway and saw a person standing at the front door. The morning sky was still dimly lit and with no lights on in the front office Jason could only see the silhouette of a stocky built man wearing a baseball cap.

As Jason walked down the hall toward the front of the office the face on the other side of the glass door became clearer. It was Glenn. Jason reached into his pocket and retrieved his key ring, inserted the heavy office key into the deadbolt and unlocked the door. "What's up, Glenn? What are you doing here this early?"

Glenn adjusted the ball cap on his head. "I was on my way to the job site and I saw your light on so I stopped."

"Isn't this a little out of your way? I thought you lived in Cayce?"

"I had an errand to run so I swung by here."

"So what's up?"

"You heard anything about whether or not they're going to finish up today?"

"I doubt I know anything you don't. You've been down there more than I have the last couple of days."

"I noticed. What've you been doing anyway? I'd thought you would've been down there tryin' to help get this job finished."

"There really wasn't anything I would do to help. You had a few guys working on the inside doing as much as they could, and I had some other projects I had to help finish up."

"You heard any rumors about what's going on?"

Jason could tell Glenn wanted to talk about more than just the schedule for the Wardlaw project. But Glenn wasn't being direct with his questions. In fact, the only time Glenn was direct was when he was yelling and cursing.

131

"You think the developers will shut us down?"

Jason looked thoughtful for a moment. "I don't know. I wouldn't think so. They have too much money invested in the project."

"People ain't going to want to bring their kids to a place where a serial killer's been burying bodies."

"Wardlaw isn't going to be a fast food restaurant with a play land inside. It's designed to appeal to white collar professionals. Adults who want to spend money in trendy shops. After the hype dies down I really don't think they'll care. If anything, some people would come for the novelty."

Glenn again adjusted the cap on his head. In the months they had worked together Jason had learned to read his body language. If Glenn pulled the brim down with a snap he was pissed. A two-handed adjustment, right hand on the brim and left and on the back of the cap, meant he was nervous. A stroking motion to the back of the cap usually was an indication that Glenn was in a good mood and ready to be friendly. A slow deliberate right-handed adjustment meant he was thinking. Jason decided Glenn didn't think much; however, this morning Glenn was thinking.

"Come on, Glenn. Any city where half the population would line up with their kids to gawk at an electric chair that had been used to kill people for years, wouldn't think twice about shopping in stores where right out the window they could get a look at where some serial killer buried their bodies."

Glenn looked at Jason as if he was considering Jason's words. "We ain't going to finish on time."

"Probably not." Jason could tell Glenn was mentally kissing his new truck good-bye.

"You going down there today?"

"A little later. I have some things I have to finish around here first."

"I've been hearing people talk about it a lot."

"Oh yeah. What are people saying?" Jason knew better than to solicit information Glenn had picked up at a softball field, but still, he wanted to hear everything he could about Wardlaw and the murdered children.

"Some of the guys think these are some of the people Gaston killed.

You know, he said he'd killed about a hundred or so people and he'd tell where they were."

"Well, he may have killed more than the police actually knew about. I read that was just a last minute ditch by him to try to stop his execution."

"I don't know. Why would he say that?"

"The guy was warped."

Glenn adjusted his cap again. "You know, I remember some of that."

"I only read about years later. I was too young to really remember it."

"Well, I better get down there. We got to get some work done today."

"I'll see you down there a little later."

"Yeah, later."

After Glenn left Jason locked the door. He didn't want anyone wandering into the office unannounced. Jason returned to the printer. A red light was flashing indicating it was out of paper. Jason replenished the paper tray and waited as the last image printed. It was another picture of Annie. She was a missing child, as was Susan; but were they ever found, or were they among the bones that were unearthed in the old playground?

"I have to find Peggy Anderson and Mark Harris." Jason looked at his watch. "Wesley might be in his office by now." Jason was so used to talking to his cat Sebastian as he walked around the house he didn't always realize when he was only talking to himself. Jason walked into his office and sat at his desk. He dialed Wesley's direct line and waited as the phone rang. Just as he started to end the call...

"Hello. The State paper. This is Wesley."

"Hey Wesley."

"Jason?"

"Yeah, it's me."

"What're you doing up this early?"

"I couldn't sleep this morning so I decided to get up and just go to the office."

"You're at work already!"

"Yes. Believe it or not. Look, I had dinner with Bess and Louise last night and we went through some of Aunt Bess's old yearbooks from

Wardlaw. She taught there for a few years."

"Did you find something?"

"Maybe. She remembered Susan, Peggy and Annie."

"Okay. Susan and Annie I remember from the article, but who is Peggy?"

"Peggy was the name on an I.D. bracelet that was found with one of the skeletons. And a little girl named Peggy just happened to be best friends with a little girl named Annie."

"No shit!"

"Exactly. So can you find someone who works there that would know how to get in touch with Mark Harris? He might have some information that would tie these together. He sure hinted enough about it in his articles."

"Consider me on it right now."

"Wesley, remember you promised. Don't say anything about this until I get all my facts straight. If the killer is still around somewhere, I wouldn't want to be responsible for letting everything leak out and then the guy getting away."

"No problem. I'll sit on it a few days. But if I get wind of someone going after the same information then I have to let the news editor know. I want to get some credit for all of this."

"Just keep quiet as long as you can."

"Okay."

"So you're going to find somebody who knew Mark Harris?"

"If there's anyone here who knew him I'll find out. I'll do it just as soon as I go get my coffee. Why are you so wound up over this?"

"I don't know. It just matters to me that I try to do something."

"Well, whatever. I'm on my way to get coffee just as soon as I hang up. I'll start checking around now."

"Thanks."

"No problem. But chill before you have a stroke."

Jason ended the call. He knew Wesley didn't understand why he needed to be involved in this case. "I don't understand it either," Jason said aloud to himself. He ran his hand through his hair, pulling it away from his eyes, and then scratched his scalp as his fingertips reached the crown of his head. The last two weeks had been hard on him. The lack of rain and the constant humidity were wreaking havoc with his sinuses. His allergist had put him on a combination of decongestants and antihistamines to keep the asthma at bay. He knew the medications were most likely heightening the level of anxiety he was feeling.

Jason stared at the phone willing it to ring. He knew Wesley had not had time to even walk to the offices which housed *The State's* on-staff reporters, but still he stared as if wanting the phone to ring with information on the whereabouts of Mark Harris. Scratching his scalp again Jason set the photos of the three little girls aside and walked to the file where blueprints were stored. With a sigh he pulled out the top drawer and removed the drawings for the Grover Stores job. Roger, his assistant, had taken over the project, but he needed to stay involved. The job was going to bring in good money.

As usual Roger had made few errors. The blueprints for Ed Grover's stores were a long way from being completed, but so far they were good. Jason scribbled a quick note for Roger, indicating a couple of calculations he wanted him to re-figure, then returned the drawings to their file drawer. Again, Jason was up pacing around the room. The work did little to relieve his anxiety. He needed to get out and do something. Maybe go for a drive or go home and water the shrubs in his yard. It still wasn't too hot for a run. Anything to burn off his energy. Jason decided the short drive was his best option.

Chapter eighteen

Angela pulled into a parking space at the Columbia City police headquarters. She had timed it just right, there was still one open space. As she stepped out of her car she saw two other people circling the long narrow lot for a parking space. "When are they going to enlarge this thing?" She asked herself. Angela held in her left hand a cinnamon raisin bagel; the melted butter seeping through the paper napkin was making her fingers greasy. In the same hand, pressing against the bagel and making the butter situation worse, was a stainless steel travel mug full with coffee.

Angela entered the building and started down the hall to the basement stairs leading to her office.

"Angela. You got a minute?"

Angela turned to see her captain, Frank Morris, standing in the doorway of his office. "Sure."

"Go ahead and put your things down, then come back up here. I need to talk to you a minute."

"Okay. I'll be right there." Her captain was a stern man and most times when he said he wanted to see her she felt like a school kid being called to the principal's office. She had noticed, in the last few months, that feeling had started to change to a small degree and Angela was astute enough to know it was because, even through her frustrations, she was gaining more self-confidence as a detective.

Angela knocked on the open door and leaned in through the doorway. "Frank."

"Come on in and close the door, please."

For a split second Angela felt her skin crawl. "What's up?"

Frank let out a sigh. "This isn't easy." He cleared his throat. "I spent some time last night at Rob Edwards' house, talking to him and his wife."

"I called there last night and spoke to Mary for a second. She sounded upset. Is anything wrong?"

"I'm afraid so." Frank looked down at a stack of papers on his desk. "There isn't any easy way to say this so I'll just spit it out. Rob has cancer."

Angela felt the blood drain from her face. "What kind? How bad is it?"

"It's lung cancer. It doesn't look good at this point. They're going to start him on some treatments and see what's happens."

"What's the prognosis at this point?"

Frank ran his hand across his thinning hair. "I think Mary and Rob are trying to have a positive attitude, but from what they were saying last night," Frank paused, "I think they're having a hard time doing that. It just doesn't sound very good."

Angela knew it wasn't good. She had watched her uncle die from lung cancer. In six months he had gone from a strong healthy man, who thought he simply had a chest cold he couldn't get rid of, to little more than a living skeleton. Then one night he started coughing and couldn't get his breath. As he gasped for air he took one last, long breath then went limp in her aunt's arms and died. It would be like that for her partner Rob Edwards.

"He hasn't been acting like himself lately. I just thought this case was bothering him." Angela stared at the floor, not really knowing what else to say.

"Angela. I don't know how close you and Rob were, but I know you all seemed to get along well together. And you worked well together."

"I guess we are kind of like the odd couple. But we made a pretty good team. At least I felt like we did. God, that sounded like I was talking about him in the past tense."

"That's one of the things I wanted to talk to you about. Whatever the ultimate prognosis… Rob won't be back at work, at least not for a while, if ever. I know chemo really takes a lot out of people and he won't be able to work at a job like this."

"Frank, I really don't want to work with someone else on this case. If that's what you're getting ready to say."

"I'm sure you don't and I can understand that. You started it with Edwards and you want to finish it with him. But I'm going to put someone else with you. I think this case has the potential to blow up in our faces if we aren't careful. The press has already been down there more than once. That Dorothy Danze has called the Chief and me a half dozen times apiece. That woman is a pain in the ass."

Frank paused for a moment waiting for a response from Angela. When he got none he continued. "Right now, they're still just snooping around and speculating. We've made no official statement other than this is a murder investigation. But it's just a matter of time before something leaks out. I'm surprised those two workmen that dug the thing up haven't been interviewed."

"Actually, it was a woman who first saw it and then the guy running the backhoe. They have been interviewed. And Dorothy Danze was on TV last night talking about items being found with the bodies and saying that the bones aren't from an old cemetery."

"Whatever. It'll probably take me a day or so to get everyone's workload shifted around so I can put somebody with you. So just keep working on what you all were doing."

"Frank?" Angela paused for a moment. "I guess the best thing I can do is just be blunt with this. Are you putting someone else with me because you don't trust me to handle this case by myself?"

"Yes and no."

"What do you mean yes and no?"

"You're a good detective. Better than some of the one's that have been here for a while, because you pay attention to details. But you do have less experience than most of the others and, like I said, this is going to turn into a sensitive case. I'm leaving you on it because you're good. But I'd have two people working on this no matter who it was."

Angela thought she was being complemented but wasn't certain. Still, she knew Frank wasn't confident in her ability to work on the Wardlaw case alone. "I can handle this by myself."

"Maybe so, but I'm still putting someone with you."

Angela knitted her eyebrows. "Any idea who?"

"Probably Randall Evans."

"Sir, if I have to work with someone I'd really prefer to work with one of the other detectives."

"What's your objection to Randall?"

"Other than he's sexist, bigoted, and obnoxious – nothing at all."

"I know he can be a problem, but I plan to have a long talk with him before I assign him to this case."

"Frank, if I can come up with some leads by next week will you let me work it alone?"

"You've already had too long on this with nothing turning up."

Angela felt desperate. Under no circumstances did she want to work with Randall Evans. "It took several days to get the first report to us. Then they found the other remains. It takes time to get six graves excavated and paperwork processed."

"Angela…"

Angela stopped Frank before he could continue. "We're just now getting started. Just give me until the end of next week."

Frank was silent. "You have until four o'clock Wednesday afternoon. If you don't have anything substantial by then, you better get used to working with Randall. At least on this case."

"I'll get something."

"Then you better get at it."

Angela took that as her cue to exit her Captain's office. "Thank you." Angela pushed her chair away from Frank's desk and walked to her office. Once inside she closed the door to the small room, something she rarely did because of its size.

She just needed a few minutes to think. To think about Edwards, her partner, and to sort out what she needed to do next with the Wardlaw case. Angela leaned back in her chair and put her feet on top of her desk. She stared blankly at a Monet print hanging on the wall opposite her desk. The pale green lilies lying in swirling pastels of water created such a tranquil scene. She thought somewhere there was a place like this. But it wasn't here in the oppressive heat of a summer drought with a schoolyard full of murdered children.

Angela looked down at her watch. It was already nine. She rubbed her eyes. They felt tired and sleepy. "I need to get some more caffeine in me." She stood up and, giving the lilies one last look, headed upstairs to get her second cup coffee for the morning.

"Angela."

Angela turned her body slowly as she sipped the hot coffee that contained so much cream it was a light tan color, like chocolate milk.

"Angela. I've got the report for you that you were waiting on." The young desk officer handed her the report and then smiled.

"Thank you, Debbie."

"I would have given it to you sooner, but you were in with the Captain. I didn't want to interrupt."

"That's fine." Angela took another sip of coffee and read the case number on the folder. It was the forensic examination of the items found with the first body.

Debbie nervously toyed with a misplaced strand of her short blond hair. "Is there anything else I can get you?"

Angela smiled. "No, this should keep me busy for a little while. Thank you." Angela had noticed more than once that Debbie always seemed nervous when she had to talk to her about anything. But other than a slight curiosity, she had never given the matter much thought. With the pressure to find a major piece of the puzzle to the Wardlaw case and a partner who was most likely dying of lung cancer, she wasn't inclined to analyze it further.

Back at her desk, Angela skimmed the report. Not much to it, but at least it helped to narrow down a window of time for the first remains. The buttons, zipper, I.D. bracelet, and shoes were all probably from the mid-sixties to early seventies. Surprisingly, the theater department at USC had provided that information.

With the time frame narrowed down, Angela went back to the missing person files and began searching for files on Caucasian children reported missing during those years.

*****

Jason finished his drive and was back at his desk. He looked at his watch. It was almost nine. He hadn't yet gotten a call or a text from

141

Wesley with information on Mark Harris. Jason picked up his cell phone and called Wesley's number.

"*The State* newspaper. This is Wesley speaking."

"Hey Wesley. This is Jason."

"Jason. Hey. I bet I know what you're calling about."

"Sorry."

"That's okay. I was just getting ready to call you."

"Did you find out anything?" Jason didn't try to hide the anticipation in his voice.

"There were only a couple people left that worked with him. Everyone else is retired or passed away. I was able to get you some information."

"So, what did you find out?"

"Well, Mark Harris didn't leave the paper; he was killed in a car wreck. Probably not long after that second article was written. They didn't remember the exact date, but they said it was some time in the late fall. That article ran - when was it? September? October?"

"I'm not sure. The date was cut off."

"Sorry about that. I'll get you another copy. Anyway, I think that's what I remember seeing, at least on one of the articles."

"Did he have any family?"

"Yes. They said he was married. Thought he might have had one, maybe two children, but they weren't sure."

"Where's his wife now? Did they know?"

"One of the guys said he thought her family was from Camden, but wasn't sure. He said it was either Camden or Lugoff. He did know that she moved back over there after Mark was killed."

"That would make sense. Did they know her name?"

"One guy said Barbara, the other guy said Brenda."

"Would personnel have any records on who his dependents were?"

"I don't know. The old records are so screwed up down there. I think it's a waste of time trying to find anything."

"Would you mind checking for me?"

"No problem. It'll just be a quick phone call. But I can't guarantee you anything."

"I know. Thanks, man."

"You want me to put you on hold while I call down there? Or you just want me to call you back?"

"I'll just call you back a little later. I have a few things to get caught up on here."

"I hear ya."

"Okay. Talk to you later. Oh, and tell Cindy hey for me."

"When are you goin' to ask her out?" Jason teasingly remarked to his friend because he knew Wesley found her attractive.

"Don't give me that, man. You're the one she's got her eye on."

Jason felt annoyed by Wesley's comment, especially after his aunt's questions from the night before. "She works for me and she's not my type."

"She's good looking. If she wasn't so hot on you, I'd ask her out. The way it stands, I wouldn't have a chance."

"Like I said, she works for me."

"Just kidding. I'll check out HR and see if they've got anything on the deceased Mr. Harris."

"Call you later. And I'll tell Cindy hello for you." As Jason ended the call, Cindy knocked on his door.

"Do you have a minute?" She had a broad smile on her face.

"Sure, what's up?"

Cindy handed a manila envelope to Jason.

"What's this?"

"Look at it. I found it on my front porch this morning."

Jason pulled the pages from the envelope and slowly began to read. "It's the forensic report on all seven sets of remains! And photos. How did you get this? Did your cop friend leave it?" Jason paused.

"Oh, let's just say cops aren't the only friends I have around town."

"You're kidding." Jason was shocked. He had never expected to actually get his hands on this much information.

Jason was quiet for a moment as he looked at the report in his hand. He leafed through the pages and pulled out two photographs. He stared at them. The first picture was of the bracelet. 'Peggy' was clearly visible. The second photo was of a child's skull with its hollow eye sockets staring up from the table where it lay. It almost didn't seem real, but Jason knew it was. He had seen for himself the first bones pulled from the earth after the backhoe began to cut its trench.

"Cindy, is there any way you can find out from your cop friend how the investigation is going?"

"I don't know. I can ask. If you want to see missing person files I know he won't be able to get you those. I already asked."

"No, I understand he can't get those. I just want to know if they have any leads at all. If they've identified any of the skeletal remains, that sort of thing."

Jason paused for a moment.

"Could you give him a call this morning and just ask?"

"I'm fixin' to do it right now."

Jason began reading the report. After about thirty minutes Cindy returned.

"I talked to him."

"What did he say?"

"He said just going over there and asking some questions was no problem. Shop talk."

"Did he tell you when he is going to do this?"

"He said he would probably make it over there today."

"Great! Then he'll call you back?"

"Yep! Did you find anything in the report?"

Cindy walked to the drafting table and looked at the photos in front of her. "I know things like this happen here in Columbia. I see it on the news. But somehow, when it's on television it always feels like it's so far away. Like it's someone else's problem. Like we're kind of protected here. But looking at this and seeing where they dug them up over at Wardlaw – it's just scary. It makes me want to go get my daughter out of daycare and tie a leash between me and her so nobody can get her."

"I don't even have kids and it scares me."

"Jason, did your aunt help you any last night?"

"No, not really." Jason wasn't sure why he lied; it was just like an instinctive response. "We looked through some of her old school photos, but she's going to have to dig some more out of the attic."

"That sucks. I thought you would probably go over there and come in this morning telling us you had solved the case."

"I wish. But that only happens on television." There was a long pause. "I'll look at these in more detail a little later. I have to get busy and make some phone calls and work on that new stair detail of yours.

"Sure. I'll get that detail for you right now. I think I have it right, or almost right."

Jason retreated to his office with Cindy's drawings and she returned to her desk. Jason tried to concentrate on checking the drawings, but found himself every few minutes looking at his watch to see how much time had passed since he had last spoken to Wesley.

Jason lifted his head and rubbed his eyes. "If Wesley was able to find anything, he should have it by now." Jason picked up his phone and called Wesley's number.

A woman's voice answered.

"Hello. My name is Jason Shealy. I'm trying to reach Wesley Fuller."

"I'm sorry, but Mr. Fuller is in a meeting right now. Can I take a message or tell him you called?"

"Actually, if you could just put me through to his voice mail."

"Hold please, while I connect you."

There was a short pause then Jason heard his friend's prerecorded greeting. "Wesley. This is Jason. I was just wondering if you were able to find out Harris's wife's name and anything else about her? Give me a call or text me. See you, and thanks."

Again Jason looked at his watch. There was nothing he could do but wait until Wesley called back. Jason stared at the envelope that contained the report, then opened the folder where he had placed the photographs of the three Wardlaw schoolgirls. Their eyes were so full of youthful innocence – that is, all but Annie's. Hers were sad and distant, as if she were somehow apart from her surroundings. A girl he dated briefly a few years ago who was a believer in Wicca and the goddess would have said Annie had an old soul. Jason looked at the sad little face and he knew it wasn't an old soul that lived in her small body. He knew all too well from his own childhood, hers was the face of pain.

Jason set the photographs aside and focused his attention to Cindy's stair detail.

Chapter nineteen

Angela lifted her glasses and rubbed her eyes. Stacks of missing person reports covered her desk. She had spent the better part of the day searching files. For the time period the artifacts were identified as being from, she had only two possible matches, but seven bodies. It was better than nothing. To go back decades without the help of a computer, Angela felt as if she would be lucky to find anything at all.

Twice she had tried to call Rob Edwards. Once there was no answer so she left a message on his phone. Her second call was to his home phone. His daughter-in-law answered. She told Angela that she had just stopped by to let the dog out and Edwards, his wife, and son were at the hospital for more tests.

"Edwards, I need your help," she said aloud to herself. Angela picked up the two files and walked upstairs. She would get someone started tracking down any additional information the department might have on files relating to the two missing child reports she'd pulled. She wanted the parents found.

Only upon reaching the top of the stairs did Angela realize how late it was. Anyone who could help her with her search had gone home for the evening. It was almost eight. "No wonder I'm hungry." She looked at her watch again and contemplated the time. She knew a run would help relieve her tension, but she was mentally too tired to motivate herself. She just wanted to go home and relax. Maybe mix herself a vodka tonic and watch television.

Angela turned and went back downstairs to her office and gathered her things. "I have until next Wednesday to figure something out," she told herself. "I can do this."

Having just exited Wardlaw's auditorium, Jason was standing in the stair well on the second floor landing when he looked out the window and saw a black Honda Accord pull into an empty parking space on Park Street. Jason watched as a woman got out of the car and walked toward the Wardlaw lot. She showed something to the uniformed officer who was guarding the excavation site, then walked under the crime tape. That was when Jason recognized her. It was Detective Angela Porter.

There was no window on the back side of the building where he could watch what she was doing, so he quickly went downstairs into the gymnasium and ran across the floor to a door at the far end of the building where the locker rooms had been located. The door was directly opposite where the first grave had been discovered and most likely, Annie had been buried. Jason watched as she left the first grave and walked to the far end of the playground and stood under the pecan tree where the six other graves had been uncovered.

While Jason silently watched the detective, he pulled his cell phone from his pocket and reread the text from Wesley. It was the name Betty Harris, Mark Harris' widow and her last known address, Clyburn Street in Camden.

Cindy's friend at the Cayce police department had come through with some information, too. He told them the woman detective on the case was temporarily working it alone. Her partner was sick or something. Through Cindy's friend, Jason also knew Detective Porter had the lab report and was searching in the correct time period for the missing children. It would only be a matter of time before she found the right match. At that point the police would know more than he did and with his avenues to obtain information exhausted, there would be no way for him to become involved.

Jason's need to be involved in the case felt almost overpowering. He knew possibly the only chance he had was to approach Detective Porter now, before she had time to start putting the puzzle together herself.

Jason closed the gymnasium door, gave it a push to make certain it had locked, then turned and sprinted across the gym floor to the door that opened into the stairwell. From there he dodged sawhorses and two-by-fours as he ran to the main entrance on the second floor of the building. Jason paused only long enough to lock Wardlaw's front door, then ran down the stone steps and across the lawn to Angela's Accord.

Jason reached the car just in time to turn and see Angela crossing under the crime scene tape at the corner of the building.

Angela looked up and saw Jason standing beside her car with his hands on his hips and breathing heavily. She approached with caution, more out of habit than genuine concern. "You're Jason, the architect, aren't you?"

Breathlessly, Jason replied, "That's right, Jason Shealy."

"Are you alright?"

"Yeah, I'm fine. I was just upstairs and saw you, and so I ran down to talk to you for a minute before you left."

"What do you want to talk to me about?"

"About Wardlaw. About the remains. I have some information…"

Angela could hear Jason starting to wheeze as he tried to talk. "Are you sure you're okay?"

"Yes. I have asthma from my allergies. I just need to get my inhaler. It's in my car over here."

Angela followed Jason to his Subaru and watched as he pulled his keys from his pocket and opened the door. His breathing was becoming more labored and she could see herself calling an ambulance instead of heading home for the evening.

Jason dug though his messenger bag and quickly produced the inhaler.

Angela watched as he sprayed its mist into his mouth and breathed the medicine deep into his lungs. It only took a couple minutes before Jason's breathing relaxed.

"Do you have these often?"

"No. They're pretty rare actually. I guess running through the school and breathing so hard around all that dust set off the attack. I never had asthma until I moved back here after college."

"Really. Where'd you go to school?"

"The University of Kentucky in Lexington."

"Nice area. I have some relatives that live up there."

"What part?"

"I couldn't tell you the street name off the top of my head, but I know their children go to Dunbar High School."

"Okay, then they live on the west side of town. Probably somewhere off Harrodsburg or Versailles Road, in one of those neighborhoods."

"That sounds familiar. Anyway, you said you had some information about Wardlaw."

"Yes. Here, let me show you this."

Jason turned and pulled a manila folder from his messenger bag and removed copies of the news articles his friend Wesley had given him.

With the sun beginning to go down and the poor quality of the copies, Angela squinted to see the words on the pages.

"Would you like to sit in the car? I'll turn my dome light on."

"Sure." Angela climbed in the passenger seat while Jason walked to the other side and got behind the steering wheel.

Jason flipped on the light. "How's that?"

"Better."

Jason watched anxiously as Angela read each article carefully, sometimes rereading paragraphs to make certain she comprehended the full meaning of what their author, Mark Harris, was implying.

When she had finished she looked at Jason. "How did you find these?"

Jason took a long slow breath then began speaking. "When I started working on this project, I did a lot of research on the building and its history. Old buildings like this are really my passion."

"Okay, so how did you find these articles?"

"I guess I remembered glancing at them when I was doing my research. After the first remains were found, I just felt like something was nagging at me. Like there was something about Wardlaw I should remember."

"Anyway, a friend of mine works at *The State* newspaper, and he helped me find the articles. The ones you just read."

"Well, I appreciate you giving me these. I'll go through them closer at the station and, hopefully, they can help." Angela moved as if she were going to get out of the car.

"Wait." Jason placed his hand on Angela's. It was only a slight touch, but it stopped her from exiting.

"Like I said, Jason, I appreciate the information, but I'm leaving now."

Jason removed his hand. "I know you probably think I'm some kind of nut, but I can help you with this case."

"I really don't see how that's possible."

"You have that article now and you didn't before."

Angela looked down at the copies of the news articles she held in her hand, then looked back at Jason. Starring him in the eye, she asked, "Let's hear it. How can you help me?"

Jason hesitated for a moment. He wasn't sure how much he should share with Angela, but he had to win her trust and get her cooperation now. If he didn't do it now, he knew he never would. "Peggy isn't one of the missing girls you need to be looking for."

Jason saw Angela's expression change as soon as he said the name "Peggy." Angela wasn't able to disguise her surprise.

Trying to control her voice so as not to betray her shock that Jason would have Peggy's name, Angela asked, "Why do you say I'm looking for the wrong person?"

"I didn't say you were looking for the wrong person. Actually, I don't know what missing children you are looking for. I just know Peggy isn't one of them. Look at the article. The names there are Annie, Susan, and Paula."

"That's only three names. I have seven sets of remains to identify."

"True. But Peggy was Annie's best friend. They went to Wardlaw together in 1967."

"You can't be much older than me, if any. You weren't even born yet. How do you know they went to school together? Are you a relative of one of the girls?"

"I just started piecing stuff together after I got my hands on the articles."

"Then how...?"

Jason interrupted, "My aunt was a teacher at Wardlaw. Last night she and I went through her old yearbooks and found photographs of the missing girls mentioned in the article. She remembered Peggy. Peggy finished junior high there; then my aunt lost touch with what happened to her after that."

Angela sat quietly for a moment not really sure what to do next. Jason obviously had information she needed. "Okay. So you have a news article, anyone could've dug that up."

"That's true, but no one has except me. Here, look at these." Jason handed the photographs of the three girls to Angela. "I made copies of those from the yearbooks."

"You said your aunt remembers these girls?"

"Yes. And I have this, too." Jason pulled his cell phone from his pocket and showed her Wesley's text message. "Mark Harris, who wrote the articles, died not long after the second story was written. This is the last known address for his widow. Also, my aunt is checking with a friend of hers who works with the Richland County school system to see if she can get a social security number for any of the three girls or their parents. We could find them and start back tracking for information."

Angela stared at Jason in amazement. "Why are you doing this?"

"I don't know. Honestly, I'm not a psycho. At least I've never been one before. I just want to do something to help. I want to be involved in finding out who did this."

Angela thought silently for a moment, still not understanding Jason's motivation. "Okay, this is the deal. I'm working on this by myself – for now. My Captain wants to put another detective with me and the guy's a jerk. I have until Wednesday to come up with some hard leads in this case." Angela looked at the papers she still held in her hand and sighed. "Honestly, other than some old case files, this is the best information I have."

"I won't do anything to screw up your investigation. I won't go to the press with anything. I just want to help."

"Why?"

"Honestly, I don't know. It's just important to me."

Angela turned to look at Jason. Even under the dome light of his Subaru she could see the bright green of his eyes and the sincerity in them. She remembered her earlier assessment of him. Handsome in sort of a boyish way, but probably just another guy who has a fascination with crime scenes.

"Every part of me that's a cop tells me not to trust you. But my gut feeling is that I need to just go for it, but I just don't know."

"Look, I gave you this information. If I were out for publicity for myself, I could just as easily given it to Dorothy Danze. She's been down here a lot talking to people."

Angela's shoulders lifted and then fell as she breathed in deeply and then exhaled. "I know. She's been calling the station. Actually, I'm surprised she doesn't already have these articles."

"Just tell me what I can do to help."

Angela stared again at Jason, then said, "Can we go talk to your aunt tonight and see if she found out anything with these social security numbers? Then, tomorrow, we'll track down Betty Harris."

"You said 'we.' Does that mean we'll work together on this?"

"For now."

The corners of Jason's mouth turned up slightly in a small smile. "Do you want to go to my aunt's now?"

"Will she be there?"

"Yes, I'm sure she is."

"Okay, I'll follow you."

Jason pulled a business card out of his planner. "Here, this has my cell phone number in case we get separated on the highway."

Angela took the card and added the number to the contacts in her phone. She then walked to her own car. "I must be stupid," she said aloud to herself. She knew involving a civilian in a police investigation was a dangerous move and, potentially, career suicide. But Jason had just handed her the best information she had come across. Assuming Jason's information and the articles were correct, and three of the murdered victims were Wardlaw students, maybe the killer was a teacher, coach, janitor, or even someone from a nearby neighborhood who hung out around the school grounds. Mark Harris, without coming out and saying so, had implied there was a connection between the girls in the article and other disappearances. Now Angela knew she had to discover the names of the other children and establish the same link Harris had found. As far as Jason was concerned, she would just have to work off her gut instincts and keep an eye on him for anything unusual.

Jason pulled out of the parking space; Angela pulled into the street and followed close behind. She hadn't thought to ask where his aunt lived. She picked up her cell phone and dialed her friend, Becky. It went to voice mail. "Hello Becky, this is Angela. I just wanted to let someone know where I was. I'm following this guy named Jason Shealy. We're going to his aunt's house. Actually, I forgot to ask her name or where she lives. Anyway he has some old news clippings on Wardlaw that have some information in them that could help with the case. Don't say anything about this to anyone. I just wanted someone to know where I was, since I don't know this guy that well. Talk to you later." Angela hung up.

After a short drive on the interstate and some twists and turns through a neighborhood, Jason slowed, then came to a stop at the curb in front of a two-story brick house. Even in the partial darkness, Angela could tell it had a well-kept yard with flowering trees and shrubs, partially hiding it from view from the street.

Jason stepped out of his car. Angela was already out of her car and walking toward Jason. "Is this it?"

"This is it."

"Nice house," Angela commented, thinking of her own second-floor apartment which, most times, felt too small even for one person. "Is your aunt home?"

"Yes. I called ahead just to make sure, and to let them know we were coming."

As the two walked up the drive to the house, Angela began to ask questions about Jason's aunt. "You said your aunt taught at Wardlaw?"

"That's right."

"What does she do now?"

"She's a professor at USC."

"Who else is going to be here in the house besides the three of us?"

"My aunt's partner Louise, two cats, and a beagle."

"Her partner?"

Jason hesitated for a moment. "Ah yes, her domestic partner, Louise. She's like my aunt, too."

"So they're gay?"

"Yes." There was a short silence between the two.

"Hope that doesn't make you uncomfortable. They're my aunts and I never really think about it."

"No. Doesn't bother me at all. I have gay friends."

Jason and Angela stood at the front door, but before he could ring the doorbell, the door swung open and a short beagle rushed out at their feet and began prancing around Jason.

"Hey, I was in the dining room and saw you pull up. Why didn't you park in the driveway?"

"Angela, this is Louise, my aunt's partner."

Louise extended her hand and Angela shook it. "You must be the detective. Please come in and have a seat. Jason, make her feel at home while I get Bess. She's in the back yard."

Jason led Angela into the two-story great room. As Angela followed, with a detective's eye, she surveyed the rooms. Everything in the house seemed to be strategically placed to give aesthetic appeal to the rooms, in addition to functionality. There were beautiful pieces of art on every wall and every table. The paintings appeared to be originals; nothing was a print or reproduction.

"Have a seat," Jason pointed to the sofa. "Can I get you anything? Coffee, juice, soda?"

"No, I'm fine. Thanks anyway."

Jason watched Angela as she continued to inconspicuously survey the room. "They collect art," Jason volunteered.

"I see. They have a lot of beautiful things."

"They like to travel, too. Every time they go somewhere they come back with a new painting or sculpture, or relief – something. The good thing is they've given me some of the pieces they've gotten tired of."

Just as Angela was going to comment, Bess and Louise walked into the room.

"Hello, I'm Jason's aunt, Bess Shealy. You must be the detective." The two women shook hands. "I'm glad to see Jason took our advice and went to the police with the information he found. But I have to admit, I didn't expect a visit from any of you."

"Sorry, if this has alarmed you in any way, but after Jason told me you remembered the girls that could possibly be two of the remains we dug up, I wanted to talk to you myself. Also, Jason mentioned you were trying to track down some names, addresses, and even social security

155

numbers of family members of the missing girls."

"Yes, that's right. I've had a little luck. I have an address for each of the girls when they were at Wardlaw and their parent's names. I'm sorry. That probably isn't much help. You could get that much from the missing person reports, I'm sure."

"Yes ma'am. Could we just start from the beginning on how the two of you put all this together?"

Jason and Bess looked at each other. "I guess I'll start," Jason replied. "I guess it starts with me."

Between Jason and Bess the two relayed to Angela the sequence of events and their assumptions which lead them to the possible identities of the remains recovered from the Wardlaw playground. Angela was amazed that the two of them were able, in such a short period of time, to come up with so much.

Finally, after taking several pages of detailed notes, Angela paused her questioning.

"So what will you do now, Detective?"

"Just call me Angela."

"Okay, Angela."

"Actually, we'll do a couple of things. First track medical and dental records for the girls, and I'll contact Professor Russell and he'll determine if we have a match. If we need to, he'll take the photographs of the two girls and superimpose them over the skeletons to see if they match. And next, we'll do just what Jason was going to do, track down Mark Harris's widow and talk to her."

"You know Angela, I never did believe the rumors that Annie had run away from home," Bess said thoughtfully.

"Why's that?"

"For one thing she was just too young."

"There are children living on the streets right now that are younger. They're abused, abandoned, or their parents don't want them and just kick them out. It happens all the time."

"I know, but it wasn't so common back then. Something about it just didn't feel right. I saw how close Annie and Peggy became and I don't think Annie would have left her – not without a word."

"Well, it looks like she didn't. Or if she did, she didn't get very far." Angela saw a sad expression wash across Bess's face. Her face showed a vulnerability which hadn't been there when Angela was questioning her and Jason. Angela liked her.

Looking at her watch, she said, "I've taken a lot of your time. I need to be going now."

"No, that's quite all right. I hope we've helped."

As Jason and Angela rose to leave, both Louise and Bess shook Angela's hand then hugged Jason and gave him a kiss on the cheek.

"Drive carefully," Louise yelled as the two walked down the driveway to their cars.

Jason and Angela stood beside her Honda. The moon was full and cast a glow across the hood of her car that made it appear to glisten.

"I like your aunt and Louise. They're nice, and helpful." Angela held her note pad up in front of her and shook it slightly to emphasize 'helpful'.

"I know. They're great. I might not have made it through my childhood with my sanity intact without them."

"Were things bad at home?"

"I have an older sister, and I had a younger brother. He died in an accident when we were children. My parents – my family, kind of fell apart after that. My mom alternated between being wrapped up in grief and wrapped up in my sister. Dad just shut down. Not like he was that emotionally available before, but that made it worse."

"I'm sorry."

"It's okay. Bess was a Godsend."

There was an uncomfortable pause between the two, then Angela spoke. "Look, I really have to get home. I'm pretty beat and I want to get an early start on this tomorrow."

"You're working tomorrow?"

"Yeah, probably."

"Would you like to go grab a sandwich or something, I haven't eaten yet?"

"No, thanks anyway," Angela quickly declined. "Look, Jason, me letting you be involved in the investigation is really breaking the rules here."

Jason felt anxiety building in his stomach and his face began to feel flush. He was anticipating Angela thanking him for his help then telling him to get lost.

"I know you're taking a chance, but I want to help."

"Jason, the cop side of me says to play by the rules and to not trust you. But my gut feeling is to trust you."

"So what are you going to do?"

"I guess I'll give it a shot and trust you – for now."

"Thank you."

When Jason smiled as he thanked her, Angela could see a sparkle in his eyes. He really is attractive, she thought to herself.

"Okay, here's what I need to do. I have to tell my Captain about what I've – we've, dug up, but tomorrow is Saturday and I know he won't be in. When I talk to him on Monday, I'm leaving your name out of it for obvious reasons."

"Okay. Then what?"

"Well, if you're available tomorrow, I thought we could track down Betty Harris."

"I'm available. Any time tomorrow. I can be free."

"Okay. Let me get into the office and see what I can run down on these names and addresses your aunt gave me and I'll make sure this is a current address for Betty Harris."

"Do you want me to meet you at the station?"

"No. It would probably be best if I just met you someplace and we rode from there."

"We could meet at my office. It's on Taylor Street. It would be convenient to hit Bull Street from there and get on I-20 and go straight to Camden, provided she still lives there."

"That sounds good. I'll call you tomorrow." Angela pulled a business card from her pocket. "Here, let me write my personal cell number on the back of this – just in case you need it."

Chapter twenty

Angela awoke early the next morning. She had hardly slept during the night – she was too excited about the information Jason had given her. As she lay in bed she began making a mental list of what she needed to do first.

"Get with the Captain and show him what I've found, but not until Monday. I have to track down files on these two girls, make sure medical records get pulled so Russell can get a positive I.D. on them. More missing person files to sort. Talk to Betty Harris. God, where's Edwards when I need him." She felt guilty. "For god's sake, he has cancer and all I'm thinking about is how I need his help. I'm a jerk," she told herself as she rolled over and pulled the sheet up closer to her neck.

Jason had been so helpful, he would be able to do more, but there was no way she could let anyone find out. Not without getting herself in trouble. She knew she probably shouldn't even let him go with her to question Betty Harris. What if something was said about it? She could jeopardize the case. She could jeopardize her job.

Angela closed her eyes to try to get a few more minutes of sleep. As Angela began to drift into a dream state, Jason's face flashed before her. She knew she would take the risk.

When her alarm finally sounded, she quickly turned it off. She was tired but, for the first time in weeks, was anxious to get to work. Angela showered and dressed quickly then dried her hair. "God – bad hair day." She applied more gel and worked it through her hair. After another a minute or two she paused.

"This is not a date. This is a murder investigation and you are putting your job on the line," she said to herself as she looked at her reflection in the mirror. "I'll put on the navy blue shirt. I look better in that."

She looked at her watch. It was nine.

"I'll call him after I get this address confirmed."

Once at the station Angela went straight to her office to sort through the missing person files on her desk. Quickly she dug through the first stack. Nothing. She sorted through the next stack setting on the floor beside her desk.

"Anna Walker. This must be it." Angela held the folder in front of her rereading the name on the tab. Opening it, she read a physical description of the young girl, "Brown hair, green eyes, seventy-five pounds, about four-eleven. "She was small," Angela thought as she continued to read. "Age twelve, missing from the house, younger brother said she walked to the store to get a soda with some change she had saved." Angela let out a sigh. "I've found you, Annie. I'm sorry."

Angela set the file aside and began looking again. Deeper into the stack she found the file on Susan Thompson's case. "Age twelve, blond hair, blue eyes, reported missing on July 13, 1969. That's why Jason's aunt didn't remember her disappearing. She disappeared during the summer just like she speculated."

Angela set Susan's file on top of Annie's then locked her office door and went upstairs. "Debbie, could you run this name and address for me.?I need to make sure it's current."

"Sure, Detective Porter. I'll get it right away."

"Thanks. I'm going to get some coffee, then I'll be downstairs in my office." Back downstairs, Angela went inside her office and closed the door behind her. She felt slightly claustrophobic in the small room, but ignored the feeling. It was more important that she have privacy as she sorted through the files. "What was the other name?" From her daily planner she pulled the article Jason had given her and, unfolding it, scanned the words until the found the name of the other girl Mark Harris had named. "Paula Groves. Let's see if we have a file on you."

Angela's search only lasted a few minutes. "This is one I'd skipped over the other day. The time period didn't match what Russell had in the report." Angela read the first page of the missing person report. "Last seen leaving a Girl Scout meeting at Wardlaw. Missing in September 1979."

Angela reached for cell phone. "I have to call Jason."

She was startled by a knock on the door.

"Detective Porter? Are you in there?"

"Yes. Who is it?"

"It's me, Debbie. I have that address information for you."

"Oh okay, thanks. Just a second." Angela shoved the three folders into her top desk drawer before opening the door. "Hey, Debbie. What'd you find?"

"The address checks out. Unless she just recently moved and hasn't reported her new address to the DMV, then this is where she lives."

Angela smiled. "Thanks, Debbie. I appreciate it."

Debbie looked around the room at the reports spread across the floor. "Is there anything else I can help with?"

"Not right now, but maybe later."

"Okay. If you need anything I'm working all day today. Just call me."

"Thank you. I will." Angela smiled again as Debbie backed away from the door then retreated upstairs.

"Jason. I have to call him."

Angela closed the door and dialed Jason. After several rings she was almost ready to end the call when she heard Jason answer.

"Hello."

"Jason. This is Angela."

"Hey. Good morning."

Angela could hear a pleasant, friendly tone in his voice. "Jason. I may've hit the jackpot here."

"Really! What'd you find?"

"I have missing person files on Annie, Susan, and Paula Groves. All three were Wardlaw students."

"No kidding. Did it take very long to find them?"

"No. They were right there in front of me. And I had Betty Harris' address double-checked and, unless she just recently moved, she's still there. So, are you ready to take a drive to Camden?"

"Sure. When do you want to go?"

"I'm going to make copies of these reports and then I'll meet you at your office. How fast can you be there?"

"I've been waiting on your call; I'd just stepped outside for a second, so I'm basically ready to walk out the door right now. I can be there in maybe twenty minutes, give or take a few minutes for traffic."

"Great, I'll see you there."

Jason turned around to see Sebastian perched on top of the kitchen counter and rubbing his head against the refrigerator. "Boy, if that's not a hint for a treat, I don't know what is." Jason scratched Sebastian under the chin the opened the refrigerator door. "Okay, so what d'you want? There's not much in here fella. How about some turkey?"

Jason tore a small piece of turkey from a larger deli slice. "Here you go, fella. I need to go out for a little while, but I'll stay home with you tonight. I promise." Jason gave Sebastian a loving rub on the head then picked up his messenger bag and car keys from the counter top and quickly exited into the garage.

Even on a Saturday during the hottest part of the summer, traffic was heavy. For the last twenty years Columbia's urban sprawl had gone unchecked and the highways had not been designed to handle the large number of motorists traveling around the city from the numerous subdivisions that had sprung up.

Jason turned his air conditioning on high and pointed the vents toward his face and chest, but still he was hot. The heat, along with his eagerness to meet with Angela, only increased his frustration with traffic. Finally, after a hurried drive to his office that felt as if it took twice as long as it actually did, Jason saw Angela's car parked on Taylor Street in front of his office building.

Jason parked his car at the rear of the building, then walked to the street to greet Angela.

"Hello Angela."

"Hi Jason."

"Would you like me to drive?"

"No. Since this is police business, I'd better drive out there. I'm taking a big enough risk just taking you along with me."

"Don't feel obligated to take me along. I can stay here if it'll get you in trouble."

"No. I want you to go, too. We'll just have to figure out how to do this."

Jason tossed his messenger bag into the back seat then climbed into the Honda. His knees hit the dash. Jason was only average height, but someone much shorter than either he or Angela must have been riding in the passenger seat.

"Where's the lever to push the seat back?"

"It's right over there on your..."

"Oh, I got it." The seat went back with a thud. "Sorry."

"That's okay. A friend of mine, Becky, was the last person to ride there. She's short so she always pulls the seat up as far as it'll go."

Jason buckled his seat belt then, with a sweeping motion, pushed his hair away from his eyes. He put on his Ray Ban sunglasses and turned to look forward into traffic.

"I'm ready, " Jason said with a smile.

To Angela, Jason's smile seemed to make his entire face come alive. She found the sparkle it gave to his green eyes disarming.

"I'm only doing this because he can help me with this case," She told herself as they pulled into traffic and drove toward Bull Street and then onto I-20 to Camden.

As they drove, the silence between them was broken by uncomfortable attempts at small talk, which ranged from where each of them had gone to school to the chance for rain. When they changed the subject to Wardlaw and the missing children, they relaxed and conversation was easier.

Jason described to Angela his passion for historic buildings and how he felt the first time he walked through Wardlaw's empty corridors. He said he could almost sense a sadness in the building. The colors in the murals in the cafeteria were as bright as the day they were painted, yet all around them there was ruin. His parents had attended Wardlaw, not that it held any great significance for him, given the state of his relationship with his parents. His connection was the emptiness of the abandoned building.

Angela was surprised that Jason spoke in terms of feelings and emotions. It was so unusual to hear that from a man. She guessed it was from the influence his aunt and Louise had on him while he was growing up. She also knew there was something more there motivating him to want to be involved in this case. There was more than just a love of old buildings and a romantic spirit, but she didn't want to ask. Not yet. Even if Betty Harris could give them any additional information, this case was far from solved. There would be plenty of time to find out what drove Jason to need to track down the identities of these children.

"Clyburn Street must be around here somewhere," Angela said as she drove slowly and tried to watch for street signs. She glanced at her GPS. "We're coming up on Clyburn Street now."

"Arriving at destination," said the voice from the GPS. Angela pulled her car to the curb.

"Well. Looks like this is it. There are two cars in the driveway. Someone has to be home. Can you see the license number on that one car? I don't have my glasses with me. I forgot and left them at the station."

"Let's see. D-M-L... Yes, that's her car. So how do you want to do this? Do you want me to go in or stay here?"

"You better stay here first. If she gets talkative I might have you come in. I don't have a problem with you coming in. But if she isn't too friendly, I just don't want word getting back to the station and my Captain that I was out here with someone, since I can't think of a good lie to explain who you are."

"OK. Call me if you need me. I'll be right here."

"Wish me luck."

Angela left the motor running in the car so Jason would have air conditioning. It was almost noon and, with the heat index, the temperature was a sweltering 101 degrees.

Jason watched as Angela stood on the front porch and rang the doorbell. When a woman answered the door Jason rolled down the car window enough to hear bits and pieces of the conversation between the two women. The woman who answered the door was average height, just a little shorter than Angela, and she had dark, reddish brown hair which was most likely dyed. Even from a distance Jason could tell it had that unnatural tint that his own mother's hair has right after she's been to a stylist to have the gray covered up.

When Angela showed the woman her badge, the woman looked first at the badge then past Angela toward the car and Jason, then stepped back from the door to allow Angela enough room to enter the house.

As Angela walked inside, she turned and looked back at Jason and smiled.

Once inside, Betty Harris led Angela into the living room. The house was modestly decorated. The furniture was old but in good condition. There was no artwork on the walls – just a couple of the mass-produced prints depicting Rainbow Row in Charleston and then some family photographs.

"Have a seat."

"Thank you." Angela watched Betty Harris closely. The body language was of a woman who was nervous. "Mrs. Harris, I would just like to talk to you about your late husband, Mark Harris."

"What about Mark?"

"Really, this has more to do with some articles he wrote before he died." Angela removed copies of the articles from her note pad and handed them to Betty Harris. "Mrs. Harris, do you remember your husband working on these articles or talking about them?"

Betty Harris covered her mouth with her hand as she read the headlines and her husband's name appearing in the byline. "I remember these stories, yes."

"Did he ever talk to you about them?

"Mark talked about a lot of his stories. I don't remember him talking about any one in particular. That was a long time ago." Betty Harris handed the copies back to Angela.

"In the stories he mentioned the names of three children, three little girls who went to school at Wardlaw and disappeared. He also implies that there are other missing girls and that somehow all the disappearances are related in some way. Did he ever talk about that?"

"Look Miss – Porter, wasn't it?"

"Detective Porter." Angela corrected her. She hated being referred to a "Miss" when a male officer would have been automatically called detective.

"Detective. Mark and I were close. We were married, but he's been gone a long time. I just don't remember."

Even as Betty Harris insisted she didn't recall anything about her husband's work Angela's gut feelings told her the woman wasn't telling the truth. She was tense, nervous.

"Mrs. Harris, do you watch the evening news?"

"Of course I do."

"Have you seen Dorothy Danze's stories that she has done on the school and the remains that have been found?" Angela watched, as the level of anxiety in Betty Harris appeared to increase.

"I think I may have seen one of them. Some of the news I listen to closer than other parts."

"Do you think it's possible those remains could be the children your husband wrote about?" Betty Harris began twisting the rings on her fingers in quick, short movements.

"Mrs. Harris, I don't want to make you uncomfortable, I just need your help, if there's anything you can tell me."

"I don't know what I could tell the police about anything."

"Your husband didn't give any names in his second story, but he must have known their names, otherwise he wouldn't have made the references he did, or connected it to the first story."

Betty Harris stared at Angela but said nothing.

Angela continued, "I don't have children of my own, but I would guess it's the most horrible thing imaginable to have a child that's missing and not know what happened to them. You wouldn't know if they were dead or alive, or if they were suffering at the hands of some psychopath."

Angela watched the woman's face as she continued to speak. She felt she had hit a nerve.

"If we can identify these children, at least their parents will know what happened to them."

"I'm sorry. I wish I could help."

The room was dimly lit with little sunlight coming in through the windows. Angela thought she could see tears starting to form in Betty Harris' eyes. "Well, I'll not bother you any longer. Here's my card. You can reach me at the station. If I'm not there just leave a message on my voice mail or call my cell phone."

"I can't imagine knowing anything that would help you."

"Take it just in case."

"Alright."

As Angela was leaving, she paused to look at two photographs hanging on the wall near the front door. "Are these your children?"

"Yes, that's Mark Junior and Karen."

"Nice looking children."

"Mark lives here in Camden. He's a manager at the chemical plant. Karen lives in North Carolina now. She is an engineer."

"Sounds like a smart girl."

"She is. Always was top in her class."

Angela could see the pride on the woman's face.

"I hope you can remember something that will help us bring some peace to the parents of those little girls. They never got to see their children grow up." With that Angela exited the house and stepped onto the front porch.

Angela had no sooner gotten inside her car then Jason began to question her about what had transpired between her and Betty Harris.

"Well? Did she tell you anything? Did she remember the articles?"

Angela buckled her seat belt and shifted the car into first. "Actually, she didn't tell me a damn thing."

"Nothing at all?" Jason brushed the hair away from his eyes.

"Nothing. But she's nervous about something. I think she does remember those articles, or at least remembers her husband working on them and doesn't want to talk about it."

"Why do you think that?"

"I'm not sure. You should have seen her. Her facial expressions, her body language; she was just too uncomfortable."

"Could just be that you're a cop. A lot of people are uncomfortable around cops, even if they haven't done anything wrong."

"Maybe. Or it could be that it brings back bad memories because her husband died not long after the last story ran. But I think there's more to it."

"So, what are you going to do?"

"We'll give her a couple of days to think about it, then I'll call her again."

"So, what we do we do now?"

"Let's go back to the station and sort through the missing person files. You can help."

"Really? That won't be a problem?"

"There aren't so many people in the offices on Saturday. If anybody says anything I'll just tell them you're my date and you're just waiting on me while I finish up some paperwork."

Jason smiled. The word "date" caught his attention. He wondered if there was anything implied by explaining his presence as her date.

"Do you want to stop and get your car first?"

"It doesn't matter. Whatever's convenient, as long as I don't leave it in the parking lot after dark, it should be okay."

"Alright, then let's just go straight to the station."

Jason was surprised by the look of the Columbia police station. He had expected something larger, more modern. Columbia's station did not match the mental image he had formed based on watching prime-time police shows.

Angela led him past the front desk to a flight of stairs that led to the basement. The long hallway snaked through the basement until it reached Angela's office.

"Well, this is it my home away from home."

Jason wasn't sure what to say. If he said "nice office" he might appear sarcastic, since it clearly was not premium office space. Neither did he want to comment that it wasn't even as large as the closet in his bedroom and insult the detective. Instead, he decided to comment on the single poster that hung on the wall opposite her desk.

"I see you like Monet."

"Yeah, I'm not sure why some of his stuff appeals to me. I guess it's because all of his paintings are sort of tranquil looking. I need that sometimes with this job."

"I can understand that."

Jason stood with his hands on his hips surveying the small office. "Okay, so what do you want me to do?"

"Well, here's the missing person files I've pulled so far. In his second story, Mark Harris said that there were three more missing girls, but he didn't give too many specifics. That would cover six of the seven graves we found on the Wardlaw playground. So, just start looking for missing girls from two years before the first disappearance up to the time the article ran in *The State*."

"Okay, I can handle that."

"While you do that, I'll see if I can get someone at the Coroner's office busy tracking down medical records for me so Professor Russell can make an I.D. on the skeletons."

"Where do I start?"

"Start with this stack right here." Angela paused for a moment to study the expression on Jason's face.

"You okay with doing this?"

"Yes, I'm fine. There's just more here than I expected."

"Well, that's over forty years' worth of reports and it's not just local. There are also printouts I got off a nation-wide data base that lists missing persons."

"I see."

"Okay, I'll be back in a few minutes. Oh, since you're my date, maybe you should pull the door closed so no one sees you in here looking through files. But if you start getting claustrophobic, then go ahead and open the door a little."

"No, that's fine. Small places don't bother me. When I lived in Kentucky I went caving a few times with a college buddy of mine."

"Great, then I'll be back in a minute."

While he waited for Angela's return, Jason began reading the reports of missing children. Since the skeletons unearthed on Wardlaw's playground were Caucasian, he separated out the files of anyone who wasn't white. Occasionally, he paused to study a photograph of the missing child or read some of the details from the police report, statements from parents or friends relating when they were last seen. Jason could remember the smile on the face of his brother Tommy as they played along the banks of the Congaree River the morning before he drowned.

"I'm sorry, I should've done more."

"You're sorry about what?" Angela said.

Jason hadn't heard the door open and Angela's voice startled him

169

instantly, bringing his thoughts back to the present.

"What? Did you say something?" he said.

"You said you were sorry about something. And you looked like you were in deep thought. Everything okay?"

"Yes, fine," he said. "I was just reading some of these. So far I've only found one that is white and fits into the right age group."

Angela watched Jason as he read the description of the child. He wasn't a law and order nut. That wasn't why he was interested in this case. There was something else.

"Patty Franks," he said. "Brown hair, blue eyes, age eleven. She didn't attend Wardlaw and went missing in June, after school was out."

"What year did you say?"

"1971."

"That would be two years after Susan Thompson," Angela said, "and Susan was two years after Annie Walker. I wonder if that's significant. Might not even be the right girl." Angela shrugged. "But set it aside. We'll get medical or dental records tracked down and see if Professor Russell can make an I.D."

Angela knitted her brow and looked at Jason again. "Are you sure you're okay?"

"Actually, I'm starting to get pretty hungry. I was kind of keyed up this morning so I didn't eat anything."

Angela looked at her watch. "Wow. It's after three. You want to sort through a few more of these and then go get some dinner?"

"That sounds great," Jason said.

Angela sat down at her desk and pulled one of the stacks of files closer to her. "We'll go through what we have here then leave. I need to take you back to your car anyway."

As Angela began to open the first file, her phone rang, a double ring that indicated an outside call.

"Hello, Columbia City Police. This is Detective Porter."

"Angela. Hello. How's my favorite police detective?" Angela immediately recognized the exaggerated drawl of Doug Brazell.

"Hello, Doug."

"How's everything going on the Wardlaw case?" he said.

"Not bad," she said. "I may have some possible matches with at least four of the remains."

"That's great. Just send them over and I'll get Russell to take a look at them."

Angela could detect a slight sound of surprise in Brazell's voice, as if he hadn't expected her to come up with anything on her own.

"Well," she said, "I already left a message at your office to have medical and dental records tracked down."

"Good, good, but I think I'll look at these files first myself. You know how it is. This could be such a sensitive case with the press and the public. I just want to make sure we keep our hands around it. But first, let me tell y'all, I just heard about Rob Edwards and even though we've had our differences over the years, I'm truly sorry to hear about his condition."

"Yeah, I…"

"How's he doin' anyway? Any good news at all?"

"Actually, I'm not sure at the moment. The times I've called everyone was at the hospital except his daughter-in-law, and she just said they didn't know much yet, other than it didn't look good."

"That's so terrible. And so close to retirement, too. You just never know, do you."

Angela was certain Doug didn't wish anything bad would happen to Edwards, but he was spreading the sympathy a little too thick. She listened as his Charleston accent came and went.

"Much more of him and I'm going to vomit," she thought to herself.

"I'll tell you what. You get those names over here and we can find the next-of-kin, and get some medical or dental records for ol' Russell to look at. Then we can get you an I.D. on those remains so you can find us a killer."

"Are you going to be in the office all day?" Angela asked.

"Actually, I was just headed out to Lake Murray. Friend of ours has a house on the lake and is having a cookout. The ol' ball and chain is already out there with the kids, swimming. I just came in to check a few things and thought I'd better give my favorite detective a call and see how she's doing."

171

"Well, I'll get these files to you first thing Monday morning."

"That'll be great, Hon. Y'all have a good weekend, too. We'll have to do dinner one night this week. You know, so we'll have more time to talk about the case and don't have to rush back to the office."

"Okay, well, I'll have to check my schedule."

"Sure thing. Bye now."

Angela tossed the phone receiver down hard on its base.

Jason looked up from the file he was reading. "You okay? I couldn't help overhearing some of that."

"Men like him just piss me off." Angela was standing behind her desk with her hands on her hips and her wire frame glasses pushed up on top of her head holding back some loose strands of hair. In that instant Jason realized how attractive he found Angela.

"The son-of-a-bitch. He mentions his wife and children in one breath and asks me out the next."

Jason felt a flash of jealously. "Who was it?"

"Doug Brazell, County Coroner, and unfortunately, by law he's in charge of any bodies that turn up."

"Really? I thought the police would be in charge of any kind of investigation."

"If its murder, then it's the Coroner, and unfortunately, everything Edwards said about this one is true."

"Who's Edwards?"

Angela's shoulder rose slightly then lowered it, as she breathed in deeply and let out a sigh. "He's my partner. The older guy. You probably saw him at the school with me when we were questioning people."

"Tall, kind of stooped a little. Smokes a lot."

"Yeah, that's him."

"We spoke briefly. Where's he in all this? He's not on the case anymore?" From Cindy's friend, Jason knew Angela's partner was ill, but he didn't know the circumstances.

"He just found out this week that he has lung cancer."

"Wow. That's awful. How bad is it?"

"I don't know. I've called a couple times, but he won't take my calls, or isn't able to take them."

"I'm sorry."

"It's okay. I should've known something was up with him. He had a summer cold that he couldn't shake. I just thought it was allergies and the smoking. Everyone's allergies are worse this summer."

"Mine, too." Jason nodded in agreement.

"Anyway, he just hadn't been himself. I think he must've suspected and then just found out for sure this week."

"Is that why you're on the case by yourself?"

"Yes. But if I don't come up with some hard leads or some information by Wednesday, my Captain will give me a new partner on this, and I don't like working with the guy he was going to assign to me."

"Why's that?"

"He's arrogant and sexist and just an all-around jerk."

"Well, maybe what we have so far will help."

"It'll help, but it's not enough. Dorothy Danze or some reporter from *The State* will probably come across the same stuff by the time I talk to my Captain."

Angela sat down at her desk. "Okay, where were we?"

"I haven't looked at these yet." Jason pointed to the files directly in front of Angela.

After another twenty minutes of sifting through reports Angela turned to Jason. "Tell you what. Let me get copies of this ready to go to the Coroner's office. Then we'll go get your car and get something to eat. How does that sound? I feel like a drink. I needed one last night and never got it."

"Sounds like a plan to me."

"Okay, just hang tight in here a minute while I get these ready to go over to the Coroner's office. Then I'll make copies of case files to take with us."

While he waited, Jason surveyed the tiny office. Since it was a basement room there were no windows to allow light from outside. On top of a two-drawer file cabinet behind her desk there was one small plant that looked to be in poor health from lack of real sunlight. The only color in the room was the Monet print on the wall behind him. The rest of the room blended in with the dark brown paneling. The overhead light cast a dim, yellowish glow around the room giving just enough light that, over time, anyone who spent much time in the little office would undoubtedly need glasses due to eyestrain. Angela had tried to make the little room more pleasing by adding the plant and the colorful print, but there wasn't much hope for the tiny room.

"I'm back. Ready to go?"

"Sure. You want me to bring any of this stuff?"

"No. I have copies for us to look at later."

Jason caught the word "later" and wondered if Angela had plans to continue working into the evening and if these plans included him.

"So, how do you want to do this?" Angela said. "You want to get your car first? You said you didn't want to leave it in the parking lot after dark."

"Well, it's not going to get dark for a few more hours. We could go eat first. Or we could get my car and either drop-off your car or mine at either of our houses, then ride together. Just depends on where you want to go."

"Where do you live?"

"Irmo."

"I'm not familiar with what's out that way, she said. "I'll warn you I'm not crazy about most of the chain restaurants."

"If you like nice cuts of steak or fish, then I know of a neat little place. It's in Chapin. The restaurant itself is in an old Victorian era house and its run by a guy that's a friend of my aunt. Good atmosphere, too."

"What are the prices like?" Angela was thinking of her car insurance bill; it was due this month.

"Very reasonable. It's not as pricey as it looks."

"That'll work. Let's go."

Traffic was light. It only took a few minutes to pick up Jason's car and then get on I-26 and drive to Irmo. Jason had told Angela there was a more direct route to his house, but even on a Saturday traffic near the mall exit would most likely be heavy this time of day, so he would take her in using a back route. It was a little longer, but they wouldn't have to stop at as many traffic lights.

Angela paid close attention to every turn as she followed Jason past Columbiana Mall and twisted and turned through two connected neighborhoods. She wanted to make sure she could remember how to find her way out, and then back in again should she need to.

After arriving at Jason's house, Angela parked her car in the drive-way and rode with Jason to the restaurant. Both the atmosphere and dinner were as good as Jason had described it to be. She wasn't sure if it was the two glasses of red wine before dinner or the relief of having possibly made the first breakthrough in the Wardlaw case, but whatever the reason, Angela felt more relaxed than she had in weeks.

The ride in the car with Jason to visit Betty Harris had been awk-ward. There were periods of uncomfortable silence between the two. Or at least Angela felt uneasy; she wasn't sure about Jason. Tonight was different, the conversation was relaxed and they talked about them-selves, their family, and hobbies - anything but police work.

When the check finally arrived, Angela offered to pay for her dinner, but Jason insisted it was his treat. After all, he reminded her, he had sat in her office under the pretense of being her date. Even though it was said in jest, Angela wasn't comfortable with Jason referring to this as a date. She didn't want to give him the wrong impression. Jason had information she needed and for that she was letting him have access to the investigation. "We'll get those remains identified and I'll just tell him it's been fun but, sorry, you can't tag along anymore," she promised herself.

When they arrived back at his house, Jason invited her in for coffee. Angela was curious about what the inside looked like and how he lived. On the outside it appeared large with a well-manicured lawn. Of course, the grass was dry and brittle, but so was everyone else's. Angela de-clined the invitation; she didn't want to give him the wrong idea. Dinner was great, but she wasn't his date and from here on out the interaction between the two of them would be strictly professional.

That night Angela's sleep was restless. In her dreams Angela saw the images of the missing girls standing over shallow graves as the dirt was brushed away from their buried bones. Then, the little girls would stand alongside their own skeletons and in a chorus they would cry out, "Who killed me?"

At one point in her dreams, she saw Jason standing under the pecan tree, smiling. He reached out his hand for her, but just as she drew close enough to grasp it, a dark figure came from the darkness around the tree and engulfed him. She saw the green in his eyes turn to red and his smile change to terror as he was consumed by the shadow. When Angela awoke it was the early-hours of Sunday morning, still two more hours before sunrise. She was cold and shaking, her body damp with sweat, and her blanket and sheet were pushed to the foot of her bed.

With her eyes only partially open, Angela stumbled out of bed and went into the bathroom. Her bladder had been full; too much water before bed she thought. Only slightly more awake, she walked to the linen closet in the hall and pulled out a heavy quilt. In bed with her blankets and quilt covering her, Angela's body began to warm and the chills stopped. Relaxed now, she drifted off to sleep.

Chapter twenty-one

Sunday morning came and went for Jason. He and Sebastian shared a bowl of cereal for breakfast. Jason ate the wheat flakes and small bites of granola. Sebastian finished off the milk that was left in the bottom of the bowl. Jason spent about an hour tidying up the house. He had a maid service come in once a week to dust, vacuum, and mop the floors. Just that much was a big help and it gave him the luxury of coming home to a clean house. Jason stood in the middle of the kitchen floor surveying the room. The dishwasher was running and everything was clean except for three stacks of assorted papers, junk mail, and bills lying on the counter top.

"I really need to sort through these." Jason pulled up a stool and sat down. He sifted through the stacks and removed three bills, water, electric, and cable. "Better pay these, huh, Sebastian. We have to be clean, eat, and watch television."

Sebastian purred and pushed his head against Jason's chin. "I love you, too," Jason said as he rubbed the cat's head and scratched behind its ears. Jason opened his laptop and logged into the first account to begin paying bills. Just as he started to fill in the amount, the phone rang. Jason rushed into the living room where he had left his cell phone.

"Hello."

"Hey Jason. It's Cindy."

"Oh, hi."

"Boy, don't sound so glad to hear from me."

"No. Sorry, I was waiting on a call from someone about some stuff and I thought this might be the call." Jason was disappointed. He had hoped the call would be from Angela.

"I just wanted to see what you were doing today. I'm fixin' to take Jamie to Finley Park so she can roller blade some, and I was wondering if you wanted to meet us there."

"What time is it?"

"It's almost one."

"Wow. I didn't realize it was that late." Jason looked at the clock on the DVR. "I don't know."

"Jamie would love for you to go so she'd have somebody to skate with. I can't get on those things. I'd bust my butt."

"I'd like to, but was paying bills…"

"Hate that for ya."

"Yeah, and then I really need to get some work done around here," Jason lied. He wanted to wait for Angela to call. She was probably searching through more missing person files right now.

"So, have you tracked down any more information on the investigation?"

The question caught him off guard. "Not yet."

"Are you going to give up on this now?"

"I don't know."

"Why don't you try to track down the guy that wrote the stories?"

"Wesley called me and told me that the guy was dead. He died not long after the last article was written."

"That sucks."

"I thought I'd told you he was dead."

"I don't know, maybe you did. With all the work we have right now, and that son-of-a-bitch ex-husband giving me more shit, I'm lucky to remember my name."

Jason suddenly felt guilty. He had been so consumed with the discovery of the remains at Wardlaw he had forgotten about Cindy's problems. "I'm sorry. I hadn't even asked you how things were with you."

"That's okay. About the same. The stupid son-of-a-bitch is saying he's going to take me back to court to get Jamie. Well, the asshole won't get her, not with all the pot he smokes, but it'll cost me more money to shut him up."

"He smokes pot? Really? You hadn't told me that."

"Well, I should say he smokes it when it's free and someone gives it to him. He's too cheap to buy his own."

"That's interesting. You ever thought about getting your cop friend to arrest him?"

"If he's in jail he can't pay child support."

"That's true."

"So, anyway are you going with us?" Cindy's tone immediately went back to cheery.

Jason looked at the clock again. "I don't know…"

"Come down for an hour. Jamie probably isn't goin to skate long in the heat anyway."

"Are you leaving now?"

"Yep. Just as soon as I can get her to put her shoes on."

"OK. I'll leave right now and meet you there. I'll look for you by the playground."

Jason walked back into the kitchen and looked at the stacks of papers on the counter top and Sebastian perched on top of one of the stacks. "I wish you had thumbs so you could help out with some of the work around here." Sebastian yawned and looked away. "Exactly my sentiments."

Jason stayed at the park with Cindy and Jamie for almost two hours. It was four when he finally returned home. Angela hadn't called. On his way home he had driven through the parking lot of the police station. Her car wasn't there.

The remainder of Sunday came and went with no calls from Angela. At one point Jason laughed at himself. He was reminded of how his older sister behaved when she was in high school waiting for some boy to call. At least he wasn't on the phone with his buddies saying, "Oh, I'll just die is she doesn't call."

*****

Monday morning Jason showered and dressed for work. He took his cell phone into the bathroom with him just in case it rang while he was in the shower. No calls.

When he arrived at work Cindy and the others were already there and busy. "Any calls for me?"

179

"Not unless there was one on your voicemail before I got here."

Jason walked into his office and looked at the mailbox light on the phone. It wasn't lit. "Shit." Jason tossed his messenger bag onto the seat of the chair opposite his desk. "She probably has everything she figured she could get from me and I won't hear from her again."

"Did you say something?" Cindy called out from the front of the office.

"No. Just talking to myself. Trying to figure out where I need to get started." Jason's phone rang. "Hello. Shealy Architects and Associates,. This is Jason."

"You gonna get your skinny ass down here and go to work, Mr. Architect?"

"Glenn?"

"Yeah, it's me."

"Where are you?"

"At Wardlaw workin' full steam ahead, which is what you ain't doin'."

"The job site isn't closed off anymore?"

"No. I got a call from the developers Friday night. And I spent the weekend getting everybody rounded up again."

"Did you get all the crew back?"

"One of the sheet rock subs has most his crew tied up on a big house out at that new golf course. But he said he could get some more out here. He just uses a bunch of illegals anyway. Won't take no time to round up another crew."

While Jason listened to Glenn explain his plan for getting caught up and perhaps even making the construction deadline, which Jason knew was impossible at this point, his mind was still on Angela and the investigation.

"Hey, college boy, you listening?"

"What?" Jason realized Glenn had just asked a question and he hadn't heard him. "I'm sorry, someone just walked in and I didn't hear that last part." Jason noticed he was starting to make a habit out of lying.

"I said we got some windows in for the third floor and I don't think they'll work. I could make them fit – that's no problem, just shim them up and seal it, but I think the historical people won't let me use them."

"Oh, okay. Yes, they have to be wood and match the original design."

"Well, this is only three; to replace the ones that got broke."

"Are they wood?"

"No."

"Then we can't use them."

"Hell. A window's a window. It keeps rain out."

"Glenn, we've been over this before. Wardlaw is on the National Register of Historic Places. You can't modify history."

"You'd think I wanted to change who won the Civil War."

"Whatever. I'll be out there in a little while or I'll get Cindy to call about the windows."

"You do that. Hey! You, Padro. Third floor with that. Tres floor." Jason moved the phone away from his ear as Glenn yelled at a worker.

"I'll talk to you when you get out here."

"Bye." Jason heard another shout from Glenn as he laid down his phone.

"What a way to start a Monday." Jason had no sooner hung up than his office land line rang. "Hello. Shealy Architects and Associates."

"Jason?"

"Yes."

"This is Angela."

Jason smiled, his mood instantly changing. "Hello. How are you?"

"Fine. Can you be ready to go somewhere with me in about ten minutes?"

"Sure. What's up?"

"Betty Harris called. I want to get out there before she changes her mind. I'll swing by and pick you up."

"Change her mind about…" There was a click on the other end. Angela had hung up. Jason hung up and, with his left hand in his pocket and his right hand pushing the hair back from his eyes, he turned, again surveying the room. "Shit." He had three sets of drawings to review and put his seal on. Roger had made good progress on the Grover store project. Cindy had finished the corrections to the stair detail and needed him to look at them again. Jason looked at his watch. Unless Angela hit every red light she would be at his office in ten minutes.

Jason breathed in and let out a sigh. "I can't get any of this done in ten minutes." Jason began to shuffle through the drawings. "At least I can organize it and then work on it tonight. Cindy was right. I am chasing ghosts."

It seemed as though he had just started looking through the stack of drawings, when Cindy leaned around the corner of his office.

"Jason. There's someone here to see you."

Without looking up he replied, "Who is it?"

"A woman. Said her name is Angela."

Jason looked again at his watch. "Shit. That was fast. Okay, I'm coming." Jason picked up his messenger bag and hurriedly walked to the front of the office where Angela was waiting. "That was fast."

"I hit the lights just right. You ready?"

"Ready to walk out the door. You want to drive or you want me to?"

"I'll drive."

Jason turned to Cindy, "I have to go out for a couple hours to run some errands. I'll see you later."

"What about the drawings?"

"I'll get them as soon as I get back. It won't take long. I'm sure they're fine. Oh, I almost forgot. Would you go down to Wardlaw and get with Glenn. He said some new windows came in and they aren't right. They won't meet the guidelines we have to follow for historic accuracy."

"Okay, but…" Before Cindy could say another word Jason was out the door.

As soon as Angela pulled into traffic and headed toward Bull Street Jason asked, "So what's up with Betty Harris?"

"She said she had time to think about it and, if I could come over there this morning, she'd give me her husband's notes."

"Notes?"

"Apparently she kept all his files. She said they've just been sitting up in the attic since she moved back to Camden."

"That's great. And she's just going to give them to you?"

"Yes, she said it was probably terrible for those parents not knowing whatever happened to their children, so if there was something in there that could help, I could have it."

The remainder of the drive to Camden was, for the most part, silent. There was little talking between the two. Jason wanted to ask Angela what she had done Sunday and why she hadn't called, but he decided he shouldn't. He knew it was his male ego that wouldn't let him ask. He didn't want to sound like his sister when she was a teenager.

Betty Harris must have been watching for them. When they pulled into the drive, she immediately opened the front door and stepped onto the porch.

"Should I stay in the car or go inside?" Jason asked.

Angela thought for a second. "I guess you need to stay here. I hate to keep leaving you sitting in the car, but I just don't want to take any chances."

"That's fine; just leave me the keys so I can turn on the air if I need it."

Angela pushed the key back into the ignition. "This shouldn't take that long." Angela then, without thinking, placed her hand on Jason's hand which was resting on the console and squeezed it.

Jason looked down at Angela's hand still resting on his. Angela realized what she had done and quickly pulled it away. "Sorry."

Jason smiled. "No problem. Really." Jason felt his face flush. He was pleased that she had touched his hand.

"Back in a few minutes."

Angela stepped up on the porch. "Good afternoon, Mrs. Harris."

Betty Harris looked around Angela to Jason still sitting in the car. "Would the other officer like to come in too?"

"No, he's fine. He's working on some paperwork."

"Come in, please." Betty Harris stepped aside so Angela could enter the house, then she closed the door behind them. The house was dark, just as it had been Saturday when she had first visited the home. This time she could smell the fragrance of eucalyptus. Had it been any stronger it would have been nauseating.

Angela noticed Betty Harris was nervous. "Mrs. Harris, I'd like to thank you for calling and offering your husband's notes."

"I started not to call, but the more I thought about it, I just couldn't keep these to myself. Not with those children's parents and the suffering they must have gone through all these years."

"Mrs. Harris."

"Please, just call me Betty. Mrs. Harris sounds so old. But I guess I am old." Betty Harris patted the side of her hair and pushed a long strand back behind her ear.

"Okay, Betty, if you don't mind me asking, why did you never give these notes to the police before?"

"Well, when Mark was killed in the accident I was just so torn up over it, and I had two young children to take care of. I just never thought about it. No one ever asked for them. Then, when I saw the news the other night, about the remains dug up at Wardlaw, and then you showed up asking questions about it…" Betty stopped talking and looked down at her hands she held clasped in front of her.

"When you saw the news, did you think there was a connection between the remains there and the children in your husband's articles?"

"Not at first. I just thought how awful. The world just isn't a good place anymore."

"Yes ma'am. But when did you first think there was a connection? Or did you think there was a connection?"

"Honestly, it'd been so long since I'd read those stories Mark wrote, I'd forgotten what was in them. It wasn't until you brought them by Saturday that I remembered. I guess I just tried to forget. I think those stories are what got Mark killed."

Angela raised her eyebrows in surprise. She hadn't expected a comment like that from Betty Harris. "How do you mean, 'those stories got him killed'?"

"Mark always did a lot of research for his stories. In some ways he was a perfectionist when it came to his writing. He said he wasn't going to sell out like other reporters did."

"Sell out?"

"Twist things around and sensationalize things just to sell papers."

"I see. That's commendable."

"When Mark was on a story like these, he always worked late. He'd stay up all hours working. Not getting much sleep. He'd meet people late at night sometimes."

"Did you know where he was when he was meeting people?"

"Sometimes. The week he died, he told me he was writing a follow-up to the articles you showed me. He had been keeping late hours researching it. The police said he must have fallen asleep at the wheel."

"I'm sorry."

Betty turned her head to look at the square banker's box sitting on her small dining room table. "My brother went to see the car and get it taken away. He said there was red paint down the side like someone had hit Mark's car."

"Was there another car involved in the accident?"

"No, just Mark's, according to the police."

"Why would your brother think someone had hit your husband's car?"

"Well, Bob used to run a wrecker service in Lugoff and he'd seen lots of wrecks. He said it just looked like someone had hit Mark or side swiped him."

"So, he thought maybe it was a hit and run?"

"Either that or someone ran him off the road. Bob tried to get someone at the sheriff's department to look into it, but they just said there wasn't any reason to. So after a while, I just told Bob to leave it alone. Keeping things stirred up was just making it harder on me and the kids."

"What happened to the car?"

"The wreck was pretty bad. There wasn't much left of it. I wouldn't have wanted to drive the thing or see it even if it could've been fixed. The insurance company totaled it and sent me a check, and then I guess it just ended up in a junkyard or sold for scrap. I don't know; whatever they do with cars like that."

"Where did your husband have the accident?"

"It was out Highway Six by the dam."

"So, it was Lexington County."

"Yes."

"Do you remember the date of the accident?"

"That isn't something you forget." Betty Harris had an almost indig-

185

nant tone in her voice as she replied to Angela's question.

"I'm sorry. I know it isn't."

"It was November 12, 1982, at around 11:00 o'clock"

"Would you mind if I talked to your brother Bob about the car and what he saw?"

"I don't see what good it would do after this long, but if you want to. His name is Bobby Shepherd. Here, I'll write his number down for you." Betty turned to look for a piece of paper.

"Here, I have a note pad and pen." Angela handed Mrs. Harris the pad and pen. She took the pad and quickly wrote down the number then handed it back to Angela. "I don't want to be rude or anything, but I really don't want to talk about this any more right now."

Angela didn't want to overstay her welcome and, in turn, have Betty change her mind about sharing her husband's notes. Angela knew she could always have them subpoenaed if she had to, but it was much better dealing with someone who was cooperative.

"That's quite alright. I know it can't be easy. If there's anything else you can think of, please call me. You still have my card?"

"Yes."

Angela picked up the bankers box and followed Betty to the front door. "Detective, when you're finished with those papers, I'd like to have them back. I hung on to all Mark's papers all these years, I guess because I thought the children might what to see what their father had done, and Mark put so much of himself into his writing."

"Of course, Betty. I'll take good care of them."

When Jason saw Angela walking to the car he quickly got out and helped her with the door. "Want me to get that?"

"No, I got it. It's not heavy."

"Anything good in there?"

"I don't know yet. Come on, let's get back to Columbia. I want to start going through this stuff, and I have a couple phone calls to make."

Jason wanted to begin sorting through the box, but Angela's car was too small to maneuver the box and sort papers without nearly standing on his head. With little leg room, even for his average height, Jason was glad he had opted for the practicality of his Subaru rather than the flashier sports cars that caught his eye.

"Jason, would you dial a number for me and then hand me my cell phone?"

"Sure, what is it?"

Angela recited the number and as soon as Jason hit "send" he handed the phone to Angela. "Hey Debbie, this is Angela Porter. I need you to track down an old accident report for me. It happened in Lexington County on November 12, 1982. It was a fatality. A man by the name of Mark Harris was killed in the accident. As far as I know it was a single car accident and he didn't have any passengers in the car with him. Thanks, Debbie. I owe you a drink." Angela ended the connection and placed the phone on the console beside her.

"Betty Harris must have said something for you to want to see the accident report."

"She told me she felt like her husband working on these stories was responsible for his death."

"How does she figure that?"

"Well, she said he kept late hours and sometimes worked without much sleep researching facts. And the police who worked the accident said he apparently fell asleep at the wheel. But her brother Bob thought it was either a hit-and-run or someone ran her husband off the road."

"And what makes her brother Bob an expert?"

"Nothing other than he used to run Bobby's Wrecker Service and worked a lot of accidents, and he said it looked like someone had hit Mark's car. She also said he tried to get the sheriff's department to look into it, but they pretty much ignored him."

"So, then what'd they do?"

"Betty said she told her brother to just drop it because she was dealing with enough just trying to handle her husband's death and take care of the children."

"What do you think?"

"Bobby sounds like a good ol' boy who may or may not know what he's talking about, but it's worth looking at."

"What are we going to do now?" Jason was anxious to see what treasures of information were in the box.

187

"The box is pretty full. We're going to need some place to spread all this out. Obviously, it isn't my office. I guess I could put it in the conference room at the station."

Angela was thinking out loud. And Jason didn't like the way her train of thought was going. If she took Mark Harris' files to the station, then his access to them would be limited at best.

"How about we go to my house?"

"Your house?"

"I have a formal living room and dining room that I hardly ever use. And I have an office with a computer and a big dry-erase board in it. I could help you get everything sorted and organized."

Angela thought for a moment. "Maybe for the first sort-through to see what's in there that wouldn't be a bad idea. But I'm still going to have to take it in to the station."

"Great! Sounds like a plan. Let's swing by and get my car then go to my house."

"Okay, but I need to do something first."

"Sure. Anything I can help with?"

"No. I want to stop by Baptist Medical Center and see my partner. Rob Edwards."

"He's the one with lung cancer?" Angela nodded. "I thought he wasn't taking your calls."

"He hasn't been, but I don't know if that's just his family trying to be protective, or if he is just going through so much he doesn't want to see me. Lung cancer is a terrible way to go. I watched my uncle die from it."

Jason's thoughts went to his brother Tommy and his own loss. "I'm sorry."

"I just want to try to see Edwards for my own sake as well as his. When my uncle was sick there were people that he had known for years that didn't come to see him. Then at the funeral they said they wished they had, but didn't want to get in the way or some other excuse."

"You think they were just making excuses?"

"I think they just didn't take the time to go see him. They were too busy. He was dying and would like to have seen some of his old friends, and they were just too busy to take time. I know there were some that stayed away because they have a hard time with illness and death, but still…" Angela paused. Jason didn't know whether to ask about her uncle and encourage her to continue or change the subject. He decided to ask.

"You were close to your uncle?"

"He was almost like a second dad. Anyway, what time do you want to get together? Probably the sooner we get started on this the better."

"How about six, or is that too late?"

"Six is good. That'll give me time to see Edwards, check in at the station and get through rush-hour traffic."

"Do you remember how to get to my house?"

"I think so. If not I'll just put it in my GPS. If I have any problems I'll call."

Angela dropped Jason at his office, then headed back down Hampton Street toward the hospital. She pulled her car into the fist available space in the parking garage then took the skywalk across Sumter to the main building. She took a deep breath as the elevator doors closed. She hated hospitals and this one was a maze. Its continued expansion over the years had resulted in a mass of corridors sprawling off in different directions like the arms of an octopus. It was difficult to find your way around unless you just knew where you were going.

Having found Edwards' room, she paused outside the door. Angela took another deep breath then slowly pushed the door open as she knocked. Her eyes met those of Mary Edwards, Rob's wife. Angela could see in Mary's face the same look she had seen in her aunt's years ago – worry, fear, and exhaustion.

Mary smiled then looked back at her husband who was sitting up in his bed, breathing heavily.

"Hey Mary" Angela said.

Edwards saw Angela and smiled. "There's my partner. 'Bout time you got your butt down here. I've been waiting on you to come ask my advice on the case. Edwards reached out his hand and motioned for Angela to come closer. "Here, pull up that chair."

"I don't want to bother you all. Did I come at a good time?"

"Hell, it doesn't matter. Damn doctor's been bothering me all morning. Gonna have to send Mary out to get me something decent to eat. If the lung cancer doesn't kill me first, their food will." Angela laughed.

"I would've come by sooner, but I kept missing you when I'd call."

"Yeah, Mary here's turned into my personal bodyguard. She's being protective."

"I'm sure she's got her hands full, too."

"Mary, honey, why don't you go get me some of that soup they've got down in the cafeteria. I'm kind of hungry now. If you don't mind?"

Mary rose and took her husband's hand. "Are you sure you want me to go?"

"I could go if you like," Angela offered.

"No, Mary knows which one I like. Don't you, honey," Edwards said with a smile.

"Okay, I'll be right back."

"I ain't going no where."

Angela was quiet for a moment, then spoke. "I feel like I just ran her off. I could've gotten the soup for you."

"Their soup isn't much better. I just wanted to get her outta here for a few minutes. She's making herself sick staying here trying to take care of me. She needs to go home and get some rest, but I think she's more stubborn than I am." Edwards' laugh quickly turned into a cough. Angela felt sick inside.

"How's the case going?"

"Not great, but not bad either."

"Who's the Captain stuck you with?"

"No one yet, but he wants to put Randall Evans on it." Edwards made a pained face. Angela could tell the expression was one of dislike for Evans and not pain from the cancer.

"I talked him into giving me until Wednesday. If I make some good progress or get any breaks, then I can keep it."

"Don't count on it, kid. I've been watchin' the news this week. News and talk shows. I saw that reporter, what's her name, Dorothy Danze. Does she know anything she shouldn't?"

"Most of what she's reported on so far she could've picked up just by hanging around the site. But I think I may have a break I want to tell you about. And I think, if we can track down dental records, then we'll at least be able to identify all the remains."

"Tell me about it, and you better talk fast. Mary's like a guard dog and she'll be back soon."

Angela began with meeting Jason and how he had given her the articles then helped track down Betty Harris. How Mrs. Harris had lent her cooperation by giving Angela her husband's notes. Edwards was pleased she had so much, but he cautioned about involving Jason too deeply in the investigation.

"He's not a cop, even if he means well he could do something to screw this up." Angela promised she would take his advice and keep a watchful eye on Jason.

"You say the reporter implied there were seven murders of children that were connected?"

"That's right. We have the three names of the girls that went to Wardlaw and I'm assuming the names of the other four will be in his notes; even though he only mentioned three girls in the second article."

"Get those other names and get Russell to confirm the identification of the remains, then just look for any common threads. Lay everything out. Could be that there's nothing the victims had in common other than where the killer came in contact with them. It could be something about where or how they disappeared."

"Don't worry. I'll keep it all in mind. I'm taking everything over to Jason's house tonight and he's going to help me start laying it out and sorting through the notes."

"His house, huh? Let me tell you, if Captain Morris doesn't see you working at the station and making progress, he'll stick Randall Evans with you. Whether you like it or not. Let me tell you, as soon as those remains are identified, you're going to have a bunch of upset relatives wanting answers. Then the press will start hounding him and he'll put Evans and probably some other detectives on it, even if you are making progress. It'll be too high profile not to."

"So regardless of what I find, he'll still give the case to someone else?"

"No, he'll just put someone with you. But if you make all the early breakthroughs, you'll be the one running it."

"Looks like I have my work cut out for me."

"If this architect friend of yours checks out okay, make good use of him. He sounds like he might be pretty sharp. Just be careful about it."

Just as Edwards finished, Mary walked back into the room with the warm split-pea and ham soup.

"You all talking about police work again?"

Angela looked up with a guilty smile. "I was letting him know how our case had progressed."

"I see. I got your soup, honey."

Angela stood up and made an awkward, hesitant movement toward the door of the hospital room. She knew Mary didn't want her there. She was understandably protective of her dying husband.

"I'll talk to you again later, Edwards. Take care, Mary. If there is anything I can do to help with anything, just call."

"Thank you, but I'm sure we'll be alright. Our son and daughter-in-law stop by every day, either here or at the house."

Angela kept her composure until she got to her car. She had tears in her eyes and was fighting to hold back a sob. "It's not fair." Angela put the key in the ignition and started the car, then backed out and wound her way down the levels of the parking garage to Hampton Street then went home.

Chapter twenty-two

After being dropped off at his office building, Jason offered no explanation as to who Angela was or where he had gone. He simply said hello to everyone and then retreated to his own office where he began checking and stamping drawings with his seal. A couple times Cindy interrupted him to ask if he needed anything.

The answer was always the same, "No, I'm fine, don't need anything and the drawings look great." Jason knew her inquiries were attempts to engage him in conversation to discover where he had been and the identity of the attractive woman. Jason didn't want to exclude Cindy. She had been both helpful in collecting information for him and in picking up the extra work that he had neglected for the last week and a half. He decided to offer no explanation of Angela's identity. Nothing other than she was a new acquaintance, which resulted in a smile from the other architect and a snort from Cindy. As for the Wardlaw remains, as they were now referred to on the news, he told Cindy that Wesley had discovered the fate of Mark Harris and had located his widow.

Cindy was excited for him. Jason wanted to tell her the truth, that in order to be involved in the investigation, even if it was an anonymous involvement, he had felt it necessary to go to the police, to Angela. But Angela had sworn him to secrecy for the sake of the investigation and possibly, her career. For her, he had to be silent.

That evening, standing in his dining room holding Sebastian and looking out the window, Jason waited for Angela's arrival and the box of files. Miscellaneous papers and hand scribbled notes that could point to the identity of the monster that killed the children buried beneath Wardlaw's playground.

"Sebastian, here she is. A little late, but she's here." With Sebastian in his arms Jason opened the door.

"Hey, we saw you pull up. Sebastian and I were watching birds out the window."

"Wow, he's a big one. Can I pet him?"

"Sure. He loves to be petted almost as much as he loves to eat." Angela scratched around the ears and under the chin of the big tan and white cat. Sebastian immediately started to purr.

"Come on in. I didn't know if you had eaten or not, so I took the liberty of picking up some Chinese on the way home. I got a couple of different things, plus egg rolls and soup, so you can pick whatever you like."

"Actually, I haven't eaten. I had a couple of errands to run after I stopped by to see Edwards, so I just ran by my apartment and changed into some shorts. I was burning up in those pants."

"You want to eat now?"

"Why don't we get started, then we can eat while we go through stuff."

"Okay, that sounds good. Want me to get the box?"

"It's in the car. I'll go get it."

"I'll help. Just let me set Sebastian down."

The bankers' box wasn't heavy, but Jason carried it into the house just the same. He told himself he wasn't trying to impress her, it was just good manners.

"I thought we could probably work in the formal living room. All I have in there right now is a sofa and a coffee table. I haven't finished furnishing the house," Jason offered in explanation for his lack of furniture in the room.

Angela's eyes surveyed the rooms as she followed Jason into the formal living room. She had a good eye for details and she noticed his taste in art was similar to that of his aunt.

"You have a nice house. You live here alone?"

"Yes. And thank you. I still need to buy some more furniture and artwork. But finding the time has been my biggest problem. So I decided to not worry about it and just find the right pieces."

"How many bedrooms?"

"Three, plus a study and a finished room over the garage. I eventually want to put a media room in there. I love movies." Jason paused. "Have you looked at any of these notes yet?"

"No, I haven't had a chance. I called my Captain and told him I'd contacted Betty Harris and she was giving me some files to look through."

Jason was worried. "So you told him about the articles, too?"

"I had to. If I don't make enough progress he will put someone on this with me. I didn't tell him I already had the notes or that there were so many. I need to keep him up-to-date without saying too much. I want to keep this case for myself."

Jason heard resentment in Angela's voice. "You really don't like that other detective do you?"

"He's arrogant, sexist, a smart-ass, he thinks he's always right and he won't listen to anyone else's ideas or opinions. Let's see, what else. I could go on; there's more."

"I get the idea." Jason set the box on the coffee table. "Can I get you anything to drink? Water, cranberry juice, soda, iced tea, wine." Jason ran through the list of everything he typically kept in the house.

"Iced tea sounds good." Angela lifted the lid from the box and began removing file folders, loose sheets of paper, and a stack of photographs. Even though it wasn't apparent that the files were in any particular order, she was careful to keep everything in the order in which it was in the box.

Jason returned with two glasses of tea. "Okay, so what've we got?"

"I'm not sure. I was looking through this and it doesn't seem to be in any particular order, but Harris could've had it organized in some way that made sense to him."

Jason took a sip of his tea then added. "One of the architects that works for me has four or five piles of papers on his desk at any given time. I don't see how he ever keeps anything straight, but he does. If I had to find something on his desk I couldn't do it. But, no matter what I ask for, he reaches down in the stack and pulls it out."

Angela continued to sift through papers. "An organized mess. Here, you take the top half and I'll take the bottom half. Let's see if Mr. Harris has the names of the other missing girls."

It only took a few minutes of sorting. Mixed in with the assortment of papers and photographs were seven manila folders, each with the name of a different girl. On three of the folders, printed in capital letters, were the names Annie Walker, Susan Thompson, and Paula Groves.

"I think we're on the right track." Angela said. In each folder was a copy of the missing person report that had been filed on the child. Angela set the three folders to the left of the coffee table.

Jason held the other four folders in his lap. "Ready to see what we have?" Angela scooted across the floor closer to Jason. He sat the folders in front of them and together they open them and scanned the various documents. Again, in each was a copy of the missing person report and a photograph of the child.

"He seems to have a lot of information on them," Jason said.

"Cute little girls, weren't they," was Angela's only comment. After a few moments of silence, she spoke. "Looks like we have possible identities for all the remains. I'll have to get this to Brazell tomorrow so he can track down dental and medical records."

"How long do you think it will take with the ones he already has?"

"Probably not long; if they can find the records. I've never worked a case like this where the victims have been dead for so long. I don't know how difficult it will be to find records from the sixties. Or even the seventies. That was forty plus years ago."

Angela and Jason now had the additional four names they needed to put faces and lives to the bones lying spread out across the examining tables of Professor Russell's forensic anthropology lab. Now the work was up to Brazell and Russell to confirm the identities so Angela, along with Jason, could find a killer.

Mark Harris had been very thorough with his investigation, just as his wife had said. For each girl there were school schedules, lists of hobbies and interests, extracurricular activities, the names of churches they attended, friends, favorite places of play, and common routes they would walk through their neighborhoods. Mark Harris may have known more about the day-to-day activities, and the thoughts and interests of these seven little girls, than their own parents.

Jason stared at the folders spread in front of them. "You know, I thought I was pretty clever when I came across those old articles. I thought I would have this whole thing figured out in a week if I could just get access to the right information."

Angela was leaning over reading the school schedule and extracurricular actives of Patty Franks, hearing Jason's comments, she looked up. "What do you think now?"

"I think it looks like a jigsaw puzzle and all the pieces are white." Just then Sebastian flopped down on the papers Angela had been reading and rolled over, exposing his small round stomach. "Hello fella. Do you want to be petted?"

"He likes you. He has good taste."

"You're sweet."

Jason wondered if Angela meant him or his cat. "Do you want me to move him?"

"No, he's fine. I love cats, actually. With my job, I was afraid I wouldn't have time to devote to one."

"When I was working until all hours of the morning, researching the history of Wardlaw and there were things I couldn't do out of my office here at home, I used to take him with me to the office on Taylor Street. He seemed to enjoy himself. The building has mice in it and sometimes at night, when I was on the computer and there weren't any other noises in the building, they would come out. Sebastian would send papers flying everywhere trying to catch them."

Angela watched the expressions on Jason's face change as he talked about his cat. He spoke of Sebastian almost as if he were his child.

"Jason, why are you doing this?"

"Doing what?"

"The news articles; the photos from your aunt's yearbooks. Why help me? Why are you so, for lack of a better expression, hung-up on this?"

Jason was thoughtful for a moment. "You know how they say everyone has something to atone for. Well, my adult brain says that it wasn't my fault, but the little kid in me still says that it's my fault for letting my little brother drown. And I'm not talking about that pop-psychology, inner-child stuff either. I grew up feeling responsible."

Angela was shocked. That wasn't the answer she had expected.

"Your little brother drowned! What happened?"

Jason spent the next few minutes describing the events of that day, over twenty-five years ago, when he and Tommy decided to climb on the rocks in the Congaree River.

"I don't even know whose idea it was to go down there in the first place. We just ended up there. We parked our bikes and started climbing around, pretending we were explorers. Tommy jumped on a rock, lost his balance and fell in."

"I'm sorry."

"It wasn't even deep; the river bottom was just slippery. He couldn't stand up and get his footing soon enough and the current just swept him into deeper water. I couldn't swim that well then, so I tried to find something to throw to him. A limb, a piece of wood – anything. But there wasn't anything. He was yelling for me to help him. Then he just went under and didn't come back up."

"What did you do?"

"When I knew for certain that I couldn't get to him, I ran for help. The rest is kind of a blur. I just remember ambulances, rescue workers, boats, Mom and Dad. I especially remember Dad. I remember seeing him cry and just saying over and over to my uncle, "Why Tommy?""

Angela turned her head slightly and knitted her eyebrows. She felt sorry for Jason and all the guilt and sorrow he must have felt.

"He wished it had been me instead of Tommy."

"I'm sure he only meant 'why' as in 'why one of his children.'"

"I would have thought so, too, but from then on, everything I did was a comparison to Tommy. To him, Tommy was the one who would have been better, stronger, faster, and more successful."

"Did you ever ask him about it?"

"Actually, one night when he had three or four bourbons too many in him, I did ask. You know what he said?" Angela shook her head 'no.'

"He said he always knew Tommy would have been better than me at anything he did. He said he still loved me. Loved my sister, too, but Tommy was special. He even said it was my fault. I was the older brother. I shouldn't have taken him down to the river." Jason was quiet for a moment as he looked into Angela's eyes. "So there you have it; the dysfunctional Shealy household in the condensed version."

"That's terrible."

"It's okay. I've learned to deal with it. My Aunt Bess saved my life. She even took me to a therapist. Of course, my parents never knew. Dad would've had an aneurysm."

"Why?"

"Are you kidding? Not only would he be stuck with his least favorite son to carry on the family name, which I haven't done yet, but that would mean I was also crazy."

"Sounds like he needed some therapy himself."

Jason laughed. "Real men don't eat quiche or see therapists."

Angela smiled and looked into Jason's eyes. They were a deep beautiful green and she felt drawn into them. She felt an impulse drawing her closer to those eyes, closer to Jason, and she knew he felt it, too. Jason and Angela drew closer still; their eyes slightly closed and tilted downward gazing at each other's lips. Angela felt a warmth rush over her. Then, just as their lips were to touch, Jason's cell phone rang. It was like a warning bell in their ears telling them their kiss shouldn't happen. Angela looked down at the floor.

"I guess you should get that."

"I guess so." Jason picked up his cell phone from the sofa behind them. "Hello."

"Hello, Jason."

"Hey, Aunt Bess." Angela waved. "Angela says hello."

"Angela, the detective? She's there?"

"Yes. We're sorting through some papers."

"Are you watching the seven o'clock news?"

"No, we're in the living room."

"They just said that Dorothy Danze is going to have some information on the status of identifying some of the remains found at Wardlaw."

"No kidding. I'll turn it on. Thanks for calling."

"Give me a call later and let me know how everything's going."

Jason heard a playful tone in his aunt's request for a return call. He knew she was referring to Angela and not the Wardlaw investigation. He too wondered how things were going.

"That was my aunt."

"I know."

"Oh, yeah. Anyway, she said Dorothy Danze is on the news with some information about the identification of the remains."

"Shit!" Angela exclaimed. "I wonder if she found the articles from *The State*."

"I don't know. It wasn't hard to do; I found them. Come on. Let's go to the great-room and turn on the TV." Jason was by now standing and looking down at Angela. He reached out his hand to help her up. When Angela's hand was firmly in his grasp he pulled upward. Angela rose from her seated position quickly and easily. She was agile and he noticed the strength in her arms that he hadn't expected. He could tell she worked out a lot.

Jason led Angela into the great-room. "Have a seat." He picked up the remote control and punched in the numbers for the correct station just in time to hear the anchor introduce Dorothy Danze with the evening's lead story.

"I'm with you tonight from the University of South Carolina campus outside the building which houses the anthropology department. Inside this inconspicuous building are the skeletons of the seven people found buried on what was once the Wardlaw Junior High playground."

"Even though officials with both the Richland County Coroner's office and the anthropology department have declined to comment, our sources tell us that Professor Bill Russell, a forensic anthropologist with the University, is close to identifying at least some of the seven remains." Dorothy paused for a moment to add emphasis to her report.

"It has been almost two weeks since the first of the remains were unearthed in a place where children once played, but for nearly thirty-one years, has been nothing more than an overgrown lot where some of Columbia's homeless would congregate. Very little information has come out of the Columbia City Police Department. They have been unusually silent about their investigation. The possibility of identifying three of what our sources tell us are most likely the remains of children, has been the first break in the case."

"Dorothy, have any of the identities been confirmed yet?"

"No, John. From what our sources tell us, the police, using missing persons files, so far have isolated possible matches for only about half the victims."

"Has any indication been given as to when the identification process will be complete?"

"Well, John, apparently this is a rather painstaking process. And from what our sources tell us, there are over four hundred active cases of missing persons in South Carolina where that person is a child. So finding a possible match and then locating the necessary dental or medical records requires a certain amount of time."

"Dorothy, you said children. Are all of the remains those of children?"

"John, we don't have that confirmed. But our sources tell us that all seven are children somewhere between the age of eleven to fourteen."

Jason looked at Angela as Dorothy Danze announced, to most of the Carolina Midlands, that the remains belonged to children. He could see the anger in her face and saw it manifest its self by Angela tearing at a fingernail on her left index finger with the nail on her right thumb.

"Have any parents or relatives of children missing from the area come forward about the possibility that one of these could be their child?"

"To my knowledge, John, no. But as I said, the Columbia police have not shared information about the case, nor have they made any public announcements."

"Thank you, Dorothy. Please keep us posted as more information comes available."

"Certainly John, and thank you."

Tragic was the last word Jason heard come from the anchor's mouth as he turned off the television. He looked at Angela who was still tearing at her fingernail. "That bitch. Don't those news people have any sense of responsibility? We're not trying to cover anything up; we just have to control the information that gets out." Jason watched as Angela stood up and started pacing around the room.

"We don't want the killer to know what we know if he's out there listening. And we don't need a bunch of hysterical parents with damn lawyers in tow coming down getting in the way."

Jason wasn't sure what to say, if anything, so he continued to watch as Angela vented her anger and frustration. "Most of those four hundred missing children she's talking about are parental abductions. She made it sound like we sit on our ass and do nothing. Nothing! While a bunch of psychos run around kidnapping and killing children. Damn it!"

"Are you going to repute her statements?"

"I just want to know who this damn 'source' is that she kept mentioning."

"So what'd you think will happen now?" Before Angela could respond she heard her cell phone ring. She looked at the screen.

"It's my Captain. I have to take this."

"Sure, go ahead. Do you want some privacy?"

"No, it's okay." Angela answered, "Frank?"

Jason listened to Angela's portion of the conversation.

"Yes, I saw the news. I have no idea. Yes sir. I've been going through the information Betty Harris gave me from her husband's old notes. Yes sir. I picked them up earlier. I don't see a lot here yet, but I haven't had time to read it all. I at least do have the names of the other four children he suspected were victims."

There was a long pause. "Yes sir. That will give us potentially all seven children. I have no idea how she knew they were children. That could have come from anyone who was hanging around the excavation site and saw the size of the bones. It could be just speculation."

Another pause. "But Frank, we agreed that I could work the case alone if I came up with some solid leads. It's Monday night, I have the names of the victims. As soon as that's confirmed, then I can start trying to find a killer." Angela was silent while she held the phone to her ear. Jason could see the frustration on her face. "Good night."

Angela pressed the 'end' button on the phone and laid it down of the coffee table. "Damn it!"

"What did he say?"

"He's putting Randall Evans on the case with me."

"That's the guy that's the problem."

"Yes, and the Captain wants me to bring in all the information Betty Harris gave us."

"Are you going to?"

"I'll have to. This might make it harder for me to keep you in the loop as far as you going places with me. Evans will be tagging along now, trying to take over the case for himself."

"Why don't we make copies of everything before you take it? At least we'll have the same information here that Evans has access to. That way we could still work together and you could still work independently of Evans on some things."

Angela smiled. "Is there a place near here where I can get copies made?"

"Don't need one. I have a good printer here. It will make good scans or copies. Whichever you prefer."

"God, were you like a Boy Scout or something? You're always prepared. I bet you even have a Swiss army knife in your pocket."

"Actually, I do have one of those, and I also have one of those combination tool things. You know, with the pliers and screwdriver and stuff, but I keep them in my car. I don't like carrying a bunch of junk in my pockets."

Angela smiled at Jason. She wondered what their kiss would have been like and where it would have led, had it not been interrupted by the phone. She was tempted to try again, but the moment had passed. She would have to wait for another time.

"Do you want to start copying this stuff?" Jason asked.

"Let's eat first. I'm starting to get a sick headache from not eating, and if I let it go too long, I'll end up with a migraine."

Jason and Angela went into the kitchen and were followed by Sebastian. Sebastian seated himself on the countertop watching them warm up dinner and waiting for a handout. Jason and Angela worked easily together. Angela made herself at home opening cabinets and drawers, looking for plates and flatware, while Jason manned the microwave and poured them each a glass of wine. As the tension that had built from the news broadcast, and knowing she would now have to work with Randall Evans, began to fade, Angela's mood slowly lightened. The headache she had felt herself developing was gone and the wine took the remaining edge off her tension. She sat at the glass breakfast table watching Jason as he cleared away their dishes and poured himself a second glass. Angela declined, one was her limit tonight.

Jason, with his back toward Angela, talked about his family while he looked for containers for their leftovers.

Angela listened as Jason talked, unaware of her gaze. He spoke of his aunt and her influence over his adolescence, and then his estrangement from the rest of his family.

Angela knew she found him attractive. She had thought so when they first met. Because of his interest in the Wardlaw case she had assumed he was just another guy who gets off watching cop shows and action flicks. Now, she at least knew another side to him, but he still carried baggage. Hell, who didn't have baggage. God knows she had her own from too many failed relationships with too many insecure men.

She wondered if Jason could handle her career. How would he feel with a girlfriend that's a cop? Angela knew she needed to slow down. They had only "almost" kissed. She couldn't even be sure he felt the same attraction. He was still a man, and she knew all too well men didn't think on the same level as women. Maybe he just wanted to hook up. After all, he did tell her he hadn't dated anyone in a while. But there was nothing wrong with hooking up on occasion. Sitting there watching him made it all too tempting.

Having found a container for the remainder of the fried rice, Jason placed the food in the refrigerator, then turned to face Angela.

"Ready to make copies?"

The question caused Angela to snap out of her sexual fantasy. "I'm sorry. What'd you say?"

"You looked like you were a million miles away."

"Not quite a million, but pretty close to it."

"Thinking about the case?"

"Yes and no. Actually, when you asked, I was wondering how you got so adept in a kitchen."

"Picking up takeout and putting away leftovers isn't adept."

"No. But I can just tell you probably know how to cook more than Hamburger Helper. Also, I noticed the gourmet cookbooks on the shelf."

"You're pretty observant."

"I'm a detective."

Jason smiled. "I guess that never really turns off, does it."

"Not really. So you haven't answered my question."

"My aunt and Louise taught me how to cook and to appreciate good food and wine. They didn't want me to grow up to be an uncultured male chauvinist pig. Did they do a good job? What'd you think? You're a woman; you judge."

Angela smiled and looked into Jason's clear green eyes that she loved so much. "Final verdict's still out, but I like what I see so far."

Jason was taken aback by the directness of Angela's comment. She was flirting with him and he liked it. Angela was a woman he wouldn't have to guess with. She would be direct. Whatever she did or didn't want, he knew she would tell him. Jason knew he wanted her, but this wasn't the night for it. It was too fast.

"Okay, Jason, where's that copier? We'd better get busy."

Chapter twenty-three

When Jason finally fell asleep that evening, his dreams were troubled, bordering on what he could almost describe as nightmares. He saw himself walking through the deserted halls of Wardlaw, pieces of fallen plaster and broken glass crunching under the soles of his sneakers and the sounds of pigeon wings in his ears as they took flight in classrooms that lay off the hall to his left and right.

He was moving in slow motion down the main corridor of the second floor. He could hear the echoes of children's voices reciting some verse, but it was indistinguishable, like a distant memory from childhood. In his dream he continued to walk toward the voices. There was a flash of a face in the burned-out school office, but when he turned, the image was gone. He couldn't turn quickly enough; it was as if his body was weighted down and moving against an invisible force.

The voices were louder now. They mocked him. As he drew nearer the classroom at the end of the long hall, he could hear the verse that was being recited. It was a poem he had memorized as a child for an elementary school play. In his dream, he knew some of the words from the poem weren't right, but somehow in his distorted dream world they made sense. He was now outside the classroom door – he hesitated. The school looked different now. The hall was clean and there was an aroma that was a strange mixture of fragrances. It was both sweet and pungent at the same time.

Jason felt fear, but he was willed inside the room. He gave the door a slight push and it swung open slowly, easily. The room was filled with rows of heavy wooden desks. The same type he remembered from his own years in middle school. Sitting in the room were eight children reciting over and over the verse he had heard in his dream, walking through Wardlaw's halls. His fear was turning to panic, but still he walked into the room, never taking his eyes from the children. As he reached the front of the room to stand behind the teacher's desk, he could see their faces. They were the little girls from Mark Harris's files. Young, innocent, but they looked strange, almost two dimensional, like a photograph. Then he saw the eighth face. It was Tommy.

His face was swollen and his eyes dark. His hair was wet and matted against his head. He looked beyond Jason, pointing. When Tommy opened his mouth to speak, dirty river water poured out.

"He did this!" was all Tommy said. Jason awoke with a start. He was cold and drenched in sweat.

It was difficult to go back to sleep. He couldn't shake the image of river water flowing from Tommy's mouth.

It was morning, and the memory of the dream was as vivid as the dream itself had been just a few hours before. Jason rolled over, turning his back to his alarm clock and pulled the blankets up under his chin. Looking at Sebastian, who was curled up on the spare pillow, Jason said, "I think the connection has to do with Wardlaw. What'd you think?"

Sebastian stood up, arching his back and stretched. He pushed his head against Jason's then curled up against Jason's neck. "It has to be someone connected with the school."

When he did finally get up he knew he would be late getting into the office, but he really didn't care. He had worked enough this week that everything was caught up. Billing had been sent out and money was coming in for the commercial jobs. Business was good.

Jason turned on the small TV in his bedroom so he could listen to the morning news while he shaved. Again, there she was, Dorothy Danze talking about the remains.

"She's getting a lot of mileage out of this one, Sebastian. It's probably time to renew her contract and she wants to look good."

The phone rang. "Hello."

"Jason. Hey, good morning." He recognized Angela's voice immediately.

"Hey, there. How'd you sleep?" he asked.

"Not worth a damn. I couldn't stop thinking about the case."

"Me either. Where are you?"

"I'm on my way to work. I just wanted to give you a call and say thanks for copying all this stuff for me last night. I'll see what's going on in here today and maybe we can get together later and start going over the files again. That is, if you're free this evening."

"I'm free until we're finished."

"Great. I'll talk to you later. Bye-bye."

"Bye." Jason hung up. "Sebastian, I think she likes us." Sebastian yawned and laid his head down on the pillow.

Jason sat on the end of the bed, pointed the remote control at the TV and turned up the volume so he could better hear what Dorothy Danze had to report. It appeared to be nothing more than a recap of the story from the night before.

"Sebastian, what do you say I call the office and take the day off. I could hang out here and we could sort through files and help Angela." Jason heard the muffled sound of the phone ringing. "Damn, where'd I put that."

He pulled back the blankets and the ringing became louder. "Here we go." Jason picked up the phone and answered the call. "Hello."

"Jason?"

He recognized Wesley's voice immediately. "Hey man, how're you doing?"

"I don't know. I just saw Dorothy Danze on television. She was talking about the investigation of the remains they found at Wardlaw."

"Yeah, I know. I have it on right now, and she was on last night, too."

"What'd she say last night?"

"Looks like it was the same tape just with slightly different editing."

"Have you talked to her any?"

"No, why?"

"She said she had inside sources."

"I'm not an inside source," Jason said. "All I have are the articles you pulled for me."

"You could've shown her those."

"Well, I didn't."

"Whatever. I just wanted to let you know that I'm going to the news editor with the articles."

"Why?"

"It's like I said, I want the credit for finding those stories and she's beating us to it. And since you haven't got anything for me; have you? Then ,I'm going to let them know."

Jason thought about what Wesley was saying. Really, at this point it no longer mattered. Through Angela, he was on the inside of the investigation and that was all that mattered to him.

"Whatever you need to do, man. If I found the stories so easily by accident, and you looked them up for me that quickly, then someone who thinks to look for them wouldn't have any problem either."

"I'm glad you're not pissed about it. But you know how it is. Say, how about we get together for a beer after work one night this week."

"I'll probably be pretty busy, but yeah that sounds good. Just give me a call."

"Later."

"Bye." Pausing for a moment, he breathed in deeply and then exhaled. He knew he should give Angela a head's up on this one. He guessed *The State* would have something in tomorrow's paper. Jason pulled a red t-shirt over his head then walked down stairs. Sebastian ran down the stairs in front of him. When Jason walked into the kitchen, Sebastian was pacing around his food dish.

"Okay, I know you're hungry." Jason retrieved a small can of cat food from the pantry. "Here you go, little man."

Jason pulled his phone from his pocket and called Angela's cell phone. There was no answer. She was probably already at work and in a meeting with her Captain. Next he dialed her office – no answer, just voice mail. Then he sent a text message. He knew he would probably have a few minutes to wait, so he decided to take the time to have breakfast, something he rarely did. Jason was standing at the refrigerator with the door open, trying to decide what he wanted to eat, and what would take the least effort to prepare, when the phone rang.

"Hello."

"Jason, you texted me?"

"Yes, I did. How's it going so far this morning?"

"I have a meeting in a few minutes with the Captain and my new partner Randall."

Jason could hear the sarcasm in her voice. "Are you going to show them the files?"

"Most of it, but I'll hold out some of the best stuff for just us."

Jason smiled. "I just wanted to let you know my friend Wesley called. He's the one that works at *The State* paper and helped me find the articles I showed you."

"Yes, I remember you told me about him."

"Well, he saw Dorothy Danze on the news this morning."

"She was on this morning, too?" Angela asked. "What did she say? Anything different?"

"Not really," Jason said. "It was pretty much a recap of last night's story. Anyway, Wesley said he saw it and he was going to the News Editor and let him know about the articles. He wants some recognition for this because it's close to raise time for him."

"You couldn't talk him out of it?"

"No. He doesn't want the TV stations to get ahead of them and him miss out on the brownie points, basically."

"Since we got to Betty Harris first, it probably won't matter anyway. Look, I have go. I'll call you after the meeting is over. Are you going to be at work?"

"I thought about taking the day off, but I need to go either to the office or to the school. I need to check on some things. It won't take long. Then I thought I'd come back here and spend some time going through Harris's files."

"It will be this evening before I can come to your house. I'll call your office and if I don't get you there I'll text you. Is that okay?"

"That'll be great." Jason and Angela said good-bye then hung up.

"She definitely likes us, Sebastian." Jason pushed his hair back from his face, then, thrusting his hands into his pants pockets, he looked at the stack of papers on his counter top. He had so many things he needed to do. Sort personal papers. Work on his yard that was becoming more dry and scorched each day. Then, there was work. But none of this was what he wanted to do. The only thing Jason was able to focus on was the Wardlaw case.

Jason called the office and spoke for only a few minutes to Cindy and then to Roger, one of his architects. He gave them both some instructions on what needed to be done, then called Glenn Stone. Glenn was in his usual mood, which wasn't good. Jason had a mental image of Glenn wearing his ball cap pulled down low over his eyes and barking instructions at the crews. He was trying to make up time and finish on schedule, which both men knew was impossible, but still Glenn pushed. Everything he needed from Jason and his firm had been taken care of for now. With that, Jason felt free to immerse himself in Harris's files.

First, Jason retrieved Post It notes and a marker from his desk drawer, then he wrote the name of each girl on a note. He then posted each card to the longest wall in his formal living room.

Sebastian sat in the floor on top of an open file folder. Jason picked up the cat and set him on a cotton throw that was lying on the sofa.

"You sit here. I don't need help with the papers right now." Jason picked up the folders on Annie Walker, Susan Thompson, and Paula Groves, the only three girls who had attended Wardlaw Junior High. Under their names he taped pictures of the girls. Their physical appearances were quite different. He had read that some serial killers select their victims based on some physical type. That didn't seem to be the case here.

Next, he attached addresses of the girls at the time of their disappearance. On the wall to his left, behind the armchair, he hung a large map of greater Columbia. On the map he highlighted the approximate street location for the residence of each girl. Yellow would represent the home of Annie Walker, pink for Susan, and blue for Paula. Annie and Susan lived in close proximity to one another, which he had expected. Paula, on the other hand, lived in a totally different neighborhood.

One of the articles he had read about Wardlaw dealt with the complaints of parents who met with the school board in an attempt to stop busing. He knew he would have to check school records. Paula might have been one of the students who was bused from another area of Columbia. If this were the case, then he and Angela might be able to exclude neighborhood as a common denominator.

Jason stood back from the wall, his hands in his pockets, admiring his work. "Now what?"

Next, he taped to the wall, photographs of the other four girls and located their addresses on the map of Columbia. Only two of the girls – Patty Franks, represented by the green, and Robin Skinner, the orange, lived in what could be considered in close proximity to each other. None of these four lived near Annie, Susan or Paula.

It was noon before Jason realized how many hours he had spent reading through files, notes, and news clippings. Some of the print from the copied news clippings was difficult to read without straining. Jason rubbed his eyes – they were tired. He was hungry, too. As he walked to the refrigerator his phone rang.

"Hello."

"Hey Jason, this is Angela. What're you doing?"

"Actually, I have been reading through Mark Harris's papers all morning."

"Anything interesting?"

"Not yet. I have sorted information and looked for anything that could connect the girls to each other. Right now the only connection is between the three that we know attended Wardlaw. How's your morning going?"

"My Captain officially assigned Randall Evans to work on the case with me. I'm still in charge, but he's my partner. And we have a positive I.D. on three sets of remains."

"You're kidding. That was fast. I thought you said it could take a long time to find old records."

"I thought so, too, but with Harris's files there was enough information to track down the parents and get dental and medical records."

"Which three?"

"The ones I gave them the other day: Annie, Susan, and Paula."

"Have you notified the parents yet?"

"No, not yet."

Jason could hear the excitement in Angela's voice and he wished he was there in the police station with her, reading the official report confirming the identities of the girls. "Now what do we do?"

"Now we go to lunch. I'm starving and I want to get away from my new partner for a while. He's on my last nerve." Angela paused for a moment. "I didn't even ask if you already had plans or had eaten."

"Actually, I'm standing in front of the refrigerator trying to decide what to eat. So, do you want to meet somewhere or would you like me to pick you up?"

There was silence on Angela's end of the phone line.

"Hello. You still there?"

"I'm here," she said. "I was just thinking about where to go."

"Have you ever eaten at The Blue Marlin?" Jason asked.

"Yes, as a matter of fact I have. I like it."

"Want to go?"

"Sure," she said. "Just call me when you get close to the station and I'll meet you out front."

"Will do." Jason spun around. "Yes!" he said, as he did a drum roll with his hands on the counter top. Sebastian raised he head and opened his eyes wide. Jason's gesture had startled him.

"I have a lunch date, little man. How about that?" Jason rubbed the cat's ears and head. "I'll be back in a little while."

Jason picked up his messenger bag from his desk chair in his office, retrieved his keys from the kitchen counter, and headed out the door into the garage.

While she waited for Jason, Angela read through some of her copies of Mark Harris's files on the other four girls. She had already pulled the missing person records and forwarded them on to the Coroner's Office for, hopefully, a positive identification.

She was looking for anything that would connect these four with the others when she noticed something. Harris had noted in the files the length of time the girls had lived at their addresses. Everyone, with the exception of Kathy Boyd, had lived at their address for most of their short lives. Robin Skinner, one of the other missing girls, had not changed addresses, but her father had moved out when the parents divorced three years before she disappeared. Kathy Boyd, however, had only lived with her parents at her address for about six months.

Angela sifted through the many pages of paper in search of a previous address. Then she read a neatly folded copy of a class schedule for Kathy. She had attended Wardlaw through the seventh grade. She knew this had to be more than a coincidence. Four girls now had a connection to Wardlaw Junior High.

The ring of her cell phone broke her concentration. It was Jason; he was on Huger Street and would be at the station in a few minutes.

Angela refolded the copy of the schedule and put it inside her portfolio. She then picked up her sunglasses, locked her office and in a fast pace, ascended the stairs. Angela was smiling when she climbed inside Jason's car.

"You look like you're in a pretty good mood. Is that smile for me or has your day just been that good so far?"

Angela felt her face flush a little. She was attracted to Jason and she knew the feeling was mutual. "Actually, a little of both maybe."

Jason returned the smile. "So what made your day go well? I know it isn't getting Randall Evans as a partner."

"This." Angela unzipped her portfolio as Jason exited the parking lot and turned on to the street. "It's Kathy Boyd's seventh grade class schedule. She went to Wardlaw in the sixth and seventh grades."

"No shit!" Jason took the schedule from Angela and shifted his eyes back and forth from the traffic in front of them to the paper in his hand. "You sure this is the same Kathy Boyd?"

"We'll have to get it checked out to make sure, but it looks like it." Angela took the paper from Jason. "It has all of her teacher's names, classes, room numbers, everything. If this checks out, which I'm positive it will, then we have four dead girls who attended Wardlaw."

"That's too big a coincidence." Jason commented. "It had to be someone who either taught or worked at the school."

"Don't get too convinced yet," she warned.

"You just said yourself that we have four that went to Wardlaw."

"I know, but there still could be something else connecting the girls. It could be nothing more than the guy who did this was driving around neighborhoods looking for an opportunity. If we get our minds set on something too soon, then we might rule out an important factor later."

"I see your point, but what is your gut telling you? Wait a minute," he said. "Where are we going to eat?"

"Blue Marlin? We'd already decided – unless you'd rather go somewhere else."

"Right. I remember," he said, "I must've just had a brain fart. So anyway – your gut feeling?"

"My gut feeling is some sick son-of-a-bitch was working at the school and picking off children, and the ones he got his hands on that he didn't kill, he probably molested."

"Then we agree. Now when are they going to I.D. the others?"

"I don't know. It'll just depend on tracking down records and how long that takes."

The restaurant was noisy and dimly lit. Jason followed close behind Angela as the hostess led them to their small table at the rear of the restaurant. Once seated, Jason looked around the room at their fellow diners.

"You know every time I come in here for lunch, the guys that are eating in here make me think of middle-aged frat guys. You know the type?"

"And they are always on their cell phones talking too loud about their business deals," she said.

Jason laughed. He liked Angela. She was attractive, smart and now that they were getting to know each other better, he could see she had a lighter side. She wasn't what he had expected to find in a woman police detective. Until Angela, his mental image of a woman police detective was something of a cross between the women officers in Law and Order and the prison matrons in old B-movies.

Jason and Angela sat in silence as they read the menus. "I hate to decide what to eat," Angela commented, then took a sip of water from her glass. "I guess I'll have the tilapia. That's about the only thing that jumps out at me."

Jason looked over the top of his menu and smiled.

Angela saw the expression on his face. "That didn't come out right did it?"

Jason, still smiling, "I didn't say anything." He saw Angela blush slightly. Jason brushed the hair away from his face then laid down his menu. "You know, this may not be the right time or place but…" He was interrupted by the waitress.

"Are you ready for me to take your orders?"

"Sure." Angela spoke first. "I'll have the tilapia, and could I get the broccoli as a side item?

"Sure, no problem. Would you like a salad, too?"

"No, thank you."

The waitress turned to Jason. "And what can I get you?"

Jason hadn't really read the menu selections; he had been too busy focusing on Angela. "Uh, shrimp and grits, but leave out the sausage."

"Sure thing. And would you like a salad?

"No. Just another glass of unsweetened tea when you get a chance." The waitress took the menus and left.

Angela leaned forward slightly. "You were about to say something when the waitress walked up."

"Oh, yeah right." Jason drew in a deep breath and exhaled. "What I was going to say was that the timing may not be the best but…" He was interrupted again. This time by someone who obviously knew Angela.

"Well, how's my favorite member of Columbia's finest?" Angela turned quickly. She was startled by the voice.

"Doug."

"Hey there, Angela. How're y'all doin' today." Doug Brazell turned to Jason.

"Doug, this is Jason, a friend of mine."

"Hi, nice to meet you," Jason said, extending his hand. "Did you just come in Doug? Would you like to join us?" Jason asked.

Angela looked at Jason and frowned.

"No, actually I was on my way out. But I'll sit down here for a minute," he said, as he turned to the man with him. "Why don't you pull the car up, Jack, and I'll be out in a second." Brazell handed the other man the keys, then pulled out a chair and sat down. He smiled at Angela and straightened his tie.

"Jason, didn't you say you work with my favorite detective here?"

"No, I'm just a friend." Jason recognized Doug from the job site, but he knew Doug didn't remember him.

Brazell gave Jason little notice. He turned his attention to Angela and, with an air of superiority, he proudly reported that he was hard at work getting Angela the information she needed. Angela didn't know if it was her imagination or not, but Doug seemed to put extra emphasis on the word "hard."

After exchanging a few comments about the weather, "Well, I guess

I'd better run. Jack probably has the car out front now."

Before standing to leave, Doug leaned close to Angela and said, "I have two more of your Jane Doe's tracked down. Just need to get the dental records in so Russell can have a look at them."

"Which two?" Angela moved back a little. She didn't want to turn her head without first moving away from Doug. She didn't want their faces that close.

"The last two." Doug winked and the stood up straight, standing above Angela. "Nice meetin' you, Jason. Talk to you later, Angela."

Jason watched as Brazell walked out of the dining room and headed for the front door.

"You know, I'm really not one of those stereotype macho guys, but I'd really like to punch him. He was hitting on you."

Angela looked into Jason's green eyes. "He's enough to get your testosterone up, isn't he?"

"God, I'll say. Man, I really want to punch him."

Angela smiled. "Well, don't punch him, because then I'd have to arrest you."

"Just so long as you handcuff me." Jason realized what he'd said as soon as it was out his mouth. "I'm sorry, I shouldn't have said that. God, I sound as bad as he does. I apologize."

Angela reached across the table and placed her hand on Jason's. "It's okay, really. Actually, I don't think it sounds like such a bad idea."

"Arresting me?"

"No. Handcuffing you." Angela saw Jason's face flush. He was either embarrassed, or excited, or both. "Did I embarrass you?"

"Sort of. Not really. I mean, what I've been trying to say is that..." He paused. "I would like us to see each other, as in a date."

"Do you think you can handle dating a cop? Most of the men I've gotten involved with got tired of it after a while."

"I don't know, he said. "I've never dated a cop. All we can do is try."

Angela removed her hand from atop Jason's. "You know, the first couple times we met I thought you were an attractive man." This time Angela felt her face flush. "But I just blew it off. It's just natural to notice people who are nice looking or dressed well."

Jason pushed his hair away from his face. "I'm flattered."

"You shouldn't be. I also thought you were probably a nut, because you asked a lot of questions about the investigation."

Jason laughed. "I guess I am kinda nuts." Jason looked down at his napkin that was folded and lying in front of him. He fingered the corner of the fold. "I'm still living through my brother's drowning. I think I'm trying to get some closure by talking you into letting me be involved in this case." Jason sighed, then looked at Angela.

Angela was taken aback by the look of vulnerability in Jason's green eyes. She wasn't used to seeing that in the men she dated. The others had tried to impress her with male bravado. Angela knew it was because a woman detective intimidated them. Maybe it was the influence his aunt had over him, but for whatever the reason, Jason wasn't intimidated by her, and he wasn't afraid to show his fears. She liked that.

"I don't think you're nuts. Going through that had to have been hard on you. That was a lot for a child to deal with, especially with the way your parents handled it."

"Don't get me wrong, I don't sit around and dwell on it all the time. I guess just seeing the skeletons of those children get pulled out of the ground got to me."

"It gets to me, too."

"Angela, seriously," Jason said, "I would like to start seeing you."

"I'd like that, too. Dating would be good. I just don't want to try to start something serious right now. I want to stay focused on this case."

Jason smiled. "Casual dating is good. Serious will come later if things work out."

To relieve the awkwardness that had been created by the momentary talk of dating, they shifted their talk to the investigation. In hushed tones so no one around them could overhear, Jason described for Angela how he had started trying to organize Mark Harris's files by posting photographs and notes to the walls of his living room. He also described how he had located the girl's addresses on the map of Columbia and how only two girls had lived in a neighborhood that would not have sent children to Wardlaw. The other girl, Paula Groves, was probably bussed in. Jason knew from his research on the school, that busing was an issue at Wardlaw as late as 1984.

"When Brazell said 'the last two' which ones did he mean?" Jason asked.

"I'm assuming he meant the last two chronologically, but that wouldn't be right, because we already have Paula identified." Angela paused. "Maybe he just meant the last two in the stack. I don't know, he never seems straight forward when he talks to me."

"That's because he wants to get in your pants."

Angela could detect the irritation in Jason's voice.

"Does that bother you?"

"Guys like that give all the rest of us a bad name," hesaid.

"Jason, my experience has been that most of the rest of you are like that," Angela smiled. "Present company excluded of course – maybe."

Jason leaned over the table slightly. Smiling, he said, "I'd still like to punch him."

Throughout lunch Jason and Angela's conversation alternated between the Wardlaw investigation, to talking about themselves. Jason hadn't felt this comfortable talking with anyone in a long time, not even with his friends. Cindy was a great friend, as was Wesley, and a couple of the other guys he hung out with, but Angela was different. He wasn't sure what it was about her that made him feel differently. He just knew the feeling was good.

After lunch Jason took Angela back to the police station. She reached for the door handle then hesitated. Leaning toward Jason she kissed him on the cheek. He smiled. "What was that for?"

"That kiss last night was interrupted. We never picked up where we left off. Also, I just wanted to say 'bye' and I'll see you later."

"Would you like to come over tonight and work on the files?"

"If you cook I will."

"If I cook? You won't come over if I don't cook?"

"I'm going to have to go home and eat. Or get something and eat on the way. But I can get there earlier if you cook. Besides, your aunt said you were a good cook. I'd like to find out for myself."

Jason gave a smile with only one side of his mouth. "Call me and let me know what time you're going to get off. I'm going to run by the school and check on a few things, then I'll be home." Angela got out of Jason's car, and turned before closing the door. "I'll call."

Chapter twenty-four

When Angela arrived at Jason's house that evening, they exchanged a light kiss then went straight to the kitchen where Jason was finishing dinner preparations.

"It smells wonderful. It looks like Italian."

"Thank you, it is. It's shrimp with a tomato sauce and feta cheese over risotto." Trying to appear modest but loving the praise, Jason assured her it was simple to prepare. While they ate, the two reviewed the information supplied by the Coroner's office. Cause of death couldn't be determined, but three of the skeletons definitely belonged to Annie, Susan, and Paula. If they were able to locate the dental and medical records and Mark Harris's conclusions were correct, then by tomorrow the identities of Kathy Boyd and Robin Skinner would be confirmed. That would leave only Patty Franks and Sarah Martin.

Angela decided to work under the assumption that all the skeletons unearthed on the Wardlaw playground belonged to the missing girls Mark Harris had identified in his files. With that decided, the two began affixing photographs, Post-It-Notes, and miscellaneous information relating to each girl, to Jason's living room wall.

Two hours later, Angela and Jason stood back to analyze their work. After some contemplation, Angela spoke. "Okay, so what do we have? Pictures, addresses, date of disappearance, hobbies, classes, friends, but what do we really have?"

Jason ran his fingers through his hair pushing it away from his eyes. "Somehow, we need to pick out the common items and organize them. Usually, I use high lighters, but I don't like the idea of high lighting my walls."

"Everything is already lined up in columns and rows like a giant spread sheet. Why don't we use colored string to tie a line between items the girls had in common?" Angela added.

"What do you mean?"

"Get yarn. Yarn comes in a million colors. We have tape holding everything to the wall. We just need to tape the yarn from one point to another to visually show the link." Jason still looked puzzled.

"Here, let me show you." Angela walked to the wall. "Pretend I have a red piece of yarn. The red yarn represents attending Wardlaw. Tape it first to the Post-It-Note under Annie that says Wardlaw student. Then tape it to the one under Susan. Next, Kathy Boyd, and then Paula. See what I'm getting at?"

"I think so." Jason stood with his arms crossed in front of him staring at the wall in contemplation. "You think this will help?"

"Can't hurt. We need a visual thing to tie it together. I don't know about you, but the visual would help me."

"It might help, but what if we don't have all the information on the wall and we miss something?"

"Then we probably would have missed it anyway, because we didn't see it as being important in the first place."

Jason, still staring at the wall, ran his fingers through his hair again. "I guess we better go buy some yarn. There's a craft store near the mall."

Angela picked up her car keys that were lying on the coffee table. "I'll drive. I'm probably parked behind you anyway."

At the craft store they bought fifteen different colors of yarn, and two packs of Post-It-Notes, one white and one multi-colored. Back at Jason's house they dumped their supplies in the floor and Angela began searching Jason's wall for commonalties between the seven girls. Just as Angela had described in her example, she used red yarn to link the four Wardlaw students. Next, she used yellow for the three girls who had lived in neighborhoods which would have supplied Wardlaw with students.

Then, they used white to connect the girls by age and grade. There were four seventh graders, one sixth grader, and two eighth graders. Three girls played softball and two were in band. After several minutes of work Jason and Angela stood back to examine their work.

Jason spoke first. "I don't see that this is getting us anywhere. We have yarn overlapping and crisscrossing, but so far there isn't any one thing that ties all the girls together."

"Don't give up yet. We just need to look at this deeper. Maybe instead of just going to Wardlaw, the similarity between the girls is the classes they took or extracurricular activities." Angela looked at the map of Columbia pinned to the opposite wall.

"Here. Here's one more thing we didn't get. Patty and Robin lived in the same neighborhood. I'll use pink yarn for that one." Using the yarn, Angela connected the Post-It-Notes with the girls' addresses.

"Look here." Angela pointed to the wall. "Patty Franks and Robin Skinner lived near each other – same neighborhood. Patty, Robin and Kathy Boyd played softball. Here's another one, Susan Thompson and Sarah Martin were both in band."

"Okay, I see what you're getting at; but Susan was in Wardlaw's band and Sarah was in band at Hand Middle School."

"Then we look deeper. There's a lot of information here." Angela's voice had an excited tone. "Who were their teachers? Who were their softball coaches? Who was the band director? Who was the janitor for that matter? Maybe there was a traveling tuba and softball glove sales-man that only passed through Columbia once every two years."

Jason rubbed his forehead and closed his eyes. He thought Angela's comment was funny, but he chose to ignore it. He was getting a head-ache. "Do you think there is one adult common to all the girls through school or outside activities, and this isn't just random?"

"Yes, I think so. There are too many similarities for this to be ran-dom. There has to be one common thread. And that's not a pun."

Jason smiled and continued to rub his forehead.

"Would you like a beer or a glass of wine or something?"

"No," she said. "I don't think as clearly when I drink. Why? Do you want one?" Angela smiled at Jason and with a gentle touch she pushed a strand of his hair away from his eyes, then with the palm of her hand, touched his cheek. "This isn't what you thought it would be, is it?"

Jason, looking into Angela's brown eyes took her hand in his. "No, not really. I guess I've watched too much television. I expected to find the killer in one hour minus commercial breaks."

Angela smiled.

Jason leaned closer. He hesitated for only a moment as he leaned closer until Angela's lips met his. Their kiss was soft, light, inviting. They both felt the warmth in their bodies telling them they wanted more. Angela slowly, reluctantly turned her face away from Jason's direct gaze.

"I'm sorry, is something wrong." Jason asked.

"No. Don't be sorry. We just can't right now. We can't get too involved; we have to stay focused on the case."

"I know. What do we do now?"

"With us or with the case?" Angela asked.

"I guess both."

"Well, I don't know about you, but I'm going to try to keep my hormones under control until this investigation is over. But as soon as it's over I'm getting out the handcuffs."

Jason blushed and smiled. "You promise?"

"Yes. And I keep my promises." Angela watched as the red in Jason's face grew deeper. It amused her that she was able to make him blush.

In an effort to make the red in his face fade Jason changed the subject. "What about the case?"

"We just have to keep trying to find commonalties between the girls.," she said. "Identify adults they all may have come in contact with. Start questioning people who knew them."

"That could be hard. If we talk to people who knew them, we'll be talking to people who were children over forty years ago. They may not remember things correctly. A child's recollection of events isn't usually very accurate."

"Sometimes neither is an adult's memory. We need to talk to teachers, too. I know some probably passed away. The others I'm certain would be retired. The girls who went to Wardlaw probably all had the same teachers. We'll start there."

Jason felt his role in the investigation was about to become very limited. "What can I do?" He asked.

"Actually, I thought you could use your aunt to get in touch with some of the teachers that were at Wardlaw when she was there. Randall and I will focus on some of the other legwork. Then, whatever you find we'll follow up on officially."

"That sounds like it would work. We have copies of their report cards." Jason pulled out a stack of papers that had yellowed with age. "The way they did their report cards back then is going to come in handy, at least for a couple of the girls."

"How so?"

"I spent some time today reading through the report cards and class schedules, just curious about what subjects they took. What kind of students they were, teacher's comments. You know, general stuff. And basically, what they did was each teacher filled out an individual sheet on the student with their grades, attendance and comments. The teacher's name, class room number, time of day they were in the class, is all listed," he said.

"Are all of them like that? I think we just had the one card when I was in school."

"Mine were like the kind you had. And no, only Annie and Susan had the multiple pages. All the rest are the one piece of paper deal, or card stock. But we do have copies of class schedules for the other girls. So we have most of the same information. It'll just take a little longer to sort through it."

"Are all of the teachers listed for each girl?"

"Yes, and so are coaches, band directors, Girl Scout leaders, neighbors. You name it. Harris put together a pretty thorough list."

"What if we had a spread sheet and could sort by the girls' names and by the people they were in contact with regularly. Do you think you could come up with something that would work?"

"I don't see why not. I could set it up to sort two ways." Jason's eyes looked past Angela as he mentally sorted out the design of the spreadsheet. "Yes, it would work and it wouldn't even have to be anything fancy, just a simple data sort. The only thing that would take some time would be typing in all the names. Mark Harris talked to a lot of people."

"We need a complete list of names anyway. How long do you think it would take?"

"A few hours. How about I start putting the list of names together while you read through some of the stuff I looked at and sorted through today," he said. "First, I'm going to call Aunt Bess and see if she's available to help.""

"Good idea." Angela picked up a folder labeled Annie Walker and began reading. There was nothing that appeared to be outstanding about the little girl other than a couple of notes from teachers. One read: very artistic and imaginative. The other, from her science and math teacher, only said, "Very quiet and well behaved in class. She's an angel."

Annie had done well in both subjects. Angela thought about the poor little girl. It sounded as though she had intelligence and talent that could've one day taken her away from her troubled young life. Instead, she was murdered and never even got to grow up.

Angela looked up. "What'd your aunt say?"

"No problem. She said she occasionally sees some of the teachers she worked with, so she'll be more than happy to do what she can."

"That's great. You know, Jason. I don't think I would have this much to work with if it hadn't been for you. I admit I was initially skeptical, but you've really helped so much."

Jason smiled, he appreciated the complement, but he felt compelled to make a joke. He sometimes wasn't comfortable with complements. "Gee, and I thought you only had me around because you are interested in me."

"I'm serious, Jason."

"Sorry. I know you are, but you probably would've found all this on your own. I just came across it because of researching the school when we were getting ready to start the renovation work."

"Maybe. But I wouldn't have made it to this point so quickly; or Dorothy Danze might've gotten to Betty Harris first."

Jason swept his hair away from his eyes. "Why don't I get my laptop out of my office and start setting up the spreadsheet. You can sit here and prop your feet up and relax while you read."

"Good idea. Let me get some of these files."

"Here, I'll help. While you read, you could write down any names you come across, then I'll check it against the spreadsheet to make sure I didn't miss anyone."

Angela sat down in the armchair with the stack of file folders by her side. There was a throw draped across the arm of the chair. She covered her legs and feet with it. She felt chilled from the air conditioning and hoped she wasn't getting a summer cold. Jason tucked the throw around her feet and smiled, then busied himself on the computer as Angela continued to read.

Angela read the missing person report on Susan Thompson. She had gone missing during the summer between sixth and seventh grade. No reported problems at home; family seemed pretty stable. Out riding her bicycle and didn't come home. The bike was light blue with a white banana seat and a white wicker basket attached to the front handlebars. According to the report, the bike never showed up. Angela knew that probably the killer had somehow managed to take the bike with him or some child found it abandoned and never reported the find.

Susan's report card from Wardlaw wasn't much for a parent to brag about. She made average grades. Mostly B's and C's with a few A's. Her best subject appeared to be music. Susan was in sixth grade band, where they just worked on basics and simple compositions. According to the music teacher's comments, she had a knack for the clarinet and should consider joining chorus. There was an additional written comment underlined at the bottom of her report card for music. The handwriting appeared to be very different. Someone else must have made the notation. It read: "She has the voice of an angel."

It was starting to get late and Angela was tired. Jason, sitting across from her on the sofa continued to work on the spreadsheet. Angela's eyelids felt as if they had tiny weights attached to them. She wanted to close them for just a few minutes, but she knew if she did she would fall asleep, and she couldn't afford to sleep -- not yet. There were more files to read through.

The next file Angela picked up was the one belonging to Patty Franks. At age eleven, she was the youngest of the murdered girls. Patty didn't attend Wardlaw. She was an honor student and seemed to be popular and enjoyed a variety of extracurricular activities. Angela wrote down the names of her teachers, Girl Scout leader, piano teacher, all of whom were women, making them very unlikely suspects. Angela grew more fatigued. Then she listed the name of Patty's softball coach, Jim Hilliard. For some reason that name sounded familiar, but she was too tired to think. Angela closed her eyes and the pin fell from her hand.

"Angela. I did a first pass on the sort. Looks like all the girls who had gone to Wardlaw had basically the same teachers. Looks like the only exception is Paula Groves. She had a different English teacher. The woman's name was Hurst. Probably she replaced someone who retired or transferred to another school or something." Jason paused, waiting for a reply. "Angela?"

He turned to see her asleep in the armchair. She had her head cocked to one side. Jason thought she looked uncomfortable and would probably have a stiff neck if she slept in that position for very long, but he hated to wake her. He knew she was tired and had been under stress.

Jason got up from the sofa and walked over to Angela. As he watched her sleep, his eyes studied the curve of her face. It was oval with prominent cheekbones and just enough tan to give it a healthy glow, even when she was tired. Jason bent down and took the folders from her lap. Just as he tucked the throw up around her shoulders, Angela moved and gave a snort. It startled him and he laughed.

Angela blinked her eyes and turned her head from side to side in a confused and disoriented manner. "Did I fall asleep?"

"Yes." Jason smiled.

"What's so funny? Was I drooling on myself?" Angela wiped the corner of her mouth with her fingers, then inspected them for saliva.

"Not yet, but you did give a big snort."

"Was I snoring?"

"No." Jason gave a mock frown. "Why? Do you usually snore?"

"Not that I've been told, but it's been a while since I had overnight guests." Angela stretched and yawned. "What time is it?"

"It's almost eleven." Jason was now seated on the ottoman. He lifted Angela's feet and placed them in his lap and began to massage them.

Angela closed her eyes. "Umm, that feels good. You found the way to this girl's heart. You better stop before I get too relaxed and fall asleep again."

"That's okay; go ahead and sleep."

"No, I have to go home."

"Home? Are you awake enough to drive?"

"Yes, I'm fine." Angela sat up. Leaning forward she rubbed her eyes.

"I don't have far to drive. My apartment isn't that far away."

"You could stay here."

Angela looked up. "We haven't gotten that far yet."

"I didn't mean like that. I have spare bedrooms, remember."

"That's okay. I need to go home so I can get up and get to work on time tomorrow."

"I could get you up early."

"No. I'm not much of a morning person. It'll be easier on me if I go home now and sleep in my own bed, then get up early."

"Are you sure?"

"Positive." Angela slid her feet into her sneakers then stood up. Checking the pocket of her shorts for her phone, she said, "I think I have everything."

"Can I at least get you some coffee for the road?"

"No, I wouldn't sleep at all if I had any this late."

Jason looked down at the file folders lying around the arm chair. "Do you want to take any of this with you?"

"No, I have copies of all this at the station. I'm pretty wiped out. I'm not doing anything when I get home except go to bed."

"Okay, I'll walk you to your car."

Once in the driveway, Angela opened the door of her car then turned to face Jason. "What're you going to do tomorrow?"

"I have some things I need to do at the office, but I'll call my aunt first and give her the list of teacher's names. I'll see if she can get in touch with some of them. Anything in particular you want asked when we talk to them?"

"Yes, but I'm too tired right now. I can't think."

"Sure you won't stay?"

"I'm sure." As if on impulse, Angela put her arms around Jason's neck. He responded by putting his around her waist. This time their kiss was deep and passionate. She ran her fingers up into his hair as he pulled her body tighter to his. Angela felt her body burning, wanting Jason's. Slowly, reluctantly, she pushed herself away. "Much more of that and I'd stay for breakfast."

"I'd like that."

"You know I promised myself I wouldn't. Not until this case is going somewhere."

"You think we can hold out that long?"

Angela placed her hand on Jason's chest. "No, but I'm going to tell myself we will."

Jason leaned closer. Angela stiffened her arm. "Don't start that again. I need to go home and take a cold shower, alone." She put an emphasis on 'alone'." Angela got into her car. "I'll call tomorrow."

"Would you text me tonight and let me know you got home okay?"

"Jason, I'm a big girl. I have a gun and I catch bad guys, remember."

"You're also a tired big girl. Please, just humor me."

"Okay, I'll text. I promise."

Jason gave Angela one last kiss good night. As she backed out of Jason's driveway and headed down the street, Angela didn't notice the black Lexus parked barely half a block away, or the man sitting inside who had watched their embrace.

Chapter twenty-five

Jason awoke to the sound of his phone ringing.

"Hello."

"Good morning. You sound sleepy."

He recognized Angela's voice. "Huh, oh, good morning."

"Boy, and I thought I wasn't a morning person. I'm sorry, I thought you'd be up by now."

"Good morning, honey. What time is it anyway?"

"It's after seven."

Jason looked at his alarm clock. "I must have forgotten to turn it on."

"Turn on what?"

"My alarm clock."

"Sorry, I woke you up."

"Don't be, I needed to get up. I need to get some stuff done at the office today or Cindy'll be on my ass."

"I need to leave for work in a minute myself. I just wanted to let you know, *The State* ran an article in today's paper about the murders and did a reprint of Mark Harris's articles."

"We knew that was going to happen."

"It also goes on to say that Betty Harris turned over her husband's research to me."

Jason was now more fully awake. "It mentions you by name?"

"Yes. Detective Angela Porter."

"Is that good or bad?"

"It gives me credit for leading the investigation. But at the same time, it blasts the police force for not being clever enough to figure out any of this without the help of a dead reporter's notes."

"I'm sorry."

"Don't be. At least we have our hands on those files before the paper or Dorothy Danze."

"This is true. Anything you want me to do?"

"No. Just get with your aunt. I'm going to see if the Coroner's office has any more dental records tracked down."

"Okay Honey, I'll talk to you later."

Angela sat on the edge of her bed tying her sneaker. "Honey." She said aloud to herself. "One good kiss and he calls me 'Honey'. Probably just that southern man thing." Angela smiled. "But, then again, maybe not."

Angela locked the door of her apartment, then walked to her car. As she laid her brief case in the passenger seat and secured her travel mug of coffee in the cup holder, she scanned the parking lot for any unfamiliar vehicles as was her habit every morning.

Angela tried to keep a mental inventory of tenant's faces and the cars they drove. Her apartment complex gave her a discount on her rent for keeping an eye on the place. This morning many of her neighbors had already left for work leaving the parking lot almost empty. The only thing she noticed was a black Lexus. She hadn't seen the car in the lot before.

She couldn't imagine anyone in her complex being able to afford a Lexus. Could be someone visiting Kim. Kim was a blond who lived upstairs in the building opposite Angela's. Kim had a married boyfriend with a lot of money, and a wife who didn't understand him.

Angela pulled out of her parking space and headed for work.

*****

Jason was almost ready to hang up when he heard his aunt answer.

"Hello Aunt Bess."

"Jason, good morning. What did you think of the news the other night?"

"It was rather general. Not that she wasn't specific with the information she did have. It seemed as if she was trying to sensationalize the story."

"I think that is pretty much standard. I was wondering who her inside

232

source was that she kept mentioning."

"You know, I thought about that and I would guess it might be some-one who worked on the team that recovered the remains."

"I see. You think someone could be selling whatever information they have to the highest bidder?"

"Or someone who just likes to talk. You know how people like to talk." Jason paused for a moment. "Anyway, the reason I'm calling is I need a favor."

"What do you need? I'll help if I can."

"The last couple of days Angela and I have been sorting through Mark Harris's files trying to organize them and see if we could figure out who the likely suspects are."

Jason's aunt interrupted. "So how are things going between you and Angela?"

"Fine."

"What's fine?"

Jason knew there was no use avoiding his aunt's questions. She would continue to ask about Angela until he confessed.

"Actually we've decided we're going to start, sort of, dating." Jason heard his aunt's voice change and take on a playful inquisitive tone.

"What is 'sort of' dating?"

"It's getting to know each other better. But not trying to get serious about anything until we can get something going on this case. We don't want to lose our focus."

"I bet. How long is that going to last?"

"I don't know."

"My guess would be, not long. I think she has the hots for you. And she's easy on the eyes."

Jason smiled. He was always amused by some of his aunt's expres-sions. "Yes she is, Aunt Bess, and she's nice, too. I really do like her."

"I'm glad. I worry about you sometimes. I want you to find someone as good for you as Louise has been for me."

"Let me ask you something. There for a while you were trying to get me to go out with Cindy. Now it's Angela. Why did you switch?"

"I like Cindy, she's a sweet girl, but you didn't seem interested in her.

Now here's Angela, who may be nice too, and who you are interested in. It's as I said, I just want you to find a person who's good for you and with whom you can be happy."

"It's a little too early to tell about Angela, but I'll keep you posted. Anyway, let's get back on track here. The reason I called."

"Oh yes, sorry."

"We've put together a list of names of teachers and other people the girls came in contact with regularly. I'd like you to help me get in touch with the teachers."

"I don't see that many of them anymore."

"I know, but you could help track down some of them and help introduce me to the ones you knew."

"When do you want to do this?"

"As soon as possible."

"As in today?"

"I need to go to the office for a little while, but yes. Actually, I do want to start tracking them down today."

"Do you have a list?"

"Yes."

"If you could email it to me I could look it over. At least fill in the blanks on the ones I know how to reach. I could call my friend at the Superintendent's office and get the rest of them. That is, if they're still teaching in South Carolina."

"That would be a big help. What are you doing later?"

"I'll be home until about eleven. I'm meeting Louise for lunch. She's showing a house in Forest Acres so we're going to Pasta Fresca. Why don't you join us?"

"That sounds good. Would you mind if I bring Angela along?"

"Not at all. I'd like to see her again, especially since she has my favorite nephew's attention." Again Jason heard the tone of his aunt's voice change to playful. He chose to ignore her comment.

"I'll email the names to you in a few minutes. See you later." Jason laid the phone down on the night stand, then picked up Sebastian and walked into the bathroom to start the water for his shower.

Angela's day wasn't starting off as well as she had hoped. Dorothy Danze was waiting for her in the parking lot. Angela ignored her requests for an interview and simply stated that the police department wasn't prepared to make a statement at this time. The scene in the station wasn't any better.

"Porter, get in here," her Captain yelled from down the hall when he saw her enter the office corridor.

"Yes sir." Angela's stomach suddenly felt the way it did when she was being scolded as a child.

"Did you see *The State* this morning?"

"If you're talking about the article on the Wardlaw investigation, then, yes sir, I have."

"Of course, I'm talking about that! It looks like the lid is about to come off this case. I've had the Mayor and the Chief of Police call me before I could even sit down. We've also had lawyers representing the parents of the three girls that have been positively identified contact me. They want to know why over forty years passed, since the first child disappeared, before we figured this out. And, why didn't we do something when the articles first appeared in the paper thirty years ago." There was a momentary pause. "Where the hell is Randall Evans, anyway?"

"I don't know, Sir, I just got here."

"Well. Do you have anything yet? I noticed you didn't work late last night."

"Actually, I was going through some of my notes trying to organize information."

"I see. And what did you organize?" Frank Morris had a "shoot-from-the-hip" style, which was frustrating to Angela at best. Angela's assessment of him was – if you had someone draw a gun on you, then Frank was a good person to have by your side, because he thought fast on his feet. But if you needed strategy and planning, then you were on your own.

"I've put together a list of names of people who came in contact with each of the girls."

The Captain's voice was now calmer. "Where'd you get the names?"

"From Mark Harris's notes."

"Have you verified the accuracy of his notes?"

"I'm doing that with the information as I go. We were able to come up with possible identities for three of the girls from the information in his notes, and the news articles. Those have proven to be correct. The forensic report confirmed those identities. I've also given Forensics possible identifications for the other four. Brazell has his people tracking down dental records on the remaining victims."

"Where'd you get the names for the other victims?"

"From the notes. I ran into Brazell during lunch yesterday and he said they had the dental records tracked down for two more of the missing girls and …" Angela looked at her watch. "I would think if he got them yesterday, then they would know something by now."

"You had lunch with Brazell?"

"No, I just ran in to him. Like I said, he should have something by now, if he received the medical records."

Captain Morris cut her off before she could finish. "I'm going to get him on the phone.

Angela knew Frank Morris and Doug Brazell had a good working relationship, but a bystander wouldn't have known from his tone.

"I'm going to call him and see where they're at on this." Before he could pick up the phone Randall Evans walked in.

"Where the hell have you been?"

Randall was visibly caught off guard. "Checking out the accident report from Mark Harris's car wreck."

Frank raised his shoulders and held his hands out slightly indicating he didn't know what Evans was talking about, but wanted to be informed.

"Mark Harris, the guy whose notes we're using. He was killed in a car wreck several years ago."

"Not too long after his last article on the missing girls ran in *The State*," Angela added.

"And?" Frank indicated he wanted still more information.

Evans continued, "Seems that Harris's widow told Porter here, that her brother-in-law, Bob, didn't think the accident looked right. He said there was something funny about it."

"Okay. And Bob is an expert in what?" Frank asked in a sarcastic tone.

"Bob used to own Bobby's Wrecker Service. He's seen a lot of car wrecks and he said this one looked funny. Like maybe he was forced off the road or something."

"Well, what'd you find?"

"I talked to Bob. He said he had some pictures of the car. It had paint on the side like it'd been hit."

"Have you seen the pictures?"

"No. He said he would try to find them. Anyway, I got a copy of the accident report and I managed to track down the officer who worked the scene. He said nothing looked unusual to him, as best he could remember."

"What'd you think?" Frank asked.

"Well, I haven't seen these pictures of Bob's yet. It was late at night on a two-lane road that he wasn't familiar with. The guy could have either got off the shoulder and lost control or fell asleep."

"Why does Bob think someone ran his brother off the road? It was his brother right?"

"No, Mark Harris was his brother-in-law. He said that Mark was about to figure out who killed those girls. He thought it was somebody with important connections and they had him killed to shut him up."

Frank put his hands on his hips and rolled his eyes. "Could be that he just can't accept the fact that his brother-in-law fell asleep at the wheel and got killed. This ain't no god damn soap opera; it's just some sick bastard killing children. Unfortunately, it ain't the first serial killer we've had around here." Frank paused and looked down at his desk. "Follow through on that, but unless something jumps out at you, don't waste much time on it. I think our best bet at this point is just to confirm the identities of the victims and start talkin' to people on Porter's list."

"List?" Evans knitted his eyebrows.

"Porter's been working overtime. She has a list of people that came in contact with the girls. That is, assuming the remains match with the information Mark Harris had in his files."

Evans spoke up; he didn't want Angela to get one up on him. "Did anyone stop to think that this Mark Harris guy could have killed those kids himself?"

Angela and the Captain looked at each other. Angela quickly retorted, "I don't think the dates and times are right for him to have done it." She paused, seeing the questioning looks of her two colleagues.

"The first girl disappeared in 1967. If the identities prove out, then the last one disappeared in 1982. Harris was what, maybe eighteen in 1967, and he's from Camden. He would have to get to Columbia and find the opportunity."

"It's not impossible. He would just need a car."

With his hands on his hips standing like a gun fighter waiting for the draw, Frank Morris directed his question at Angela. "Have you checked him out?"

"No but…"

Morris cut her off. "Randall, while you're checking on the car, look into Harris's background. See what you can find out. Maybe he killed these kids and was writing these articles to get attention or point the finger at somebody else."

"I'm on it."

Morris turned to Angela. "I think that's a good idea of yours to put together a list of people who came in contact with the girls. Most serial killers don't know their victims. They work off opportunity. Keep working on it. Something might turn up."

"Is that it, boss?" Randall asked. He was clearly proud of himself for posing the Mark Harris theory.

Angela felt as if she were being pushed off the case. "Frank, I thought you were going to let me lead this investigation. I mean I've gotten us this far."

"I know, but I've got everybody starting to breathe down my neck on this. There're other detectives with more experience on murder investigations than you've got. If I leave you in charge, then it'll look like I'm not giving this priority."

Morris nodded to Randall. "Why don't you go ahead and get on that and let me know what you find out." When Randall Evans exited the room Frank Morris again turned his attention to Angela, who immediately began speaking.

"You said if I came up with some leads then I could have the case.

Well, I did. We wouldn't have names for any of them if it weren't for me finding those articles." The tone in Angela's voice showed that she was clearly frustrated and Morris noticed it.

"You're right. And you're still on the case. Frankly, this one is so old, if it wasn't Harris who did it, then I don't think we'll ever solve it. But I'm not letting this department take any heat for not doing everything it can to get some justice for the families of those children."

Angela looked her Captain in the eye. "When someone is dead, there's never any justice. You can't give them back their lives."

Morris was surprised by her comment. He tended to think of justice in terms of catching the criminal and seeing them punished, not compensation for the victim.

"You might be right, but our job is to catch them and lock them up. I'll save the morality part for God." Both were silent for what felt like a long moment, then Morris spoke again.

"Look, Angela, you're a good detective, but you don't have any experience with anything like this. Now, you have some good information there." He looked down at the list of names in her hand. "Start tracking people down, you may find something there."

Angela knew she was being dismissed and she felt as if her Captain had just told her he didn't have confidence in her. Right now she wasn't sure she had confidence in herself. She hadn't found the news articles; Jason had approached her with them. She hadn't pieced together clues; a dead reporter had. With her list of names, Angela walked down the short hallway to the stairs leading to the basement and her office to begin making phone calls and track down the people on her list.

Chapter twenty-six

When Jason arrived at his office both Cindy and Roger were, for lack of a better term, buzzing over the morning news and the article in *The State*. Roger was the first to greet Jason. "Man, did you see the paper this morning?"

"Yeah, what about it?" Jason tried to act as if he didn't know what Roger's question was in reference to.

"The Wardlaw articles. It's all over the front page."

"Yeah, I know. Wesley called me yesterday and told me to expect it."

"Aren't you pissed? I thought he'd promised he would keep this quiet?" Now Cindy had entered the room and took a position beside Roger. She listened to the exchange and waited for an opportunity to add her opinion.

"He did, but he said he could only keep it quiet so long. He has a job to do and I guess they didn't want the TV stations getting one up on them."

"I still think they shouldn't have run the story." Cindy was now in the conversation.

"Why?" Jason asked. "Dorothy Danze has been blasting it all over the airwaves for days now. At least this way, Mark Harris gets some credit for what he found years ago." Jason thought for a moment. For several days he had wrestled with telling his friends he was working with a detective on the case, but he wasn't sure how they would take it. Would they expect him to share everything he knew and then be upset when he didn't?

"So, have you found anything else?" Roger asked.

Jason inhaled a large breath of air, making his shoulders rise and fall as he exhaled. He knitted his eyebrows and swept his hand back through his hair. "No nothing."

Cindy looked at Jason. He could tell Cindy didn't believe him. But he knew, for Angela's sake, no one could know they were secretly working together.

"I know I haven't been putting in enough time here at the office lately. I'll talk to you all later. I have some catching up to do." With that, Jason exited the room. He knew he would be spending even more time out of the office in the next few days while he helped track down and interview former Wardlaw teachers.

When Jason finally noticed the time, it was almost noon. If he didn't hurry he'd be late for his lunch date with his aunt and Louise. Just as he picked up his messenger bag, his phone rang. He saw Angel's name appear on the screen. An instant smile came to his face. "Hello Angela, how has your day been?"

"Not worth shit!" Was the reply from the other end of the line.

"What's wrong?"

"Morris and Randall Evans."

"Why don't you meet me for lunch? You can tell me what happened. I'm going to meet my Aunt Bess and Louise." It took only a little coaxing to persuade Angela. She wanted to see Jason as much as she wanted to get out of the station for a break.

When Angela arrived at the restaurant, Jason, his aunt, and Louise were already seated at a table at the far end of the room, away from the other patrons. She knew her mood showed on her face, but she didn't care. Frank Morris had made her feel like a little girl being dismissed to the back yard to play, while the grown-ups did their grown-up things. Seeing Jason made her mood lift only slightly.

After a quick glance at the menu, Angela ordered a salad, as did Bess. Jason chose a club sandwich and Louise went for the daily special.

The three gave Angela time to vent her frustrations. Jason wanted to do something to help, but there was nothing he could do other than listen and help track down information.

After Angela had finished, Bess shifted the conversation to her search for the teachers. "Here you go, Angela. Here's the phone numbers of about fifteen of the teachers on the list."

Angela was shocked. She hadn't expected so many so quickly.

"How did you get all of these?"

Bess took a drink of iced tea and then began to explain. "It really wasn't that hard. There are about four of them that I still see from time to time. Some are on Facebook, one teaches at Benedict College, so all I had to do was just call their information number. The others I got just by calling my friend at the superintendent's office. So that leaves about nine or ten still unaccounted for."

"This will really help speed things up." Angela scanned the list. "Let's see, there are three Wardlaw teachers you don't have."

Bess leaned over and pointed to the names. "I should have made a notation here. Janice Hopper died, I think about five years ago, of cancer. And Mr. Tipton, I'm not sure what happened to him. I think he may have retired and moved to Georgia. Let's see, there's one more. Oh yes, Jim Hilliard. I don't know where he is, but I think he still lives in Columbia.

Angela knitted her eyebrows. For some reason that name stood out. "What's his story? Is he still teaching?"

Bess considered the question. "Honey, at our ages, everyone has retired or died." Bess pointed to a name on the list. "I run into Liz Ivins periodically. She was the librarian at Wardlaw. That gave her a lot of time to wander around the school and keep up with everyone else. Anyway, whenever I see, her she fills me in on all the teachers who were there when I was there, and what they are doing now."

Jason and Angela looked at each other. "She sounds like a good one to talk to," Angela said with a positive tone in her voice.

"Anyway," Bess continued. "I believe she said Mr. Hilliard had to leave teaching because of some kind of nerve problem."

"You mean something neurological?" Angela asked.

"'Nerve problem' is the term they used years ago for anxiety or stress. I don't know. He always seemed a little odd. But who knows, it's easy to get burned out teaching. Especially when you volunteer to help out with as many clubs and extracurricular activities as he did."

"He did a lot of activities outside school?"

"Yes, I looked back through the old year books this morning. You know, the ones I showed you," Bess nodded to Jason. "I wanted to jog

243

my memory on who some of these people were and what they taught. He sponsored the math club, or was it science club? I don't remember now. Anyway, he helped with band, too, and I think he did some stuff in the summer with the ball leagues."

"Was he the only teacher that did all of these activities?"

"Oh gosh, no. When you're a teacher you always have to help with something. Bake sales, field trips, help coach a sport, because they need another adult there, even if you don't know how to play."

"What about the other teachers? Could you tell me what they did? What kinds of activities, clubs. A little bit about them."

"I can try." Bess went down the list of names. She was only able to provide sketchy information about the teachers she worked with while she was at Wardlaw. Classes they taught, how they interacted with their students, and what clubs they sponsored, was about the extent of it. There were a few she had kept in touch with. For those she had a little more information – children, married, single, and a little about their personalities. There were a few teachers she knew through mutual friends. For these she had some information, primarily through Facebook.

Angela took notes and asked questions while Bess continued to talk. Jason and Louise listened. Angela didn't set her pin down until Bess could recall no new information regarding her former colleagues.

"That's about all I can remember. I hope it helps."

"The state police, SLED, are preparing a profile for us. I'll take this information and compare it to the profile and see if anyone is a likely match."

Louise, who had finished her chicken wings and was wiping her fingers with a moist wipe, asked, "Do any of these sound like a potential suspect."

Angela looked at her note pad and list of names. "Honestly, I just don't know. I don't really know much about serial killers other than what I've read. Statistically, most serial killers are heterosexual males of European descent, which means almost every man on the list. At least there aren't a lot of male teachers on the list. Most of the teachers were women."

"Do you still want me to contact these people?" Jason asked.

"Yes, definitely. We still need to talk to everyone."

"Is Randall Evans going to talk to some of these also?"

Angela frowned. "No. That's the rest of the story. He came up with the idea that Mark Harris could be the killer and was writing the article as a way of getting attention."

Jason, Louise, and Bess were silent. They looked at each other, then at Angela. Jason was shocked; the thought had never crossed his mind that the person whose notes he was reading and was hailing as brilliant for discovering the connection between the disappearances, was actually the killer. It was also obvious to Jason that Angela had already dismissed this theory and was angry because her Captain accepted it as a possibility. To Jason it sounded plausible, but he didn't what to question Angela. Right now she needed his support.

Fortunately, Louise asked for him. "Did you look at him as a suspect?"

Jason watched Angela's face as it changed.

"No, I didn't look at him. I don't think it's necessary. Randall and my Captain are wasting time. They're only looking at Mark Harris because it's the simplest solution." Angela swirled the ice cubes in her glass before she took a drink of tea.

Louise continued. "When did the murders stop?"

"I don't know that they did," Angela retorted. "All I know is Mark Harris wasn't alive to find a connection between these and any others."

"But there are only seven bodies."

Angela was becoming defensive. "The guy could still be killing kids right now, but just doing it somewhere else." Angela looked down at her note pad and folded it closed, then slid the clip of the pin under the cover securing it to the pad.

"I'm sorry. I didn't mean to offend you or question your judgment," Louise began. "I was just asking questions."

"It's okay. I'm used to having everything I do questioned."

Jason now felt he needed to come to the defense of Louise, but still be supportive of Angela. "Angela, Louise didn't mean anything by it. From what you've said about him, it sounds like Randall was just trying to suck up to your Captain. He wants to be the hero."

Jason could see that, even though Angela appeared calmer, she was still bristling. Angela swirled the ice cubes in her glass again then rubbed the bridge of her nose with her thumb and index finger.

"Louise, I shouldn't have been so defensive. I've just been second guessing myself all morning. I just keep asking myself why I didn't eliminate Mark Harris first"

Bess, who had been quietly watching Angela, now spoke. "Dear, there must be something that stood out to make you not consider this reporter as a suspect. You appear to me to be too thorough in your work to just overlook something."

Angela was softening. "I don't know." She shook her head, "I don't know. I just know it has to be someone listed in his files."

Bess straightened in her chair and took a more upright posture. "Then you have to find them, don't you."

"Yes, I do."

Bess waived for the waitress. "Well then, we're wasting time here, aren't we? Louise, you have another house to show and Jason and I have some phone calls to make and people to see."

A look of confidence began returning to Angela's face. "And I have to get with the Coroner and Professor Russell on the I.D. of the other remains, then check with SLED on that profile."

Louise took the check. She insisted, since she had just sold a home for over three hundred thousand and, as the listing agent, she was going to make a hefty commission.

Once back at the station, Angela searched out Debbie Amick, the young desk officer who was always so eager to be of assistance. "Debbie, could you help me with something, please?" Angela smiled. Debbie was caught off guard and almost dropped the folders she was carrying.

"Huh, sure anything. Whatever you need."

Angela smiled again. "If I give you a social security number could you track down the person's current address for me?"

"Are they in state or out-of-state?"

"I don't know. Will that matter?"

"Not really. Do you want me to do it now?"

"If you're not too busy."

"Oh no, not at all. Anything for you. I huh, I mean, to help out."

Angela handed Debbie a folded piece of notebook paper. On it was the social security number of Peggy Anderson, the number Bess had gotten for her.

Debbie took the paper, then turned to face her computer screen. Angela watched as the young officer quickly pulled up the appropriate screens. She was good on the computer.

"Okay, here we go." Debbie recited the numbers to herself as she typed them. "Two five zero...." Her voice trailed off. "Enter. Now we just have to wait a minute."

Angela knew Debbie was nervous with her sitting there leaning against her desk so she engaged the woman in some light conversation. Just as Debbie began to become more relaxed, the screen flashed the name and address. "Here we go. Margaret L. Anderson of Cleveland, Ohio."

"Cleveland. Are you sure that's the right one?"

"Social security number is the same."

"Can you print that out for me?"

Debbie clicked the mouse. "It's on its way to the printer now." Debbie hesitated for a moment. "What are you trying to track her down for?"

"If this is the same Peggy Anderson I'm looking for, then she was the best friend of one of the murdered girls."

"Really?"

"Yes."

"You think she might know something?"

"It has been a long time. But I have to look at everything. Most people don't remember things correctly after that long."

"Sometimes I think I'd like to work my way up to detective, but I don't know if I can do it."

"You mean be a detective?"

"Yeah, it seems pretty hard."

"Don't sell yourself short. If you want it bad enough, you can do it. You'll always have doubts. Some mornings I wake up and wonder if I can do it."

Angela could tell Debbie was surprised to hear that she, too, had self-doubts. Angela patted Debbie's shoulder in a friendly gesture of encouragement, then thanked her for the help and left for her own office. Once downstairs in the confines of the small room, she googled a phone number for Margaret Anderson in Cleveland, Ohio. There was M. Anderson, a M. L. Anderson, and a M. C. Anderson.

Angela wrote down the numbers and dialed the number for M. L. Anderson. A man answered.

"Hello. Is this the residence of a Margaret or Peggy Anderson.

"No. This is Mitch," responded the deep male voice.

"Sorry, I have the wrong number." Angela dialed the second number. An answering machine with a woman's voice answered. "Hello, I'm sorry I couldn't come to the phone, but if you leave your name, number and a brief message I'll return your call as soon as possible." Angela hung up without leaving a message. "Who uses answering machines anymore? Someone from that age group," she answered aloud. Angela wrote the number and address in her note pad so it wouldn't be misplaced.

While Jason and his Aunt contacted former teachers, Angela placed phone calls to anyone else on her list of names for which she could locate phone numbers. A couple of the older ones were deceased and for a few, she had Debbie track down motor vehicle records. Most of the people she spoke with remembered the girls but could recall little else. Angela scribbled notes beside each name to indicate if she still needed to contact the person, or if she had made contact and thought they were a potential source of information worthy of a face-to-face meeting.

Finally, just before going off duty, Angela received the call she had been waiting for. It was Brazell. He confirmed the identities of the remaining girls. And now the grim task of officially contacting the surviving parents, or other family members to confirm that their daughters or loved ones had been buried on the Wardlaw playground. Angela took off her reading glasses, rubbed her eyes and then straightened her shoulders. She could feel the tension setting in. She thought of Jason and wondered if he had made any progress.

As Angela exited the police station, she was met by Dorothy Danze.

"Detective Porter could you give me the status of your investigation?

Have the police come up with any new leads?"

"I'm sorry; no comment at this time."

"Detective, my sources tell me that the former reporter for *The State,* Mark Harris, had linked together seven disappearances, and now all seven have been identified as the girls found on the Wardlaw school grounds. Would you like to comment on that, Detective?"

Angela stopped dead in her tracks. She was completely caught off guard by Dorothy Danze having the information on the identities of the bodies so quickly.

"I told you I have no comment at this time. Now if you'll excuse me." Angela pushed past Dorothy and her cameraman.

Having securely locked herself in her car, she hit her hand on the steering wheel. "Damn it!" She called Jason as she pulled out of the parking lot.

Angela told Jason all the girls had now been positively identified. Mark Harris was right. She also told him about her brief encounter with Dorothy Danze. As they talked and Angela drove toward Jason's house, she didn't see the black Lexus that had pulled into traffic behind her as she left the station.

Once at Jason's she took off her gun and laid it on the counter top, then sitting on one of the barstools, she removed her sneakers and began rubbing her feet. "I haven't been for a run in days and I'm starting to feel like a slug."

Jason was staring at the gun. "I know what you mean. I usually run at least every other day, but lately, I haven't made time for it."

"You run? With your asthma?"

"Yes, it doesn't bother me that much. At least not like what you saw that evening at the school when I met you at your car and then had an attack."

Angela noticed Jason looking at the gun. "Does the gun bother you?"

"No, it's just big."

"It's a nine millimeter."

"I could tell. My father has guns. One more thing he and I don't agree on. I don't think private citizens should be allowed to own guns. Only law enforcement officials. He, on the other hand, is a card carrying NRA member. He thinks he should be able to deer hunt with a bazooka if he wants."

Angela raised her eyebrows and laughed. "I'd like to get guns off the street, but there are so many in this country now that I don't know if there are any good answers at this point. Anyway, how did you and Bess do?"

"We had some hits and misses. There were three teachers we couldn't reach and one was deceased. But of the ones we did talk to – they all remembered the girls. Some remembered them better than others. With Annie, Susan, and Patty, the ones who disappeared longer ago, the people we spoke with couldn't remember as much; but I would expect that, wouldn't you?"

Angela nodded in agreement. "Anything significant?"

"Not really. Just more general stuff."

"The teacher that was deceased, was it a man or woman?"

"Woman. That was the one my aunt mentioned."

"Who weren't you able to find?"

"Jim Hilliard, Bernice Boyd and Dick Johnson."

"Where did they teach?"

"Let's see," Jason opened his note pad. "Hilliard was at Wardlaw, Boyd was at Hand Middle School, and Johnson was at Heyward Gibbs."

Angela was surprised. "So you got through all the teachers at all the schools?"

"Yep. The one's we couldn't reach by phone, we just went to their houses."

"That's great. Did anyone know how to get in touch with the others?"

"One woman we talked to said she thought Bernice Boyd was living in Virginia with her daughter. She's retired of course."

"We can track her down through retirement checks."

"Dick Johnson, we're still looking for. Bess is contacting her friend at the superintendent's office to try to get a social security number for him. A librarian at Heyward Gibbs said she remembered him. He was a teacher when she was a student there and she said someone told her he had moved out of state. And no one has a clue what happened to Jim Hilliard."

"Is Bess checking on a social security number for him also?"

"Yes, she'll get all three."

"That's great. That will help, hopefully."

Jason's voice now took on a more somber tone. "Have you contacted the families of the girls?"

Angela sighed. "Not yet. I guess I'll do that tomorrow."

"Would you like me to go with you?"

"You can't. This will be an official police call. Not that I wouldn't prefer you be there instead of Randall." Jason took Angela's hand in his.

"If I can help in any way, let me know."

"I will. This will be awful you know. At least now they can stop wondering if their children are still alive somewhere."

Jason and Angela were both silent for a moment, each contemplating how it must feel to have a loved one, a child, lost all those years only to learn they had lain in a shallow, unmarked grave, posed like a sleeping angel. Angela broke the silence. "It's just so sad. I was looking at an old yearbook I had from middle school. We just looked like babies. How could someone hurt an innocent child like that?"

Jason, sitting with his fingers still entwined in Angela's, shook his head. "I don't know. I don't know how anyone could hurt an animal either, for that matter."

Angela pushed a loose strand of hair back behind her ear with her free hand. "You know, that's the age just before they start growing up. They're still so impressionable, so innocent. In some ways they are like little angels."

Jason began to tell Angela about the dream he had a few nights before, where his brother was in the Wardlaw classroom, but Angela didn't hear him. She was focusing on her own words. Something she said had a familiar ring, but she wasn't sure why. She interrupted Jason. "Did you hear what I said a minute ago?"

Jason realized she hadn't been listening. "Yes, but said about what?"

"About the children being angels."

"Yes, I heard it. What about it?" Jason knitted his eyebrows.

"Someone else called them angels."

Angela stood up and turned to face Jason. "Someone made a reference to the girls as angels."

"Was it someone you talked to?"

"Let me see here." Angela walked to her computer bag which was leaning against the edge of the bar. "I know I made a note about this."

Jason watched as Angela scanned first one page of her note pad then another. "Here, here it is."

Angela began to read aloud to Jason. "It was Tina Graham."

Jason shrugged. He didn't recognize the name.

"She is one of Professor Russell's students. She worked on the excavation of the grave sites."

Jason suddenly remembered her. "I remember now. What did she say?"

"I'm getting to that. I wanted to talk to her because she was the one who actually noticed the six additional graves and alerted the rest of the team. When they were removing the remains, she made the statement to me that all of them were posed in the same way."

"What do you mean?"

"All of them were laid in their graves exactly the same way. Annie was the only one who had any clothing or other artifacts with her, but they were all lying on their sides in a semi-fetal position their hands together and in front of their face. Tina Graham commented that they were lying there, as if in a pose. A pose you often see in photographs or on cards of sleeping children. They make them up to look like angels."

"She said they looked like angels?"

"No, that was just what she used to describe the pose they were in."

"So, how does this help?" Jason asked.

"We'll compare it to what the state police, SLED, says in their profile of the killer. Then compare it to the backgrounds of the people we have on our list. Maybe something will jump out at us."

"When do you get the profile?"

"I'll have it in the morning."

"Is there anything else you want to work on tonight?"

"Not really. I do want to try to contact Peggy Anderson again. Do you mind?"

"No, of course not."

Angela again seated herself on the barstool beside Jason and turned to the page where she had written the phone number of Margaret L. Anderson. "I tried her today while I was at the station, but no one was home."

Jason listened. He could hear the phone ringing. Angela was almost ready to give up when she heard a sudden voice on the other end.

"Hello."

"Ah hello. Is this Margaret Anderson?"

"Yes it is, and if you're selling something, I'm not interested."

"No, I'm not selling anything. Did you at one time live in Columbia, South Carolina?"

There was a momentary pause. "Yes. Who is this?"

"I'm sorry to bother you Ms. Anderson, but my name is Detective Angela Porter with the Columbia Police Department and…" Before Angela could say another word, Margaret Anderson had interrupted her.

"Has something happened?"

"No ma'am, I just need to ask a couple of questions about an old case that I'm looking into that you might be able to provide some information on."

"I haven't lived in Columbia since high school. I don't know what I could help you with."

"If I could just ask a couple questions…"

"Alright, but please make it quick. I was just on my way out."

"Did you go by the name Peggy when you were a young girl?"

"Yes. I still do. That's why I thought you were a phone solicitor. No one who knows me calls me Margaret."

"Were you a student at Wardlaw Junior High in 1967?"

"That sounds about right. I did go to Wardlaw. Yes, I think sixty seven is one of the years I was there."

"Were you friends with a girl by the name of Annie Walker?" There was silence on Peggy's end. "Hello, Ms. Anderson. Did you hear my question?"

"Why are you asking about Annie? How do I know you're a police detective?

"Ms. Anderson, I am a police detective. If you like I can give you may badge number and you can call the station to confirm that I am who I say I am." Angela paused.

"Go ahead," Peggy replied.

"The old police reports state that Annie Walker ran away from home."

"Annie did not run away from home. You people asked me about her then, but you wouldn't listen to me."

Angela could hear the pain and anger in Peggy's voice. "I can't change the mistakes the officers may have made back then, but I'm listening now."

"Why are you asking me about her now?"

"I hate to be the one to tell you this now, but Annie Walker has been found."

"Oh my god! Is she…" Peggy's voice trailed off.

"I'm sorry, but her remains have been positively identified. We believe she was murdered."

"Oh god, no. How? When?"

"We don't know that for sure. We found an identification bracelet with her remains. She appeared to be wearing it on her wrist at the time she was buried. Your name was on the bracelet and there was an inscription on the back."

"It said 'Happy birthday,' didn't it," Peggy blurted out.

"Yes. Was it yours?"

"Yes. All the kids had them. My parents gave me the bracelet for my birthday the year before."

"Why did Annie have your bracelet?"

"I'm sorry, Detective. I really can't talk right now."

"But I need to ask you some questions."

"I sorry. I just can't right now."

Angela heard Peggy hang up the phone and then, only the sound of a dial tone. Angela laid down the phone and, bending her head downward slightly, closed her eyes as she rubbed her temples. "I'm getting a headache."

"Can I get you something?" Jason asked with concern. He had heard her describe how bad her headaches could get.

Angela looked up and, taking Jason's hands in hers, gave him a light kiss on the lips. "No, I think I just need to go home and get some sleep. Maybe eat something and then sleep it off before it turns into a migraine."

"I could fix something for you here."

"No, it's okay. I'm just tired and I hate having to tell people someone is dead."

"How did she sound?"

"I could hear her voice cracking like she was starting to cry. She said the police talked to her when Annie first disappeared, but there was nothing in the old report about it."

"Shouldn't they put everything in the report?"

"Technically, yes, but no one does. Officers always keep their own notes. Notes that are separate from what gets officially filed. Maybe I should track down the investigating officer, if he is still alive after all these years."

"Couldn't hurt."

"No, it couldn't. And maybe you could talk to your aunt again and see if she remembers anything else about the disappearance, or about Annie and Peggy."

"Do you want to work on anything tonight?"

"No, I just want to go home. I'm tired. Being pissed off all day takes a lot of energy out of me."

Jason smiled. He found Angela's comments like that one amusing. Jason had noticed a gradual shift in his focus regarding the Wardlaw case. He seemed to find himself thinking less about his brother Tommy and his family, and more about Angela and his desire to help her and simply spend time with her. She was beautiful, intelligent, and could be funny. He had dated several women over the years, but Angela was different. His feelings for her were different than what he had experienced in the past.

Angela's voice broke his train of thought. "I'm going to try to talk to Peggy Anderson again tomorrow. Maybe even try to get her down here. And I'll get Debbie to track down our three missing teachers."

"Debbie?" Jason questioned.

"She's an officer at the station. She's young and can find anything on the Internet. I think she has a little crush on me."

"A crush?" Jason was surprised. "At least she has good taste."

Angela returned his smile. "Don't worry, I already have my eye on you." Angela gave Jason another quick kiss. "Now I do need to go, but I will take a couple Tylenol, if you have any."

"They're upstairs in my bathroom, I'll be right back."

While she waited, Angela's eyes surveyed the kitchen. With the exception of some papers spread across one side of the countertop, everything was very tidy. The kitchen was spacious, but not too big. She wondered if Jason was normally this neat or did his cleaning lady keep it in this condition.

Jason returned with the Tylenol and Angela washed them down with water. "Okay, time to go."

"I'll walk you to your car."

The night air was damp from the humidity and still no rain in the forecast. Jason watched Angela's car drive away and watched as the brake lights illuminated as she pulled to a stop at the sign at the corner, then took a right onto the next street, which would lead out of his neighborhood. He had wanted her to stay. Jason stood in his driveway and looked up into the night sky. There were only a few stars visible. The lights from Columbia obscured most of them from view. As Jason turned to go inside, two houses down, he saw a black Lexus pull away from the curb, turn its lights on and then drive to the corner then make the same turn to the right.

He cast only a passing glance at the car and the driver, noting it was a white man, but not someone he recognized. He gave it no further notice other than to think to himself that he hadn't seen someone come out of either the Martin's house or Mr. Boone's house and get in the car. Probably they had gotten in the car while he was kissing Angela good night.

"I guess the neighbors will have something to talk about now," he said to himself, as he walked up his driveway and went inside.

Chapter twenty-seven

When Angela arrived home, all she could think about was her conversation with Peggy Anderson. Peggy had to remember something that would help. She would try again tomorrow. Try to get Peggy to talk to her. As Angela walked up the stairs to her apartment, she made a mental list of what she needed to do the next day. She would start with Debbie. Have her track down the teachers Jason and his aunt weren't able to locate. Then try to track down coaches, ministers, Sunday school teachers; anyone else who was left on the list. Compare the people they had talked to with the SLED profile and – what she was dreading most – talk to the parents and tell them the identities of their long missing children had been confirmed. She knew she was stuck with that assignment because she was the woman on the case. But, better her than Randall Evans. He had the sensitivity of a slug.

As Angela started to insert her door key into the deadbolt lock, the door opened slightly. Angela remained still, more out of surprise than fear. Her mind raced. Had she pulled the door securely closed when she left that morning? Yes, she remembered double checking it. Had maintenance been in? Possibly, but they were supposed to call at least a day in advance. Had the exterminators come to spray? No, it wasn't the end of the quarter; they weren't due for two more months. Had someone broken into her apartment, and if so, were they still there?

Angela backed away from the door. She pulled her nine-millimeter from its holster and slowly pushed open the door. The apartment was dark with the exception of the light from the DVR. With her left hand Angela reached to her side and flipped up the light switch. A small end table lamp came on casting a dim light over the living room. Angela's eyes scanned the room. There didn't appear to be anything missing, but something about the room looked out of place. Had she come home in the middle of a robbery? Again the question, were they still in her apartment?

Angela stepped into the living room and moved sideways to her left so that she could get a better view across to the kitchen. All clear, as was the small balcony, which was off the living room. Next was the hallway leading to the two bedrooms. It couldn't have been more than twelve feet long, but now it might as well have been a mile, and as dark as a cave.

Angela started first with her bedroom. She readied herself, then flipped the light witch. Nothing! Her heart was still racing, Angela kept an eye on the bedroom door to ready herself in the event that someone was still in the back room and tried to make a break for the open front door. Walk-in closet and master bath were all clear. Now for the hall bath and the back bedroom. Angela first checked the hall bath. She was glad she had forgotten and left the shower curtain pushed back when she cleaned the tub a few days ago. The scene from Psycho flashed in her head, only this time it would be reversed with someone behind the curtain coming from out of the tub after her.

All that was left was the back bedroom that doubled as a spare bedroom, and her office. Angela readied her nine-millimeter. As she hit the light switch, she saw papers strewn across the room and the drawers to the file cabinet hanging open. She checked the closet. No one here! The apartment was clear. Whoever had broken in had either found what they were looking for, or found nothing and left.

Angela returned her pistol to its holster, then stood looking around the room. She was careful not to touch anything. Better to call for a uniformed officer, have photos taken and file a report. If anything were missing she'd need the report for insurance.

She called Jason from her cell phone while she waited for the officers to arrive. He was insistent about her not spending the night in her apartment, or that he would come over there. She told him "no." Even though she was certain she had locked her door, somehow she must be mistaken. Probably just neighborhood kids passing through and trying doorknobs.

As Angela sat on the edge of her sofa, still careful not to touch anything, she began visually scanning the room, trying to identify anything that might be missing. The more Angela looked around the room, the less she believed what she had told Jason. As a uniformed officer, she had worked an office break-in where they were looking for information – not equipment or valuables.

Papers on her coffee table had been sifted through and some were left scattered on the floor by the sofa. The drawer in the bottom of her entertainment center was open and the DVDs had been removed and tossed to one side. Angela stood up and walked the half dozen steps it took to cross the small living room. Everything had been moved, but nothing was missing.

She then walked down the short hall to the spare room. When she had first entered the room, she was more concerned about who might be waiting inside. Now, as she stood there with her hands on her hips, what she saw finally registered. Whoever had broken into her apartment had searched through her personal files and from the looks of her desktop, probably her laptop as well.

"Damn it." Her first fear was that they had wiped out or corrupted her hard drive. The second monitor was turned off, but the power light on the laptop was still lit. Her first impulse was to turn on the computer to see what damage had been done. No, she had to wait. The mouse and the power button could be a good source of prints. She thought it was strange that they didn't just take the laptop.

Angela turned quickly when she heard the doorbell. It was probably the uniformed officers.

For the next hour and a half she talked with the officers, gave her statement, and looked around her apartment for anything else that might be missing. They dusted for fingerprints turned up nothing. Whoever had been in her apartment had most likely worn gloves. There were no visible signs of forced entry and "yes," she told the officers, she was certain she had locked her door. Angela was more certain now than ever.

After the uniformed officers left, she called Jason. She knew him well enough to know he wouldn't sleep until he knew she was alright. Angela again repeated to Jason, she didn't want him to come over. She was the one with the gun, not him, and she could handle it alone. When she did finally go to bed at midnight, Angela left the light on in the living room. For the first thirty minutes she lay there, every noise in the apartment, every pop and crack, every footstep from the apartment above, made her eyes open and dart first to the door and then around the room. Finally, exhausted, Angela fell into a deep sleep. She would go in late tomorrow. She deserved it.

Chapter twenty-eight

"Angela, I have at least ten messages for you." The desk clerk handed her a small stack of pink four by five pieces of paper. "Sorry to hear about your apartment getting broken into last night."

"How'd you hear about it so soon?"

"When I came in this morning, night shift told me."

"Oh." Angela continued walking, not giving the clerk a chance to ask more questions. She should call Edwards, she thought to herself. He would know what to think about all this. But first, she had to find Debbie and have her track down the few remaining people on her list.

"Debbie. I'm glad you're here today, I need your help again."

"Oh sure, anything. Just let me take these back to my desk." She looked down at the stack of files she was carrying in her arms. "You want me to come down to your office?"

"Yes, please. That'd be good." As Angela continued down the stairs to her tiny office in the basement, she began reading the pink sheets of paper. There were two calls from her sister in Aiken. She probably saw the stories about the murdered children in the paper and wanted to know if she could get the inside scoop to share with her country club friends. There was one call from Rob Edwards' wife, which surprised her. Angela hoped he wasn't worse. There were three from a Ms. Anderson with an out of state number written under the name.

"Two-one-six area code," she thought. "It has to be Peggy Anderson." Angela sat down and quickly called the number. There were only two rings before a woman picked up.

"Miller, Jackson, Heart and Associates, how may I direct your call."

"I'm calling for a Peggy Anderson."

"One moment please. I'll see if she's available. Who may I say is calling?"

"I'm Angela Porter, uh, Detective Angela Porter."

"Oh yes, she told me if you called to put you right through. Hold one moment please."

Angela's wait was only for a few seconds, but it felt much longer.

"Hello. This is Peggy Anderson."

"Ms. Anderson, I'm Detective Porter. We spoke last night."

"Yes, thank you for returning my calls this morning."

"Actually, I think I should thank you for calling me back. I'm sorry if my call to you last night was upsetting."

"It's not your fault. Annie was my best friend. It was just hard after all these years to suddenly hear…" She paused and collected her thoughts. "To hear that she was dead and had been dead all these years."

"Yes, I'm sorry. I know it has to be difficult, but I'm glad you asked me to call. I would really like to ask a few questions."

"Yes, of course. I want to help in whatever way I can. For Annie's sake."

"How was it that she was wearing your I.D. bracelet?"

"I gave it to her."

"Why did you give it to her?"

"As I said, she was my best friend and I loved her. Let me tell you something about Annie. Her family was very poor. Her father drank a lot and I think her mother tried to hold everything together as best she could."

"Was her father abusive?"

"I think so, but I think it was more physical and psychological. I don't think it was sexual, at least it hadn't gotten to that point yet."

"So Annie shared a lot with you?"

"Yes."

"Did she ever talk about running away?"

"No. She didn't run away."

Angela heard tension in Peggy's voice. "The police report listed her as a runaway."

"Look, I know you weren't involved in the initial investigation, and from the sound of your voice, you probably weren't even born when Annie disappeared. But Annie wouldn't have run away."

"Did she ever make a comment that she would like to run away? Not that I'm implying that she attempted to, but something must have made them think she did."

There was silence on the phone for a moment. "Once she did say that, but she was just upset."

"What was she upset about?"

"I guess it was a day or so after I'd given her my bracelet. One of the teachers took it away from her and accused her of stealing it."

"What happened?"

"They had her in the office. I remember it was upstairs. They had me come up there and told me they had found her with my bracelet. I remember feeling the teachers were rather mean to her about the incident. It was embarrassing, too."

"How so? Could you explain?"

"Being the center of that kind of attention. Having the other kids stare at you when they take you out of the classroom to the office."

"I can see where she would have been upset by it."

"Of course she was upset, and I felt bad for her. She was one of these children that you see too many of now. No one really cares about them. Anyway, I remember one of the teachers, I think he was the one who actually saw her with it, kept saying how disappointed he was with her. The jerk! Then, I got the third degree on why I'd given it to her. Poor Annie."

Angela could hear Peggy's voice falter with emotion. "Do you remember a teacher by the name of Bess Shealy?"

"Miss Shealy. Yes, I remember her. She was always nice. She seemed to really care about Annie. I remember she used to give Annie little art lessons during lunch. Until Annie and I started having lunch together every day."

"Miss Shealy spoke with a lot of fondness for Annie and you."

"You know her?"

"She's one of the people I've spoken with while investigating this case." Angela didn't want Peggy to know Bess was actually helping her track down people.

"Is she still teaching at Wardlaw? I guess that's a silly question. She probably retired a long time ago."

"Actually, Wardlaw was closed years ago. It's being renovated and turned into upscale shops and restaurants."

"They're putting something like that in Elmwood?" Peggy was surprised. Her last memory of the Elmwood neighborhood was that of run-down houses that had been converted to duplexes and triplexes.

"Middle and upper middle class families are moving back into Elmwood. They're restoring the houses."

"I bet it looks nice then. When I was a small child it was a pretty neighborhood."

Angela thought it odd that Peggy didn't know about how the River Vista area and Elmwood had changed in the last few years. "When was the last time you were in Columbia?"

"I moved away to go to college. Other than a few trips home while I was in school, I haven't been back. My family and I don't really see eye-to-eye on some things and its best this way. I have a cousin who still keeps in touch. So I know to send flowers when someone dies, but that's about it."

"I'm sorry. What happened between you and your family?"

"Detective Porter, I really don't want to talk about my family. I called because of Annie."

"Yes, of course. Do you remember when you saw Annie last?" Angela heard Peggy's voice falter as she spoke.

"I remember. It was the night she disappeared."

"She disappeared in the evening? The police report doesn't say anything about that. It lists her disappearance as during the day."

"I told you the police just blew this off because she was poor."

"Ms. Anderson…"

"Please, just call me Peggy."

"Okay. Peggy, please don't be offended by my question, but are you sure you remember this correctly? It was a long time ago and the memories of children are sometimes less than accurate."

"I understand that, but Peggy and I sneaked out of our houses the night she disappeared and wemet a few blocks from the school. The next morning when she didn't show up for school, I thought maybe she had gotten caught sneaking back in the house. And her father may have beaten her again and she stayed home. It wasn't until later that night that I heard they were saying she might have run away from home."

"Do you know any reason why they may have said she ran away?"

"It was because of a note she had written to me."

"A note?"

"Yes, when they had her in the office accusing her of stealing my bracelet. They went through her book bag looking for other things she might have stolen." Angela could hear the sarcasm in Peggy's voice. "Anyway, they found a note she had written. She wished we didn't have to wait until college for us to go away together. She wished we could run away now."

"So from that, they assumed she ran away?"

"That, and that idiot putting his two cents worth in."

"What idiot?"

"The same teacher that saw her wearing my bracelet."

"Who was that?"

Peggy paused. "You would think I'd remember his name. Especially since I didn't like him. You usually remember the names of the teachers you don't like."

"I think that would be true for me," Angela added.

"Hillman, Hillson, Hilliard. That's it. Hilliard. Mr. Hilliard. I always thought he was strange."

"Strange? In what way, and why didn't you like him?"

"He seemed to not like the fact that Annie and I were friends. I never could figure out why. It was odd. He seemed okay with us individually, but when we became friends... he was just different after that." Peggy paused. "I remember he had this ceramic angel. One like you would expect a grandmother to have in a curio cabinet. Not a male teacher. Anyway, I remember Michael Murphy broke it. I thought the man was either going to cry, or have a nervous breakdown."

"You said he had an angel?"

"Yes, I think he had a thing for angels. Once I remember, and this was before Michael broke the angel, Annie and I walked in and caught him taping a picture of one of the girls in music class to the angel."

Angela felt a chill run down her back. "Taping a picture to the angel? How? What do you mean?"

"A school picture, one of the little wallet size ones. He was taping it over the face of the ceramic angel. Funny how I remembered that. I hadn't thought about that in years. Annie and I had a pretty good laugh about it. I'm certain he knew we saw him."

"What did Mr. Hilliard teach?"

"Let's see, he taught science; I was in his science club."

"Did he teach anything else?"

"I don't remember. That was all I had him for. Oh, he did help out with the band and chorus."

"Peggy, I'd really like to talk to you in greater length. Would you consider coming back to Columbia so we could talk in more detail? Maybe look at old photos, yearbooks, and anything else that might jog your memory."

"Do you suspect, Mr. Hilliard?"

"Right now, everyone is a suspect, and no one is a suspect. But you've really helped by giving me so much information on Annie. I wish I had as much on the other girls."

"Others? You said others? Are there other children?"

"Actually, we found a total of seven. Even though Annie wasn't buried in a group with the other six, we strongly believe the same person is responsible for all the deaths."

"My god!" Peggy was silent for a moment. "I don't know. I'll have to think about it."

"That's fine. You have my number here at the station. Let me also give you my cell number." Angela recited the number. "Please, call me. I think talking with you more could help." She could sense Peggy's reluctance.

"I don't know. If I don't come to Columbia, I'll at least talk with you on the phone again. Now if you excuse me. I have a meeting in a few minutes."

"Peggy. Thank you." Angela laid the receiver of the phone in its cradle, then pushed back from her desk as far as her small office would allow. She felt tense, anxious; her thoughts were racing and she began to voice her thoughts as if saying them out loud would help clarify where her mind was going.

"Angels! He had a thing for angles, taught science, helped out with band." She remembered some of the girls were in band. "If he was involved in outside activities, then he could have come in contact with girls from other schools. I have a suspect!" Angela was startled slightly when she heard a knock on her door. "Hello."

She stood up and opened the door.

"It's me, Debbie."

"Hey, what's up?"

"I just wanted to let you know, I found everyone except this one here."

Angela took the piece of paper from Debbie. "You couldn't find Jim Hilliard?"

"No, nothing at all. I can go in and look again, but it's like he dropped off the face of the earth. All the records I tried just end in 1985. And there was a gap in information between 1977 and 1978 where I couldn't find anything either. It's almost like he just disappeared for a while."

"Could he have died in eighty-five?"

"It's possible. I'll have to do more searching."

"Would you try? And I'll try to find a relative and track him down that way."

Debbie noticed Angela's heightened anxiety. "Is everything OK? You seem kind of tense."

"I'm fine. Just wound up over the case and not getting enough sleep. Especially last night."

"I bet. I don't think I would've stayed there by myself."

"A friend kept asking me to come over and spend the night. I thought about it, but it's like getting back on a horse after it throws you. If I hadn't stayed there last night it might've made tonight worse."

Debbie nodded her head acknowledging she understood Angela's perspective.

"Besides, I'm the one with the big gun. Right."

Debbie laughed. "Do you want me to keep looking for him?"

"Please. Could you get me his last known address?"

"Already did." Debbie handed Angela a Post-It Note with an address scribbled on it. "This is the last address that his tax returns were filed from."

"Thanks."

As Debbie turned to exit the tiny office, she paused, then turned again to face Angela. "I know you're real busy right now with this case and all," she paused. "If you want to take a break from it one night and go get a bite to eat or have a drink, then just let me know."

"Sure, that sounds good. I'm kind of swamped right now, but yeah, that'd be great." Angela saw a smile spread across Debbie's young face. A smile that looked as if she had just had a prom invitation accepted.

As Debbie walked away, Angela closed her door. She wanted to talk to Jason and didn't want her conversation overheard. She dialed his cell number. He had told her the night before that he planned to go in early to get some work done. As soon as she heard his voice she started talking and relayed her conversation with Peggy Anderson. She asked him to call his aunt and have her find out as much about Jim Hilliard and his after school activities as she could. She didn't want to jump to conclusions. It was all too obvious. She just had to find proof and something that would connect him with the other girls at the time of their disappearances.

After Angela finished her conversation with Jason, she transferred the address to her notepad, then quickly exited the office, locking the door behind her and headed for the stairs.

Just as Angela pushed on the cross bar of the glass door, she heard her Captain. "Porter! Get in here." Angela looked up and saw Randall Evans standing in their Captain's office. "What've you been doing the last day and a half?"

"Checking out the names on this list, locating people, and getting statements. Why?" Angela walked into the office.

"Because I need to know if you have come up with anything. Evans here has been looking into the possibility that reporter could have done this."

"Mark Harris?" Angela interrupted.

"Yeah, Mark Harris might've been the killer."

"Yes, I know. You said that yesterday." Angela crossed her arms and looked at Evans.

Before Evans could answer, their Captain spoke. "Look, whether you all want to work together or not, doesn't matter. I've put you together and you're going to cooperate. All of a sudden I've got reporters, the Mayor…everybody's kicking my ass over this. Hell, I even had a call from Thorton Collins, the former U.S. Senator."

Angela raised her left eyebrow. "Why is he calling? He's not even in office any more; he's a fossil."

"Well, he's still pretty powerful. He's looking into it out of concern that 'something like that could go on in the Midlands,' was all he said."

Angela rolled her eyes. "He's probably just trying to get his name in the news again."

"Alright Porter, what've you got?" It only took Angela a split second to decide not to share with Frank and Randall her theory on who the murderer really was.

"Nothing yet. I'm still checking names and making contacts."

"I want the two of you to get out there and make face-to-face contact with all the families of the victims. And I want it done today! One of the things they're busting me for is not letting the families know something sooner. Since the word is out that we got all the remains identified, every person in five counties wants to know if it's their missing relative."

"I still have some people I haven't talked to."

"I don't want to hear it! Get with the families. Take statements from them. Then Porter, I want you to help Evans out with his theory on the reporter."

"But sir, I really think I could better spend my time trying to find some commonalties between the girls. There has to be something connecting them to each other."

"Porter, I understand that. I can appreciate your dedication. But you've never worked a serial killer case before. Most of the time there is nothing connecting the victims to each other. Nothing other than opportunity for the killer."

"I don't think that's the case here. If we just approach this systematically, I think it will make it easier to…" Her Captain cut her off before she could finish her statement.

"I'm running this and you all are going to work together. You're going to investigate the reporter first. And find out who is leaking information while you're at it!"

"Yes sir." Angela resigned herself to working with Randall and wasting valuable time chasing down his theory. It was now mid-morning. She had wanted to meet Jason for lunch. She needed to see him; she needed to see the warmth and caring in his green eyes.

Angela and Randall walked out of their Captain's office.

"Well Porter, when do you want to get started telling the families? I gotta' get back to checking out the accident." Angela gave Randall a questioning look. "You know, the accident Harris was killed in."

"I thought you'd already made up your mind on that?"

"Yeah, but I just want to take a look at it one more time. I've been spending a lot of my time going through Harris' notes. There's so much detail there, I don't see how he could've gathered all that if he wasn't stalking them."

"You really think so?"

"Well, yeah! I mean why would he have all that? How would he see a connection between kids that turned up missing over that long a period of time when no one else did?"

"I don't know. Maybe he was just smart…did his homework." Angela was becoming increasingly irritated by her new partner. Angela paused. "I need to run back down to my office for a second. I'll meet you in the car."

"Sure, I'll get the air conditioner going. I bet it's a hundred out there already."

Angela went back downstairs to her office and left Randall to start cooling off the unmarked car they would drive to the homes of the families of the murdered girls. Once in her office, she quickly sent Jason a text then left a voice mail message for him.

She didn't have time to wait for a reply. Hopefully, he would see the message soon.

Chapter twenty-nine

For the remainder of the day Angela and Randall went from the home of one victim's family to the next. Sometimes they stayed long enough to ask a few questions; sometimes the parents were too upset to talk. Each time they would get back into their car, it would already be heated up to the point that Randall had difficulty gripping the steering wheel without burning his hands. Even with her tan, the intense South Carolina sun stung the skin of Angela's forearms. It was days like this when the idea of moving north didn't seem so bad. The heat was physically draining and with each family they visited, even though she maintained a professional and controlled exterior, Angela felt as if her heart were sinking.

She was surprised to find that most of the families of the murdered girls still lived in the neighborhoods where they had originally lived at the time of the disappearance, even though the parents of the first victims were now elderly. A couple of them still lived in the same house. Patty Franks' mother took Angela and Randall through the house and showed them photographs of Patty. A picture of Patty in her softball uniform was in a small frame setting beside her softball trophy on the mantel above the fireplace. Mrs. Franks' had a strange calm about her that was unlike the other parents they had spoken with. It gave Angela a strange feeling. Then, at the end of the hall, Mrs. Franks unlocked and opened a door. Behind the door was Patty's bedroom, perfectly preserved as if Patty had just that morning left for school.

Angela watched as Mrs. Franks walked around the room and touched with gentle reverence the small hairbrush and ribbon that still lay on the dresser. Then Mrs. Frank spoke in a soft Charleston draw.

"You know we had a little spat that morning," she said. "I wanted her to pull her hair back and tie it in a bow. But she wanted to wear it down like the other girls. She said only little kids tied their hair back."

Mrs. Franks put her hand to her face and began to sob. Angela went to her and put her arms around her and let the older woman cry into her shoulder. Randall coughed and excused himself from the room.

After a few minutes, Mrs. Franks assured Angela she was alright and would call her sister to come over and stay with her awhile. Angela again gave her sympathy and stated that she would like to ask a few questions when she felt more like talking. Then Angela left to join Randall in the car. "Boy, you were in there long enough."

"It was only about ten minutes."

"Well, it was hot as hell out here in the car."

Angela could feel her face flush with anger. "The woman was upset! She just found out her only child was murdered forty-three years ago and buried on a playground." Angela pulled down the visor to block the sun from her face. "Come on, we've got one more to go."

"Hey, don't yell at me. I don't like this shit any more than you do. Dealin' with the tears and stuff. You women are better at all that."

Angela rolled her eyes. "Let's just go." Angela rubbed her forehead. The heat combined with a lunch that consisted of only a bag of chips and a diet soda was causing what felt like the beginnings of a migraine. "I should've done this by myself," Angela said in a low, barely audible voice.

Randall heard her comment. "Hey, I'd rather be out chasin' leads, too, but I got stuck with this. I thought the Captain would send you out by yourself to do this, too."

"You mean give me the shit job so you can play Law and Order and save the day – I don't think so. This should've been mine and Edwards' case."

"Well, he ain't going to be able to come back."

"I was making progress on my own."

"Progress with what? Charts and graphs? While you're sitting there saying stuff like 'there's got to be a system to this,' there could be a killer out there that knows we're looking for him, and now he's in a damn other country."

"If that's your opinion, then why are you wasting time investigating Mark Harris."

"Because with all that shit he had on those little girls, it was like he was stalkin' them."

Angela responded with, "Whatever," and then fell silent for the remainder of the ride to what had once been Annie's home. Angela didn't buy into Randall's theory. It didn't make sense. To have been the killer, Mark Harris would have committed the first crime at around the age of eighteen. And while she knew eighteen-year-olds were very capable of killing, she had never met an eighteen-year-old who had thought processes that were logical and systematic enough to commit the murder and dispose of the body without getting caught. Eighteen-year-olds were more spontaneous; they made mistakes.

"Here we are." Randall pulled the car to the curb and threw it in park.

They both looked out the car window to survey the exterior of the small house before getting out. Of the seven homes they had visited, the home of Annie was by far the smallest and in the worst state of repair. While some of the other houses were older houses and needed some paint or the shrubbery cleaned back, they appeared to be in good condition. This house needed more than touch-up work.

The front yard was almost devoid of grass with only a few scattered patches remaining. Angela could see beer bottles setting in a row on the front porch beside a beat-up, brown, vinyl recliner. The screen on the porch door was torn, and even from their parking place at the curb, rotted ends of floorboards on the porch and a rusted set of bedsprings leaning against a tree at the side of the house were clearly visible. From what Peggy had told her about Annie's family, she wondered if the house, with its peeling paint and dirty windows, had not looked this way forty-seven years ago when Annie was still alive.

"Real gem ain't it." Randall pulled the keys from the ignition. "Last one; let's get it over with."

As the two detectives walked up the cracked and buckled sidewalk to the front porch, they could see the house was in even worse condition than it first appeared. The shingles on the roof were buckling and had moss growing on them. Walking across the front porch to ring the doorbell, they were careful to watch where they placed their feet so as to not fall through the rotting boards.

Randall tried the doorbell. Looking back over his shoulder, "Don't work, imagine that." Randall knocked hard three times on the door. Hearing nothing, he knocked again. This time he heard the doorknob rattle and begin to turn. As the door slowly opened, Angela and Randall saw the face of a gray haired, slightly overweight woman who was probably in her late seventies.

The woman, still holding the door partly closed, cautiously looked first at Randall and then Angela.

"Can I help you?"

Randall, who was standing slightly in front of Angela, spoke first. "I'm Detective Evans and this is Detective Porter. We're with the Columbia City Police Department and we're looking for a Harry and Evelyn Walker."

"I'm Evelyn Walker and my husband Harry is inside. If you're here about Harry Junior, he's a grown man and I can't make him do nothin."

"Ma'am we're not here about Harry Junior…" Before Randall could finish his sentence he heard the loud, raspy voice of a man yell out from inside the house.

"Who the fuck's at the door? Goddamn dinner's goin'ta get cold while you're standin' there yackin."

"I'm sorry. I've got to get Harry's dinner. He's got sugar and the doctor took his foot off last year so he can't get up and get things for his self."

Now Angela spoke. "Ma'am, do you have a daughter named Annie?"

Evelyn Walker stopped and stared at Angela with a sad and distant look in her eyes. It was the look of a woman who had probably known little happiness in her life.

"Yes, I have a daughter Annie, but she runned away from home when she was little. Do you know where she is?" For an instant there was a small glimmer of hope that appeared in her sad eyes.

Angela felt her heart reach out to her. To tell a woman like this that she was going to have yet another tragedy to deal with seemed too cruel, but Angela continued, "Ma'am, may we come in?"

Evelyn looked down as if embarrassed by her appearance. Wiping her hands on a tattered dishtowel hanging from the pocket of her faded flower-print housedress, she said, "Well, you'll have to excuse the house. It's kind of a mess right now. I don't get too much time to clean - with Harry and his foot, and all..." Evelyn opened the door wider and stepped aside to allow the two detectives to enter the small living room.

From the kitchen, Harry pushed his wheelchair into the living room. "Who the hell are they?"

With an apologetic tone Evelyn said, "Harry, hush now. These are detectives from the police department. They're askin' about Annie."

"What about her?"

Looking at Harry, Angela replied, "We're here about what happened to her."

"The school and the police said she run off. She had somebody at school she was moonin' over all the time. They kept givin' her presents. She wouldn't tell us who he was. Probably some boy, whose mama and daddy had some money, got her knocked up so she took off."

"Harry, please," Evelyn said again.

Angela wished she could pull her nine-millimeter out and put a bullet in his vulgar mouth. He abused his daughter and now he was slandering her. Unfortunately, the law didn't allow her to do this favor for Mrs. Walker.

"Mr. Walker, you may have heard about some children's bodies being found buried on the old grounds of the Wardlaw Junior High."

"Yeah, what about it?"

"Mr. and Mrs. Walker, I'm very sorry to inform you that," Angela shifted her eyes to Evelyn, "your daughter Annie has been positively identified as one of the victims. Apparently, she's been buried there probably since the time of her initial disappearance."

"Oh no, God no!" Evelyn gasped, covering her mouth with her hands - hands that were still grasping the tattered dishtowel. Harry fell silent.

Angela moved toward Mrs. Walker who now suddenly appeared more frail and stooped than before.

"I am so very sorry."

"I'm going to get me a lawyer!"

"Pardon me, Mr. Walker?" Angela asked.

"You heard me. I'm goin' to get me a lawyer. You police said she done run away instead of lookin' for her like you was supposed to do.

It's your fault she wasn't never found. Now I'm goin' to get what's due me."

Angela could feel the anger inside her. "I hope you do get what's due you, Mr. Walker." Angela turned again to Evelyn Walker. "Mrs. Walker I know this has got to be a shock for you, but I'd like to come back at a better time and ask a few questions. Maybe there's something you can remember that might help us figure out who did this to your little girl."

"Yes, of course."

"She don't remember nothin'. And she ain't talkin' to you till we get a lawyer. Now I think you just better leave."

Once inside the car, "Well Porter, what'd you think of the charming Mr. Walker and his lovely wife?"

"I felt sorry for her. Too bad they amputated his foot and not his head."

"Yeah, no wonder the cops on the case thought the kid ran away. I would've, too, if I'd dealt with that son-of-a-bitch."

Their encounter with Harry Walker gave Angela and Randall some common ground on which to communicate. But even with this more casual exchange, as they made their way through traffic back to the station, Angela still wasn't ready to relinquish ownership of the case or include Randall and their Captain in on her speculation as to who the killer may have been.

By the time they were back at the station, it was after seven and Angela's headache was worsening. She needed to call Jason and see if he had any new information from his aunt. Jim Hilliard had to be the killer; she needed to find him and then prove it. But first there was paperwork to fill out and she wanted to study the SLED profile on the killer.

When Angela finally left the station to go to her car, Dorothy Danze was again waiting for her. This time, however, she didn't have her camera crew with her.

"Hello, Detective Porter. I've heard you and another detective were making rounds to the families of the victims. It must be terrible for them." Dorothy paused to add effect to her words. "Waiting all those years. Hoping your child will somehow come home. Then you find out they were murdered and buried in one of the places where they were supposed to be safe – a school playground." Another pause. "Kind of ironic isn't it."

"Is there some point to this conversation?" Angela's head was pounding. The Tylenol she had taken earlier had done little more than take the edge off. All she wanted was to get to Jason's house. She hadn't been able to reach him on the phone and he hadn't responded to her text.

"Do you have anything you'd like to tell me – off the record?"

"There isn't anything to tell," Angela answered as she squinted her left eye slightly from the pain in her head.

Dorothy continued, "You're a woman in a traditionally male profession. You know how it is. It's the same for me. The first sign of a wrinkle around my eyes and they'll put me on late night doing human-interest pieces. Maybe we could help each other out."

"I'm sorry, but I have a headache. It's late. I'm going home and I really don't see how we could help each other."

"I know your apartment was broken into. Did they take anything or were they just looking for information."

The comment shocked Angela. For that instant she almost forgot just how badly her head was beginning to pound. "How'd you know about that? Unless you had something to do with it!"

"I didn't do it. If I had, I wouldn't have left such a mess. Maybe whoever did it knows who the killer is, and they want to see how close you are. Did you ever think of that?"

"You know, Ms. Danze, some police officers are smarter than you think they are. And actually, yes the thought did cross my mind. But now I'll be keeping an eye on you, too." Angela pushed by Dorothy and hit the unlock button on her keyless entry.

Angela could see Dorothy standing in the parking lot watching as she drove away. As she drove, Angela debated whether or not to go straight to Jason's house or home to her apartment. When she reached the intersection where she had to make the decision to get on I-26 or I-20, she took the split and headed to Jason's. Her head pounded. She hoped he was home, she needed a mega-dose of Tylenol and then some sleep in a dark room. It was after nine o'clock, she hadn't eaten and, with the migraine, she was now becoming nauseated.

Angela decided to take the shortcut Jason had shown her. There would be a few more twists and turns on the two-lane road, but at least she would be out of any traffic, especially at that hour. Angela could feel the migraine now moving behind her eyes, the pain was intense. She reached up and adjusted her rearview mirror to dim the reflection of the lights from the car behind her.

She could see it was coming up fast and had its bright headlights on. Angela tilted her head down and looked straight ahead. It was then she felt a nudge on her bumper, it was light at first, then harder. "Shit!"

She looked first in her side mirror then her rear-view mirror. This car was right on her tail and intentionally hitting her. Angela down-shifted into fourth and sped up. His second attempt to hit her missed.

She tried to get a good look at the car, but it was too dark and there were no streetlights. All she could see was that it was an older model car and a dark color. Then she felt the hit from the side. He had side swiped her. She swerved and went off the road. The shoulder was soft and she had to fight with the wheel to keep her car out of the ditch. As she forced her car back onto the highway, she looked over into the car beside her. The windows were covered with a dark tint and a dark silhouette was all that was visible before she saw the sedan position itself to come at her again.

This time Angela threw on her brakes and locked up her car. The sedan went by her and she saw its break lights come on. Angela looked for some way to turn her car around quickly. The highway wasn't wide enough to make a U-turn, even in her small car. Then she saw the car speed away. Angela pressed down hard on the gas. She knew it might be tempting fate, but she wanted to get close enough to get a license number.

The car disappeared around a turn and when Angela rounded the turn, the car was nowhere in sight. It had vanished into the night. Angela slowed her speed and drove the three more miles to Jason's house. Her hands gripping the steering wheel until her knuckles turned white. She was shaken and mad at herself for being so.

When Angela pulled into Jason's driveway the garage door was up and he was climbing out of his car with his messenger bag in hand.

Jason walked to the back of his Subaru; she could see the smile on his face. She needed that smile right now. As she came to a stop in his driveway, he saw the damage to the side of her car and the smile instantly vanished.

"Are you okay? What happened?"

Angela got out of her battered car. "I think I'm going to be sick!" Jason took Angela's hand and with his arm around her walked her into his house and led her quickly to the bathroom.

"Here, let me help."

"No, just wait outside."

Jason stood outside the bathroom. He could hear Angela's coughs and gagging sputters. After what seemed like forever, the coughs stopped.

"Are you okay in there? Do you need anything?" Jason heard the toilet flush and then water running in the sink.

"I'm okay," Angela replied in a weakened voice. Then the doorknob turned and Angela slowly opened the bathroom door. Her face was pale and her eyes sunken. Her face was framed with sweat-drenched wisps of hair and her hand shook as she lifted it to Jason's shoulder.

"I'm taking you to the hospital."

"No, I'm fine. It's just one of my migraines."

Jason put his arm around Angela to help steady her. "Is that what caused your accident?"

"No. Someone was following me and tried to run me off the road."

"What?" By the tone in Jason's voice, even through the haze of her headache, she could hear the worry in his voice.

"Just let me lie down first." Jason led her to the sofa in the great room. Angela lay down and he positioned a pillow under her head and wrapped her in a woven cotton throw.

"Did you hit your head?"

"No. Just nothing in my stomach, migraine, and scared to death."

"Can I get you anything? What would help?"

"Four extra strength Tylenol if you have them. And a cold cloth to go over my eyes."

Jason hurried up the stairs to retrieve the items, taking two stairsteps at a time. When he returned, Angela thanked him and washed down the four capsules with water. "How long does it take for those to start working?"

"It may be a while. Usually, I just have to sleep these off. Do you not get migraines?"

"I get them once in a while, but not like this. Is there anything else I can do?"

"Well, actually." Angela hesitated. "I hate to sound like a whiner, but I think this started because I didn't really eat anything today. If you don't mind I'd like to borrow your kitchen long enough to fix myself something."

"I think you need to just lie there and rest. Tell me what you want and I'll get it."

"I really don't want to impose."

"Angela." Jason's voice took a serious tone. "I know we really haven't known each other that long, but I think we've already progressed to the point that you can let me wait on you when you're sick."

Angela's eyes were closed and her brow furrowed with pain, but she smiled. "Okay, you win. I'll have soup if you have it."

"What kind? I have tomato, chicken noodle, and clam chowder."

"Chicken noodle…and some crackers, too, if you have them."

"Coming right up." Jason wanted to ask more about the car that tried to run her off the road, but he thought it best to let her rest first.

"Jason. One more favor? Could you hand me my phone. I need to call the station and report that guy running me off the road." Jason handed Angela her phone then exited to the kitchen.

Angela finished her soup and had only a few minutes to nap when the first Lexington County Deputy arrived at Jason's house. They had to be called since the incident was within their jurisdiction. It wasn't long before a state police officer arrived, only to be followed by Angela's Captain.

By the third time Angela recounted the events of the evening her headache was beginning to subside. Still, she didn't tell her Captain about her suspicions, nor did she share with him her conversation with Dorothy Danze. Angela knew she was close and someone else knew it, too. Now came the tough part – proof.

Chapter thirty

Angela spent the night at Jason's. She took his room - he had insisted - and he slept in the guest room. She wasn't yet ready to start a physical relationship with him. They barely even had a date that didn't involve looking at crime files. Besides, she was still feeling the after-effects of the migraine and the physical exertion of sex might set it off again. Lying there in Jason's bed, smelling the scent of him on the pillow, she could think of worse ways to get a headache.

Morning came too quickly. Angela rolled over and opened her eyes only to find a large furry head and some whiskers not more than an inch from her nose. Sebastian had apparently, sometime during the early hours of the morning, decided he would spend the remainder of the night with Angela. She was startled for only an instant, then reached up and began petting the large feline who was standing guard over her. Petting Sebastian reminded her of how much she missed having a pet.

As a child, she was always bringing home strays. At any given time her parent's back yard had two or three dogs and an assortment of cats and their kittens. Her job was too demanding of her time. There were too many nights when she worked late, and wouldn't get home in time to walk a dog, and she felt like her apartment was too small to be fair to the animal. But she was putting money away and interest rates were good. By the spring she should be able to buy something.

Angela heard a knock on the bedroom door, which drew her out of her daydream of a small home with flowerbeds in the front yard.

"Come in."

The bedroom door was slightly ajar. Jason opened it wide enough to stick his head inside. "Hi there. How are you feeling?"

"Like a new woman." Angela propped her head up with her hand and smiled at Jason as he sat down on the side of the bed.

"I see you made a friend."

"Yes. He startled me a little. I woke up and there were these big eyes and whiskers in my face." Angela extended her other hand and Sebastian rubbed against it.

"Sebastian, were you a bad boy and scared our guest?" Sebastian purred.

"Oh, it's okay. I used to have lots of pets growing up. I miss having one."

"Why don't you get one?"

"Too many long hours. It wouldn't be fair to the pet." There was an awkward moment of silence as the two suddenly thought about being in a bed together.

Then Jason spoke. "How about breakfast? Are you hungry? I can cook something."

"No, I've imposed on you too much already. I had you waiting on me last night and I kicked you out of your own bed. I'll get something later."

Jason frowned and pushed his hair back from his eyes. "First of all, you haven't imposed. And, last night, since you introduced me to your Captain as your boyfriend, I don't think me cooking breakfast is too much."

Angela closed her eyes and wrinkled her nose tightly. "I said that. I'm sorry. It sort of slipped out."

"Don't apologize. I liked the sound of it." As Jason smiled Angela was taken with how his green eyes seemed to sparkle and his face lit up. She returned the smile.

"Okay, I give in. What's on the menu."

"Do you like omelets?"

"I love omelets."

"Good! Then its omelets, toast, and hash browns."

"What! No grits?"

"Actually, I'm not a big fan of grits, but I might have some instant ones in the cabinet. So I can do grits, too."

"No, I was just kidding. What you're making is more than I usually eat for breakfast in three days. The time you spent away from South

Carolina - you must have been brain washed. You don't drink sweet tea and you don't eat grits."

"And I don't have a bumper sticker with a rebel flag." They both laughed. It felt good to have a light-hearted moment. Angela was seeing a lighter side of Jason and she liked what she saw.

"Would you like some help in the kitchen?"

"No, you can just hang out here and relax. If you need a toothbrush I have a spare one in the right hand drawer in the vanity. It's still in the package. It hasn't been opened."

"Thanks." As Jason exited the bedroom, Sebastian ran after him. Angela brushed her teeth and washed the sleep out of her eyes and, in the process, washed away what little eye make-up she wore. Looking in the mirror she commented to herself. "Well, Angela, if he can't take you after a night of being sick and no make-up, then he isn't worth it." She knew however, make-up or no make-up, Jason wasn't the type of guy who would care.

Angela looked at the clock radio sitting on the nightstand beside Jason's bed. "Shit. I'd better call in." Angela made a quick phone call to the police station and left a message with the desk that she was calling in sick. She knew that, given the events of the night before, her Captain, even with his sometimes rough exterior, would understand. She could smell the food cooking in the kitchen. It made her stomach rumble. Angela walked to Jason's office and began sifting through the papers she had left lying beside the chair the last time she was at his house. Jason had disturbed nothing.

Picking up the report cards from the girls who had attended Wardlaw, she began reading the comments of the teachers. She started with Annie. For the most part the teachers gave pretty generic remarks. 'Pays attention in class,' 'Needs to speak up and participate more,' and 'Always turns work in on time.' Then as she read the comments from Annie's science and math teacher, she closed her eyes and whispered, "My god."

There it was in front of her. Why hadn't she noticed it before? Maybe she did, but its significance didn't register until talking with Peggy. Jim Hilliard had described Annie as an angel. Angela quickly pulled the file folders of the other girls from the bankers' box. There it was on each girl's report card - Annie, Susan, Kathy, and Paula. Hilliard had in some way described each of them as angels. She gathered up the folders and rushed into the kitchen.

"Jason, look at this. I know it's him."

"Ouch! Shit!" Jason grabbed his hand.

"You okay?"

"Yes, I just burned myself." Jason put his finger in his mouth.

"You're supposed to put that in cold water."

"It's okay, it's not that bad. Now, what do you have?"

"Look at these report cards." Angela, standing beside Jason, held them out in front of her. "For all the girls that went to Wardlaw, look what Hilliard wrote."

Jason read the comments on each of the report cards. "Okay, I get your point, but just let me play devil's advocate here. How do the way the skeletons were positioned and his comments about the girls being angels, make him a murderer? He may have written that on all the report cards."

"He didn't write it on Peggy's." Angela held up Peggy's report card. "For the entire year she was in his class; not one reference to being an angel."

"Still, that doesn't mean he did it."

"I talked to Peggy Anderson yesterday morning. She called the station and left a message for me that she wanted to talk."

"And?" Jason inquired as he buttered bread for the toast.

"She said that Annie had been accused of stealing her I.D. bracelet. She brought up Hilliard's name. She said he was the main one accusing her of being a thief."

"Okay, so what else? Why then call her an angel?"

"She also told me that Hilliard ridiculed and belittled Annie over that incident. She almost made it sound like it was something personal to him. It sounds almost like he was jealous. She also told me that the whole bracelet thing happened not long after she and Annie had walked into Hilliard's classroom when he was in there by himself. They caught him taping a photo of a girl to the head of a ceramic angel he kept on his desk."

"That's weird."

"Exactly. And when one of the kids in their class accidentally broke the ceramic angel, Hilliard went ballistic.

"Okay, so you think all this adds up to him killing little girls because he wants to turn them into his angels."

"That sounds like it to me. And I think there's more Peggy might know. I just need to get her to talk to me and open up. I suggested she come to Columbia, but as far as I know, she isn't going to take me up on it yet."

"What else do you think she would know?"

"I'm not sure. Maybe she could help pin point what happened, some event. Maybe it was the bracelet thing that set him off. Something made him go from taping pictures of girls' heads to ceramic angels… to killing them and burying them on the playground."

"I don't know. That was a long time ago for someone to remember little details. Especially, since she was just a kid at the time. I think our best bet would be to connect him to the other girls. See if something pops up."

Jason transferred the omelet to a plate and then spooned the hash browns into a serving bowl. "Why don't you grab the jelly out of the refrigerator while I get the toast." Jason bent down and peered into the oven to make sure he wasn't burning the toast.

The two sat down to eat. "This is great. Do you cook like this all the time? I almost forgot to ask. Did your aunt track down anything on Hilliard for us?"

"As a matter of fact, she did. She has his sister's address, and where he worked after Wardlaw closed. Apparently, he left teaching. He lived with his mother after that. And no, I don't cook that often. It's not much fun cooking for just myself."

"Does she know why he lived with his mother?"

"Actually, I called some of the other teachers that used to work with my aunt. One of them said they thought Hilliard had some sort of nervous breakdown. He had to leave teaching."

Angela straightened up in her chair. "Oh, really?"

"Yes. This woman went on and on about what a caring teacher he was. How awful it was to loose someone like him from the profession.

She laid it on so thick I thought I'd puke. Anyway, she said that she'd heard he suffered some financial setbacks. He had to live with his widowed mother after he got out of the hospital."

"That's interesting. We'll have to check that out."

"Actually, I already did. I checked out the deeds and he did sell his house in 1979. I couldn't find a record of him having bought any other property. That's what I was doing yesterday afternoon."

"You really have been busy!"

"Louise helped with the deeds."

Angela smiled and shook her head. "Anything else?"

"Oh, yeah. Apparently, Jim Hilliard is the younger half-brother of the former Senator Thorton Collins. Hilliard's mother was married twice. The Senator's father, her first husband, was killed in World War II."

Angela laid her fork down and swallowed hard, then stared at Jason. "You're not going to guess who called my Captain yesterday wanting to know about the case?"

"Who?"

"Senator Thorton Collins."

"You're kidding."

"No, I'm not. I think this is starting to add up." Using her fingers, in the air Angela began counting off her assumptions like she was clicking off items of a grocery list.

"Hilliard is a teacher for four of the seven murdered girls. He has an incident, for lack of a better word, with one of them. Writes about all of them being angels. Cuts out pictures of little girls and tapes them to a ceramic angel. He has a breakdown and disappears from sight for a while. Senator Collins calls about the case. Senator Collins just happens to be the older half-brother of Jim Hilliard. On top of that, my apartment is broken into and all they go through are my files. Then I almost get run off the road. Just like Mark Harris may have been run off the road."

"Okay, so what do we do next?"

Angela took a gulp of orange juice, then said, "We find Hilliard's connection to the other three girls and then we find Hilliard. Did the teacher you spoke with know where he was?"

"No. She just said that he went to work for his brother, the Senator, after he recovered from his breakdown. And I have his sister's address for you."

Angela took her last bite of hash browns. "Great! Let's start going through the last of Mark Harris' files, then maybe I'll just go pay Hilliard's sister a visit and see what her brother has been up to the last few years."

"I thought you were calling in sick today?"

"I did. Now let's get started, partner." Angela picked up her glass of orange juice and headed for Jason's formal living room. Jason and Sebastian followed close behind. With one hand on her hip and the other holding the half-empty glass, Angela stared at the wall displaying the brightly colored yarn. "Okay, if you follow the red yarn you can see the connection between Annie, Susan, Kathy, and Paula. All of them were Wardlaw students either before or at the time of their disappearance."

"Have we looked that close at extracurricular activities?" Jason offered.

"No. No, we haven't. Didn't you do a spreadsheet for that the other night?"

"Yes, I did that and all the adults the girls had regular contact with. At least the ones Mark Harris had on his lists. I'll go print a copy." While Jason retrieved his laptop, Angela began to compare information and follow the multiple colors of yarn taped to the living room wall.

"Here you go, copies for each of us." Jason handed a copy of the spreadsheet to Angela.

"That was fast."

"It's a pretty fast machine. I need something with a lot of horsepower because of the applications I run."

Angela returned her attention to the spreadsheet. "Okay, so tell me what I'm looking at on this one."

"Well, if you look at it here you can see each girl's name and the hobbies, then I did the reverse and sorted by hobbies and the girl's name. And I included everything that Harris had down. Church youth groups, band or music lessons, school clubs, sports, Girl Scouts; you name it, it's on there."

Angela looked from one page to the other. "Okay, let's go through

287

this together." One by one Jason called out the activities and, anywhere there were commonalties between two or more girls, they highlight their names. "This isn't getting anywhere. We know Susan was a Wardlaw student and she was in band. Sarah Martin was in band, but wasn't a Wardlaw student. Patty, Kathy, and Robin all played softball, but not on the same team and only Kathy went to Wardlaw."

Then Jason, looking at his copy of the same spreadsheet, added. "Patty and Robin lived near each other and looks like all three were in the same league."

"We need to know for sure what Hilliard's activities were." Angela pulled the banker's box closer to her. "I don't see any files on Hilliard in here."

"Maybe Mark Harrris hadn't gotten that far yet. Maybe he just saw the connection between the girls, but not who might have done it."

"That's possible. He might not have picked up on the angel connection. As thorough as these notes are, I find that hard to believe."

"So, what next?" Jason pushed his hair away from his eyes.

"I'll go home. Shower. Put on some fresh clothes and pay Hilliard's sister a visit and find out where her brother is these days."

"I don't think you should go alone."

Angela smiled and touched Jason's cheek. "I can handle it. But I do need your help. Your aunt had mentioned that Hilliard volunteered a lot with extracurricular things, like school clubs, and stuff."

"Right. She said a lot of teachers did."

"Okay, so what I need you to help me do is find out exactly what he was involved in. Who he may have worked with."

"Well, we already know he helped out with the band. So I guess I'll start by finding the full-time band teacher. Wait a minute! Didn't your aunt already talk to him when she contacted the other teachers?"

Jason flipped through the copies of notes his Aunt Bess had given him. "Yes. Here it is. Art Franklin was the music teacher and band director until 1980 when he retired. He is in Columbia and Aunt Bess did talk to him."

"Anything significant?"

Jason read the notes carefully. "Actually, this is interesting. Aunt

Bess said that he remembered both Susan Thompson and Sarah Martin."

"Sarah Martin didn't go to Wardlaw." Angela reminded Jason.

"He said she was in a band camp he did one summer. As a matter-of-fact it was the summer she disappeared."

"Let me see." Angela took the paper from Jason's hand. "Why didn't I pick up on this before?"

"I don't know," Jason answered. "You haven't really had a lot of time to go through this in any detail. And when we had lunch with Bess and Louise the other day, we just kind of skimmed through the high points."

"Yes, but Franklin knew both girls and Hilliard helped with the band. Damn, I should've caught this."

Jason could see Angela was coming down on herself for missing what she considered a key link. "Angela, honey, don't beat yourself up. You didn't have the link to Hilliard yet. Franklin was on the list because he came in frequent contact with one or more of the girls."

Angela wasn't paying attention. "Do we have a picture of Hilliard?"

"Probably in one of the yearbooks."

"Can you make a copy of it like you did the other ones?"

"You mean scan it in and blow it up?"

"Yes!"

"Sure, if it's clear enough." Jason and Angela began flipping through the one yearbook he hadn't returned to his aunt. After a few minutes Angela found what she was looking for. It was a clear, sharp black and white photo of Jim Hilliard. Even though it was small, they would probably be able to blow it up enough that she could flash it to some of the people who may have known Hilliard back then, and jog a memory. She knew it was him. She knew he was the killer. She just needed more than what she had to get anyone to believe that a senator's brother preyed on children.

Jason placed the small photo on the scanner. "Okay, it's in there. Now let me see what I can do with it. You know if this doesn't work, then I have a better scanner at work we can try."

"I only need it a little bigger."

With only a few clicks Jason had the first of the enlarged photos coming off his printer. "How's that?" The small photo was now about a three and a half-inch square, but had amazing clarity.

"I think that'll work."

"You want a couple more?"

"Sure." Jason printed out two more copies.

"Are you going to go see his sister now?"

"No. Let's go through these notes a little closer. There could be some other links there that we haven't seen yet. I want to get as much as I can first."

For another hour Jason and Angela carefully sifted through the file of each of the murdered girls. They started first with Annie since she was the first to go missing. They had begun to feel as if they knew her. They had so much more information on her than the other girls.

Angela stretched her arms high into the air. "My back is stiff. I'm not used to sitting this long at one time."

"Would you like me to rub it?" Jason watched as Angela began to stand.

"No, I just need to stand up and get the blood through my rear end again." Angela placed her hands in the small of her back and arched slightly backwards. Straightening her stance, she again contemplated the trails of colored yarn on the opposite wall. "You know, if you follow the colors, there are overlaps with some of the girls."

Jason rose and stood beside Angela. "What'd you mean?"

"Well, look. There isn't one thing common to all seven girls, but there are overlapping connections. Like this, for example. We have four Wardlaw students. One was in band and one played softball. Now we have another girl who was in band, but didn't go to Wardlaw. We have three girls who played softball and only one went to Wardlaw. I think we're on the right track. We already know Hilliard was a teacher at Wardlaw for at least three of the girls. Now we find out if he had contact with the others through softball, or band."

"I'll track down the band director for you, since my aunt sort-of knows him." Jason offered.

"What are you going to say if he asks you why you're asking about Hilliard?"

"Maybe just that I'm the architect on the project and we thought it would be a neat idea to get some of the old teachers together for when we have the grand opening."

Angela nodded her head. "That sounds good. I'll take the softball angle. I was at Mrs. Franks' house yesterday and she had a lot of photographs of Patty on the wall. Little trophies and awards sitting around. It was sad."

"I bet. I can't even imagine."

Angela's voice took a somber tone, "You know, I don't think she has changed anything in Patty's room since the day she disappeared. It was like stepping back in time to 1971. There was even a faded out Bobby Sherman poster on the wall."

"My sister had New Kids on the Block posters. Tommy and I teased her about it. Of course, I was the one doing most of the teasing. He just said what I said."

Angela could see the love in Jason's eyes when he spoke of his sister and brother. She could also see how quickly it changed to sadness as his thoughts obviously trailed off to a less pleasant memory. Angela cupped his hand in hers. "Do you see your sister much?"

"Not like I should."

"When all this is over, you could invite her out to eat, or over for dinner or something. Maybe you two just need to reconnect with each other."

Jason was reflective. "Yes, I should. I should do that. She's probably forgiven me by now for drawing a mustache and black eyes on Jordan."

Angela smiled. "That's probably a safe bet." Angela bent down and picked up her notes. "You know, yesterday when I spoke with Robin Skinner's parents, I only talked to the mother. I think I'll talk to the father this time."

"Was the father not home?"

"No, they're divorced. Mark Harris' notes said that they divorced about three years before Robin disappeared. Robin's father coached softball."

"Was she on his team?"

"I think it would be worth it to talk to him. We know three of the girls played softball. By now I'm sure he's been told about Robin."

"Maybe not, if they aren't on friendly terms."

Angela shrugged. "We'll see." She paused. "Oh, I did tell you about seeing Annie's parents?"

"No, why? What happened?"

"Seeing Mrs. Franks was bad enough, but the Walkers' – it was awful. That poor girl. I wonder if she ever had a happy minute." Angela began to relay the details of her visit to the home of Harry and Evelyn Walker. Jason was appalled, but at the same time, not surprised. He had gone to school with kids who lived like that. He knew a couple of them had managed to break out and make a better life for themselves, but most just continued the cycle.

Chapter thirty-one

As much as Jason hated to see Angela leave, he knew they both needed to work on finding the evidence that would connect Hilliard to the murders. When he first heard Randall Evans' theory that Mark Harris could be the true killer and the information he collected on the girls was from stalking them, he did have some doubts about Angela's conviction that he was not the killer. However, he was now convinced she was right. There were too many things to connect Hilliard to the girls. And now there was evidence of emotional problems.

"We'll get him, Angela," he said aloud to himself as he drove to Art Franklin's house on Zimalcrest Drive near Seminole Road Elementary School. Jason pulled his Subaru into the steep drive and engaged the emergency brake. Pulling the photograph of Jim Hilliard from a manila folder and fishing out a note pad and pen from his messenger bag, Jason braced himself for the blast of humidity that he knew would hit him as soon as he stepped from his car.

The one hundred percent humidity felt as if he were breathing in water. Walking up the incline past the two other cars parked in the drive, Jason could feel sweat start to run down his back. He patted the right front pocket of his khakis for reassurance – yes, his inhaler was there. The house was typical for the area. A mixture of tall straight pines and hardwoods shaded the front yard, the grass was patchy, and overgrown azaleas surrounded the house.

Jason rang the bell and pushed his hair back from his eyes while he waited. When Art Franklin opened the door, Jason was surprised by the man's appearance. Even though Jason knew his approximate age, Franklin looked much younger than his voice on the phone would lead one to believe. Franklin greeted him in a warm, friendly manner and invited him to come in. "Here, let's go in the den and have a seat. I've been out in the back yard doin' a little yard work and the Missus doesn't like me to sit in the living room with my dirty pants on. You married?"

"No, I'm not."

"Pity. Every man needs a wife to keep him in line. Men do stupid things when women aren't around to stop them, at least that's what my wife tells me." Franklin let out a laugh. "Here, have a seat." He pointed to an over-stuffed armchair.

Jason took an instant liking to this man. He thought to himself that he might actually have learned to play an instrument if Mr. Franklin had been his music teacher.

"So, what can I do for you?"

"I think my aunt, Bess Shealy, spoke with you the other day."

"Yeah, yeah. I remember her, but not too well. She didn't teach there long, did she?"

"No sir, I don't think she did. Anyway, what I'm trying to do is get some information on the old school. Track down some of the people who taught there. I thought it would be interesting to maybe set up a display in the old school after the shops open. Maybe if I can talk the developers into it, have some of the former teachers as guests at the grand opening."

"Well, if it's got anything to do with shopping, my wife will drag me there." Franklin laughed again.

Jason gave a broad smile. Yes, he liked this man. "Could you tell me a little about what you did there, music programs, band, extracurricular stuff, old stories? Just anything you can think of."

"Wow, thirty-some years' worth of teaching, I don't know where to start."

"Well, how about at the beginning. My aunt told me you pretty much built the music program there." Jason saw a look that was unmistakably pride wash over Franklin's face.

"Well, I don't like to brag but, yep. There wasn't much of a music program when I got there."

"Then tell me about it. I'd love to hear."

For the next two hours Jason and Art Franklin conversed about the Wardlaw music program, which included a chorus that Franklin's wife volunteered to teach in the evenings. There was also a small concert band, a string quartet, and an attempt to form a marching band; but it never actually got off the ground.

Jason found the stories interesting and he promised himself he would create a display for the opening of the shops. It would be a shame to let so much history be forgotten. He could sell it to the developers as a draw for people who had gone to school or taught there.

From a storage closet in a back room, Franklin pulled out two large boxes full of mementos from his days as a music teacher. In each box was an assortment of ribbons and medals and a few small trophies the band had won in competitions with other area schools. The principal had given them to him when the decision to close had been made. Mixed in with all this was a large collection of photographs.

"Do you have photos of every band class you had?"

"Yep. I took pictures of all of them. You never know when one of your kids is going to become famous."

"I guess that's true. Did any of these kids become famous?"

"A couple of them have done pretty well in music. I wasn't able to keep up with all of them. I've got one that's writing songs for some of the big names in Nashville and one of them is playing in New York."

"That must make you feel pretty good."

Franklin smiled, "It sure does."

"Can we look at some more pictures?" Jason wanted to see if there were any pictures of Susan Thompson.

"Sure, here we go." Franklin reached in and pulled out a disorganized stack of photographs. Franklin began to tell the story behind each one as Jason listened.

After a few minutes Jason stopped him to ask a question about one of the photos. "This photo here; is that the marching band you tried to start?" It was a large group of students standing on the Wardlaw grounds.

"Let me see." Franklin adjusted his glasses as he read the description he had written on the back of the photo. "No, this is the band camp we hosted."

"Band camp?"

"Yeah, me and some of the other middle school and junior high music teachers wanted to have a day camp for that age group. So we organized our own. The wife helped out and so did some other teachers."

"What year was that?"

Franklin tilted his head back slightly, then extended his arm about another half-inch. "Let's see; it says 1973. Yep, that's right. My sister got breast cancer that summer, I remember."

Jason had gone to see Franklin specifically about Susan Thompson, but now he wondered if Sarah Martin could also be connected in this same way. She disappeared the summer of 1973.

"Did Jim Hilliard help with the band camp?"

"Jim Hilliard." Franklin repeated the name. "That's a name I haven't heard in a long time. Yes, he did help with it. He was always a big help with anything having to do with the band. Good voice, too. He sang in the church choir over at…" Franklin paused. "Over at - I believe it was that big Presbyterian Church on Divine Street."

"Have you heard from him? No one seems to know where he is."

"I don't know. He had a breakdown of some kind years ago. I don't think he was the same after that. He couldn't take a lot of stress after that. Of course, he was an odd one anyway."

Jason smiled so as to give the impression that he was only interested in hearing another amusing story. "Oh, really, how's that?"

"Well, I don't know, some people might say I'm odd. Just ask my wife."

Jason laughed and gave Franklin a firm pat on his shoulder. "All women think men are odd."

"Ain't that the truth," Franklin smiled and shook his head then continued. "I don't know. A couple of the women teachers that worked there, that were single, thought he was good looking. They wanted to catch his eye. But he never seemed much interested in them."

"Oh really? You think he didn't like women?"

"No. I don't think he was gay or anything. He wasn't much interested in the men either."

"What did he like?"

"Beats me. We had this one teacher there, taught French. She and my wife were pretty close. That's how I know about this and all. Anyway, she went out on a date with him a couple of times. Even went to his house once. I think that was the last date. She said he had a couple of girl's bicycles in his Florida room. She said he had some dolls and girls clothes lying around."

"He just had it lying out in the open?"

"Well, I think she said she was looking for the bathroom and opened a door to one of the back rooms and saw the stuff."

"What'd she think about it? Did she ask him about it?"

"Oh, he said something about Salvation Army donations or collecting for the church; something like that."

Jason pushed his hair away from his face. "That's possible."

"Well, she told my wife that's what she thought too, then…" Franklin stopped with his story, leaned closer to Jason and in a hushed tone continued. "Well, that's not the worst part. I guess when she did make it to the bathroom, she was looking for some toilet paper or something. I think she was just going through his cabinets. People do that, you know, when they're being nosey. And she was a nosy one. Anyway, she opens the cabinet by the toilet and a bunch of Polaroids fall out. She said some of them were a little fuzzy because they looked kind of old, but they were of young girls."

Jason felt as if his heart had just skipped a beat. "You mean he had pictures of young women?"

"No. She said it was girls, young girls. Young like the age of the ones in our classes."

"My god! Did she report this to anyone?"

"I don't think so. People didn't talk about stuff like that back then. When some of those celebrities started talking about it on television, people started speaking up, but not back then."

"Were they suggestive photos? Did she think he was molesting girls?"

"If my memory serves me, they were just girls on the playground, or the ball field. So, I'm not sure what she thought. My wife was the one that talked to her. I didn't say anything either, and I should have. Looking back on it now, he must've been molesting the girls at school or maybe with the softball team, or at his church. Had to have been." Franklin looked down at the floor and shook his head.

Jason felt sorry for this man who in just a couple of hours he had grown to like. "Things were different then. Like you said, people just didn't talk about that kind of stuff."

Franklin lifted his head and looked Jason in the eye. "You know it's no excuse, but I don't think anything would've been done about it if we had said something."

"Why's that?"

"Well, with his half-brother being a senator and all. They probably would've just moved him to another school, if that much. And that would've been the end of it."

"What was the teacher's name?"

"Gloria something, I think. You'd have to ask my wife. But she's over at her sister's right now."

"Could I call you later and get her name?"

"Sure."

"Mr. Franklin, my aunt told me that you may have known Sarah Martin, a young girl that disappeared several years ago."

Franklin had a faraway look in his eyes. "I didn't really know her, but I do remember her. Sweet girl. Kind of quiet, but still friendly. Did they ever find out what happened to her?"

"Actually, I don't know if anything official has been announced or not, so I'd like you to keep this to yourself. But a friend of mine on the police force is investigating those remains that were found on the old Wardlaw playground." Franklin nodded, acknowledging he had heard about the case. "Well, it's my understanding that one of the remains was Sarah Martin."

"Oh my god. I just can't believe it."

"I know, it's terrible. But I'd like to know how you were acquainted with Sarah. She didn't go to Wardlaw?"

"She was at that band camp we ran that summer."

"Are you sure she was at the band camp?"

"Positive. Your aunt and I got to talking about it. She mentioned the two girls we had disappear from Wardlaw. I'm not sure why, but somehow we got on the subject of Sarah Martin, and I went back through my old pictures and there she was."

"Are you sure it was her?"

"Positive." Franklin flipped over the group photograph he was still holding. "See, right there's her name – Sarah Martin. I write names and dates on the backs of all my pictures. Always have."

"It's good to do that."

"Yep, I knew, one of these days, I'd get old and wouldn't be able to remember things. So I made a habit a long time ago of writing everything down."

Jason squinted and looked at the photograph. The hair was slightly different than the photograph he had, but the face smiling out of the group for the camera was, without question, Sarah Martin. Jason pointed to the man standing at the rear left corner of the group. "Is this Jim Hilliard?"

"Yeah, that's him." There was a short moment of silence. "You don't think he had something to do with what happened to Sarah?"

"I wouldn't know about that, Mr. Franklin."

"You do, don't you. That's why you've been asking all these questions."

"Sir, like I said, I'm just trying to get information on the school. But I would appreciate it if you wouldn't talk to anyone else about this."

Franklin stared at Jason with what boarded on a look of horror. "No, no, I won't."

"Could I borrow that photograph? I'll take good care of it. I'll make a copy and then get it back to you in a few days."

"Well, I suppose." Franklin reluctantly handed Jason the photograph.

"Thank you. And I'd like to get the name of the French teacher if you could talk to your wife for me." Jason handed Franklin a business card.

"OK, I'll do that. I just can't believe this. I should've said something."

"No one has said that Hilliard was responsible for what happened to Sarah. And even if he is, it's not your fault," Jason said as he and Franklin began walking to the front door. Once in his car, Jason picked up his cell phone and dialed Angela's cell. There was no answer. What should he do next? He decided to go home and wait for her.

*****

No sooner had he walked in the door, his phone rang. Jason glanced at the screen. He didn't recognize the number so he opted to try to reach Angela again. Before he could dial his cell rang again.

"Hello."

"Jason! This is Angela."

"Hey. I tried to call you earlier, but couldn't get you."

"I forgot to take my cell phone in with me. Why didn't you just call me at work?"

"I didn't know if that would be a good idea."

"It's okay for you to call me. Guess what? Mrs. Franks just happened to have a photograph of Patty's softball team. And make a guess who the coach was."

"Who?"

"Jim Hilliard."

"Are you sure?"

"Very sure. The photograph was a big eight by ten. The faces were very clear. It's him alright."

Jason interrupted. "Now, guess what I have. Jim Hilliard helped Franklin with the band. One summer Wardlaw was the host for a band day camp. Sarah Martin attended the camp. Hilliard was in the group photograph standing beside her."

"No shit! I think now we need to find out where that son-of-a-bitch is hiding. We have him connected to all the girls with the exception of Robin Skinner."

"She played softball, didn't she?" Jason inquired.

"Yes, but Hilliard wasn't her coach. I already checked that one out. Her father coached her team."

"He still could have come in contact with her at the softball field if he was coaching. But anyway, let me tell you this. This will blow your mind. Franklin said one of the teachers that was friends with his wife went out with Hilliard on a date. Even went to his house. She opened a door and saw a couple of girl's bicycles and some girl's clothes."

"Did she say anything about it?"

"He said Hilliard told her he was collecting the stuff for charity or something. But get this. Franklin said this teacher was kind of nosy. Apparently she opened some cabinets in his bathroom and found Polaroids of young girls. Like middle-school age girls."

"Does he know if she reported it? Didn't she think it was strange? I mean, apparently she did if she talked to Franklin's wife about it."

"He said he didn't think she reported it, because people didn't talk about things like that back then."

"What was the teacher's name?"

"He said Gloria something. He's going to ask his wife tonight and get back to me."

"Would your Aunt know her?"

"I don't think so. I think this was after she quit teaching there. But I'll check with her just to make sure."

"Damn!" Angela said loudly into the phone. "I'm coming over. We need to find that teacher and connect Hilliard with Robin Skinner." Angela was both excited and disgusted. She knew if she could just find physical evidence that would connect Hilliard to the murders, she would have the case solved. If the teacher truly did see what she had described, the clothes and the bicycles were probably his trophies. The photographs, if they were of the missing children, probably allowed him to relive whatever it was he did to the girls before he killed them.

By the time Angela arrived at Jason's house, she felt as if her head was spinning. She wanted to get a search warrant, but to search what. They didn't even know where Hilliard was, and she didn't want his sister to tip him off that they were looking for him.

Jason greeted Angela with a kiss.

"What's for lunch? I'm starving and I don't want to do a repeat of yesterday's migraine.

"How about sandwiches?" he said. "I haven't been to the store in the last few days. The cupboard is getting a little bare."

"That sounds good. Let's get out the file on Robin while we make lunch." Angela hurried into the living room to retrieve the folder, while Jason made sandwiches. Angela read the file as she walked into the kitchen, "None of this matches up. Nothing that we know about him ties in with Robin."

"Then maybe it's something we don't know about him. Hey, do you want olives or pickles on the side?"

"Pickles are good. I don't like olives." Angela lifted her eyes from the page to look at Jason, then directed her attention back to the file. "That could be about anything, since we don't even know where he lives now."

"Then let's find out where he lives."

The expression on Angela's face grew reflective. "This morning, I was all fired up to go see his sister. Now, the more I think about it, someone knows I'm on the right track. If I go see his sister, she might tip him off."

"You want me to talk to her? I could do my, 'I'm trying to track down old teachers' routine."

"No. Because if he's living there, then I'll want to get a warrant to search everything, so it would be better if I went."

"Okay, if you think so." Jason reluctantly agreed. He enjoyed talking to Franklin. It felt like playing secret agent when he was a child. "When are you going to question the Senator?"

"Right after the sister," Angela said. "I think I could get further with her. The Senator is slick. I don't think he is likely to slip up. Besides, Hilliard's last known address was with the sister."

As they talked and speculated about the connection between Robin Skinner and Hilliard, Angela hurriedly ate her sandwich, washing it down with a glass of iced tea. "Sweetie, I hate to eat and run, but it's after one now." Angela rubbed Jason's cheek.

"Where're you going?"

"To see if I can catch Hilliard's sister at home."

Jason frowned. He wanted to go, but he knew Angela was right, so he didn't bother to ask if he could go, too. "Is there anything I can do?"

"Try to find that teacher Mr. Franklin told you about. But leave the questioning to me. I think I'd better do that one, too."

"Will do."

Angela left just as she had arrived, in a flurry, leaving Jason to feel alone and, suddenly, like he was playing second fiddle to the investigation. He turned to Sebastian.

"Well little man, here we are again. She left us at home alone. But she does like us. And we are helping, aren't we?"

Jason picked up the tan and white cat and rubbed his face into its fur. "Come on; let's get back on the computer. Franklin told me some things about Hilliard. We can check those out and put them in our spread sheet." Jason's voice changed to baby talk. "And my little Sebastian can help me with everything. He's my big boy."

After a half-dozen phone calls and a few lies about how he was looking for a long lost teacher who had been so influential in his life, Jason was able to confirm that Jim Hilliard had indeed been a member of the church Franklin mentioned. But no one he spoke with knew how to reach him. They had just assumed he had moved away. After another call to Franklin and a long chat with his wife - she liked to talk as much as her husband - Jason secured the full name and last known address she had for Gloria Wells, the teacher who had seen the photographs of the young girls.

With Sebastian in his lap, Jason leaned back in his chair and propped his feet up on his desk. After only a couple of minutes of reading his new notes and comparing it to the spreadsheet of information on the girls, he saw the connection they had been looking for.

"No shit. Sebastian, I think this might be it." Sebastian purred upon hearing his name. Jason picked up the phone and called Angela.

"I've got it! I have the possible link!"

"What? There's some static. You're breaking up."

"I said I think I've found the connection between Hilliard and Robin Skinner."

"What is it?"

"Church! Robin went to two churches. One with her mother, and one with her father. Hilliard was a member at the church her father attended. She was probably there the weekends she visited her father."

"We have her father's address. Try to track him down and see if the address is still current."

"Already working on it. Oh, and I have Gloria Wells' address for you."

"Gloria Wells?"

"Yes, the teacher Franklin told me about." Jason continued to raise

303

the volume of his voice so he could be heard over the static.

"That's fantastic! Wait a minute, hang on. I'm getting static again on this phone. I need to get out of this dead spot. I will call you again as soon as I get a chance. You're a dear. I owe you."

"I'll remember you said that." Jason yelled into the phone trying to be heard over the cracks and pops.

With the static, Angela wasn't sure what Jason said next but she thought he said something about handcuffs. The image that came to mind made her smile.

Chapter thirty-two

Angela pulled up and parked at the curb in front of the home of Cecilia Miller. Earlier, Angela had called Debbie at the station and asked her to dig up as much as she could on Jim Hilliard, and anything current on the former Senator Thorton Collins.

Again, Debbie came through. She didn't have a lot of information, but she did get the basics. Thorton Collins was retired from political life. A polite way of saying he had lost his last election and was too old to really do anything else, and too rich to care. Collins' only sister was Cecilia Miller. Her husband had been a partner in several business ventures with the former Senator. Cecilia's oldest child, a daughter, was a partner in Collins' law firm; her middle child, a son, was a surgeon in Charleston; and then there was Jim, the brother, who had been a teacher, but now no one knew where he was.

While Angela sat in the car and made some notes for herself, she surveyed the grounds. The front yard was well kept and appeared to be freshly mowed. Angela made a snorting sound. Most people in the less expensive neighborhoods were observing the restrictions on watering and letting their yards dry up. Mrs. Miller was probably running her sprinkler full blast every day.

Angela got out of her battered car. The creaking and popping of the door hinges of her once new vehicle made her get a sudden sick feeling in her stomach. The stone sidewalk that led from the street curved gracefully through azaleas, day lilies, and beds of iris and heather. The front porch was filled with dusty white rattan furniture that obviously saw little use. Angela rang the doorbell and waited.

The house itself was old, but well maintained. It was a two-story brick with tall, square columns that supported a second floor balcony and stretched upward to a porch roof that extended a good eight feet out from the front of the house. There were four dormers jutting outward from the roof, most likely a large attic room ran the length of the house. Her grandmother had dormers like these in her farmhouse in Ohio. Of course, her grandmother's home was a modest wood frame house that had been in the family for three previous generations, but to Angela, when she was a child, it had appeared as large as this one did now.

A middle-aged woman came to the door. "May I help you?"

"Hello, I'm Detective Angela Porter with the Columbia Police department. I was wondering if I could speak with Mrs. Cecilia Miller."

"Is there anything wrong?" The woman had a worried look on her face.

"No ma'am, I just need to speak with her for a brief moment; there's something she might be able to help me with. And you are?"

"I'm Jean Kerr. I'm her nurse. Mrs. Miller's health hasn't been the best in the last few months and the family hired me to stay with her."

Angela gave a sympathetic smile. "I won't stay long. I just would like to speak with her a moment."

The nurse looked over her shoulder. "Let me see if she'll see you."

After a few minutes the nurse returned. "She'll see you. But please, she gets tired easily."

"Thank you, I'll keep that in mind." Angela smiled again then followed Jean into the sitting room where Cecilia was reclining in a chair. The room was cool from a steady flow of air-conditioned air. There was a gray tabby cat, that appeared to be almost as old as Cecilia, stretched across the woman's legs. Light streamed in the room through large plate glass windows that reached from floor to ceiling. There was a slight aroma of lilac that made Angela feel as if she might sneeze. Original artwork hung on the walls and there was a small stack of books on the table beside the old woman's chair.

"Mrs. Miller," the nurse said softly. "The police officer is here to talk to you."

Angela stepped forward. "Hello Mrs. Miller. Thank you for seeing me." Angela bent down and took the elderly woman's extended hand to shake it. Angela gently clasped the slender bony fingers in her own. She was careful not to squeeze too tight; the hand looked frail.

"Have a seat dear," she pointed to a chair opposite her.

"Thank you." Angela sat down. "Mrs. Miller, I won't take up much of your time. I'd just like to ask you a couple of things you could maybe help me with."

"I don't know how I could help the police. Is this about the break- ins in the neighborhood.

Angela smiled. "No, I'd like to ask you about your brother."

"Thorton? Is everything alright with him? He is such a great man. He has helped South Carolina so much."

"Yes, ma'am. But I'd like to ask about your younger brother, Jim." Angela watched as the smile faded from the woman's face. Her eyes looked away from Angela and seemed to transport her to a dark place.

"Ma'am, I'm just trying to locate him. It seems no one knows how to get in touch with him."

"I'm not sure how to get in touch with him."

"But you do know where he is, don't you?" Angela questioned.

"Not right off hand," Cecilia paused. "I am not my brother's keeper."

"If you could try to locate him, it would be a big help to me. I just have some things I'd like to talk to him about."

Cecilia reached over to the end table beside her chair and picked up what looked like a pager. Within moments the nurse had reentered the room. "Yes, ma'am?"

"I'm tired. Jean, would you show this lady out. I don't feel well."

The nurse turned to Angela. "It's best you go now. She's tired."

"Yes, but I need to locate your brother, Jim."

Cecilia Miller turned her head and waved her frail hand in a dismissing gesture. "It's best you leave now."

"Yes, alright. Mrs. Miller, I'll leave my card with you. If you think of anything, please give me a call." There was no response from the woman.

As the nurse escorted her to the door, Angela attempted to obtain information under the guise of small talk. "She certainly got tired quickly. I hope I didn't say something to upset her."

"I think it was asking about her brother, Jim. She doesn't talk about him. Never shuts up about Senator Collins."

"Why's that?"

"I'm not sure. They have never talked to me about it."

"They?"

"The family. Senator Collins, her children, and the rest of them."

"I see. I'm just trying to locate Jim. You wouldn't know how to get in touch with him, would you?"

As the nurse stood with her hand on the open front door, she appeared nervous. "I really can't say."

"So then, you might know where he is."

"Please, I really need this job. The hours and the pay are good and I have children to get through school."

"I promise I won't mention your name."

The nurse nervously looked around then lowered her voice. "I saw a letter come from a psychiatrist at the mental hospital."

"Did you read the letter?"

"No, I wouldn't dare. Mrs. Miller got upset when she read it. She called her brother, the Senator, and he came over with his son and Mrs. Miller's daughter. You know, the one that's the lawyer."

Angela nodded in acknowledgment. "What was in the letter?"

"I don't know. The Senator's son took it with him. He's a lawyer, too, you know."

"But, it was about Jim Hilliard?"

"I'm pretty sure of that. They were angry and they kept talking about the letter and talking about him."

"What'd they say?"

"I didn't really hear that much. I was only in and out of the room a couple of times, because Mrs. Miller called for me when she got upset. They were upsetting her pretty bad."

"Do you remember the doctor's name?"

"No ma'am, I don't."

"Okay, if you do think of anything, please call me." Angela handed the nurse her card.

"Please don't tell anyone I talked to you. I have to have this job."

"Don't worry. I won't." Angela smiled then walked down the stone walkway to her car.

Once she had pulled away from the house and was headed toward the intersection with North Trenholm Road, she let out a yell.

"Yes! Damn yes! You did it you son-of-a-bitch and they know you did it, and now you're hiding out in a mental hospital. Son-of-a-bitch."

Angela didn't see the black Lexus that was following her.

She picked up her cell phone. "I wonder if he's had any luck tracking down that teacher," she said aloud to herself. No answer. "Shit! Well, I guess I'll go to the mental hospital."

*****

Angela pulled into the main entrance and parked her car in a visitor's slot. She took in a deep breath as she stared at the brick building. She picked up her cell phone and sent a quick text message to Jason telling him where she was. She then sent a second message to her best friend, Beth.

Visions of walking through the wrong door and trying to convince someone she really was a police officer raced through her head. She knew it was absurd, but she could picture men with white clothes and large biceps dragging her down the hall saying, "Calm down. It's okay if you want to play police officer, but you have to go back to your padded cell now." She suddenly felt claustrophobic. Angela took a breath and got out of her car.

The security guard at the door, seeing Angela's nine-millimeter in a holster on her waist, stepped in front of the door. Excuse me ma'am, you'll have to stop here. Angela held up her badge and I.D. card identifying herself as a police detective. The officer studied the badge.

"You can go in detective, but you can't go past the front lobby without checking your gun. Security reasons."

Angela smiled. "That's fine, she said, and continued through the door.

Angela clipped her badge to her shirt. "Excuse me," she said to the receptionist. "I'm here to see a patient. His name is Jim Hilliard. Or it might be listed under James Hilliard."

"Just a minute, I'll check." The receptionist accessed the computer screen, studied it for a moment, and then looked up at Angela. "What's your name please?"

Angela showed the receptionist her police identification. "I'm Detective Angela Porter."

"I'm sorry, but you're not on the approved visitors list."

"I'm a detective and I'd like to speak with Mr. Hilliard."

"I'm sorry, but I don't have the authority to allow that. You'd have to talk to his doctor or his family."

"Who's his doctor?"

"That's Dr. Kirkpatrick."

"Then can I see Dr. Kirkpatrick?"

The receptionist looked back at her computer screen. "I'll see if she's in." While Angela waited, the woman dialed the doctor's office.

"Dr. Kirkpatrick, there's a police detective here to see you." The woman paused and looked up at Angela. She then swiveled in her chair to a point where her back was almost completely turned to Angela and, in a hushed voice, she said into the receiver, "She wants to see Jim Hilliard." Another pause. "I don't know; she didn't say." The receptionist swiveled back around in her chair. "She'll be right up, if you'd like to take a seat."

"Thank you." Angela took a few steps away from the desk and continued to stand while she waited.

"Detective?"

Angela turned around. "Yes. Doctor Kirkpatrick?"

"Yes." The two women shook hands. Angela was surprised by the appearance of the doctor. She was more attractive than she had pictured. Karen Kirkpatrick had short, dark brown hair and light blue eyes that appeared almost transparent with the light reflecting off her glasses. She wore makeup, not too much, but one could tell it was there. "How may I help you?"

"I'm here to see a patient of yours. Jim Hilliard."

"And what makes you think I have a patient by that name?"

"Well, when I walked in and asked to see him the receptionist said I needed to see his doctor and called for you. So that would tell me he's your patient."

"I see. Why do you want to talk with Mr. Hilliard?"

"First of all, I'd like to know what you're treating him for?"

"I'm sorry, but that information is confidential between the patient and myself."

"Okay, then can I talk to him?"

"I'm sorry, but you'd have to talk to his family about that."

"Okay, I'll do that, but let me ask you a question. Does he ever talk about angels, or about liking little girls?" Angela smiled; she could see the doctor's body shift and her back become straighter, less relaxed. She was clearly on the defensive. "That's what I thought. We'll talk again. Have a good afternoon."

Back inside her car, Angela slapped her scorching hot steering wheel. "Damn, I've got him! Now I have to prove it."

She picked up the cell phone. "Jason where are you?" There was no answer. Angela looked at her watch; it was getting late. If she hurried, she could beat some of the rush hour traffic. Where should she go? Maybe Jason was at his office. She wasn't far from Taylor Street. Angela turned her air-conditioning on high and pulled into traffic.

Jason wasn't at his office and she had gotten a chilly reception from Cindy. Jason had said there was never anything between the two of them. Maybe not for him, but Cindy was definitely viewing her as competition, Angela was sure of that. Angela looked at her note pad. Debbie had given her Senator Collins' home address. Maybe she should just drop in on him. She knew it would probably be interesting to see what he had to say about his younger half-brother. Angela made a U-turn and headed back to Forest Acres.

His house looked only slightly larger than his sister's, with a yard that was better kept. A maid wearing a pale blue uniform dress and crepe-soled shoes answered the door and led Angela into a study that was off the foyer. Angela looked around the room as she waited. The wall around the door and the opposite wall were consumed by bookshelves that reached from floor to ceiling. There were law books, literary classics, and books of regional interest. Looming over the room, from above a fireplace surrounded by a heavy oak and marble mantel, hung a painting of a much younger Senator Collins. The painting appeared to show the Senator in what Angela believed to be the Senate chambers in Washington.

"Miss Porter."

Angela turned to see a frail and stooped old man enter the room. She was shocked. This was not as the Senator was portrayed in the painting.

"Senator?"

"Have a seat Miss and we can chat about what I can do for you. I love to meet with my former constituents." The Senator put an emphasis on "former."

"It's Detective Porter. I'm with the Columbia Police Department."

"Oh, yes. Let me think." The Senator shook his finger in the air as he walked past Angela to seat himself behind his desk. "Aren't you the one who's working on that case with the remains buried out at the old school?"

"Yes sir. How'd you know that?"

"Well, I make it a point to know what's upsetting the people in my district. I may not represent this part of the state anymore, but I haven't lost my concern for the people."

"Yes sir."

"Now how can I help you?"

"Actually, I'm here on business. I'd like to talk to you about your half-brother."

"And what would you like to know about my brother?"

"I would like to know why he is in a mental hospital."

"Jim. Yes, that's such a sad story, too. So much promise, that one. So bright, too."

"Why is Jim at the State Mental Hospital?"

"Well, you see, I knew you'd ask that. His doctor - lovely woman - said you'd stopped by earlier asking about him."

"Senator, why is he in the hospital?"

"You see, he was always a high strung boy, even when he was a little thing; always wanting to do everything. Always trying to be the best at everything. You know, sometimes it's best to pick one thing and just be good at that," the Senator smiled.

"You haven't really answered my question, Senator. Why was your brother committed to a mental hospital?"

"Well, it's like I was telling you; he was just too high strung. He just couldn't take the pressure of always working too hard. Always trying to help everyone. You see, don't you?"

"Are you saying he had some sort of breakdown?"

"Not at all. The grounds of the hospital are quiet and it provides a more relaxing environment for my brother."

"I see. Did you know that we've positively identified all the remains that were uncovered from the Wardlaw school playground?"

"No, I didn't know that. I had inquired a few days ago."

"Did you know that your half-brother, Jim Hilliard, was associated with each of the dead girls?"

"I wasn't aware of that, but if that is in fact true, I'm sure there were lots of other people besides my brother who also were acquainted with those poor girls."

"Actually, Senator, I haven't been able to find anyone else who has a connection to all seven girls. And I think you know that. I also think you know your brother is responsible for the deaths of those little girls. That's why he's hidden away in that hospital, isn't it?"

"Miss Porter."

"That's Detective Porter…Senator."

"Detective. I know this is probably an emotional case for you, you being a woman in your child-bearing years. I'm sure this case upsets you. But that's no reason to slander my family by pointing blame at my poor half-brother just because he's high strung."

"Senator, think about the parents of those murdered children. Missing all those years… not knowing if they were alive or dead. If they were being abused or tortured. The things that sick adults do to children are horrific. Don't you have any sympathy for those families?"

"Detective, I really don't like the things you're saying. I think you should leave now. And if you continue to say these things, I'll be forced to have a word with your Captain. I'm sure you've worked very hard to become a detective. It is, after all, a man's job. It'd be terrible to waste all that hard work only to end up behind a desk, filing papers."

"Don't threaten me, Senator. If I find out you knew about your brother, I'll charge you as an accessory, and your sister, too."

The Senator's face hardened. Angela knew she had struck a nerve. Now, it was just a matter of finding physical evidence to a murder case that had begun over forty years ago.

Angela saw the Senator look past her. She turned to see a stocky, muscular man standing in the doorway of the study. "Jose, would you please show the detective out. She was just leaving."

Upon seeing Jose, Angela felt as if she were in the presence of a mob boss, not a retired Senator. She stayed calm.

"I guess I've worn out my welcome. I'll be back to talk to you again, Senator."

The Senator smiled and stood up as Angela prepared to exit the room.

"You have a good day, Detective, and be careful driving. There's lots of bad drivers out there always running into other cars."

For a moment Angela ignored his comment, then the force of its meaning hit her. She felt a chill go down her back and her stomach suddenly become weak. Angela spun around. "Keep your thugs away from me, or you'll regret it!"

The stocky man stepped to the side as Angela walked past him and out of the study. He then followed her out the door and to her car to make sure she actually left. There was a black Lexus parked behind her in the circular drive. Angela glanced at it, then climbed into her car and drove off.

Angela waited until she was two blocks away before she picked up her cell phone to again try to reach Jason. "Where the hell is he?"

Angela suddenly became worried. She knew the Senator had threatened her. It was obvious. Maybe he had gotten to Jason. She dialed his office – they hadn't seen or heard from him all day. Angela felt her anxiety level increase. She looked at the clock on her dash; it would take a good thirty minutes to get to his house. But if he wasn't home, what then?

As Angela made her way through traffic her phone rang. "Hello."

"Angela?"

"Jason, is that you?"

"Yeah, it's me. Where are you?"

"I'm on I-26 right now headed for your house. Where are you? I've been trying to call you all day."

"Sorry, my phone isn't working right. I don't know what's wrong with it. Sebastian knocked it off the counter top this morning. I'm going to do a hard reset. If that doesn't work, I'll have to run by the phone store and get it checked. I can receive text messages and voice mail, but not calls. "

"Okay, so where are you?"

"I'm having lemonade with Miss Connors."

A flash of anger went through Angela. She had been worried about him and he was with some woman drinking lemonade. "Miss Connors? Who the hell is that?"

"Gloria Wells Connors. Guess what? She was my French teacher in high school!"

"I'm really happy for you that you're having such a good time. Did you know I've been worried that something could've happened to you? Senator Collins just threatened me!"

Jason's tone changed. "What'd he say?"

"I don't want to get into it now."

"Okay, but I think you need to come over here."

"What for?"

"Miss Connors is the one Franklin told me about. She's already talked to me. I know you said you should be the one to talk to her and ask the questions. But since she was one of my teachers, I thought it might be okay. Anyway, I think you should hear this, too."

"Where are you?"

"I'm over on the northeast side of town in the Summit."

"Text me the address."

"She lives in one of the older sections. It'll be easy to find."

"With traffic, I'll be there in about twenty minutes."

When Angela arrived, she parked in the driveway behind Jason's Subaru. As was her habit, Angela made a mental note of the appearance of the exterior of the house. The grass was dry, but still green. She must still be watering. Before Angela could ring the bell, Miss Connors had opened the door. She had a pleasant but nervous smile and was dressed in a loose-fitting, flowered, cotton skirt and a white scoop-neck T-shirt. Angela followed her back to the kitchen where Jason was seated at the breakfast table with a full glass of lemonade and a plate of cookies in front of him. The flowers in the windows, the smell of fresh bread, the plate of cookies, even Miss Connors' clothes, made Angela feel as though she had stepped back into the television ideal of the 1950s.

"Can I get you a glass of lemonade and some cookies?" Miss Connors smiled as she nervously clasped her hands.

"Lemonade would be great. It's pretty hot out there." Angela seated herself at the table and looked over at Jason who gave her a big smile. Angela wasn't sure if the smile was from information his former teacher had given him, or if it was because this older woman was, for the moment, playing the role of mother.

"So, you were one of Jason's teachers?"

"Yes, when he was a sophomore in high school."

"I thought you taught at Wardlaw Junior High."

"Well, I did for three years, but I taught at other schools after that."

"I see." Angela wasn't sure what to say next. "So you and Jason have been reminiscing?"

"Yes. I was so surprised to hear from him."

"Believe it or not, Miss Connors' class was one of my favorites."

"Really?"

Miss Connors brought two glasses of lemonade to the table and seated herself in the chair that was opposite Angela. "Detective Porter? I believe Jason said you are a detective."

"Yes, that's right, but why don't you just call me Angela."

The woman smiled. "Alright, if you'd call me Gloria. Jason asked if I'd talk to you and tell you about what I saw at Jim Hilliard's house. I should've said something a long time ago. Back then we weren't really trained as teachers to recognize problems like that. And we weren't encouraged to get involved in those kinds of matters. People kept their problems in their own families."

Angela could hear the slight southern drawl as Gloria spoke. "Yes, Gloria, things have, fortunately, changed a lot in the last several years."

Gloria looked up; she had been nervously playing with the condensation on the outside of her glass.

"Gloria, what I'd like first is to get some background information. Just some basics about how well you knew Jim Hilliard. How long you had dated. How you came to see the things I've been told you saw at his house."

"That's fine. I've already talked to Jason about a lot of this. Actually, it is such a relief to finally tell someone about it. This has bothered me for years."

"Let's start from the beginning. How did you meet Jim Hilliard?"

"He and I were both teachers at Wardlaw Junior High. He taught science and math in seventh grade and I taught French for a small group of honor students in the eighth grade, and I also taught English. French had been my major and I was waiting for an opening at one of the high schools."

"You didn't know him other than through the school?"

"No."

"Okay, why don't you just start from there; tell me how you ended up going to his house."

"I was single at the time. I knew Jim wasn't married either. He was a very handsome looking man. He always seemed so nice and pleasant. One of the other teachers started encouraging us to talk on a more social level. I think she thought we would make a nice looking couple."

"How long did the two of you talk before you went out on an actual date?"

"Oh, I suppose for about a month or so. Jim was so nice and all. But there was something that was a little standoffish about him. Sometimes it was hard to tell if he was really interested in going out. I just thought maybe, him coming from money and all, made him a little like that."

While she listened, Angela both recorded the conversation with her cell phone, and took notes.

"Anyway, we finally went out to dinner a couple of times. He was very mannerly. I'd never had anyone order wine for me with dinner. I guess being from the kind of family he was from, he was just used to those kinds of things. Anyway, after a couple of dinner dates and a movie, he invited me over to his house."

"Did you drive yourself on these dates or did he pick you up?"

"Oh, he always picked me up, and opened the car door for me, too." Gloria returned her gaze to her glass of lemonade. "Anyway, this was the last time he and I went out. He picked me up. He had invited me to his house; I'd never been there before. Then he asked if I'd rather go out to his parent's house on Lake Murray. He said we could go by Kentucky Fried Chicken and have a little picnic, then go out on his father's boat."

Angela continued to write. "So you agreed to this?"

"Yes. I mean, he'd never given me a reason to not trust him. Anyway, he picked me up and we picked up the chicken and drove out there. It was a longer drive then, or at least it seemed longer. When we got there, I saw a little girl's bicycle in the Florida room. You know the kind that used to have a banana seat and little straw basket and all."

"Yes ma'am, I have seen those."

Gloria smiled. "I think this one was blue. I don't know why I remember it being blue. I asked if it belonged to a niece, and he said no, he was picking up donations for charity. He left it there because he didn't have room at his house. Then, after we ate, he noticed that I'd seen some children's clothes in a little storage room that was off from the Florida room."

"What'd he say about the clothes?"

"Again, he just said that they were for charity. He kicked at them and pushed them back in the room and closed the door. You know, that was the first time I'd seen him act like he was mad or upset about anything. Before going out on the boat, I wanted to use the restroom. He showed me where it was and I went back there."

"Is this where you saw the photographs?"

Gloria closed her eyes and took in a deep breath as if she were reliving the memory. "Yes. I could tell the lake house didn't get used much because everything was so dusty. I went to the bathroom. I didn't see any toilet paper and so, instead of going back out and asking where it was, I just started looking through cabinets."

Gloria paused. "It's okay, go ahead," Angela encouraged.

"I opened one of the cabinets and some of those men's magazines fell out. I wasn't shocked by them. I guess most men have them. My brother used to hide them in his room. Of course, the ones then were tamer than what they have now. I started to pick them up and put them back in the cabinet when I saw some Polaroids sticking out of one of them. I guess

I was just being nosy. I opened the magazine to look at them."

Gloria looked straight into Angela's eyes. "There were probably thirty pictures of young girls. I recognized some of them as girls from school. Some of the pictures were old, too, black and whites, and some were newer and in color. It was just strange to have those pictures in the men's magazines. It seemed dirty."

"Were the girls posing in any way? Where they provocative photos? Or were there just standing there, or what?"

"No. They weren't like that at all. Some were taken on the playground. Some were in the class room. I do remember there were some with…" Gloria paused. "It looked like he had used a marker and drawn angel wings on some of them." Gloria continued to describe, in as much detail as she could remember, the content of the photographs. She explained she hadn't gone for the boat ride that Saturday afternoon. She had complained of a stomachache and the possibility of eating bad chicken. She told Angela the car ride back into Columbia with Hilliard had been mostly silent. She could tell he knew something was wrong. That was their last date. For the remainder of the school year, their contact was limited to passing in the halls and a cordial hello or good-bye.

Gloria's transfer to a high school came through by the start of the next school year. She had no contact with Hilliard after that.

"You said the lake house belonged to his parents. Do you think someone else could've put the photographs there?"

"No. No, I'm sure that they were his."

"What makes you so sure?"

"Because there were pictures of him with some of the girls."

"He was posing with the girls?"

"Yes. Now they call it a 'selfie.' Their faces would be close together and sort of whited out. They looked like he had held the camera out himself and taken the picture."

"What were the expressions on their faces?"

"They were laughing or smiling."

Angela thanked Gloria when they finished. Jason hugged his former teacher and also thanked her. As Angela left, she asked the woman to not speak to anyone else right now.

Gloria Connors agreed, but had one parting question for Angela. "This is about those skeletons they found buried at Wardlaw, isn't it?"

"Yes ma'am, I'm afraid it is." Angela saw a tear form in Gloria's eye. "If the pictures you saw were of those same girls, which we don't know that yet... then probably, by the time you saw the pictures, it was already too late."

"Thank you for that. If I can help in any other way...."

"Thank you, I'll call."

Angela and Jason walked down the driveway together. Angela lifted her sunglasses and rubbed her eyes as she squinted from the sun. "Jesus Christ! I can't believe this."

"It's pretty bad, isn't it?" Jason ran his hand through his hair pushing it away from his face. "I've read about these things. I've heard about them on the news. I never expected to come in contact with it myself."

"I wonder if they still own that lake house."

"I already have Louise checking deeds for us."

Angela smiled. "Boy, you're on top of things, aren't you?"

"It pays to have an aunt whose partner is in real estate."

"Let's go. I need a drink."

"Your place or mine?"

"How about mine? It's closer and you haven't seen it yet. I'll warn you though; it's small and not as clean as yours. I don't have a maid that comes in."

Chapter thirty-three

It was late, nearly ten, and Jason was still at Angela's apartment. He was enjoying the quiet time with her - relaxing, talking, and reflecting. He had wanted so much to be involved with this case. The renovation of Wardlaw Junior High was his project. It was personal, but more than that, the discovery of the seven remains on "his" project resurfaced emotions about his brother's drowning and his feelings of guilt that he hadn't experienced in years. Meeting Angela was a plus he hadn't bargained for.

The music from the Bose was low; it could barely be heard. The only light in the living room was from a candle on the coffee table. Angela, with a quilt around her shoulders and her head resting against his chest, had fallen asleep. The last few days had been hard for her. They had the address of the lake house and, tomorrow, Angela would try to convince her Captain to let her get a search warrant. Probably everything was long gone; maybe even dumped in Lake Murray or burned, but it was worth a try. Something had to have survived.

Jason could hear the soft drone of the air conditioner as it came on to keep the apartment at a constant seventy-three. He felt a chill, but it wasn't enough to prevent his eyes from slowly closing.

He awoke with a start. His sudden movement woke Angela. Sleepily, she raised her head. "What is it?"

"I don't know. I think my phone just went off."

"I didn't hear anything."

"I had it set on vibrate. Yes, there it goes again." Jason sat up and pulled the phone from his pocket.

"Who is it?"

"I don't know. It's a text message. I don't recognize the number."

"What does it say?" Angela asked through a yawn.

"Vandalism inside Wardlaw. Third floor."

Angela was now fully awake. "Who sent it?"

"I don't know; they didn't give a name. It could be from the security company the developer hired. They have my number on file. Could be someone from the developer's office."

"Are you going down there?"

"Yes, I think I should."

"I'll go with you." Angela tossed back the quilt and stood up.

"No, there's no point in you driving down there, too. It's probably the security guard. The developers hired a security firm to patrol the place and the guard probably looked up my number. I bet that's what it is. They've found something torn up and called me."

"I still think I should go with you."

"Jason brushed the hair away from his eyes. It's not that far out of my way and I need to get going anyway; it's late. I'll just stop for a minute and talk to the guard. Make sure everything is okay and then go on home." Jason looked squarely into Angela's eyes. "Don't worry. I'll text as soon as I get there."

"Promise?"

"Scouts honor."

"I want you to promise me you will text or call."

Jason smiled, "I promise, I will text."

Angela returned the smile. "okay, and text me when you leave."

"I will."

"Next time, I'm going to make sure you don't want to go home."

Jason felt his body warm at the thought. "Promise?"

"I promise." Angela held up three fingers, "Scout's honor."

Jason knew from the message conveyed, not only by Angela's joke, but also by her eyes, that they wouldn't wait until the investigation was over.

Angela walked toward Jason and put her arms tight around him. He was only slightly taller than her. She liked this in her relationships. It made her feel more like she was on even footing with the men she dated. After a long, slow kiss and a reluctant parting, the two said good night.

Chapter thirty-four

When Jason pulled his car onto the school grounds, he had expected to see a security officer's car, or perhaps even a police car, waiting for him. Instead, the lot was deserted except for a beat up van one of the sheetrock contractors drove. The van was constantly breaking down.

"At least it's now breaking down after he gets to work," Jason commented to himself. He looked at his watch. It was almost eleven. He watched the building as he waited for the security guard to arrive. "Probably getting coffee," he thought. He continued to wait and watch the building.

Jason turned his attention to a set of headlights that were approaching on Park Street. His eyes followed the car as it continued to drive by, then turned left onto Elmwood Avenue. As Jason looked back toward the school, he saw what appeared to be the beam of a flashlight reflecting against the glass in one of the third floor classrooms. Jason looked at his watch again; it was now about five after. Remembering his promise, he picked up his phone to text Angela. The text didn't go through. "Shit!"

Jason reached in the back seat and pulled out a large metal flashlight. He tested the beam to make sure the batteries were working, then got out of his car. He looked around, the street was dark and the lights on the school grounds weren't working. He hesitated. Should he go inside the school or wait for the security guard? Jason looked around the grounds and then up and down the street. The air was warm and still; there was no one else on the street. Not even the usual homeless from the mission a few of blocks away. The only other car in sight, besides his own and the broken down van, was a black Lexus parked down the street in front of the church.

Jason pushed back his hair. The ends around his face were damp with sweat. He took a deep breath and walked toward the side entrance of the old school. Jason tried the door. It was unlocked. Either the security guard had unlocked it when he checked the inside of the building, or someone on one of the crews had left it unlocked. But Glenn was pretty good about locking everything up before he left in the afternoon. At this stage of the renovation, they were so close to finishing, they couldn't afford to leave any door unlocked, especially with the publicity the project had received since the first remains were discovered.

Jason slowly pushed open the door and entered the stairwell. To his left was an entrance into the auditorium. He stepped through the doorway and aimed his flashlight around the room. He smiled when he saw that the first of the velvet-covered seats had already been installed. Glenn must have been really cracking the whip the last three days to get caught up. He stepped back into the stairwell. The third floor was where he had seen the light. Of course, if there was someone else in the building, they could be almost anywhere at this point.

"Hello, is anyone in here?" His voice echoed up the stairwell. "My name's Jason Shealy. I'm the architect on this job. Is anyone in here? I'm coming upstairs. Don't shoot," he smiled and laughed quietly to himself.

Jason slowly walked up the first flight of stairs, then paused to shine his flashlight down the second floor hallway. "Hello, this is Jason. Is anyone in here?" Better to yell out and give an intruder time to get away, or notify an edgy security guard of his presence, than get shot. Jason stepped back onto the wide landing. He leaned over the brass-topped handrail and looked both below him and above. He could detect no other sounds in the building. Jason proceeded up the stairs to the third floor. Once he had reached the top and was standing on the landing, he could feel his heart start to pound.

"Hello. This is Jason, the architect on this job. Is anyone up here?" He listened. There was only silence. The magnolia trees on the front lawn were buffering even the sounds from the street. He stepped into the long, wide corridor. The beam from his flashlight bounced off sculpted glass transoms at the tops of the doors which opened into the former classrooms. Jason walked slowly down the hall, his heart beating faster with each step.

"Hello. Is anyone up here?" He thought he heard a noise in what had been the science lab and was now going to house a bookstore. With his heavy, black metal flashlight in his left hand, he slowly pushed open the door with his right. Jason took short deliberate steps as he entered the room. With the flashlight pointed to his immediate left he began a slow sweep of the large room. The room still had the scaffolding set up where the sheetrockers had just finished the ceiling. There were a few pieces of sheetrock, and buckets of joint compound on the very top of the scaffold.

Just as Jason took another step into the room, at the edge of his beam of light he saw what he thought was a person move away from the beam and disappear behind a sheet of plywood which was leaning against the scaffold. Jason felt his chest become tight and his breathing labored. Damn, this was no time for an asthma attack.

In a raspy, breathless voice he called out. "Hello. Who's there? I work on this project. This is private property. Please come out, because I'll have to ask you to leave." He had barely finished his sentence when he felt a hard force across his back. Jason fell forward onto the dusty floor and he felt a hard impact against the side of his head as it struck a stack of sheetrock.

The flashlight flew out of his hand and rolled into a corner of the room. Jason rolled off the sheetrock onto his back and looked up only to see a dark figure rush toward him. As Jason flung his body to the right, he could hear the impact of something hard against the floor where he had fallen. He stumbled to his feet only to see the figure rush at him again and swing something at him. This time it made contact with his left shoulder. It felt as if he had been hit with a board. Jason's right knee hit the hard floor and he caught himself with his right hand before he went down completely. His only advantage was his assailant was having as much difficulty seeing him in the dark as Jason was in seeing him. As the figure swung around to bring the board down on him again, Jason regained his footing and, with two quick, sprinting steps, rushed through the door into the hallway.

Jason ran for the stairwell with his attacker close behind. Just as he reached the landing he slid in some sawdust that hadn't been swept up, and lost his footing. This time his attacker brought the heavy board down straight for his head. Jason saw it coming and put his arms up to shield himself. Jason heard a loud metal ring as the end of the board had caught on the brass handrail. The attacker had missed. Half running and half falling, Jason scrambled down the stairs taking two to three steps with each stride. He didn't have time to think; he just knew he had to get out of the building if he wanted to live.

As Jason's feet hit the second floor landing, he heard two loud blasts from a siren. The dark figure, which was half a flight above him, stopped and appeared to look up to the third floor and back down to Jason. This was the few extra seconds he needed to put more distance between himself and the person on the stairs. Jason ran down the stairs to the ground floor. He paused only long enough to see the dark figure that had pursued him look over the handrail from the second floor landing, then run back into the hallway. Once on the ground floor, Jason flung open the door and fell onto the sidewalk. He could barely breathe.

"Stop! Hold it right there!" He heard the officer yell out.

Jason couldn't move. He lay on the ground gasping for air. One officer stood over top of him with his gun drawn; the other reached for handcuffs. Jason gasped the word, "Asthma!" The officer ignored him and fastened the handcuff tight on his wrist. Jason yelled as loud as his lack of air would allow. The pain in his left arm was excruciating.

"Help! Can't breathe!" Jason gasped again.

"No! Let him go! He works here!"

Jason saw Angela run toward them. He closed his eyes and winced from the pain as the officer tried to pull him to his feet. Angela shoved her badge into the uniformed officer's face. "I said he works here! Let him go!" Jason fell against Angela then slumped to his knees. Angela saw the blood on his face. "What happened? Are you alright?"

Jason was wheezing and struggling for every breath. "Can't breathe! Inhaler! Please."

"Where is it?"

"Bag – messenger bag! Car… keys…pocket."

Angela shoved her hand into the front pockets of Jason's slacks. "Got them. Get those cuffs off him now, and call an ambulance!"

Angela ran faster than she thought possible. She grabbed the messenger bag from the front seat and ran back for Jason. By now the cuffs were off his wrists, but he was still struggling to breathe. Angela put the inhaler into his mouth. Jason put his right hand over Angela's and squeezed. He was in too much pain; his hand had lost all its strength. Quickly Angela helped him compress the inhaler. She sat there on the ground holding him and stroking his hair as his breathing slowly began to calm and return to normal. "Are you okay?" Jason closed his eyes and moved his head up and down.

"What happened? You're hurt."

"Someone, someone tried to kill me. Hit me with, I think, a two-by-four. I was up on the third floor. I saw a light up there."

"Get some back-up out here! I want every inch of that school and the surrounding neighborhood searched!"

"He took off; heard the siren."

"Do you know who it was?"

"No. It was too dark. I only got one short look at his face." Jason closed his eyes and gritted his teeth in pain. "Stocky build, dark hair, maybe a mustache. I just couldn't see much."

Angela saw the ambulance pull up. One of the officers reminded her they needed to get a statement. "You just keep looking for someone in that school. He's hurt! You can get a statement at the hospital!"

Angela wanted to ride in the ambulance with Jason, but she knew she would need her car later. She followed close behind and cursed each time an inattentive driver failed to yield the right-of-way to the ambulance.

Once at the hospital, with Angela flashing her badge, it took little time for a doctor to examine Jason. His arm was badly bruised, but nothing was broken. He had a slight concussion and some cuts to his forehead. The doctor told them both that, overall, he was very lucky and should be observed during the night due to the concussion.

By the time the butterfly bandages were placed on his head and a prescription for pain medication had been written for his arm, Angela's Captain came bursting through the door.

"Porter! I want to know exactly what's going on here!"

Angela and her Captain exited the examining area and retreated into a nearby office and closed the door behind them. There were two windows which extended the entire length of the room. Jason watched as Angela and her Captain, sometimes talking calmly, sometimes obviously arguing, discussed what had happened.

Angela began from the point where Jason had first approached her with the news stories he'd uncovered, through the photographs of the girls, to her conviction that Jim Hilliard was the murderer, and the attempt on first her life, and now on Jason's, was all connected to her investigation. Her Captain was angry. First, that she had involved a civilian, and second, that she hadn't told him about her independent investigation. She reminded him that he had promised her she could work independently, and then had dismissed her out of hand when she tried to talk to him about taking the case in this direction. He was reluctant, but in the end, did agree to allow her to get the search warrant for the lake house.

"You know, we're both going to be in a pile of shit if we get a warrant and don't find anything."

"I now that, Frank, but don't you agree with me? Don't you think Hilliard is the murderer?"

"It looks like it. First we gotta get an affidavit from, what'd you say her name was?"

"Gloria Wells Connors."

"From this Connors woman, then go to the magistrate to get the warrant. We ain't likely to find anything. It's been a long time."

"I know, but we have to try."

"Go home and get some sleep. And don't talk to anyone else about this. If it is Hilliard and somebody really did try to kill you two because they figured you were getting close, we don't want them to find out about the warrant and start destroying anything that might be left."

"Don't worry. I kept it quiet this long, didn't I."

Her Captain looked through the window to Jason who was still seated on the examining table. "Obviously, not quiet enough." He turned back to Angela, "Where you gonna be tonight?"

"Well, I thought I'd better stay with Jason. The doctor said he should be checked through the night, because of his concussion."

"Give me the address and I'll make sure the house gets patrolled tonight."

"Thanks, Captain."

Chapter thirty-five

Jason's night had been a restless one. The pain in his arm and shoulder hadn't allowed him to sleep well. Angela woke up at least every hour to check him. The doctors had told her they didn't feel he was in any danger, but best not to take any chances. She could tell a couple of times he was having a nightmare, probably because of the attack. She wished she had never agreed to let him be involved in the investigation. Angela had known almost from the start, that she would fall in love with Jason if she let herself, and now she had nearly lost him. She wouldn't allow that to happen again.

Angela awoke early Saturday morning. She had to get to Gloria Wells Connor and get the affidavit before someone close to Hilliard and the Senator figured out what this woman knew and pressured her not to talk. Angela and her Captain had made their plans before they left the hospital. They would have to move simultaneously in order to not give the Senator time to react. They probably wouldn't be able to connect the car that tried to run her off the road and the attempt on Jason's life to the Senator, but damn, it they could get him for hiding his half-brother away in a mental hospital and covering up seven murders.....

Angela first met her Captain and another officer at Mrs. Connor's house in The Summit and took her statement. Then they headed for the magistrate's office for Jim Hilliard's arrest warrant and the search warrants for his hospital room, his sister's house, the lake house, and any other buildings on the properties. They weren't able to obtain a warrant for the former Senator's home. It was too politically volatile. Angela didn't have prior experience with serial killers, but from all she had read from experts on the subject, unless his family had found and destroyed the evidence, Hilliard had most likely kept trophies.

Angela wanted to be present for both the search of the properties and the arrest, but the arrest meant more. Hilliard was a sick bastard who had brutalized at least seven little girls and then murdered them. He was hers!

Angela, in an unmarked police car and accompanied by another detective, pulled into the parking lot of the mental hospital. Uniformed officers in squad cars pulled in beside them. With long quick strides, Angela walked across the small front lawn and swung open the double front doors. Angela was wearing her badge on a chain around her neck.

"I'm detective Angela Porter with the Columbia City Police Department and I need someone to take us to Jim Hilliard's room."

The young receptionist was shaken. "Yes ma'am, just a minute; let me check. Uh, I'm sorry, but he isn't allowed any visitors."

"Look, I went through all that bullshit yesterday and I'm not a visitor. We're here to place him under arrest. If you don't get someone to take us to his room right now, then I'll arrest you for interfering with a police officer!"

Angela could see the receptionist's hands start to shake. "Yes ma'am. Right away, ma'am." The girl hit a button on the phone and, with a trembling voice, spoke into the receiver. "Paul, could you come up here, please? You need to escort some people to a patient's room." She turned to Angela, "It'll be just a moment."

Within a minute or two a muscular young man, dressed in white pants and white T-shirt, walked into the lobby. He looked at the receptionist who was nervously twirling the phone cord in her fingers. "Paul, they need to go to Jim Hilliard's room. He's in three-fifteen."

Angela and the other officers followed Paul to the elevator, then to the wing of the hospital where Hilliard was housed. "This is his room."

Angela tried the doorknob. "Unlock it!" Paul reached into his pocket and pulled out a key. He unlocked the door. They then followed him into the room.

"Jim, you have some visitors here."

Jim Hillard was standing at his window with his back turned to Paul, Angela, and the officers. Angela didn't know what to expect. She didn't know if he would become violent or hysterical, so she wanted to be as calm as possible.

Hilliard turned slowly to face them. The face that greeted them was not what she had expected of someone who lived in a mental hospital. He was clean-shaven; his hair receded slightly at the temples and was grayed, but nicely combed and trimmed. His arms were folded casually across his chest. As he looked first at Angela and then at the other officers accompanying her, he gave a slight smile. "Well, I certainly have a lot of visitors today. Why don't you all come in. It's not a big room, but I think we can all fit comfortably; although we might need to call for extra chairs."

Angela took a step forward. "Are you Jim Hilliard?"

"Yes, I am. And you are?"

"Mr. Hilliard, I'm Detective Angela Porter of the Columbia City Police Department. I'm here to place you under arrest for the murder of seven children. Mr. Hilliard, I'd like to ask you to come with us down to the police station. We'd like to talk to you and have you answer a few questions."

Hilliard unfolded his arms and placed his right hand on an armchair positioned by the window. He took in a deep breath and expelled it in a sigh. Angela was alarmed by his calm.

"Well, I'm sorry you've gone to all this trouble, but you don't have the right person. I'm sure my brother, Senator Thorton Collins, will tell you that. You do know the Senator, don't you?"

"I'm familiar with him."

"I see. Well, if you'd like me to go with you, I'd be happy to oblige. I'm sure I'll enjoy the ride. I don't get to take many trips. Just holidays, birthdays, special occasions, you know." Hilliard smiled again.

The other detective stepped forward to secure handcuffs around Hilliard's wrists. Just as the second cuff clicked into place, Hilliard's doctor, Karen Kirkpatrick rushed through the door. "What's going on here? What are you doing in my patient's room?"

"Karen, they've just arrested me. Imagine that," Hilliard smiled.

"You can't take him out of this hospital. He's under treatment!"

Angela took a step closer to the doctor. "I can take him out of this hospital, and I will. I have a warrant for his arrest for the murder of seven children."

"I won't let you take him out of here. It could be too traumatic for him!"

"You want to see traumatic, Doctor? Then go talk to the parents of those little girls. Now get out of my way before I arrest you, too!"

"Don't worry, Karen. It'll be alright. Just call my brother or someone at the firm and they'll take care of it. They always do." Hilliard looked straight into Angela's eyes and smiled. "Detective, do you have any daughters?"

"No."

"That's too bad; they can be such angels."

Behind Hilliard's smile, Angela could see the cold stare of someone who understood what he'd done, knew it was wrong, but enjoyed it too much to care.

"Take this bastard out here and book him at the station."

The other detective and two of the uniformed officers escorted Hilliard out the door of his room and down the hall. Angela then turned to the doctor, "I also have a search warrant for his room and your office. So you'll need to step aside and let these officers do their work."

"I'm getting the Director! You can't do this!"

"Oh yes, I can."

One of the uniformed officers interrupted. He was standing with his rubber-gloved hand on the doorknob of the closet. "Detective Porter, there are some shoe boxes of photographs up here on the shelf. Do you want me to get those?"

"Take everything! Johnson, come on, you can drive me to our next stop." Angela left, leaving the four other officers to collect any possible evidence. She wanted to get to the lake house as quickly as possible.

Just as Angela opened the door of the squad car. "Detective! Detective!" Angela turned to see Dorothy Danze walking toward her at a quick pace.

Angela closed her eyes. "Son-of-a-bitch."

"Detective, I need a minute with you!"

"I don't have time right now." Angela turned to get in the squad car.

"The black Lexus that followed you home from work the day you had your accident. It is registered to former Senator Collins." Angela stopped and turned. "That's right and a man who works for him named

Jose is usually who drives it."

"How do you know that car followed me the other day? I didn't see a car!"

"After we had our discussion in the parking lot of the police station, I stood there and watched you drive off. No sooner had you pulled onto the street, than that car pulled in behind you. I just thought it looked odd, so I followed you both. I got the license number. When you headed out toward Irmo, the car stopped following you, so I stayed with it. It went right back to Collins' house."

Angela's mind began to race. There had been a black Lexus in the driveway of the Senator's home when she left yesterday. But there was something else. Where had she seen that car before? There had been a black Lexus parked at her complex just before her apartment was broken into.

"Okay, so the Senator had me followed," Angela turned to get in the car.

"The same car was at Wardlaw last night when someone tried to kill your boyfriend."

Angela spun around. "How do you know about that?"

"Police scanner. I was just leaving the TV station and had it on in my car when I heard the call to send cruisers out to Wardlaw. I probably pulled up just a minute or two after you did. I saw you down on the ground with him. He looked pretty bad. Is he okay?"

"He'll be okay. So what about the car?"

"After you left with the ambulance, I hung around. Talked to the officers, asked questions. As I was leaving, that's when I saw the Lexus parked down the street in front of the church. I checked the license number and sure enough, it was the same car."

"That bastard. He threatened me yesterday. I never thought he'd go after Jason."

"He's been using some of the same sources for information that I've used. He probably knows Jason was helping you. Now, I know you have search warrants. I just don't know for where. Since I've just shared some of my information with you – how about you let me be the first reporter on the scene?"

Angela looked long and hard into Dorothy Danze's eyes. She bit her

333

lip, then looked at the uniformed officer who had been listening to the conversation. He shrugged his shoulders. Angela looked down at the ground then back to Dorothy.

"Okay, get in the car. You can call your crew and tell them where you are once we get there."

Dorothy smiled. "Great! I'll owe you one."

Angela looked over her shoulder at the reporter in the back seat of the police car. "Don't think I won't remember that."

Frank Morris had two teams of officers. One was with Randall Evans at the home of Cecilia Miller. The warrants to search her home and the lake house were both presented to her since both properties were in her name alone. The officers tried to be polite to the woman, but she understood all too well why they were there and quickly became nervous and distraught. Her nurse called for Cecilia's daughter. Within fifteen minutes of placing the call, Cecilia Miller's daughter, along with the Senator and another lawyer from the firm, were at the house threatening legal action against the police department. Randall and his team ignored them and continued with the sweep of the woman's home.

As Angela, Officer Johnson, and their passenger, Dorothy Danze, made their way down the winding lake road, Angela could see just ahead of them, disappearing around a curve in the road, what appeared to be a black Lexus. "Johnson, is that a Lexus up there in front of us?"

"I'm not sure, ma'am; it might be. I can't really tell this far away."

"Slow down a little bit, I want to see where it's going."

Johnson backed off the accelerator and Dorothy leaned forward to get a better look. "If they're going the same place we are, then they'll have to turn soon."

Angela looked back at Dorothy. "That's what I'm thinking. From what the Captain said, there's only the one long drive in and out. If that's the Senator's Lexus, then once whoever it is gets down there, they won't be able to get back out with us behind them."

Dorothy leaned closer and squinted her eyes. "Can you make out the license tag? I have the tag number of the Senator's Lexus with me."

"No, I still can't see it. Let's just see where they turn."

As Johnson slowed his speed again, the three watched the black car slow almost to a stop, make a right turn and disappear into the woods.

"Give him time to get down the drive, then go in behind him."

Johnson followed Angela's instructions. As Johnson entered the long dirt drive that would lead to the lake house owned by Cecilia Miller, the three quickly lost sight of the black car which had been in front of them. Within twenty-five feet of the highway, the dirt road bent to the right. Trees and underbrush were so thick they could barely see three or four feet past the edge of the drive. Long branches extending over the dirt drive formed a low-hanging canopy which, in some places, caught the squad car's antennas and whipped them back and forth.

Suddenly, they came upon the black Lexus with its backup lights illuminated and the driver looking over his shoulder in an attempt to back out of the long drive. Johnson turned on his blue lights. The driver turned around and looked straight ahead. Angela and Johnson stepped out of the car. Angela walked up on the right-hand side of the car to watch the hands of the driver. Johnson went to the driver side window. Dorothy watched anxiously from the back seat of the squad car, not able to hear what either Johnson or Angela was saying to the driver.

After a short conversation, Angela and Johnson pushed back through the weeds and returned to their car. "Who was it? What'd he say?"

"His name is Jose Mendez and he works for Senator Collins. He said he was down here to check on Miss Miller's lake house for her, just like he does all the time."

"That's the same car that followed you. And it's the same car that was at Wardlaw last night."

"Are you sure of that?" Angela asked.

"Positive. Are you going to let him go?"

"No. My guess is, once the Senator saw we also had a search warrant for the lake house, he sent him down here to see if he could find anything and destroy it before we got here. What he didn't count on is my Captain and another team are already here. We hit all three places simultaneously."

"So, what now?"

"He's going to join us at the house." The three watched as the brake lights of the Lexus went out and the car began to move forward down the drive.

The Lexus came to a stop in the small clearing in front of the run-down lake house. To the far right of the house were two sheds and a delapidated boat house and dock. One shed looked to have been a garage; the other, which was smaller, was probably for storage.

Jose stepped out of the car and was quickly accompanied by Officer Johnson. Angela and Dorothy walked the few feet to the house and were greeted by Captain Morris. Morris looked at Dorothy, and then at Angela. "No offense, Ms. Danze, but what the hell is she doing here?"

"She was at the hospital when we arrested Jim Hilliard. Seems somebody tipped her off we were going to be there."

Dorothy smiled. "And I had some information I thought Detective Porter might find interesting. In exchange for letting me break the story of Hilliard's arrest, of course."

With his hands resting on his hips like a gunslinger, Morris shot an angry scowl at Dorothy. "And what might that be?"

Dorothy looked in the direction of Jose and the black Lexus. "That Lexus over there is owned by the Senator. It followed Angela from the police station the day someone tried to run her off the road. The same car was parked down the street from Wardlaw last night when someone tried to kill Jason Shealy. If my source knew Jason was looking into these murders with Detective Porter… then you can bet the Senator knew that, too."

"So you're implying the Senator tried to have them killed?"

"Don't you already think the same thing?"

"Who's this guy?" The Captain nodded his head in the direction of Jose.

"He was the one who escorted me out of the Senator's house. Right after Collins told me to drive carefully."

"So, what's he doing down here?"

"He was in front of us and pulled in. He was backing out when we blocked his path. I'm guessing he came down here to get rid of evidence before we could get here. But he saw your cars and tried to back out before anyone saw him."

The Captain loosened his tie. The sun was getting higher in the sky and even though the lake house and what was left of the overgrown lawn were shaded, the heat index made it feel like one hundred.

"Alright, just don't get in the way and, before you say anything on TV, it gets cleared with me first.

"No problem."

Angela looked through the front door of the house. "You all find anything yet?"

"No. We're just now really getting started."

"What about the out buildings? You get those yet?"

"Not yet. There's a rusted up chain and pad lock on the shed. It doesn't look like it's been touched in years. The chain and lock on the old garage is new."

Dorothy jumped into the conversation. "So then, someone could've put something in there recently."

"Or taken something out," Angela added. "Why don't we see if Jose has a key? He was in a hurry to get out here for something."

Angela, her Captain and Dorothy walked to the Lexus where Jose was still standing with Officer Johnson. Jose had sweat beading up on his forehead and a small drop had started inching its way down his face from his sideburn. Morris, in his usual gruff tone, practically shouting at Jose, asked for the keys to the old garage. For a moment, Jose hesitated, then from his pants pocket he produced a key chain with three keys. The group, with Johnson, Jose, and another officer, walked to the garage.

"Open it!" Morris commanded.

Jose, with shaking hands, fumbled with the keys, dropping them once then picking them up and inserting one into the pad lock. It sprung open.

"Open the door!" Again, another command from Morris. Jose pulled the wide doors back. Inside was an early model Chrysler sedan with deep scrapes and dents along the passenger side of the car. The windows were tinted and the license tag was missing. In its place was a piece of cardboard with the words "tag applied for" written in large letters with a marker.

"Well, son-of-a-bitch," was all Angela said.

Morris turned to Jose. "What'd you know about this?"

"I don't know nothing. That's not my car! I didn't run her off the road!"

"How'd you know she got run off of the road with this car?"

337

Jose froze. His eyes were wide with fear when he realized what he'd said. "I don't know nothing!"

"Johnson, take him down to the station and hold him for questioning." As Johnson led Jose away and placed him in his squad car, Morris turned to Angela. "You think this is the car?"

"It sure does look like it. The side here would have paint on it from my car. Can we get it analyzed to see if it matches?"

"Yep, looks like we need to."

Angela shoved her hand into the front pocket of her navy slacks. "Okay, so now we have a car. Let's see what's behind door number two."

Morris had one of the officers cut the rusted pad lock off the storage shed. It was dark and full of cobwebs. A thick layer of dust covered everything. In the far-left corner of the building sat a rusted lawn mower, some rakes and shovels. Several brown clay pots were thrown about the floor, along with several small hand-held gardening tools. There were boxes and a wooden crate stacked in the back, and with them were two rusted bicycles.

"Let's see what we have here." Morris stepped further inside the shed, "Get me some light in here." One of the uniformed officers quickly brought a heavy-duty flashlight. Angela and her Captain pulled the bicycle away from the crates. The tires on the bikes were flat and dry rotted. The spokes were entwined with cobwebs and the egg sacks from spiders.

"Gross! I hate spiders," Angela brushed a web away from her face. "This is an old one."

"You ever have a bike like this, Porter?"

"No, they were before my time." Her Captain cast a sideways glance at her.

"Look at this, Frank. It has one of those little plastic souvenir license tags from Smokey Mountains attached to the sissy bar in the back."

Angela rubbed the plate with her finger to see it more clearly through the years of dust and dirt.

"The name on it is Susan. One of the missing girls was Susan Thompson. We need to see if the parents can I.D. the bike."

Angela and Morris looked at one another. "You got him, kid. Looks like you were right."

"Thanks." Angela was on an emotional rush. She'd done it! She'd found the killer! "What else do we have over there?"

Morris pried open the top of one of the crates. After years of neglect, a family of mice had taken up residence and built a nest out of some of the contents. The crate was filled with shredded paper, cloth, and mouse droppings. Morris was thankful he was wearing rubber gloves. Angela was looking over his shoulder. "Is there anything in there?"

"I don't know. Let's get some light on this stuff and start photographing and bagging." They could see that the clothes that had been thrown into the crate were in poor condition. "Looks like this stuff here is all girl's clothes - shoes, hair ribbons; but we'll have to get the lab to sort through it. The mice have eaten it up pretty bad."

As they photographed and pealed through the layers, "What's that in the bottom?" Angela pointed to a metal object that was buried under a portion of a mouse nest.

"I don't know; let's pull it out and see."

"Are you afraid of mice?"

Morris frowned. "I'm not afraid of them, I just think they're nasty vermin. I don't want to put my hands into anything a mouse has shit on."

A large smile appeared on Angela's face. "You are afraid of mice, aren't you?"

"Would you keep your voice down."

"Sure." This time, a broader smile. "Here, let me. I'll get it." From underneath the old clothing, Angela pulled out a rusted metal cash box. The box was unlocked and opened easily. What Frank Morris and Angela saw next would both delight and disgust them.

Jim Hilliard had placed in this box, his collection of photographs of the murdered girls. Lying in the box beneath some of the photos, wrapped in tissue, was a broken ceramic angel.

Chapter thirty-six

That evening, Angela sat on the sofa at Jason's house and watched the news as Dorothy Danze began her report. "Jason honey, she's on!"

Moving slowly, his body stiff with pain, Jason limped into the room and joined Angela on the sofa. With his one uninjured arm around her and his still aching head resting on her shoulder, they watched the report. Dorothy kept her promise. She reported the story and betrayed no information that would be important to the prosecution's case. There were clips of her attempting to get a statement from former Senator Collins and questions about his knowledge of the murders. She spoke with one of the parents who broke down in tears of both sorrow and relief. Overall, it was a dramatic piece.

"Well, this should get her a raise. Maybe even a job in a larger market," commented Angela

"I'm surprised she didn't talk about all the stuff you all found out at the lake house."

"I think she was as sickened by those photographs as we were, and I think anyone who has even half a heart can't help but be upset when children are the victims in something like this."

"I guess you're right. The families will have to hear enough of that when the trial starts." Jason was silent for a moment. "So, tell me. What do you think the Senator's role was in all this?"

"Actually, Cecilia Miller has already started talking to us, against the family law firm's advice. Apparently, her husband discovered that Jim had murdered some of the girls; or, at that point, he thought just molested, some little girls. I guess he found some other pictures. That's when Jim disappeared for the first time. The family had him shipped out of state for treatment. Supposedly, he came back cured."

"I didn't think you could cure sex offenders."

"We know that now, but they didn't then. Anyway, he came back and

341

didn't have a job for a while, so that's when he moved into his sister's house, temporarily. Everything gets kind of fuzzy here. I'm still not clear on whether or not they suspected he murdered some of those girls or not. Anyway, when Mark Harris started putting things together, the family got nervous again and I think that's when Senator Collins came into the picture. He wanted to protect the family name. He was up for reelection and didn't want the bad publicity."

"So, he covered this up to protect his career."

"I think that was the true motivation."

"Do you think he had Mark Harris killed?"

"I don't know. Unless someone talks, we may never know. We're pretty sure we can identify the car we found at the lake house as the car that tried to run me off the road. And again, unless someone talks, we may not be able to get enough to connect them to the attempt on your life."

"I wonder why they went after me."

"They were probably watching both of us and had tried to get me. I guess they thought it might be too risky to try to kill me again. If they made it look like you'd surprised a vandal, then it wouldn't be connected to the case. I'd be too distraught or distracted to continue on the case."

"I still think they would have gone after you again."

"That is possible."

Carefully, so as not to touch his cut and bruised head, Jason pushed his hair away from his face. "It's scary to think about it. If you hadn't decided to worry about me and send those other officers out there when you did. I might be dead right now."

Angela didn't want to think about it either. She knew she was falling for Jason and she didn't want to think about how close she had come to losing him.

"Do they know what set Hilliard off? Why he would go after these girls? There seems to be almost a pattern of every two years."

"My guess is he was molesting girls in between murders. Some of that may come out as more information gets out to the public. Women may come forward and say he molested them. His current doctor might know some details. And what it was that set him off, but she doesn't have to talk."

"I guess that's good and bad. I mean, a doctor not required to share client information."

"I think it's important, too. But this time, I sure would like to know what she knows. His first doctor passed away years ago. This one only started treating him in the last few years. I did do one thing before I came over tonight. I called Peggy Anderson in Cleveland."

"Really, what'd she have to say?"

"Not a lot. She was relieved that Annie's killer has been caught. I asked her if she would come back here. She said she would. She can maybe identify the ceramic angel as the one Hilliard had. While we were talking, she did tell me something interesting. I think I have a clue about why Hilliard killed Annie."

"Oh, really!"

"Yes. What she didn't tell me the other day when I talked to her is that, at least initially, Hilliard seemed to dote on her, and not on Annie. But then he started showing Annie some extra attention and calling her an angel. Then, just before the stuff about the supposedly stolen I.D. bracelet happened, Hilliard caught Annie and Peggy kissing."

"You're kidding!"

"No. Apparently their relationship wasn't sexual; however, it was the beginning of a romantic relationship - as romantic as kids were at that age, back then. She said Hilliard was really upset when he saw them. He said some pretty vulgar things to them."

"Aunt Bess was right then, I mean about the two of them. You know, she's always said you're just born that way and sometimes you know as early as elementary school."

There was a silence that fell between Jason and Angela as they thought about all that had transpired in the last two days.

"So what happens now?" Jason asked.

"Tomorrow, I'm going to go see my partner Rob Edwards. They sent him home today. He is under hospice care at home."

"Is he any better? At least feeling better? Not in pain?"

"Not really. But he wanted to go home and be around his family. My uncle did that. He died at home. It was hard on my aunt and cousins, but in the long run, I think it helped them deal with it."

Jason and Angela were interrupted by the ring of the phone.

"Hello."

"Jason have you been watching the news?"

"Yes, Mom."

"I just can't believe it. The Senator's brother arrested for murder..."

Jason stopped his mother before she could continue. "Mom, can I call you back later; I'm kind of tired. I was up late last night."

"Alright. But call me tomorrow and don't keep such late hours. It isn't healthy."

"Okay, Mom. Bye now."

"Your mother?" Jason rolled his eyes. "You know, I was thinking. We need to take your aunt and Louise out to dinner so I can say thank you for helping. I may not have done this without them. Certainly, not without you."

"You would have."

"Maybe so; but not so soon. I definitely need to give you a proper thank you." Angela paused and smiled. "I was wondering how your head and your arm are feeling."

"They hurt, but they work. Why?"

Angela reached into her computer case that was on the floor beside the sofa. She pulled out her handcuffs and suspended them in the air with one finger.

Jason's green eyes narrowed as he smiled, "Are you going to use those on me?"

Angela laid the handcuffs on the coffee table. "No. This is just a reminder for you."

"A reminder of what?"

"A reminder that I will use them if you're bad."

"I promise I'll be good."

"I don't doubt that," Angela replied as she reached past Jason and turned out the lamp on the end table.

Jason smiled, "You are so bad."

- End-

OTHER NOVELS

by

LEIGH M. ROSE

The Third Floor

and
COMING SOON:

Red Riding Hoods

Angels' Playground

www.ingramcontent.com/pod-product-compliance
Lightning Source LLC
Chambersburg PA
CBHW051329250626
47155CB00007B/2523